The Giles Wareing Haters' Club

Tim Dowling was born in Connecticut in 1963. He moved to Britain in the early nineties, cutting short a promising career in data entry to work as a freelance writer, until he gradually became unfit for any other form of employment. He writes regularly for the *Guardian* and is the author of a biography of King Camp Gillette entitled *Inventor of the Disposable Culture*. Dowling lives in London with his wife and three sons. *The Giles Wareing Haters' Club* is his first novel.

TIM DOWLING

The Giles Wareing Haters' Club

PICADOR

First published 2007 by Picador

First published in paperback 2008 by Picador

This edition published 2016 by Pan Books
an imprint of Pan Macmillan,
20 New Wharf Road, London N1 9RR
Associated companies throughout the world
www.panmacmillan.com

ISBN 978-1-509-83753-3

A CIP catalogue record for this book is available from
the British Library.

Printed and bound by CPI Group (UK) Ltd, Croydon, CR0 4YY

Visit **www.picador.com** to read more about all our books
and to buy them. You will also find features, author interviews and
news of any author events, and you can sign up for e-newsletters
so that you're always first to hear about our new releases.

For Sophie, for all time
(DEDICATION APPLIES TO HARDCOVER EDITION ONLY)

1

It began in the first joint of my left toe, up near the ball of the foot. I was in a dark, snow-dusted wood trying to lift a log off my foot, a log whose icy sides caused it to slip from my grasp and drop back down on the toe from a height of several inches. With a rising sense of panic I repeated the action over and over, helplessly, even as I argued with myself in favour of another approach to the problem. Then I woke up.

The scene evaporated, along with the pain. The thudding of my heart was all that remained. Then the pain returned, pulsing in time with my blood. At first I thought it possible that some version of the incident with the log had actually happened, but I could not locate any memory of such an injury. I turned on the light and examined the toe. It might have been a bit swollen; it was hard to tell. The skin felt taut and strangely dry. Caroline stirred, but did not return to consciousness fully enough to grasp the seriousness of the situation. The extent of her sympathy was a drowsy suggestion that I remove myself to the spare room. After a few minutes she retreated there herself.

Lying still did not help. The weight of the duvet on my foot had become unbearable. Deep in the joint there was an unyielding pressure, a pinpoint crushing, but soon the pain began to outgrow the toe, forming a bubble of threat. At 4.25 the tinkling rasp of glass on stone as the milkman gathered up yesterday's empties brought a hot twinge: I could feel the noise in the toe. By this time I was sitting halfway up in bed with my right foot on the floor. I went through the motions of reading a book, but most of my concentration was now given over to protecting the toe, even as circumstances forced me to leave it out in the open, throbbing in the faint, unwelcome breeze. At 5.14 the partially open sash window shuddered lightly in its frame. I looked over and saw Carrot slither in from the ledge.

Carrot sat down on top of the dresser and contemplated my elevated, exposed toe. 'Don't even think about it,' I said, but I could tell he was already thinking about it. His purring grew louder, turning ominous, as he readied himself. 'No. No!' He was in the air. He landed on the bed, stepped over my leg and began to turn tight circles alongside my knee. The pain seemed to change pitch in response to his proximity. Carrot clawed horribly at the duvet.

'Go away.' I nudged him with my book. He sat down and licked his orange fur. I prodded. He looked past me and then turned and stalked toward the toe. 'Not that way. Off. Get off.' He stepped off the duvet onto the bare, taut sheet at the foot of the bed. His shifting weight on the mattress was now seismic, minutely measurable. He turned forty-five degrees and, as I watched in mute horror, dragged the right side of his face along the sole of my foot. In the effort not to contract my leg muscles I issued an inhuman whinny which frightened me. I gave up and thrust my heel in his face. Carrot reared up and batted the toe between his paws then bit the tip. I thrashed. He streaked off toward the bathroom. It felt as if my toe had been amputated. When I opened my eyes I was actually disappointed to see it still there.

'What?'

'How much do you drink?' The doctor looked away after asking this, preparing to be embarrassed by my answer. I should not have told her about the cat acting on the force field.

At dawn I had got myself dressed, motivated by a burgeoning fear that the pain was a symptom of something that would ultimately claim my life. I gingerly pulled an old woollen sock over my left foot – a shoe was out of the question – and quietly hobbled downstairs and out to the car. I drove the half a mile to the surgery in second gear so as to avoid unnecessary use of the clutch. When the doors were finally unlocked thirty minutes later I hopped to the desk and demanded the immediate attentions of a doctor.

'Do you have an appointment?' asked the receptionist.

'No.'

'Early bird surgery is appointment only.'

'There's no one else here.'

'Is it an emergency?' She looked me up and down, raising an eyebrow at the absence of gaping wounds or protruding implements. A child with a lump the size of a peach over one eye was ushered into the waiting room. I flexed my toe and flinched, and told her it was.

After a twenty-minute wait I was taken to a Portakabin, where I was examined by a GP I'd never met, and then left alone. I heard distant wailing, the faint rumble of a calm adult voice, a short silence and then a piercing shriek, which I took to be the kid with the eye. Eventually the doctor returned and embarked on a series of questions. Even as I answered them my mind began to wander. This is a known failing of mine: at those times when I should be most present – when the subject at hand is serious and concerns me directly – I am prone to a sort of inward drift. It's not wilful inattention, although it may be partly defensive, compounded in this instance by the fact that I'd had no sleep at all, apart from a ten-minute nap in the car before the surgery opened. The portable consulting room was airless and overheated, and the pain in my toe had finally begun to subside slightly. The doctor also seemed genuinely irritated, which I took as a good sign; she wouldn't dare take such a dismissive tone with me if I was dying, appointment or no.

'A fair amount, I suppose.'

'And how much is a fair amount, do you suppose?' She was looking directly at me now.

'I don't know. Half a bottle of wine a night?' I knew she would automatically double the figure I'd automatically halved, but I wondered which number she would write down. I didn't want to speculate on how the lie might jeopardize my recovery. As she made her meandering way towards divulging the cause of my night of agony, I allowed myself to think about where I might have left the radiator key. Although it was still warm for October, radiator-bleeding season was approaching, and I'd spent a good few hours the previous afternoon looking for the little brass key, with no success. I tried to picture it sitting in the blue cup in the loo on the landing, under a layer of summer dust. I tried to imagine myself putting it there for some reason. The boiler was adjacent, hidden behind a sliding panel, so there was a kind of logic to it. I could see the cup clearly enough, lopsided and unevenly glazed, a relic from two weeks in Portugal, the sole survivor of a set of four. As I narrowed my eyes in concentration, I noticed that the doctor was staring blankly at me.

'I'm sorry, what did you say?'

She repeated herself in an impatient staccato, as if she were spelling it out in chalk: 'I said we'll need a blood test to confirm it, but it looks like gout.'

Gout. Gout was not even on the list of possibilities I had dared to consider. I was struck by how little the word meant to me.

'I'm forty,' I said quietly. This was not even strictly true; I was still thirty-nine, but with less than a month to go I had made a decision to meet inevitability halfway, to attack forty at a run. It was supposed to help me conquer the fear, but in truth I'd only given the fear a four-week head start. Every time I said, 'I'm forty,' it was like pitching a stone into the pit of my soul just to hear the echo; incalculably distressing, but oddly habit-forming.

'Yes, well, it's not that unusual in someone your age,'

said the doctor. 'Some people get it in their twenties. It's caused by crystals which form in the joints, high uric-acid levels, but there can be a lot of factors. You're probably predisposed.' She went on, but a buzzing in my brain drowned her out. The depressing absurdity of the situation began to soak through. This was only my third visit to a doctor's surgery as an adult. I'd always been quietly pleased with my reluctance to trouble the health service, but now I felt cheated, deprived of some significant milestones in my own deterioration: knee trouble, lower back pain, a stern cholesterol lecture, stress-related skin complaints, a lingering, life-sapping mystery virus, perhaps an expensive scan to rule out a possible brain tumour. Six years ago I'd presented with an ear infection, a child's holiday ailment, and now I was back with gout. I was ageing by bounds. The buzzing grew more insistent. Gout. Is there no other name for it? Do Americans call it gout?

'Is that you?'

'What?'

'Is that your phone ringing?'

'Oh.' The noise was coming from my coat. 'It must be. Sorry.' I fished out the phone and answered it.

'Where are you?'

'At the doctor's.'

'Have you got the car?'

'Yes.'

'How am I supposed to get the kids to school? I thought the fucking car had been stolen.'

'I'm coming back now,' I said, standing up. 'I've got gout.' The line went dead. I fixed the doctor with an apologetic look. 'I've got to go.' She smiled, not warmly, and inclined her head, which I took as an altogether sarcastic gesture of welcome to the world of people who find themselves somewhat pressed for time.

'If it is gout,' she said, 'the pain should subside by itself in a few days. We'll take some blood then. You'll need to make an appointment.' Again she spoke in chalk, underlining the word appointment. I said nothing. I took the proffered bit of paper and left.

The handover of the keys was tense and necessarily hurried.

'I've got gout,' I said.

The boys were already standing in the hall, hair on end, coats askew. The older one filed past me without a word, half asleep, wholly unaware of the single Cheerio lodged in his eyebrow. The youngest looked at me, unplugged his thumb from his mouth and said, 'Where's your goat?'

'It's in my foot.'

'In your foot?'

'In my toe.'

'Is it.'

'Yes.'

'Can I see?'

Caroline prodded him past me. 'Not now, Freddy,' she said. 'We're late.'

2

The radiator key was not in the blue cup. After this disappointment I rummaged through a few drawers and upended the vase full of pencils in the kitchen. Nothing. I went up to my office, searched in likely boxes and mugs, turning up only a few lire and a tiny clay horse. I pulled the bit of paper out of my pocket. I had assumed it was a prescription for painkillers, but it was blank except for a handwritten website address: www.gout.co.uk. I was being encouraged to take responsibility for my gout.

A few minutes later I was sitting in front of the computer, reading an online pamphlet entitled *All About Gout*, with the afflicted foot resting on a low stool. Gout, I learned, afflicts 840 out of every 100,000 people, and is the most common inflammatory joint disease in men over the age of forty. The word comes from the Latin *gutta*, meaning drop, a term once applied to diseases characterized by a perceived discharge of humours. The high uric-acid levels which cause gout may be attributed to diet or eccentric kidney function, or both. Attacks can be triggered by stress, injury, unusual exercise, obesity or sudden weight loss. I scanned the list of proscribed, purine-rich foods, looking for favourites, developing perverse cravings. I searched further afield: one website contained the promising sentence 'How to spread the gout'. I hadn't realized it was in any way contagious, but I was certainly keen to take as many people down with me as possible. The web page, it transpired, was from an American DIY store's website. From the context it was clear that it was meant to say 'How to spread the grout.' I read it all the way through anyway. The phone rang.

'Hello?'

'Giles, hi. It's Ken.' Which Ken? Ken from the paper or Ken from the food supplement? Play it safe.

'Hi.'

'I enjoyed your piece about recharging disposable batteries.'

'It's a conspiracy,' I said. 'They want you to think it can't be done.'

'So I gather. Now, you're down for Rare Objects today . . .' Ah: Ken from the paper.

'Am I?'

'You are. I wondered if you had an idea so we could get started on a picture.'

'Oh. Hang on. Let me think. I did a have a sort of . . . let me just, let me see . . .' I let the final vowel drag on until it became coarse-grained, while typing 'rare valuable object' into the search bar at the bottom of my screen and hitting Return. The phrase 'rare books and coins' caught my eye; I'd done a book the last time. I replaced 'object' with 'coin' and hit return again. 'What about,' I said, quickly scanning the results, 'the 1913 Liberty Head nickel?'

'We've done it,' said Ken.

'Recently? Since the missing fifth nickel turned up?'

'I'm fairly sure.'

'Well, then. What about. What about the 1804 silver dollar?'

'Will we be able to find a picture of it?'

'I should think so. It's known as the King of American Coins,' I said, reading off the screen. 'And it's 2004, so we're celebrating the two hundredth anniversary of its, um, coinage.'

'Outstanding. Everything else all right?'

'Yes. Actually, no. I've got gout.'

'Christ.'

I bookmarked a web page detailing the fascinating story of the dollar of 1804, and then turned my attentions back to gout, searching out British sites, with their reassuring terminology and familiar telephone exchanges. Not that I would be ringing anyone up for further information on the challenges of living with gout, or to request educational materials for people with gout and their families. I had no intention of becoming professionally gouty, or known in gout circles. In fact I had made up my mind not to tell anyone else about it. I would suffer in silence, nobly. Already the pain had become so routine that I hardly noticed it.

I clicked on a link to the UK Family Health Net and found 2 Search Results for Osteoarthritis, Gout and Poly-myalgia: Gout. Both took me to places I'd already been. I tried my luck at www.wellness.co.uk. I typed a G in the 'search the site' box. Before I could type an O the computer impatiently attempted to second-guess me, offering up 'g-spot', 'Giles Wareing', 'gout' and 'gout UK'. I misclicked, accidentally searching the UK Wellness Coalition's site for my own name. There was, to my surprise, one result for Giles Wareing. I didn't even believe in wellness. The underlined, clickable text said, 'This cheered me up no end!' I clicked. Of course I clicked.

It was a link to an article I'd written three years before, about going to a naturist dinner party in Kent, posted on www.wellness.co.uk's Depression forum. There were several comments under the link: 'very funny', 'we all need a laugh sometimes – great medicine!' and 'wareing is a genious, whoever he is!!' One woman had even written that after reading the article she had been emboldened to leave the house for the first time in four days. I clicked on the link and re-read the piece. It was quite funny, funnier than I'd remembered, and infused with a new poignancy now I knew it had brightened the outlook of some chronically depressed people. It certainly put things into perspective, especially all those letters from naturists the newspaper ran at the time. Yes, the article may have been, as one angry naked person had put it, 'patronising, prurient and inaccurate in several of its particulars', but if it gave a few agoraphobics the strength to pop down to the shops, then it had served a larger purpose. If shut-ins can laugh at men who eat with their tackle out, there is hope for us all.

I heard the front door open and close, followed by the sound of Caroline's footsteps on the stairs, coming closer, changing tone with each flight. She stopped short of the final dog-leg which led up to the office, and spoke through the ceiling.

'There are pencils everywhere.'

'I was looking for the radiator key.'

'Anything to report?'

'I'm not supposed to eat mussels.'

'Has the dog been out?'

'I've got gout.'

'She needs to go out.'

'I'm gout-stricken.' In fact the pain was a shadow of its former self, mounting only the occasional sharp twinge, just enough to announce its location, to reserve its place. 'I'm goutish.' Goutish was a word. I'd been at the dictionary. So was goutify.

A burnt-out van decorated the entrance to Roundworm Park, blackened wiring spewing from its crunched bonnet. Tyre tracks through the thick mud showed the series of skids and turns that had brought it to its final resting place on top of a flattened park bench. A sofa bed had been pushed out of the back doors and set alight, but had not combusted successfully. I walked to the next bench along and sat down, resting the gout foot on the heel of its untied boot. The dog sat down and stared at me, then stood up and stared, tail waving expectantly. She'd never seen me sit on a bench. Normally we took a single brisk turn around the crumbling perimeter path, a walk of less than a mile, before heading back out of the gates. Very occasionally I went twice round, but taking my ease was not part of the routine. Eventually she trotted off in a long arc, avoiding a dog with whom she did not get on.

The sun had come out and was drying the rolls of extruded mud squeezed out by the van's tyres as it veered and narrowly missed a rusting litter bin. Roundworm Park was scrubby and unkempt, a threadbare swatch of green on London's western fringe, but it had a loyal constituency of dog-walkers, truants and old men who met for pre-lunch drinks. The police seemed oblivious to its existence, which was clearly the secret of its popularity.

At the other end of the field I could see the dog assume its customary strained arch, inching gently forward through the tall grass. I closed my eyes and let the sun beat against the lids, seeing warm red. I felt old and tired, but with a little undercurrent of elation because someone somewhere thought I was a 'genious'. The combination of exaggeration and poor spelling made it a hard opinion to respect, perhaps, but the hyperbole seemed playful rather than ill-judged and the spelling mistake might easily have been a typo. Whoever this depressive was, I was inclined to think the best of him. Or her. And for the first time in many months I was moved to reflect for a moment on the fact that I'd done all right for myself. I'd achieved more than an essentially ambition-less person could hope to expect. I had a wife, children and a little occupational niche where I could work untroubled by the possibility of real success: my phone rang, but not too often. All that remained for me to do was contract gout and die, and here I was well ahead of schedule. The bench rose sharply under me. Someone else had sat down.

I opened my eyes and recognized the woman instantly: the sharp, ageless features, the unkempt thatch of dyed black hair with its strip of grey along the crooked centre parting, the huge bosom which sloped downwards from right to left, the shapeless coat, the immaculate black-leather trainers. I saw her most days, waddling around the park or sitting at her usual bench. Initially I found her suspicious because she had no dog. Almost everyone who came to Roundworm Park had a dog; its general lawlessness made it ideal for dogs. Anyone without a dog was, I imagined, up to no good.

But there was another thing about her: she never acknowledged me in any way. It was customary to exchange guarded greetings with anyone you regularly met along the path, but she never returned mine, and I had taken to avoiding her because of it. If she was in the park I usually checked to see which way round she was going before I set off. She usually went anticlockwise, and in response I changed to anticlockwise, following her at a distance, slowing down to prevent the unbearable proposition of having to overtake. In general I preferred to maintain a two-bench gap. If ever we did cross paths due to a miscalculation on my part, courtesy would force me to mumble hello and endure another blanking. At first I pitied her, thinking she must be in some way deranged, until I noticed that she chatted animatedly to almost everyone else she met. Why did she single me out? Lately, the fact that I was doing all the evading had begun to annoy me. Sometimes she slowed down or stopped on the path, forcing me to do the same.

Now she was sitting next to me. This was not even her usual bench. I thought for a moment she might have been deliberately trying to provoke a confrontation, until I realized her bench was now under the burnt-out white van. Still, why would she sit down at a bench occupied by a person she had wilfully ignored on dozens of occasions? Why didn't she find the situation as embarrassing as I did?

The awkwardness was becoming acute; after a too long pause I said, quietly, 'Nice day,' and glanced in her direction. She was looking at the ground. Was she smiling? Almost, perhaps, but not quite. She said: nothing. She looked over toward the park entrance, swinging her head so that her eyes raked right across my face, unseeing. I looked straight ahead, felt sweat prickle along my hairline. The dog was trotting back towards us, but she stopped to sniff at something in a plastic bag. 'Come on, dog!' I shouted. I never used the dog's name in public, because the dog's name was Philippa.

The dog took several detours, turning in tight circles, nose to the ground, before finally approaching the bench. I stood up and took a few steps toward the front gate, but the dog did not come to heel. I walked a few yards further, hoping the dog would appear at my side, but she did not. I turned around and saw her sniffing the outstretched hand of the black-haired woman. The woman lowered her head toward the dog's and quite distinctly mouthed the words 'Hello there'. She was talking to my dog! Infuriated, I turned and took the most direct route to the entrance, picking my way through a minefield of dog shit and mud. A hot current pulsed through my big toe. When I got to the gate I whistled, loudly and insistently, until the dog finally wandered over.

A search on 'Giles Wareing naturist' did not return any further results. A search on plain old 'Giles Wareing' turned up, as I knew from experience it would, many hundreds of documents, littered with references to people who shared my name, but were demonstrably not me, fished up from some online family tree, or from a list of entrants to a 1997 Canadian fun run. There was the Reverend Giles Wareing from Frome and the brilliant astronomer Dr Giles Wareing, an expert on the topography of Jupiter. There were pictures of other Giles Wareings visiting Machu Picchu, posing in front of starter homes, or backed against the wallpaper in some dingy function room, accepting awards while simultaneously shaking hands, pupils glowing red. I picked through the first few dozen, but I'd seen all those that referred to me before. None were recent, most were tortuous links to the Amazon page for my book, *The Story of Irish Whiskey* (sales rank 236,981). I tried to narrow the search by adding more terms, but it didn't help. I tried other searches, other search engines, search engines that searched other search engines, but after ten years as a freelance writer I seemed to have left less of an impression on the world, or at least on the Internet, than most Giles Wareings, including one who died in the late sixteenth century. If any more mentally ill people had been uplifted by my work, they were keeping quiet about it. The phone rang.

'Hi, Giles, it's Ken.'
'Ken.'
'Any danger?'
'Of what?'
'Of your copy arriving before we go to press?'

3

Rare Objects: The King of Coins

America's most valuable coin has, like all rare coins, a curious history: mints do not create rarities on purpose. In fact, they usually take great pains to avoid it. According to US mint records, 19,570 silver dollars were struck in the first few months of 1804, before it was decided to discontinue the denomination altogether. It seemed that no one was spending their silver dollars; virtually all of them were being exported to Europe via the West Indies, where they were prized beyond their face value for their silver content. With the similarly sized Spanish 8 real piece in wide circulation in America, the government decided the country could do without a silver dollar.

In 1804 the United States was still very much a fledgling nation.

Thomas Jefferson, the third President, was seeking re-election. America was also making its first significant military stand after the War of Independence, choosing to wage war with the kleptocratic Barbary States of the North African coast rather than pay protection money to the pirates who harried shipping in the Mediterranean.

By a stroke of fate almost all of the 1804 silver dollars minted were exported to Africa, where US naval forces were engaged in action against Tripoli. Legend has it that the most of the money was used to fund a daring overland attack on the Tripolitan city of Derna by a collection of Arab and Berber mercenaries led by American seamen. For this reason few, if any of the silver dollars sent to

Africa were ever returned to American soil. Today only 15 genuine examples are known to exist, though several counterfeit dollars have turned up over the years.

In 1999 one particularly well-regarded example fetched over $4 million at auction, the highest price ever paid for a single coin. Because of its rarity the 1804 silver dollar has long been known as the King of American coins, a reign which will almost certainly last another 200 hundred years.

Giles Wareing

The gout returned in the night, though with none of its former intensity. I had prepared by taking four Nurofen and drinking a bottle of wine. I also took the precaution of retiring to the spare room. When I finally fell asleep dawn was imminent and when I woke up the house was empty.

The coffee in the pot was cold. I heated up a cup in the microwave, took the papers up to my office and turned on the computer. I turned to the silver-dollar piece in the newspaper. They'd removed a few words from the final sentence, but this was probably just for space.

After checking my email, I typed a g in the box at the bottom of the screen. The computer responded by offering

g-spot
Giles Wareing
Giles Wareing +clever
Giles Wareing +excellent
Giles Wareing +fan
Giles Wareing +favourite
Giles Wareing +funny
Giles Wareing +genius
Giles Wareing +great

Giles Wareing +journalist
Giles Wareing +moving
Giles Wareing +respected
Giles Wareing +respected − Jupiter
Giles Wareing +writer
gout
gout UK

I needed to figure out how to get rid of these. I could perhaps disable the facility if I knew what it was called. I sent an email to the help address at my Internet service provider, BubbleNet:

> What is it called when you type something in a box and the computer keeps trying to guess what you are about to write, offering a list of 'helpful' suggestions based on things you have typed in that particular box before (ie search engine)? How do I make it stop? Giles Wareing.

Then I went back to the search engine and typed 'Giles Wareing +inspired'. Nothing. The phone rang.

'Hi, Giles, it's Linda from the paper.'

'Linda. How are things in property?'

'I'm doing health now.'

'Are you? Since when?'

'About two years ago.'

'I guess it's been that long since I've seen you.'

'Actually I don't think we've ever met in person.'

'No. You're right.'

'I was wondering.'

'Yeah.'

'Could you do us a wee piece for next Tuesday's health page?'

'What on?' There was a long pause. I was on the verge of repeating myself when she finally spoke.

'Well, a little birdie tells me that you have gout.'

'Who told you that?'

'Ken.'

Bloody Ken from the paper. The toe throbbed three times in heartbeat succession. A version of the future flashed before my eyes: talking about my gout on the radio, displaying my misshapen toe on morning television, addressing the annual conference of the UK Gout Society and calling for gout-only carriages on public transport. Young people would ignore my stern and repeated warning that gout doesn't only happen to the old, because they would look at me and see that I was old. I would be forever associated with gout, even as I tried to branch out by speaking on other diseases of the joints. Whenever I was interviewed subeditors would put forced puns in the headlines, awful things like Rheum With a View. People would nudge each other in shops and whisper: Isn't that you-know, the gout guy? Even my friends would call me Gouty Giles in order to distinguish me from the other Gileses they knew. This is how it would be. Unless, of course, I said I was too busy. Or I just said no. No was always an option.

'How many words?' The dog, lying behind me in a square of sunlight on the floor, suddenly snapped at a dozy fly. A CD case on my desk caught a reflection of flashing white, creating the impression of a bird fluttering in a confined space. I flinched and turned around. Philippa looked up at me and beat her tail against the carpet, her eyes filled with a hopeless, desperate longing.

The burnt-out white van still guarded the entrance to the park. The black-haired woman was exactly as I'd left her the day before, sitting on her new bench, staring across the expanse of grass with her dazed, inscrutable half-smile. I attacked the path clockwise, in the hope that she might have departed by the time I got round. But I couldn't make it round. My gout flared up. I fingered the blister pack of Nurofen in the breast pocket of my shirt. There were three left. I sat down on the nearest bench and took them all.

It was cloudy and cold, but the air had a pleasant leaden stillness which gave everything an immediacy of presence. From somewhere the distinct scrape and crack of building work was conducted with an odd, echoless fidelity. The old black-haired woman was now talking to someone who now stood behind her bench. I could immediately tell it was Colin from his lime-green windcheater and his silver-white hair, a combination usually distinguishable from twice the distance. His head went back, his laugh arriving a split second later. They seemed to exchange something. One of his cards? Did the old woman want some painting done?

The dog arrived with a purple tennis ball on a rope. I'd never seen it before. 'Where did that come from?' In the distance a large woman and her lurcher were trudging toward me. 'That isn't yours,' I said firmly. 'Drop it.' I reached out to grab the rope. Philippa growled menacingly.

There is something wrong with the dishwasher. Caroline had evidently come and gone while I was at the park. The note ended with a curly arrow which pointed to a glass standing on the piece of crisp A4. The glass was flecked with sandy matter, hardened lees which the rinse cycle had failed to disperse, and which had been subsequently baked on during the drying phase. I opened the dishwasher and discovered several more glasses with similar encrustation, but the phenomenon was confined to the upper rack. I had encountered this problem a few times before and I knew its cause immediately: lemon pips.

The dishwasher's rinsing action is performed by two free-whirling plastic propellers driven by the pressure of the hot water which jets out of precisely angled holes at intervals along their blades. One hangs just under the upper rack; the other sits just below the lower rack. Lemon pips which find their way into the dishwasher are eventually sucked into the intake and drawn through the hollow blades where they become lodged in the holes, blocking the flow of water. When enough of the holes are blocked the propellers simply cease to turn and incomplete rinsing results. In my experience only lemon pips are big enough to block the jets and yet small enough to work their way into the blade intake. Occasionally you get unpopped popcorn kernels, but they're heavier than lemon pips and more likely to end up in the debris trap at the bottom of the machine. They don't present the same threat to effective rinsing. Pine nuts could be a problem, theoretically.

The two propellers snap in and out of place easily enough, but dislodging the lemon pips takes a while. It's a bit like trying to get a plectrum out of the body of a guitar: invert, shake and wait for them to find their own way out through the central intake hole. By the time the rinse cycle is noticeably impaired it's not uncommon to find up to a dozen pips in each blade. As an activity it is marginally preferable to writing about your own gout, and produces a rather more tangible sense of achievement. In the end I set aside an hour for the procedure, including telly breaks.

When I finally went upstairs again I found an impressively thorough email from Vikram at BubbleNet Support waiting for me. He ran through three different ways to disable what he called the 'Inline AutoComplete Facility'. 'Hopefully this should resolve the issue. Assuring you of the best intentions at all times, Vikram.' The least confusing method was simply to erase each suggestion manually by highlighting it and hitting delete. In a matter of seconds I had got rid of all but

Giles Wareing +funny
gout uk

I highlighted the former. Then I clicked, leaving the cursor backed hard up against the left side of the f in funny. And then I altered the entry to 'Giles Wareing +unfunny' and hit return. There was just one result, from the archive of someone's weblog – Ben's Blog. The relevant sentence read: 'And don't get me started on that unfunny twat Giles Wareing.'

A small stone dropped into the pit of my soul, and I heard its faint echo.

Gout got me out of a Sunday-morning trip to the swimming pool. The pain had largely disappeared since I'd started taking the anti-inflammatory pills prescribed after the blood test, but I needed to do a bit of work on the gout piece for the paper, transcribing a brief phone interview with a twenty-nine-year-old gout sufferer – the youngest I could find – who I'd tracked down through the UK Gout Society. At eleven, after a long bath, I hobbled up to the office. The computer was already on. I was surprised to see an empty bottle of red wine on my desk, and a half-full glass. I didn't even remember coming up the night before. I accessed the Internet and saw that I'd made the search engine my home page. I didn't remember doing that either. With a sense of foreboding I typed a g in the box and got

Giles Wareing +awful
Giles Wareing +bad
Giles Wareing +cliche
Giles Wareing +dreadful
Giles Wareing +hate
giles Wareing +loer
giles Wareing +loser
Giles Wareing +old

giles Wareing +rubbish

giles wareing +shit

Giles Wareing +smug

Giles Wareing +sucks

Giles Wareing +tit

Giles Wareing +twat

Giles Wareing +unfunny

Gilse Wareingshit

gout UK

I was able to summon only the vaguest recollection of the previous evening's investigations, a fragile memory propped up almost entirely on the available evidence: the glass, the bottle, the hangover, the entries helpfully supplied by the Inline AutoComplete Facility. But I did seem to recall a definite feeling of horror and resentment, and a quickening of the pulse which was now recurring. It was like a dream reinforced by tangible pain, like the icy log and the toe, except that this had clearly actually happened, and the icy log was, strictly speaking, a literary device.

I had no idea which search terms had prompted these feelings, however, and at that moment I lacked the courage to find out. Instead I slipped on the headphones and dutifully redacted the whole twenty-minute interview with gout sufferer Julian Garrett, now thirty, of New Alresford in Hampshire. In his voice I recognized the cagey weariness of the reluctant spokesman, and in mine, undisguised glee.

4

A Right Pain In The Toe
Giles Wareing gets gout

The pain struck in the first joint of my largest left toe. I lifted the huge stone off my foot and carefully stepped back, but when I dropped it the toe had somehow moved forward again to take the full weight of the boulder. I repeated the action over and over again helplessly, even as I argued with myself in favour of another approach. Then I woke up.

The scenario evaporated, but the pain remained, pulsing in time with my blood. I was at home in bed. The alarm clock's LED readout bobbed gently in the blackness: 2:04AM. I turned the light on and examined the toe; it might have been a bit swollen, but I couldn't tell. The skin felt taut and strangely dry. My wife Caroline woke, but did not return to consciousness fully enough to grasp the seriousness of the situation. Not wanting to keep her up, I offered to go to the spare room, but she volunteered to go herself.

The pain got steadily worse. Soon I could not even lie still. The weight of the duvet on my foot had become unbearable. At 4.25 I could hear the milkman collecting empties. Just the noise of it made me wince: he was too close, carrying dangerously heavy objects. The pain was intense, searing, physically impossible, like hot butter through a knife.

By the next morning things had improved slightly, but at

Caroline's insistence I took myself off to the doctor. To my surprise, he diagnosed gout.

The word gout comes from the Latin gutta, or drop, a term once applied to all diseases which were thought to be characterised by a downward flow of humours. Today gout affects 840 out of every 100,000 people – about 150,000 in Britain – and is the most common inflammatory joint disease in men over 40, although it is by no means confined to those of middle age. Julian Garrett, from Hampshire, was first diagnosed with gout at the age of 29 . . .

'I thought the doctor was a woman.' Caroline had come up and was reading over my shoulder as I sat at the kitchen table. She read faster than I did.

'The first doctor was a woman, but the one who took my blood at the hospital was a man. One has to conflate a bit.'

'And I never suggested you go to the surgery. You were gone before I woke up.' She sat down opposite me, picked up the main bit of the paper and flicked through it.

'Yes, I know, but if I come across as a hypochondriac, then it's no longer about the gout, it's about what a twat I am.' I paused to give her a chance at dissent, but she chose to abstain. She turned the page of her paper. 'It's a health piece,' I said. 'It's meant to be informative, not confessional.' I stopped there. Caroline did not appear to be listening any more, and I could feel myself beginning to plead. Anyway, the rest of the piece was true. Except for the weight of the duvet. The weight of the duvet did not become unbearable. I just read that somewhere.

The caption under the picture of a very sombre Julian Garrett read, 'Sloane Danger: Garrett's party-boy lifestyle led to gout at 29'. He would doubtless be very unhappy about that, but I didn't write it, and that's what you get for living in Hampshire, having gout at twenty-nine and wearing a bow tie for a newspaper photo.

'You got a letter,' said Caroline. I looked up. She'd clearly had her hair cut recently, probably the day before. She folded the paper inside out, then in four, then she spun it round like a tray on the tips of her fingers and slid it under my nose. I looked down at the top half of the letters page.

> *One does not necessarily expect Giles Wareing to be an expert numismatist, but is it too much to ask that he check his facts (Rare Objects: The King of Coins, Oct 21)? While readers may have enjoyed his tale of piracy and American naval derring do, the story overlooks a single, rather important point: there were no 1804 silver dollars minted in 1804. No "genuine examples" exist.*
>
> *David White*
>
> *London*

Normally I'm immune to complaints from pedants, especially pedants who employ the phrase 'derring do', but this did seem a rather big mistake on my part. I felt a flush of embarrassment, a brief wave of nausea, the heat from the stares of thousands of pairs of unseen eyes, the eyes of people who were reading this at this precise moment, and reflecting on my comic incompetence. How did I miss something so basic? On the other hand, was this really my fault? When presented with a silver dollar with the date

1804 stamped on it, what am I supposed to think? Why the hell weren't any 1804 dollars minted in 1804? Where did I get that pirate story from? Caroline was smiling broadly at me.

'Don't like getting it wrong, do you?'

For a moment it seemed as if there were no limit to my capacity for error. What else had I got wrong? I'd never heard of the Barbary War before last week. Perhaps that didn't happen either.

The doctor at the hospital had also given me some crutches, but I hadn't used them yet. Now, in need of some sympathy, I pulled them from the coat closet and levered myself over to Roundworm Park, with the dog barking and biting at the right crutch each time it touched the ground. I received a few stares, none of them sympathetic, exactly. I ran into Colin at the gate. 'All right, Guy? How you keeping, mate?' He always called me Guy. He looked down at the dog, who had by now chewed most of the varnish off the bottom of the crutch. I waved the tip at her menacingly and hissed, 'Stop it!' She grabbed the crutch and ran off into the park with it.

'You know, can't complain,' I said. We both paused to watch the dog readjust her grip before resuming an angled canter through the tall grass, the crutch's rubber tip skimming the ground behind her.

'Yeah. I've been meaning to drop by, mate, to speak to your missus about your kitchen.' Colin had painted our house inside and outside, devoting the better part of four years to the project. By the time he finished the back of the house last summer the kitchen ceiling, where he'd begun, needed repainting, but various pressing and mysterious business ventures had prevented him from making a start.

'Whenever you're ready, Colin,' I said. 'There's no emergency.'

'Nice one, mate, yeah,' he said. 'Handsome.' The dog was now lying in the grass at a safe distance, chewing industriously on the upper part of the crutch. They had mostly metal crutches at the hospital, the bent forearm rest sort that I automatically associate with either permanent or degenerative conditions. I'd asked for the wooden ones especially.

'I saw you talking to that black-haired woman the other day, the one who sits over there.'

'You mean Maria? Know her, do you?'

'No,' I said. 'She refuses to acknowledge my existence.'

'Oh. Do you want me to put in a good word or something?' He suddenly became distracted, looking up and then down Roundworm Road like a meerkat. It was his way, I guessed, of bringing the conversation to a close.

'No, don't,' I said. 'There's no need.' He was already halfway across the road.

'I'll drop by,' he shouted, one thumb in the air. 'Stay lucky, mate.'

Back at home there were no messages, which I took as a good sign. Once online I discovered more good news:

there was such a thing as the Barbary War. Then I went back to my home page and, with a deep breath, I typed a g in the box.

When paired up with awful, bad, cliché and dreadful, the name Giles Wareing produced no untoward results, but each successive click was like another round of Russian roulette. I was wincing by the time I got to rubbish, and I jumped when, as I steeled myself to click again, the front-door bell went. It was four o'clock.

On Tuesdays I stopped work at four to look after the boys until Caroline came home from the bookshop. As I opened the door the younger one was shouting into his brother's face: 'I'm, not, STUPID!' I looked over their heads and saw a mother from the school – Helen, or Harriet, or something – waving at me from her car. 'Thank you,' I said, waving back. As I shut the door the little one handed me a brown envelope. 'This is for you, Dad.'

'What is it?'

'It's a bump letter,' said the older one. The little one ambled past me, dropped his book bag, pulled his shredded baby blanket off the banister and walked silently into the sitting room. The television snapped to life.

I opened the envelope. Inside was a form letter on heavily photocopied school stationery with its several blanks completed in blue biro:

Dear parent:
Your child DARBY was sent to the school nurse today for HEAD INJURY RECVD IN SCHOOL PLAYGROUND.

Action taken: COLD COMPRESS APPLYED.

Please monitor your child for any further symptoms and seek the advice of a doctor if necessary.

Sincerely,

Vivienne Flynn

School Nurse

I went into the sitting room and casually ran my hands through the little one's hair, looking for contusions. He unplugged his thumb.

'Stop it, Dad.'

'Can I ask you a question?'

'What, Dad.'

'Who's Darby?'

'He's my friend but he's not my friend any more.'

'Did you have a fight with Darby today?'

'Yes but I didn't get blood on my head, but he did get blood. On his head.'

'What did you hit him with?'

'I can't see, Dad.'

'Answer me,' I said, trying a deeper register. 'What did you hit him with?'

'A bit of brick.' His brother wandered over to join in the interrogation.

'Was it a play brick or a real brick?' he demanded. An important point, I had to agree.

'Real brick.'

'Why did you hit him with a brick?' I asked. 'That's not very nice.' His eyes suddenly went liquid with outrage.

'But he hitted me with it first when he was throwing it and it went on, my, head!' He touched a spot on his crown and began to sob dramatically.

'All right, don't cry,' I said, gently finding the bump with my fingers. 'Is Darby a very naughty boy?'

'No, Dad. He's a girl.'

Caroline rang at seven.

'Hi.'

'Hi.'

'Listen, it's Lisa's last day, so we're all going to the pub for a bit after work.' Her voice had already acquired the clotted sunniness of warm champagne. She exhaled suspiciously. 'I won't be late.'

'Are you smoking?'

'No. Are you?'

'No.'

'Well, then. Any news?'

'No. Oh: we got Darby's bump letter by mistake. Do I need to do anything?'

'She's a nasty piece of work, that one.'

'I found the school list. Do I need to call her parents? She and Freddy had some kind of altercation.'

'Christ. No, don't worry. I'll sort it out tomorrow.'

'OK.'

'OK. Bye.'

'Bye.' The older one was at my elbow.

'Was that Mum?'

'Yes.'

'Is she coming back?'

'Not till late.'

'Can I stay up?'

'No.'

'Can I have sweets, then?'

'Yes.'

This time I took the precaution of filling the wine glass to the brim and leaving the bottle in the kitchen. The office was bathed in a purplish sunset light from the computer screen, which had a picture of a purplish sunset on it. This faded and was replaced by a clutch of lurid pink flowers. I bumped the mouse and my home page snapped into view with a faint audible pop. In the box it still said

giles Wareing +rubbish

I replaced 'rubbish' with 'shit' and hit return: eight results. As I scanned the list, my stomach tightened and my heart began to speed up: '. . . more shit from Giles Wareing . . .'; 'the unbelievably shit Giles Wareing'; 'that untalented little shit Giles Wareing . . .'. The next few were online reprints of a very old interview I'd done with an actor who swore a lot, but at the very bottom of the list there was a final blow, simple and direct: 'Giles Wareing = shit'.

For a moment I allowed myself to entertain the forlorn hope that the nastier comments were written by disgruntled astronomers who had fallen out with Jupiter Giles

Wareing, but they were all from the same website, the archive of a mailing list called MediaStormUK. In fact each was simply a link to something I'd written, with the comment typed underneath and the username of whoever had posted the link. They were all posted the by same person: Salome66.

I clicked on every link and read through every article, working up from the bottom of the list. I failed to see how Salome66 could read a six-hundred-word essay in praise of the cassette tape and conclude from it that I was untalented and small. There was nothing remotely objectionable about it. All the commas were in the right places. There was, I immediately felt, something unbalanced in her throwaway malevolence, an unnecessary emphasis on me. I rarely wrote the sort of things which would cause the reader to retain the author's name, much less a firm opinion of him. It seemed as if Salome66, however, had somehow divined a repulsive creature from my few words on a variety of benign subjects, and had come to see me as a figure worthy of resentment and abuse. Though I was not famous and had, in that sense, no public to answer to, I had stumbled across – I'll admit, after many hours of searching – a little clearing where my merits were being debated anyway: a place of summary judgement which had heretofore only existed in my most speculative nightmares.

Or perhaps not. No one else had offered further comment, supporting or dissenting, though there appeared to be such a facility available. While her tone implied that she expected other users of the site would be broadly in agreement with her assessments, there was no evidence in the archive – every corner of which I scoured – that anyone had ever shared or even acknowledged the opinions of Salome66, or indeed cared much one way or the other. For her to broadcast such opinions, with such vehemence, into an unanswering void, seemed transparently mad.

I could feel pity for someone who had the free time and inclination to expend such vituperation on a nonentity like Giles Wareing, but not without feeling even more pity for Giles Wareing, a subject unworthy – even by his own assessment – of criticism, considered or otherwise. Much as I disliked admitting it, strong feelings aroused by me or my work were, by definition, inappropriate. In one sense it was perversely flattering that someone cared enough. And yet I could not so easily dismiss that crude but ultimately irreducible equation still floating in front of me: Giles Wareing = shit. Sitting in front of a computer screen at one in the morning, forty, gouty and drunk, it seemed about right.

I don't remember what happened after I went down to get the bottle.

5

I was dreaming that I couldn't sleep. It was terribly real: Caroline's familiar landscape silhouetted against the gloom, the slice of street light from the gap in the curtains, the drag of the damp sheets as I rolled from side to side in mounting frustration, unable to let go of the idea that Darby's parents were not on the lookout for further symptoms of trauma. Only when the alarm went off did I realize that daylight was pouring through the open curtains and that Caroline was not there. That was why the alarm did not stop.

I found Caroline in the spare bed, looking small and matted, like an animal left in a cardboard box with some water after the dog has roughed it up. A squirrel that expires in the night. I prodded her gently. Then less gently.

'What time is it?' she said, her vocal cords grinding over the vowels.

'Seven thirty.'

'You'll have to take them to school. I'm ill.' I suddenly noticed that I wasn't feeling too clever myself, but it seemed a bad time to mention it.

Freddy sat zombified in my lap as I pulled his school

uniform on. At breakfast the older one repeated the same phrase over and over, trying out a variety of announcer's stresses.

'Dad, I want Shreddies.'

'How are you feeling today?'

'Minimal disruption.'

'Not fine.'

'Does your head hurt?'

'Yes.'

'Minimal disruption.'

'Mine too.'

'But, Dad, I don't want to go to school today.'

'Are you worried about Darby?'

'No.'

'Minimal disruption.'

Darby was not hard to spot at the school gates: a very tall, red-haired five-year-old with a butterfly bandage over one eye. I thought of the girl at the surgery on the morning of my gout attack and felt a pang of guilt, followed by a twinge in my toe.

Neither was Darby's mum difficult to pick out, given that she was engaged in a protracted argument with Darby, which Darby appeared to be winning. She was possessed of the sorts of looks which immediately silence reason, the kind of woman who could knock on my front door and get me to switch electricity suppliers against my will. I have always avoided such women, or tried to. It had never been particularly difficult.

Unfortunately Freddy had run up and was now tugging at Darby's arm, trying to get a good look at her wound. Darby, rounding off a passionate defence in what appeared to be a packed-lunch-orientated dispute, had begun to flail. I was forced to sidle over and scoop the boy up out of the way.

'Hi!' I said, a bit too cheerfully. 'I'm Freddy's dad. Giles.'

'Oh, hi,' said Darby's mum, gazing at me with an odd searching expression. I felt myself going red. 'Thanks for ringing last night.'

I forced down a rising sense of panic. Did I really ring? When? When did I ring?

'Sorry it was so late,' I said, fishing for an explanation that would cover all eventualities. 'I didn't find the letter until after everybody went to bed, but I thought I'd better let you know, just in case.' For some reason Darby was hitting me with her book bag, but I couldn't bring myself to look down.

'That's OK, I was up late anyway.' How late?

'She's all right today, I take it.' Darby was repeatedly swinging her book bag into my leg. There was something heavy in it, like a billiard ball.

'It's not as bad as it looks,' said Darby's mum. 'I went in to see the nurse about it after school yesterday.'

'So you said,' I guessed.

'Yeah.' Darby managed to catch me directly on the shin. I looked down. She looked up at me with wide, blinking blue eyes.

'Are you Freddy's daddy?'

'Yes.'

'Freddy is my boyfriend.'

'No I'm not,' said Freddy.

Darby took a giant step in Freddy's direction, planted her feet, stuck her face in his and screamed, 'YES YOU ARE!'

There were no messages. I took the opportunity to clear some damaging evidence from my office: two empty wine bottles and three glasses. Caroline intercepted me on the landing outside the spare room as I came down.

'I thought people with gout were supposed to cut down on alcohol.'

'Only beer,' I said, a screw tightening in my head. She followed me down the stairs, watched in silence as I tried to jam the bottles into the full recycling cupboard. The possibility that I might have said or done something for which I needed to apologize presented itself, but I couldn't recall a specific incident. Caroline stared intently at the calendar. She didn't seem at all angry, but there was definitely something in the air, a topic waiting to be introduced. I started to reorganize the recycling cupboard in earnest, dragging out some poorly stacked tins and the apple-juice cartons.

'They don't take the cartons anymore,' I said. 'Because of the wax.' This was true; a balding man with a clipboard had come to the door to tell me the news. When you're home all day this sort of information is often delivered in person. I thought of the willowy girl with the grey eyes who had rung the bell and convinced me to switch electricity suppliers. I thought of Darby's mum, with her cool searching stare, pale freckles dusting her collarbone.

'You have to make a decision about your birthday,' said Caroline. I shut the cupboard and stood up.

'No, I don't think I do.'

'It's your fortieth. You should do something. In a week's time it'll be too late to invite people.'

'I don't think there's anything to celebrate. I'm forty. I have gout. These are the highlights so far.' I let something unpleasant slide into my voice. Caroline paused to change tack.

'When your friends find out you're forty they're going to wonder why they weren't invited to your party.'

'What party? Come to that, what friends?'

'I'll just get a pen and we'll make a list, shall we?' My head began to throb. The inside of my mouth felt freshly plastered. I yanked open the dishwasher and felt a waft of warm, moist air hit my face.

'It's clean,' said Caroline, a little metallic ring of triumph in her voice. I picked a hot, sparkling tumbler out of the top rack and held it up to the window.

'And whom,' I said, 'do we have to thank for that?'

That morning I decided that for my own well-being I should never again look upon the words of Salome66, but my resolve loosened over the course of the day; by lunchtime I had checked the site twice, to see if she had logged any fresh sentiments. She hadn't. I added the web page to my list of favourites to facilitate access.

I took the dog to the park. Rain looked imminent and I seemed to have the whole place to myself. I left the path and found a place to sit, out of sight among the brambles. I thought a moment of painful reflection might reset my sense of self, but it only brought the remains of my hangover to the fore. Drops of cold rain began to land in the grass around me. I looked up and let them streak down my face. It was pleasant, like letting someone else do your crying for you. The dog appeared from a thicket of brambles, covered in fox shit. I looked at my watch: eighteen days to forty.

When I returned there was a message from gout boy, complaining about the picture caption, which I chose not to return, making a mental note to answer him by email later, and secretly knowing I never would. It was late afternoon before Salome66 surfaced again, this time with a link to the gout piece alongside the comment, 'more self-regarding tosh from Britain's second-worst journalist'. There was no indication who Britain's first-worst journalist might be, but I felt a perverse disappointment in being relegated to runner-up. I clicked on the link and read the piece again. How could anyone call it self-regarding? Didn't she have anything better to do? I clicked Back and then Refresh and found that Salome66 had posted another comment in my brief absence: 'if you hate this btw, you'll love this!' the final 'this!' picked out in clickable red. I brought my cursor over the word. A long web address appeared in the lower left-hand corner of the screen, only the beginning of which was familiar: it was the paper's website. A heavier rain began to rap against the skylight, speeding up like a drum roll. I clicked.

I'd known that the paper had a sort of chat room of its own, as other papers did, but I had never looked at it before. If I'd thought about it at all I suppose I imagined loyal readers discussing topical cultural issues with tiresome earnestness, all the while trying to pick each other up – a lonely hearts club dressed up as a debating chamber. I might have guessed there would be separate areas for people to discuss music and film. I might have deduced that some small section would be reserved for criticism of the British press in general, and the paper in particular. What I was not prepared for was a thread entitled The Giles Wareing Haters' Club, initiated by Salome66, with more than 180 separate posts. In retrospect, I suppose it was what I was looking for all along. A lifetime of inchoate paranoia suddenly gelled: here was confirmation that the mysterious anti-Giles Wareing forces I had hitherto only imagined not only existed but had taken the time to set up some kind of informal HQ. I could only bring myself to skim through it, but it was all here: 'my cat could write better than that'; 'smug, unfunny, pointless'; 'Agree abt Wareing. He's a cunt.' I smiled grimly at the last one. And then I vomited into the dustbin. The phone rang. It was Ken from the paper.

'Hi, mate. Fine gout piece yesterday.'

'Thanks.'

'How's the big toe?'

'It hurts more when you ring.' I felt dizzy. The smell of sick swam under my nostrils. The rain turned to hail.

'Listen, I'm sorry to call so late in the day, but can you do us a quick Words I Hate?'

'No. How long?'

'Only two hundred and fifty words, but I need it in the next hour.'

'I can't today. What's the word?'

'Your choice. It doesn't have to be topical.'

'I can't think of a word I hate.'

'Go on. You can do it standing on your head. You're the master of this kind of shit.'

I put the phone down, opened a file and typed 'Wareing/Words I Hate'. I tried to concentrate but another wave of nausea swept over me and I had to close my eyes and rest my forehead on the keyboard. I breathed slowly and steadily, waiting for the sickness to pass. I don't know how long I sat like that, but when I finally looked up the screen was filled with lowercase Ys. There were seventeen pages of them in all.

Caroline and the boys came home an hour later and found me in the garden hosing out my office dustbin.

'What are you doing, Dad?' asked the older one.

'Yeah, what are you doing, Dad?' asked Freddy.

'Hosing out my office dustbin.'

'Very fastidious,' said Caroline. She and the older one went back inside.

'Why are you doing that for?' asked Freddy.

'It was beginning to smell a bit.'

'Smell?'

'Yes.' Carrot slithered through my legs and poked his nose into the bin. I gave him a blast with the hose and he shot back into the house.

'You don't like Carrot very well don't you, Dad?'

'No.'

'But you did like Stick.' Stick was Carrot's brother, sleek and grey and playful, full of mysterious intelligence.

'I did like Stick, yes.'

'But Stick died.'

'Yes, he did. He died.' He'd been missing for two days when we found him at the bottom of next door's garden, halfway home after being hit by a car. When Caroline picked him up he was as stiff as a salt cod and flat on the underside. The breeze lifted his fur as she held him. Caroline laughed at her own tears, but something in me gave way on that night two years ago. The weight of all future tragedies, potential and inevitable, of all misfortunes, reversals and untimely deaths, pressed down for a single moment and something caved in. It somehow seemed utterly pointless to carry on living now that Stick was dead, although obviously I didn't mention that to anyone at the time. Fear rose in me like floodwater, and receded only slowly, leaving everything dank and damaged. Two years on my only thought was that it should have been Carrot.

Caroline leaned out of the back door.

'Somebody needs to go to Tesco,' she said.

'And I suppose I am somebody,' I said.

'Say it like you believe it,' she said. 'I'll make you a list.' The sun dropped into the slit between the low cloud and the horizon, illuminating a knot of small bugs churning above the lawn, looking for all the world as if they were about to spell out a message.

'I am somebody.'

'Of course you are, Dad,' said Freddy. 'You don't have to just keep on just saying it.'

6

Words I Hate No 871
Derring-do

Given that there have been no verifiable instances of derring-do since the biplane fell out of fashion, it's about time we retired this ungainly, cod-medieval word. Nowadays it tends to be used, if at all, by the sort of work colleague who thinks it's funny to say things like "Whither goest thou for lunch today?" and then wonders why you won't tell him. Even today no one is quite sure what it means. Does it refer to the deeds themselves, or the reckless courage required to perform them? Does one possess derring-do, or do derring-do? Does one dare derring-do, without knowing?

It may be of some small comfort to those who dislike such pseudo-archaisms to know that derring-do was brought into existence through a series of hideous accidents. It crops up first towards the end of Chaucer's Troylus and Cressida, in the line "In duryng don that longeth to a knyght", or "in daring to do that which is appropriate for a knight." John Lydgate borrowed the phrase for his Troy Book in 1415 – "in doring do preved a coward" – using it without an object (in daring to do what, exactly, John?). In 16th century printings of the Troy Book it was often spelled "derrynge do", and consequently came to be interpreted as an archaic substantive phrase, that is to say as a stand-alone noun. Spenser defined "in

48

derring doe" as "in manhood and chivalrie" in his notes for The Shepearde's Calendar (1579) and Sir Walter Scott's hyphenation in Ivanhoe (1819) – "a deed of such derring-do" – cemented the misapprehension.

So knights of old never indulged in derring-do, because in their day there was no such thing. It's all been a terrible misunderstanding. Case closed.

Giles Wareing

THE GILES WAREING HATERS CLUB
Started by Salome66 at 5.40 PM on 19.09.04
Membership open to all!

PavlovsKitty – 11.11 PM on 26.10.04 (193/201)
If anyone in this world deserves gout, it's Wareing

---

moretoastplease – 11.15 PM on 26.10.04 (194/201)
I read that piece. Most excruciating. He'll be writing about his fucking piles next

---

Grotius – 11.23 PM on 26.10.04 (195/201)
Why does he think we're interested in what's wrong with his body? We're not.

Salome66 – 11.30 PM on 26.10.04 (196/201)
If he could write we might be, but it was typical Wareing fare: self-obsessed, scantily researched, desperately trying to be clever and failing. 'Like hot butter through a knife'. Yuck.

---

moretoastplease – 11.39 PM on 26.10.04 (197/201)

Giles Wareing is extremely WEARING

Salome66 – 11.44 PM on 26.10.04 (198/201)

Indeed. My personal least favourite still has to be
that idiotic piece he wrote a while back in which he
tested some new voice recognition software by
writing the whole article in a strait jacket – one
lame joke, lamely executed.

---

moretoastplease – 11.47 PM on 26.10.04 (199/201)

Didn't see that. Actually sounds quite funny,
though I'm sure it wasn't.

---

moretoastplease – 11.49 PM on 26.10.04 (200/201)

200! Hooray!

Salome66 – 8.05 AM on 27.10.04 (201/201)

Morning all. Read the latest bollocks yet?

Back / Top / Add a comment

It was not a good way to begin the day, although it already
felt like part of my morning routine. I had forgotten
entirely about the straitjacket piece. It was true enough
that the concept was more amusing than the execution, but
it hadn't been my idea originally and I'd never harboured
any feelings of responsibility for the way it turned out.
Until now. I was suddenly drained of will, overwhelmed

by a sense of grinding futility. The future seemed to fall away, the past felt cancelled, the present was weighted with ache. The phone rang.

'Hi, Giles, it's Margot.' Margot from the paper. Acting deputy something or other.

'Hi.'

'How's the toe?'

'Fine.' I glanced at the crutches, now propped up in the corner, dog-chewed and flecked with dried mud. I couldn't return them like that.

'Listen, I'm ringing on the off chance. I've got a really great piece lined up and no one to do it. How would you like to interview Cher Fitzpaine?'

'A Boy Named Cher?' Cher Fitzpaine was a journalist who'd written a bestselling rehab memoir at the age of thirty. I knew people who knew him. It was possible I'd even met him a few times, although I couldn't remember any specific occasion.

'The same. He's got a new book coming out. A novel. The only thing is you'd have to turn it around pretty quickly. We want to run him on Friday.'

'When's the interview?'

'Half-past one.'

'Today?'

It was already half past when I got to Tottenham Court Road, and I still needed to buy batteries for my tape recorder. I was a quarter of an hour late by the time I got to Fitzpaine's agent's office. I was still kept waiting for a further fifteen minutes, which gave me a chance to read the first page of *A Boy Named Cher* four times without taking any of it in. I was reading it for a fifth time when he appeared.

'Hi, Giles. How are you? Nice shirt.' He stuck out his hand. I couldn't tell if he remembered me or not. I couldn't really tell if I remembered him or not. He was small. His hair and his suit were both expensively cut. His shoes were large and shiny, his eyes small and dull blue behind black wire frames. The shirt was plain white, and crisply laundered if not brand new. In fact he himself looked newly minted. As I shook his hand I realized the vague mental picture of him I'd carried around for years was in fact someone else. A chunky watch hung loosely on his wrist.

'Hi, Cher, it's good to . . .' I couldn't decide between 'see you' and 'meet you', so I let the sentence die in the air, and then coughed. 'Shall we sit at that table?'

'It's pronounced chair,' he said. I looked blankly at him.

'What is? Table?'

'My name.'

'Is it?'

'It's short for Cheriton.'

'Oh. I knew that,' I said, and I did. I knew it from somewhere. Perhaps we had met after all.

'It's the first line of the book,' he said, gesturing with his head at the paperback I still held in my hand. I looked down at the cover: the title was spelled out in lines of cocaine on a black background. The book had the sprung, dog-eared look of an oft-consulted favourite. I'd bought it second-hand not forty-five minutes before.

'That's right,' I said.

So we sat at the table, with ominous clouds gathering behind the sooty windows. I was about to ask him what it was like growing up as a boy named Chair when he reached out and touched my sleeve.

'It's a really great shirt,' he said. 'Where does it come from?' I looked down at my shirt. It was blue. Was he being sarcastic? He smiled, and I suddenly noticed that he was chewing gum. I wondered if I should make a note of it.

'The laundry basket,' I said. 'I was in a bit of a hurry.' Her face stayed blank. He chewed for a moment. Did he know I was joking? Did he just think it wasn't very funny? Was I meant to ask about his shirt? It was white. Plain white. I didn't need to know anything else.

'OK,' he said, leaning over to one side to look down my left flank. 'Talk me through the trousers.'

I tuned out at some point, letting the tape recorder listen to Fitzpaine's answers, asking the occasional question from my scribbled list. He didn't need much prompting; he talked on, one anecdote eliding into another. Occasionally I made a cryptic mark on my pad, as if something he'd said had struck me as particularly telling or noteworthy. He finally stopped talking after about forty minutes, and stared at me expectantly. I shifted in my seat, dropped my pen, whacked my shoulder on the edge of the table as I went down to retrieve it.

'So,' I said, looking past Fitzpaine's squared-off head, trying to concentrate. A handful of raindrops spattered against the window. 'So. How do you handle your, um, notoriety? Does all that bother you?'

Twenty minutes later I was in a Burger King in Oxford Street, drinking a coffee and feeling unaccountably sorry for myself.

When I opened the front door a bubbled envelope was laying on the mat. Inside was a proof copy of Cher Fitzpaine's latest book, a novel entitled *Come With Me to the Cash Bar*. 'Hilarious and harrowing by turns' was the back-cover verdict of a female author who, I happened to know, shared Fitzpaine's agent – the paperback version of her most recent fashion-fiction mid-seller figured prominently in their office display. The dog was crouched on the landing, tail thumping expectantly against the carpet.

'All right,' I said. 'Come on.'

The black-haired woman was on her bench. In what had now become an awkward little ritual, Philippa trotted over to her to be patted and spoken to, while I hung stupidly around the gate, pretending to be interested in a laminated sheet of A4 flapping on the chain-link fence of the dog run. 'SAVE ROUNDWORM PARK' it said, announcing that a meeting of the Friends of Roundworm Park would take place in the play hut to discuss crime, vandalism and the planners who were scheming to introduce evils including quad-bike racing and tennis courts. I wondered if the pleasant ping and pock of tennis balls might carry all the way to my office window of a summer afternoon. I retreated to a faraway bench and pulled out *Come With Me to the Cash Bar*, by Cher Fitzpaine:

The girl walked through his dreams at night, a foggy land-scape softened by pills and booze and peopled with nameless, sponge-faced ghosts. Only the girl remained in focus: her green eyes, the diaphanous dress, the high-spiked black Manolos she'd just bought that day they had first met . . .

It was at least as bad as I had expected. Beyond the cliché and the obsession with clothing, it was depressingly wrong-headed. The main character was a better-looking Fitzpaine, fresh out of rehab, the love interest a Czech model with a coke habit and a gangsterish boyfriend. Her pubic hair, the reader learns on page nine, is mown in the shape of a question mark. I imagined the savaging the book would endure, the additional fame Fitzpaine would accrue as a result, and the further hatred this would inspire in total strangers. I tried to imagine him enjoying the attention he had invited while ignoring its central message: your book stinks, you're a prat, you equal shit. He was probably thick-skinned enough, but I shivered at my own fragility when I thought about it.

Behind the book the dog was sitting expectantly before a soggy, split tennis ball, her eyes unfathomably hopeful.

THE GILES WAREING HATERS CLUB
Started by Salome66 at 5.40 PM on 19.09.04
Membership open to all!

---

moretoastplease – 11.14 AM on 27.10.04 (202/212)
Daring to do what, exactly, Giles? Daring to be shite?

Salome66 – 1.04 PM on 27.10.04 (203/212)
A sad little man, in love with his own opinions

Lordhawhaw – 2.22 PM on 27.10.04 (204/212)
What has this fellow got against derring-do? Is he
some sort of coward?

---

sploot – 2.43 PM on 27.10.04 (205/212)
I read that crap this morning without knowing who
it was by. Sloppy, tossed-off toss.

Salome66 – 3.17 PM on 27.10.04 (206/212)
Could this explain why he hates it so? It's from the
letters page, a few days back:

*One does not necessarily expect Giles Wareing
to be an expert numismatist, but is it too much to
ask that he check his facts (Rare Objects: The King
of Coins, Oct 21)? While readers may have enjoyed
his tale of piracy and American naval derring do,
the story overlooks a single, rather important point:
there were no 1804 silver dollars minted in 1804.
No "genuine examples" exist.*
David White
London

Grotius – 3.26 PM on 27.10.04 (207/212)
Ha ha! What a twat! Well done, David White of
London! How did you find that, Salome?

---

moretoastplease – 3.29 PM on 27.10.04 (208/212)
I didn't see that article. What was the mistake all
about?

Salome66 – 3.32 PM on 27.10.04 (209/212)
I just searched on derring-do in the archive.
Amazing what you can find.

Grotius – 3.38 PM on 27.10.04 (210/212)
Toasty: it was some filler about the "world's most
valuable coin" which Wareing clearly lifted straight
from the web, while still managing to mangle the
basic facts in the process.

---

moretoastplease – 4.01 PM on 27.10.04 (211/212)
Sack Giles Wareing!

Grotius – 5.56 PM on 27.10.04 (212/212)
Giles, if you're reading this, please kill yourself.

Back / Top / Add a comment

I was reading it. It was two in the morning, and the direct-
ness of the suggestion took me by surprise. It was as if I
had been caught eavesdropping. And still my ears burned
with the injustice of it all. I had been given precisely one
hour to write the derring-do piece, and its pointlessness was
not in dispute. Dozens of pointless pieces appeared in the

paper every day. Why single out this one? Why single out me? Why were no 1804 silver dollars minted in 1804?

I clicked on the phrase "Add a comment" at the bottom of the screen, and was greeted with the words

YOU ARE NOT LOGGED ON
You must be a registered user in order to post comments on the talkboard. If you are not registered click here to sign up.

I clicked there and filled out the required fields. My username was accepted. I logged on, clicked 'Add a comment', typed a few words in the box and clicked 'Post'. After a minute I went back to the thread and there it was.

MisterBlister – 2.22 AM on 28.10.04 (213/213)
I thougt the derring do thingwas funny.

It might have had slightly more impact with a little subediting, but in this company it was bound to be controversial. It would definitely stir things up.

Although perhaps not at half-past two in the morning. I refreshed the screen several times over a period of some minutes, waiting for a reply. I reached for my wine glass and knocked it over, smashing it on the floor, bringing my little vigil to a natural conclusion. I made it out of the room in my socks without turning on a light, in three lucky steps.

*

When I came down the next morning the boys were already at breakfast. I watched Freddy post cereal into his mouth and make his angry, chewing face.

'Morning.'

'Hello,' said the older one, without looking up.

'You look terrible,' said Caroline.

'Where are my gout pills?' I asked.

'What time did you go to bed?'

'I thought I left them just here.'

'Is it still bothering you?'

'What?'

'Your toe.'

'Oh. Yes. It is.'

I collected the shards of glass one at a time and laid them on an old newspaper while the computer warmed up. The dog sniffed at the splotches of wine on the beige rug. I felt dizzy. The computer pipped as the modem engaged. I saw that there were two new messages on the Giles Wareing Haters' Club thread. My heart started to pound, and I began to hum as if to distract myself from it. I clicked.

Grotius – 3.38 PM on 27.10.04 (210/216)

Toasty: it was some filler about the "world's most valuable coin" which Wareing clearly lifted straight from the web, while still managing to mangle the basic facts in the process.

---

moretoastplease – 4.01 PM on 27.10.04 (211/216)

Sack Giles Wareing!

Grotius – 5.56 PM on 27.10.04 (212/216)

Giles, if you're reading this, please kill yourself.

MisterBlister – 2.22 AM on 28.10.04 (213/216)

I thougt the derring do thingwas funny.

Lordhawhaw – 9.11 AM on 28.10.04 (214/216)

Traitor in our midst!

---

moretoastplease – 9.32 AM on 28.10.04 (215/216)

MisterBlister, I think you ARE Giles Wareing

Salome66 – 9.40 AM on 28.10.04 (216/216)

Ha! Spot on, toasty! You can just imagine the self-regarding prat posting his own pro-Giles propaganda (scuse alliteration) in the dead of night!

Back / Top / Add a comment

The time was precisely 9.41 AM. Salome66's comment had been written less than a minute earlier. I disconnected from the Internet, and then, with an idiotic superstition born of fear – it still shames me to write this – I unplugged the modem from the computer. Then I summoned up a blank screen, slipped the headphones over my ears and relived my interview with Cher Fitzpaine. Much of it was new to me.

CF: not really. Fame, at this level anyway, is quite enjoyable. Tell me about the shoes.

Me: How do you deal with negative reviews?

CF: I don't mind. Thankfully, the reviews for *Boy* were actually quite good.

Me: Well they weren't all good.

CF: The ones I read, that mattered to me, were, on the whole . . .

Me: What about the personal attacks?

CF: What do you mean?

Me: People slagging you off on the Internet and things.

CF: Erm. [unintelligible]. I don't really look at that stuff. I suppose it's sort of inevitable these days.

Me: But how does it make you feel to know that people are, that they're out there constantly criticizing you, insulting you, even actually hating you, without even knowing you?

CF: I don't know. I don't think about it. I mean, I don't even know that they are.

Me: Trust me. They are. [very long, awkward silence] So. Is that a new suit?

I stopped the tape and searched the talkboard for Fitzpaine. There were no results. I checked the Hate Club again. Another fan of the word derring-do had stuck his oar in – 'This is how many elements of our language come into being. What's wrong with this arsehole?' – but nothing else. The phone rang.

'Hi, Giles. It's Margot. Just called to see how you were getting on.'

'Fine.'

'Did you manage to get hold of a copy of the novel?'

'Yeah. The publisher biked it over yesterday. I haven't really got very far with it yet. Be a shame if it were any good.'

'Don't worry. It isn't. Can you file to Ken by five? I'm out all afternoon.'

As I hung up the seven hours until five o'clock stretched out before me; the allotted time seemed luxuriously ample, particularly after side two of the tape proved to be completely blank. I looked at my notes for that portion of the interview, which read in full, 'Smell? Fake tan?' and began thinking about a poached egg. The dog sensed the change in mood and began thumping her tail.

'Fuck off. It's raining.'

There were no eggs in the fridge. There was no bread in the bin. The fruit bowl was empty and the cupboard contained nothing of interest. The kitchen seemed a barren, cursed place. I stared into the sodden gloom of the back garden and weighed up the idea of taking the dog to the park after all. That's when I saw it, standing atop the lower sash of the kitchen window, next to a dead rosemary cutting in an egg cup.

The radiator key. I took it down and put it in my pocket, a small brass talisman giving off settled masculinity, quiet purpose. I had half a mind to wear it on a chain round my neck.

7

The phone rang at half-past five. Ken from the paper.

'Just a nudge,' he said.

'It's done. I mean it's basically done.'

'Fantastic. Is it vintage Wareing?'

'I don't know about that.'

'Is it patronizing, prurient and inaccurate in several of its particulars?' He'd loved that letter.

'It conforms to the house style, yes.'

'I look forward to it.'

The boys were already in their pyjamas when I came down, the younger one lying on the sofa, thumb in mouth, eyes on telly, his blanket arranged on his head like a loose turban. The older one was furiously thumbing his wooden portable games console.

'What are you playing?'

'Galactor. I'm on level 4, which is actually quite difficult.'

Having been denied a games console by Caroline, who had gone so far as to instruct several godparents not to provide him with one, he had struck back by fashioning his own out of a rectangular bridge support from the sturdy wooden train set he shared with his brother, carefully drawing on a screen, a four-arrowed toggle and buttons labelled stop and start and A and B in black biro. It was a faithful representation of the latest model, the Advantage II, a name it coincidentally shared with the current account I had been granted by virtue of my ongoing commitment to indebtedness. He spent hours working through the myriad levels of the various games he had only watched others play at the school gates. I had originally been in full accord with Caroline on the subject of the games console, but I found this a creepy and disturbing form of protest and longed to give in.

'At least he's using his imagination,' Caroline had said when I first brought it up.

'But not in a good way. He's using it to confound us.'

'He's happy playing with it.'

'That's what bothers me.'

Caroline came into the sitting room now, looking strangely fresh-faced.

'Have you finished for the day?'

'Yes.'

'Can you put them to bed? I'm just going to run over to the Forp meeting for an hour.'

'Forp?'

'Friends of Roundworm Park. I said I'd go.' She was wearing earrings. Did she usually wear earrings?

'Will you put me down as pro-tennis?'

'It won't make you very popular.' She strode over to the boys. 'I'm going out now,' she said. 'I need a kiss from you, and a kiss from you.' The older one carefully set his block of wood on pause before tilting his face toward hers. She turned to look at me. Her left ear poked out of her hair, making her look girlish and distracted. 'The microwave is broken,' she said, and left.

I went into the kitchen and poured myself a glass of red wine. The smell of it made my stomach lurch. The microwave door opened at the push of a button and closed firmly, but the start button was unresponsive. For the moment, its repair seemed beyond me. I went over to the radiator by the far wall, pulled out the radiator key and loosened the little square nut on its right flank by a quarter turn, hearing the satisfying, fizzy hiss of escaping air. I put my hand on the radiator and felt warmth spreading upwards and outwards from the centre.

'What are you doing now, Dad,' said Freddy flatly, a note of Caroline's disapproval ringing in his unconscious mimicry.

'I'm bleeding the radiator.'

'Why are you doing that for, Dad.'

'It's just one of those things you have to do from time to time.' A thin stream of hot black water jetted out of the valve. I turned the key. 'There.'

'Is it fixed?'

'Yes.'

I heard the distant burble of my office line, followed by the worn-out monotone of my own voice on the answering machine. There was an abrupt beep, and almost instantly the kitchen phone began to ring.

'Hi, Giles, it's Margot.'

'Hi.'

'Listen, I just read your piece, and it's lovely, but I do have a few queries.'

'OK. Go on, then.'

'Did you really like his book?'

'Well, I thought, I mean it was . . .'

'If you did, you did, that's fine. I just found it irredeemably awful, so I'm a bit surprised.'

'It wasn't the best thing I've ever read, no. Did that not come across?'

'I just thought you might be pulling your punches for some reason, and I wanted you to know you don't have to. We don't have any kind of deal with him.'

'No, I know.'

'Fine. And the other thing.'

'Yeah.'

'Did you really like him?' I tried to bring the piece to mind, to remember what I'd written a few hours before, but it was already a closed file.

'Not, um, not particularly. No.'

'I mean he's famously a bit of a prick, and you have him saying a lot of things that, I don't know, sound really horrible, but you kind of let them pass without comment? It's hard to tell what you think.'

'Well, I didn't want to . . .' I stopped. I could think of no way to finish the thought.

'The whole thing of, "I've met a lot of important people, but now that I'm as important as they are, it's not as much of a thrill". Who says things like that?'

'I thought I'd let him speak for himself, but if you want, I'm happy to amend.'

'Just to say a bit about how you found him, really, is all. No more than thirty or forty words. We haven't got the space.'

'No problem.'

It was a problem, however. Back upstairs I could summon nothing but a desire to defend Fitzpaine to his detractors, to carve away at the unpleasant surface until something human and forgivable remained. Where he gave me soundbites calculated to enrage the reader, I ignored them in favour of blander pronouncements. I knew he probably wouldn't thank me for it, that he was in some way encouraging, even abetting, a pithy character-assassination that would generate some publicity and move a few thousand books. With a tide of bad reviews almost certainly on the way, his sales figures were largely dependent on the bitter curiosity of his enemies. He needed more of them.

I couldn't do it. It wasn't sympathy; I had come away from the interview feeling as though something slimy had been rubbed on me. It was fear. I was already anticipating what response any vituperation on my part would bring from Salome66. It would provide another excuse to attack, to draw unfavourable comparisons, to sum me up. To criticize Cher Fitzpaine too casually, after a seventy-five-minute encounter, would only serve to legitimize the presumptuous calumny of the Giles Wareing Haters' Club. I'd spent the day imagining their callous rants, centring on the notion that I was unfit to shine Cher Fitzpaine's square-toed shoes, much less to take him apart in print. I had gone out of my way to be fair, dull and businesslike, if only to thwart them. I didn't dare offer an opinion. I'd lost my nerve.

The solution, from a journalistic point of view, was obvious for a seasoned professional like myself: I made a few minor changes that failed to address the problem, and waited a half-hour before emailing it, too late for any further revisions to be made.

In the swirling fog only the girl remained in focus: her grey eyes were still; I stood locked in their level gaze. She smiled and I felt my stomach float free.

'I don't understand this,' I said, leaning toward her. She came closer; there was now nothing between us but the threshold. I could feel her warmth, hear her skin moving against her clothes. Her smell was intoxicating. The air around us was effervescent with expectancy.

'It's simple,' she said. 'No standing charge means you only pay for the electricity you use.' The words meant nothing. There was a tiny mole between her eyebrows, just off-centre. 'In addition,' she continued, her voice now a playful whisper that made me want to close my eyes, 'there is a £10 annual discount if you use the paperless billing facility. Do you have Internet access?'

'Yes.' I broke away from her gaze, feeling the force of its magnetic pull, and looked down at the spray of freckles across her bare collarbone, sheened with perspiration. She smiled.

'Of course you do. Everybody does. Then if you add in the direct-debit discount and the cheaper rate for receiving both your gas and electricity from us, you'll be paying up to ten per cent less than you do now.'

'What do I have to do?' She was already holding out her clipboard, exposing the cool white skin on the inside of her arm. I heard a distant keening.

'You just need to sign here to confirm what we discussed. There is a fourteen-day cooling-off period, so you can change your mind any time during that. We'll take care of everything else. You'll receive a final bill from your current supplier which you should pay in full.' I heard the pitiful wailing again. Was it a woman? A child? 'There won't be any changes in your actual supply – you keep the same meter, same wires, everything. The only thing you'll notice is cheaper bills.' She knelt suddenly, and began to undo my trousers. I tried to ignore the wailing, to concentrate on what was happening. I said the words 'Like hot butter through a knife' and everything stopped.

I woke up on my front, a full erection wedged painfully under one thigh, my left arm beneath me, paralysed and unfeeling. I still heard distant cries, the words urgent but indiscernible. It seemed to be coming from as far away as the middle of the park. I held my breath and listened, until I realized that it was only air whistling through Caroline's nostrils. I rolled onto my back and lifted my lifeless arm above my head to stretch it. It fell back down, the knuckles of my hand cracking me across the nose. It was like being hit by someone else. My eyes watered.

Sometime later I heard glass tinkle on the stone steps, and the muffled whir of the milk float moving off. Caroline's breathing imitated the whine of a far-off siren, then a kitten trapped in the wall cavity. The clock's LED readout bobbed in the darkness: 5:55. I got out of bed. Grabbing the previous day's trousers from the floor, I opened the bedroom door, pulling upward on the knob to stop the hinges from creaking. The dog was already standing in the hall, looking optimistic.

'OK,' I whispered. 'Let's go.'

The centre of the park was pitch black, the wind warm and wild. My bare feet slipped inside my boots as I walked along the damp path. A powdery mist lurched violently across the open space, trees rolled and bent, branches cracking. A takeaway polystyrene box shot into the air, whirling on the axis of its hinge. To the east the dawn was just breaking pale green against the far edge of the cloud. My heart sped up; I felt light, lifted by the wind. The dog flushed a fox from under some illegally dumped construction waste near the fence and chased it in broad zigzags through the brambles. The wind dived and leapt, driving the fine rain up under my chin. I stuck my hands deep into my raincoat pockets and discovered an ancient fag packet containing three stale, curved cigarettes. Further down, deep into the lining, I found a small lighter. I smoked my first cigarette in two years sitting under a big lopsided oak which churned as if it would come down. It made me so dizzy I had to close one eye.

By sunrise the far end of the park had shaken itself dry, but the rainy night still clung to the area around the entrance, where the terraces across the street blocked out the sun's horizontal rays. The black-haired woman stood alone by the gates, leaning heavily on the handle of her tartan trolley, a long cigarette dangling from her lips, seemingly frozen in the act of rummaging through her bag. The dog circled her, sniffing the ground. I had an impulse to step in front of her and light her cigarette now I had a lighter, but I resisted. She remained in the same posture when I looked back from halfway down the road and I was suddenly struck by the idea that I didn't want her to see which house I lived in. I carried on to the newsagent's and bought a paper.

Money and Cher

Four years after his controversial rags-to-rehab chronicle made him a household name, Cher Fitzpaine is back with a novel. Giles Wareing meets him.

One is predisposed to dislike Cher Fitzpaine; his awkward, combative nature riles the bully in all of us, enjoins us with the schoolmates who, when he turned up in the middle of a term after a two-year stint in California (his mother's second marriage, to a Hollywood agent, had collapsed spectacularly), possessed of shoulder-length hair, an American accent and a name which amounted to an invitation to the take the piss, taunted him by singing I Got You Babe and Half Breed in the playground. His sullen mantra in those dark days – "It's pronounced 'chair'," he would tell them, over and over – didn't prove much of a deterrent.

The subsequent tale of isolation, extreme nightlife, celebrity-by-association, drug abuse, spiralling debt, petty crime, breakdown, rehab and true love, recounted to bestselling effect in *A Boy Named Cher*, did not exactly endear him to the literary world (one reviewer called it "insanely bad"). Fitzpaine, with studied arrogance, wrote off his detractors as jealous failures. Waiting in his agent's offices, I am expecting the sort of monster success sometimes makes of the bullied; previous interviewers have billed him as imperious, shallow, vain, self-satisfied, vindictive, smug (this is a partial list, by the way), unaware, materialistic, childish, spiteful, evil and a bore. What more could you ask for?

It is disappointing, therefore, to come face to face with a soft-spoken, polite, self-effacing, engaging and intelligent Cher Fitzpaine, who bears not even a physical resemblance to the bumptious party-boy of popular imagination. His trademark tresses are shorn; his suit sober and non-designer. "I had it made for me," he confesses, in response to unseemly prodding about its provenance, "but it's not Savile Row or

anything. I'm just a weird shape." Fitzpaine's new novel, *Come With Me to the Cash Bar*, is a romance set in the same drugged-up demimonde which numbered the author amongst its celebrity casualties, but the man who wrote it now has little in common with his protagonist, and he's hardly living up to his reputation as an irksome self-publicist. What could have happened?

"I don't suppose I was ever quite as nasty as all that," says Fitzpaine now, smiling at the thought. "But when I was doing drugs I guess I made a lot of enemies, and when I started recovery I made a few more. I deserve what I get from the first lot, but the second lot, I realized they were people who just didn't want me to get better. Pleasing them would have killed me. They're my only real enemies."

While these periods form a big part of the backdrop of *Come With Me To The Cash Bar*, the novel covers several other themes not usually associated with Fitzpaine, including gangsta rap, the post 9/11 zeitgeist and the redemptive power of fox hunting. Its scope will surprise many of his critics, as will the deftness of the writing. It's destined to be one of those rare books which comes to represent a whole generation. Fitzpaine's detractors may not recognise it as such, but he has never taken much heed of criticism. He does say this is his final statement on his wild days, a way of closing a door on them. Has the Boy Named Cher finally put his past behind him?

"I think so. I hope so. I'm steadier, calmer. I've got a girlfriend, we're getting married next year. My domestic house is in order." Yet the pressures of fame are set to intensify, with a television adaptation of *Boy* in the works. For someone in recovery, isn't all the attention a danger? "Celebrity is not as glamorous as it looks," he says. "It becomes rather routine. Sure, I've met a lot of important people, but now that I'm as important as they are, it's not as much of a thrill." This is one of those things, I suspect, that Fitzpaine says for effect, hoping perhaps that journalists won"t report the playful, ironic half-smile tugging at his mouth, that yet another of his outrageous displays of self-regard will be taken at face value. It would be remiss, if not downright unprofessional, to let him get away with it.

Cheriton Fitzpaine was born in London in 1969. The death of his father at the age of 6 and the subsequent "highly confusing" California years turned him into a shy and uncertain boy, but it was the isolation and bullying which commenced on his return to England, he says, that formed the basis of his character: he became aloof, superior, strategically irritating. "I guess the intention was to be too awkward to bully," he says now. "I couldn't fight. I saw it as my only option. It even worked to an extent; people would start in on me, and I would just make it very hard work for them."

Fitzpaine's mistake, as he sees it, was to carry this strategy into adulthood. "At some point I probably should have realised I didn't need to be such an arsehole any more," he says, "but it took two years of therapy before I felt I could stop." He drank liberally, initially to suppress his defensiveness. Cocaine enabled him to drink even more. As the night wore on he became arrogant, then cruel, and then a witless loudmouth. If he had stayed this way, the set with which he ran – mainly journalists and artists of the self-consciously louche sort – would probably have tolerated him indefinitely. His flirtation with psychosis, however, frightened the in-crowd, and he quickly found himself alone, broke and, in the famous climactic scene of *A Boy Named Cher*, naked in Borough Market, in possession of stolen celery.

"I actually had a shirt on," he says now, chuckling, "which came halfway to my knees. And some trainers. Adidas, I think. But yes, I was trouserless, and therefore walletless, which is why I stole the celery. Why I wanted it in the first place I don't know, but if I'd remembered my trousers, I'm sure I would have paid."

But then you might not be sitting here today, I venture.

"It's true," he says. "Getting arrested saved my life."

The last five years have been kind to Fitzpaine. Boy sold tolerably well in spite of the critical abuse, but the film rights made him wealthy overnight. These days his well-respected, waspish magazine column keeps him busy, though he has plenty of time to indulge his newfound interest in fashion. While he admits clothes have become a bit if an obsession (designer labels figure heavily as a leitmotif in *Come With Me to the Cash Bar*), he insists it's a just a temporary hobby, a carryover from the research he did for the book, and nothing to do with vanity. "Look at me. I"m not tall enough to be vain," he says. "I couldn't carry it off."

* *Come With Me to the Cash Bar* is published by Collop & Sprague on November 12.

'Where have you been so early?' asked Caroline. I was reading the paper in the kitchen, standing up. 'Is there more coffee?'

'The park, I couldn't sleep,' I said. 'And no.'

'Well, then, you can bloody well take them to school. I've got calls to make and things.' The older one entered with a somnambulist's gait, his hair like a bonsai spruce.

'I don't mind.'

Mothers gathered in a knot where the road dead-ended alongside the school gates, while besuited fathers came and went purposefully. I was still in my raincoat, still in boots without socks, and already beginning to feel my early start. Freddy ran off into the playground without a word. The older one joined the games-console crowd just outside the gate, standing behind a classmate to observe his thumb-work. I scrutinized a yellow police sandwich board stationed on the pavement, announcing a crime which had taken place two weeks previously. Large wet leaves artfully obscured the details.

'I think I must live near you,' said a voice. I looked up. It was Darby's mum.

'Really?'

'Where's Freddy?' asked Darby, peeling the leaves off the sign.

'He's gone in,' I said.

'I saw you this morning with your dog. I live on Gorham Road, on the corner opposite the newsagent's.' The school bell began to toll.

'Oh yeah,' I said. 'Not far.'

'What is assa-you, luh, tuh,' said Darby.

'Assault,' I said. 'Serious assault.' At the gate mothers confiscated portable games consoles, amid much argument. I caught the older one's eye as he broke off and moved toward the gates.

'Bye!' I shouted. He rolled his eyes theatrically, and spun on his heel.

'We only moved in last June,' said Darby's mum, 'I really like it round there.'

'It's nice, yeah.' I looked at my hands. I was still holding the older one's book bag.

'We really ought to organize something for the mornings.'

'Absolutely,' I said, without quite knowing what she was talking about. 'See you.'

I took the dog for another full turn around the park when I got back. Colin stopped me by the entrance.

'You all right, mate? You look a bit funny.'

'Yeah, fine,' I said. 'I didn't sleep well. Much.'

'Tell your missus I can make a start at the beginning of the month. If she's happy with that. Know what I mean.'

'No idea. I'll pass it on.'

I delayed my visit to the Giles Wareing Haters' Club until midday, in order to give its members a chance to digest the morning papers. By the time I got there, it was gone. The thread was simply missing from the list. I searched the talkboard for Wareing. There were five results, all from a brand-new thread:

TWAT MEETS TWAT

Started by moretoastplease at 10.12 AM on 29.10.04

Today our favourite very bad writer Giles Wareing interviews the celebrated very bad writer "Chair" Fitzpaine. Can anyone think of a more profligate way to waste newsprint?

Grotius – 10.21 AM on 29.10.04 (1 of 19)

Dearie me. Hard to decide who comes off worse, but I'd say Wareing edges it by a very brown nose.

Salome66 – 10.31 AM on 29.10.04 (2 of 19)

Oh my God! I haven't even looked at the paper yet!

---

moretoastplease – 10.32 AM on 29.10.04 (3 of 19)

Fitzpaine: "my domestic house is in order . . ." And what other kinds of houses might there be, Chair? This guy calls himself a writer?

Grotius – 10.35 AM on 29.10.04 (4 of 19)

He was speaking off the top of his head. GW actually had a chance to sit down and work out what he wanted to say, and this steaming pile of shit is the result

---

FritsZernike – 10.42 AM on 29.10.04 (5 of 19)

A new GW Haters clubhouse! What happened to the old one?

Grotius – 10.43 AM on 29.10.04 (6 of 19)
Deleted last night. Watch your libels please, people

Salome66 – 10.49 AM on 29.10.04 (7 of 19)
It's more horrific than anything I could have
imagined. Might one dare to describe it as 'insanely
bad'?

---

moretoastplease – 10.53 AM on 29.10.04 (8 of 19)
go on, twist me arm – It's insanely bad

Salome66 – 10.59 AM on 29.10.04 (9 of 19)
I had the misfortune to read Fitzpaine's first book
and it was truly awful – smug, badly written, full of
unpleasant self-justification – I can only imagine his
novel will be ten times worse.

Grotius – 11.00 AM on 29.10.04 (10 of 19)
To judge by Wareing's assessment it's a work of
singular genius and lasting import.

FritsZernike – 11.03 AM on 29.10.04 (11 of 19)
Guarantied to be rubbish, then, innit.

Grotius – 11.08 AM on 29.10.04 (12 of 19)
But it takes in "gangsta rap, the post 9/11 zeitgeist
and the redemptive power of fox hunting". How
could it fail to be anything but marvellous?

Lordhawhaw – 11.14 AM on 29.10.04 (13 of 19)
Morning all. Are Giles and Cher by any chance related? I think we should be told.

Salome66 – 11.16 AM on 29.10.04 (14 of 19)
It would certainly explain GW's excruciating, erm, deference

RhymeMaiden – 11.21 AM on 29.10.04 (15 of 19)
No matter what our Giles pretends
He with Fitzpaine must be friends
How else can we explain the farce
Of Wareing crawling up his arse?

Grotius – 11.22 AM on 29.10.04 (16 of 19)
It's a bit early for verse, RhymeMaiden. Though I agree with the sentiment.

Salome66 – 11.31 AM on 29.10.04 (17 of 19)
If one reads between the lines (it's less painful than reading the actual prose, I find), one can detect in Wareing a certain snivelling envy. He clearly both worships and despises Fitzpaine for his undeserved success, but he doesn't dare begrudge him it, because he knows undeserved success is the only kind he could ever hope to aspire to. Apologies for the dangling preposition.

Back / Top / More / Add a comment

I had reached the bottom of the page. My throat was dry, my heart thudded as if I had run a mile. I could dismiss all of this as casual, recreational cruelty, the electronic equivalent of drawing a moustache on a bus-shelter movie poster; all of it, that is, except the last post. I realized that Salome66 not only hated me, but had my measure. Everything she'd written was right. The phone rang.

'Hi, Giles, how's it going.' It was Ken from the paper.

'Hi.'

'Nice piece today. You auditioning for the back of Fitzpaine's book?'

'No.'

'Well, it was jolly kind. You do know, of course, that he's fallen off the wagon hard.'

'Really.'

'And that his novel is going to get crucified in next Saturday's paper.'

'I can imagine.'

'And that he is famously a cunt of the first water.'

'I had heard, yes.'

'It's great that you were able to see another side of him, I think.'

'Is this call about anything?'

'I'm just ringing to RSVP in the affirmative.'

'For what?'

'For your fortieth, mate. I've been asked. See you Friday week.'

'Great,' I said. 'Any idea where?'

When he was gone I held my breath and clicked on *Next*. There were now twenty-two posts in total.

PavlovsKitty – 11.47 AM on 29.10.04 (18 of 22)
A Cher Fitzpaine apologist! I didn't know there was such a thing!
Apart from Fitzpaine himself, of course

Lordhawhaw – 11.54 AM on 29.10.04 (19 of 22)
Or perhaps they're lovers

Salome66 – 12.03 PM on 29.10.04 (20 of 22)
Too cosy for words, isn't it? But I imagine it's just a case of one terrible writer coming to the rescue of another out of instinct, being unwilling to criticise someone whose manifest inadequacies so closely mirror his own. Unless the idiot Wareing has a book coming out soon and they've made some sort of deal.

Lordhawhaw – 12.09 PM on 29.10.04 (21 of 22)
I still think they are b*mming each other

---

moretoastplease – 12.17 PM on 29.10.04 (22 of 22)
Unless the idiot Wareing has a book coming out soon . . .
Heaven forefend!

Back / Top / Add a comment

My hands were shaking. I itched all over. Sweat was gathering in the runnels of my ears. It was clear to me that

I had to stop reading this stuff. I could see it turning into a peculiar form of self-harm. I was already obsessed. Me, who avoided all confrontations that might involve criticism, who knew better than to listen at locked doors, who knew all the barked places on his thin veneer of self-regard. I took a few deep breaths, and tried to look at things realistically. The ability of Salome66 to peer directly into my soul was probably, most likely, coincidence: two lucky punches landed in a row. She didn't, couldn't really know me. I was just feeling vulnerable because my birthday was approaching, and because there was an article by me in today's newspaper which I knew was not exactly my best work. Salome66 was in all likelihood a sad, lonely woman with too much time on her hands, perhaps even a failed writer who drew comfort from attacking someone who had what she didn't. I should feel sorry for her. I should think more generously of her. I should, at the very least, ignore her.

I clicked the refresh button. There were two new posts:

Grotius – 12.26 PM on 29.10.04 (23 of 24)
Here we are – the Wareing opus in its entirety:
http://www.bookbargains.co.uk/-/Wareing_Giles_
The_Story_of_Irish_Whi/009–14–3.html
*"Giles Wareing's enthralling history of distilling in
Ireland traces the roots of* uisce beatha *from its
humble beginnings to present-day manufacturing
methods . . ."*
Order yours today!

83

Salome66 – 12.34 PM on 29.10.04 (24 of 24)
How utterly perfect! His "book" is nothing more
than a distillery-sponsored pamphlet – no doubt the
product of some boozy four-day junket in Dublin –
designed to be sold in "heritage site" gift shops.
I imagine he's extremely proud of it nonetheless, but
wonders from time to time if he should continue to
rest on his laurels! You've made my day, Grotius!

Back / Top / Add a comment

I believe this was the point when I first entertained the idea of finding Salome66 and killing her.

The phone rang. It was Caroline, calling from downstairs.

'The microwave is still broken.'

'I've looked at it.'

'And?'

'I need to look at it again.'

'Well, if you've got nothing better to do, perhaps you could look at it now.'

The dog dragged herself up, stretched and followed me downstairs. Caroline was at the kitchen table, making another party list.

'I'm not sure about this,' I said. 'I don't want my face to get melted off.'

'We need a microwave. If you can't fix it, I'll buy a new one.'

'It's just not my area of expertise, radiation.' Again the keypad responded normally, apart from Start. It bleeped as usual, but there was no fan noise, no satisfying thunk of engagement. The light stayed off.

'The Goslings can't come,' said Caroline.

'That's a blow. Who are they?'

'You know. They were at thing's dinner last week. They're both tiny. Tiny little pepper-pot people.'

'Maybe I just didn't see them.'

'You've met them loads of times. Anyway they can't come, so it doesn't matter.'

The microwave door opened easily – perhaps too easily – at the push of a button. 'Who is coming?'

'Almost everybody else. Lisa and Claire. Sam and Gabby. Next door, the Skeldings, Jake, Libby. All your work people said yes. About thirty so far.'

'Christ.' On the inside of the microwave door there were two plastic hooks like crooked fingers, aligned vertically, which slid into two identical slots in the frame, where they communicated with two unseen locking mechanisms. One of them, the uppermost, had lost its rounded tip. This, I deduced, had to be the problem. The top latch was clearly essential to the function of the oven: apart from locking the door, it probably served to disengage the safety mechanism that prevented the microwave from operating when open. Without its tip, it couldn't interact with that mechanism. If this were true, then the only reason the microwave wouldn't work was because it didn't know its door was shut.

'I can fix this,' I said. 'I can do it.'

'Marvellous,' said Caroline. 'Take that sorry-looking dog out first.'

Roundworm Park was empty but for three uniformed schoolgirls, two of whom were having a fistfight. The third stood to one side and whooped obscenities. I decided to give them a wide berth, walking halfway round the path in the opposite direction and then turning back. The dog strode directly into the middle of the field, where the last of the mist shrouded a large man with a heavy limp and a stick. I recognized his silhouette and knew that he was hobbling in attendance behind a tiny terrier, invisible in the tall grass, waiting patiently for it to complete its peripatetic late morning toilet. I winced as Philippa sniffed his hand and then proceeded to hunch her back and drop a turd at his feet. Then I saw him reach down and pick it up, using a carrier bag as a gauntlet. Then he stood up and waved in my direction. I waved back.

Shamed by the way he had spared me a chore which I was never going to perform anyway, my face grew hot as I continued along the path. I tried to imagine being the sort of person who would selflessly pick up the turd of another man's dog, but I couldn't. Distracted by my own embarrassment, I forgot to turn around and found myself bearing down on the schoolgirls. Only two were left; they sat smoking on a bench while one dabbed at the bloodied earlobe of the other. My conscience still stinging from the turd incident, I felt a sudden surge of civic wherewithal course through me. I forced myself to slow down, to lift my eyes from the path. The dog sidled up to the girls, tail wagging her back end, and sniffed at their bare knees.

'No school today?'

'Fuck off, Granddad,' said the injured one with an accomplished snarl, before turning her attention to the dog. 'Aw. In't you sweet.'

I mixed the epoxy resin and the hardener on a magazine using an ice-lolly stick, the sickly raspberry taste of the lolly still on my tongue. The letter box snapped, spewing post onto the mat. I gathered up the letters and catalogues and brought them back into the kitchen. Most of them were addressed to the Slovakian au pair who'd given her notice in June. Five months later she still got more mail than I did. Only one was addressed to me: a small, stiff, square grey envelope. Inside was a square grey card:

> You are invited to the launch of
>
> Cher Fitzpaine's new novel
>
> COME WITH ME TO
> THE CASH BAR
>
> Published by Collop & Sprague
>
> On November 12, 2004
> 7:30 til late at The Surgery
>
> Please bring this invitation WITH YOU.

The date leapt out at me, because it was my birthday. My fortieth birthday. I stared at the card, thinking of many other things, hundreds of other things, until I was thinking of nothing at all. In the meantime the epoxy went hard on the stick.

TWAT MEETS TWAT

Started by moretoastplease at 10:12 AM on 29.10.04

Today our favourite very bad writer Giles Wareing interviews the celebrated very bad writer "Chair" Fitzpaine. Can anyone think of a more profligate way to waste newsprint?

PavlovsKitty – 1.24 PM on 29.10.04 (25 of 28)

A friend of mine works at Collop and she says everyone is shitting it because the Fitzpaine book is so bad.

FritsZernike – 1.29PM on 29.10.04 (26 of 28)

Wareing is terrible. Why is he everywhere? Why is he anywhere?

Salome66 – 2.11 PM on 29.10.04 (27 of 28)

Ah, but you'll note he never writes anything remotely serious or worthwhile. They wouldn't trust him with it.

He never writes anything funny either, but that
doesn't stop them.

Back / Top / Add a comment

'Go on,' I said, handing Caroline a mug full of water. 'Try
it.'

She put the mug in the microwave, shut the door, typed
in twenty seconds and hit Start. There came the satisfying
thunk, the whir of the fan, the interior light illuminating
the spinning cup.

'A triumph,' said Caroline. 'What was wrong with it?' I
wanted to tell her, to describe how I'd isolated the problem
by a process of elimination and deduction, how I'd used
epoxy resin to reconstruct the teardrop tip of the top latch,
sanding it back until it perfectly matched its mate, at one
point taking too much off and having to start again.

'It was the door,' I said. The microwave beeped and
went dark. It was as if a little play about a rotating mug
had come to the end of Act I.

8

The bedside lamp was shining directly into my eyes, and moving in lopsided circles. All around it was dark.

'Wake up, Dad. It's your birthday.' The bare bulb was inches from my face.

'Happy birthday,' said Caroline, in a singsong voice you would use on a child.

'Please don't burn me.'

'You are fifty today, aren't you.'

'Forty.'

'Yeah, forty.'

'Can you put the lamp down?'

'Try not to be totally joyless in front of your children,' said Caroline.

'Ow!'

'Sorry, Dad.' Caroline's weight came off the bed. The overhead light went on. I could see blackness beyond the gap in the curtains.

'What time is it?'

'Quarter to six.'

'Christ.'

'Show a little bit of enthusiasm. They're really excited.'

'Where's the other one?'

'Here!' he said, coming through the door dragging a huge wrapped triangular box. 'Happy birthday.' The package hit the bed with a lingering, faraway hollowness.

'I need to pee.'

'Help Dad open it,' said Caroline. They began to claw at the paper, rending it from the box in strips.

'It's a violin!' shouted Freddy.

'No,' said the older one. 'A guitar.'

'Oh yeah. A guitar. It's a guitar, Dad.'

'Wow. So it is. Thank you. I can't play the guitar.'

'You'll have to learn,' said Caroline. 'It's what men your age do.'

'Open this now,' said Freddy. He handed me a book-shaped package.

'What could it be,' I said, shaking it.

'It's a book,' he said. 'But not a real book. A pretend book.' I opened it up. It was a black hardbound book with blank pages.

'I see.'

'You have to write it yourself. It's a trick book.'

'Thank you.'

'It's called a diary, Freddy,' said the older one.

'Yeah. It's a diary, Dad. It's funny isn't it.'

'You're very hard to buy for,' said Caroline.

'I know.'

I was allowed to stay in bed after I finished opening my presents, but I couldn't get back to sleep. I resented the theme of my birthday so far, and I resented having to pretend not to resent it, but as I lay there I began to experience an odd stirring, a tiny flame of optimism guttering in the pit of my stomach. I tried to quench it, but it kept reappearing. Finally, it coalesced into a proposal: why not ride out the next year on a wave of self-improvement? Learn the guitar, keep a diary, master whatever little dark arts take my fancy? The list of possibilities grew: French, car repair, kung fu, poker, stage hypnotism, bread-making, quantum theory. By the end of the year I would be so improved that I would barely be me. I pulled off the duvet and sat up, possessed of a strange energy, and also a terrible, terrible sense of dread. I decided to ignore the latter, to fight it, choke it back, suck it up, to destroy it through force of will. I remember I had to sit there for quite a long time.

12.11.04

Today, on my fortieth birthday, I am inaugurating my diary for the year, a year of self-improvement, achievement, success and yes, well-being.

Having received this diary not two hours ago, I have had little time to firm up my manifesto. However, my sincere intentions include, but are by no means limited to, the following:

I will aim to become a better writer, of longer and more serious things, with the ultimate goal of rendering all criticism of my work, be it Internet-based or otherwise, laughably wide of the mark.

In the meantime I will disregard any criticism, be it

Internet-based or otherwise, which is based on the work of or preconceptions held about the old GW.

I will strive to be honest with myself or, failing that, this diary, at all times.

I will strive to get more and better friends so that I will never again have to approve a birthday guest list comprised largely of Caroline's friends, people from the paper with whom I have never previously socialised and couples from the school gates.

I will from now on make a sincere effort to clean up after the dog. It's the future.

I will try to drink less and exercise more. In addition, I will re-give up smoking after tomorrow night.

I will learn to play the guitar Caroline bought me for my fortieth birthday, and I mean properly.

I will become a better, more engaged father. I meant to put this one right at the top, by the way.

I will strive to improve my appalling phone manner.

I have not written this much in long-hand since I was twenty-two, so I will stop now.

GW

The Chord of the Day is Amaj7.

I rang the features editor and left a message on his voice mail, saying I had an idea for a longish piece which would be ideal to run in the coming weeks. I left my number twice, trying to keep the sweat dampening my hairline out of my voice. Then I left an embarrassing silence before hanging up.

I looked at my newly cleaned and empty desk, at my

new black diary, then at the guitar lying on the floor in its cardboard box. I picked it up and began to tune it. This took me a while, even with the little machine that Caroline had given me. I ran haltingly through the five chords I knew, the five chords everyone knows: C, A, G, D, E. Then I set about learning a new one. I'd chosen Amaj7 because it looked simple in the little book of chords that came with the guitar, a variation of A requiring the single fret displacement of one finger, but the chord itself was not so straightforward: it had a troubling, incomplete quality, open-ended, undecided, as if one chord were trailing warily into the territory of another, evoking a weird, sinister optimism not unrelated to what I was feeling at the time. It's possible that whatever chord I had chosen that day would have struck me as being infused with the same sieved mixture of hope and menace, apart, I think, from F. I strummed Amaj7 over and over, worrying it like a loose tooth. I played it alongside some other chords and found it had a pleasing affinity with D. I strummed them alternately and they sounded good, apart from the long, dry gaps when I stopped to reposition my fingers. The simple composition only seemed to grow richer with repetition. The phone went.

'Hello.'

'Hello, can I speak to Giles Wareing, please?'

'Speaking.'

'Hi, this is Amanda from London AllTalk? From the Duncan White programme?' I had never heard of either.

'Hi.'

'Giles, I don't know if you know this, but Duncan does a health spot every Friday at midday, and we were all just reading a recent article you'd written with great interest.'

'The fireworks thing?'

'No. It was about gout?'

'Oh, yeah.'

'Giles, we wondered, as both an expert and a sufferer yourself, if you would be willing to come on and talk about it?'

'You mean today?'

'It would be here at our studio? We will send a car for you.' I had a question, which was about money, but I didn't know how to ask it. I had dreaded the notion of becoming Mr Gout, but now the title had been conferred I felt oddly proud.

'Um, OK, yeah. Why not.'

'Great! Let me take your address.'

I was too jittery to pursue Amaj7 further. I wandered downstairs. Six cases of wine and several boxes of glasses were stacked up in the hall. Caroline was talking on the phone while Colin painted the ceiling above the extractor hood, his pink forehead speckled with ivory dots.

'All right, Guy?'

'Fine, yeah. Fine.' I reached round him to get the coffee pot, a small Italian model with half its handle melted off. 'Want coffee?'

'Tea, please, mate. Big four-oh today, is it?'

'That's right.'

'Many happy returns. I still haven't had me invitation, you know.' Caroline put down the phone and regarded us both.

'Don't think I can't hear you up there playing that bloody guitar all morning,' she said. She picked the phone up again. 'Colin, if you don't finish that fucking ceiling by this afternoon I'll kill you.'

On the way back up the stairs I stopped to bleed the radiator on the landing. Water gurgled up lazily as the air hissed out of the valve. The bubble in the system was shrinking, but it was also consolidating, gathering in the radiators higher up.

I chased the ringing phone up the stairs, splashing coffee on the skirting boards. I grabbed the receiver on the fourth ring, but it was too late. 'You've reached Giles Wareing,' said the worn voice, now no longer mine, a register too deep and cloudy with sediment. 'Please leave a message or try me on 020—' I hit the stop button.

'Hello?'

'Wareing. What's new?' It was the features editor.

'Hi, Brian. Fine.' I realized that I was answering the wrong question, but I pressed on. 'You?'

'An idea for a piece, you said. Tell me about it quickly.' I regretted ringing him, as always.

'It's basically,' I said, 'it's sort of a history piece.'

'Uh-oh.'

'About the Barbary War.'

'OK. What's that?'

'The Barbary War? Basically it was America's earliest attempt at a pre-emptive foreign policy. They decided to engage the Barbary pirates in the Mediterranean, rather than pay tribute. It was also their first adventure in the Middle East; there are a lot of parallels with what's going on right now.'

'When are we talking about?'

'1800. Straight after the Revolution, pretty much.' There was a pause.

'It sounds boring.'

'It's not, though. It's narrative non-fiction, history come to life, with lessons relevant to the current situation.'

'Is this like, some sort of hobby of yours?'

'It won't be boring. It will be fun.'

'OK. Don't do more than eighteen hundred words. Now I have an idea for you.'

'What is it?'

'VHS. Why we still love it. Eight hundred words.'

'For today?'

'Yes. Remember your ode to the cassette tape? Same piece, different format.'

'Got it.'

'Good. See you tonight.'

I turned on the computer.

TWAT MEETS TWAT
Started by moretoastplease at 10.12 AM on 29.10.04
Today our favourite very bad writer Giles Wareing interviews the celebrated very bad writer "Chair" Fitzpaine. Can anyone think of a more profligate way to waste newsprint?

Salome66 – 11.31 AM on 8.11.04 (78 of 91)
Agree – the Bonfire night piece was awful, if not quite his worst. It's the same old formula: strike a mildly contrary position, waffle on for a bit, throw in 5 or six obvious "jokes", then use some meaningless, inelegant turn of phrase to find your way out at the end.

FritsZernike – 2.35 PM on 8.11.04 (79 of 91)
If only it were that good . . .

Salome66 – 3.21 PM on 8.11.04 (80 of 91)
I think our Giles might be having some kind of mid-life crisis. There's a terrible weariness about his writing, don't you think? All that bollox about preferring the "naked transaction of trick or treating" – it's so cynical, so lazy, so painfully second-rate that I'm beginning to suspect it might be a cry for help.

Lordhawhaw – 5.04 PM on 8.11.04 (81 of 91)
He's gone a bit quiet since, has Giles

FritsZernike – 5.13 PM on 8.11.04 (82 of 91)
maybe he's seen this thread and decided to give up journalism . . .

---

moretoastplease – 11.44 PM on 8.11.04 (83 of 91)
fingers crossed

Grotius – 10.32 AM on 9.11.04 (84 of 91)
It's here! It's finally arrived!

LOLOLO – 2.07 PM on 9.11.04 (85 of 91)
what has?

Grotius – 2.39 PM on 9.11.04 (86 of 91)
I thought you'd never ask!

Grotius – 2.49 PM on 9.11.04 (87 of 91)
Only a rare, out-of-print, first (and only) edition of
The Story of Irish Whiskey by Giles Wareing! It took
a fortnight to get here, but at last it's mine! All
mine!

Salome66 – 3.11 PM on 9.11.04 (88 of 91)
Oh my word, Groty! You didn't pay for it, did you?

Grotius – 3.13 PM on 9.11.04 (89 of 91)
I did! And it was worth every penny. Excerpts to
follow shortly . . .

Salome66 – 3.20 PM on 9.11.04 (90 of 91)
Looking forward to it.

Lordhawhaw – 8.04 AM on 12.11.04 (91 of 91)
Take your time, Grotius, why don't you

Back / Top / Add a comment

Poring over the latest entries, I discovered that each username was clickable, and that clicking took one to a page where posters listed any personal information they cared to divulge. Some left positive CVs; others provided links to websites of their own; Salome66, predictably, gave away nothing at all; her personal page was blank apart from a webmail address. It did open a door, however, to the possibility that all my Internet enemies could be unmasked, investigated, their hatred of me explained away by the discovery of their own grand failings. But it would take time. The phone rang.

'Is that Giles Wareing?'

'Speaking.'

'Hi, Giles, it's Molly Brennan.' Who?

'Hi.'

'Your GP.'

'Oh, hi.'

'I've just got your test results back.'

'Oh, great. That took a while, didn't it?'

'They lost the samples for a bit, apparently.'

'Huh. Typical.' I'd tried to use an us-against-them tone, but it didn't come out right. She inserted a brief, deliberate pause.

'Anyway, they make quite interesting reading. Your uric-acid levels are more or less normal.'

'Meaning that the gout isn't as bad as we thought?'

'Meaning that you haven't got gout at all.' I couldn't think of a reply made of words.

'Eaammhhh.'

'The joint fluid confirmed it. I also had you tested for pseudogout, just in case.'

'Pseudogout. You mean false gout?' I couldn't believe it.
'Hysterical gout?'

'Pseudogout is actually an arthritic condition caused by
calcium deposits. It can be rather debilitating, and potentially degenerative. It usually starts in the knee, which is
why I didn't suspect it at first.'

'So pseudogout is worse than gout?'

'It can be. Fortunately, you don't have either.' Was she
making a game of this? Was she smiling on the other end?

'So what do I have?'

'You don't appear to have anything. Everything looks
normal.'

'But you said I had gout.' I heard the door buzzer go
downstairs.

'That diagnosis was preliminary, and based on the symptoms you described,' she said.

'So I was lying?'

'This is meant to be good news. You're supposed to be
happy.'

'I am happy. Thank you very much. I've got to run.'
Caroline's footsteps were already trudging upwards, towards
her preferred shouting post.

'THERE'S A CAR HERE FOR YOU.' I put down the
phone, stood up and instinctively patted myself for keys.
I passed Caroline on the stairs without a word, or
even eye contact.

9

The office was strangely understaffed. Only three desks out of perhaps twenty were occupied, one of them by me. Amanda from AllTalk had given me a cup of coffee and left me there. The fluorescent lighting seemed to be at half-strength, insufficient to dispel the matt-grey gloom which pressed against the windows. Two people in coats and scarves stood by the door in hushed discussion. Phones burbled briefly before answering themselves. The current radio programme – the one I was about to be on, *The Duncan White Show* – pattered away in the foreground, emanating from high-mounted speakers with the persistence of drizzle. No wonder no one was here. Someone from Barking was on the line to Duncan, complaining about unauthorized travellers' sites, or bendy buses, or the unnecessary signage spoiling our historic high streets, or perhaps all three. The subject didn't seem to matter once you were on the air. The whole business, he said, had gone too far. It had gone beyond a joke. They were closing all the post offices. Football clubs no longer cared about their supporters. Everything was about money. The water had been coming out brown for two months, but no one did anything. Pizzas were getting smaller. Kids were haring up and down the road all night on mini-bikes. Asylum-seekers were eating swans. No one listened.

'Coming up in the next half hour,' said Duncan, 'we've got journalist Giles Wareing talking about the perils of gout.' My heart thudded, even as my eyelids itched with tiredness. My breath was slow and shallow. I wanted to be somewhere else.

The heavy door at the other end of the room broke its seal with a squeak. Amanda stepped through and held it open with her back.

'We're ready for you,' she said. 'Do you want to come through?'

I was forty. I did not have gout. They were ready for me.

THE DUNCAN WHITE SHOW – TRANSCRIPT

London AllTalk Radio 98.6 FM – Taking London's Temperature
A subsidiary of Featherbed Communications plc

TX: 12.11.04 – Health Issues: Gout on the Rise

Producer: Amanda Jennings
Presenter: Duncan White

Guest: Giles Wareing

THIS TRANSCRIPT WAS PRODUCED FROM A RECORDING, NOT FROM A SCRIPT. FEATHERBED COMMUNICATIONS PLC CANNOT BE HELD RESPONSIBLE FOR THE ACCURACY OF ITS CONTENTS.

WHITE: Thank you, Carole. Now gout is a disease normally associated with overweight men in powdered wigs, but there are at present an estimated half a million gout sufferers in the UK, many of them surprisingly young, and there are indications that the numbers are getting bigger. What's causing the great gout epidemic? With me today is journalist Giles Wareing, something of an expert on the condition as he is, in fact, a sufferer himself. Welcome, Giles.

WAREING: Thank you.

WHITE: And how's the gout today, Giles? Playing you up at all?

WAREING: No it's fine today, thanks (laughs).

WHITE: Glad to hear it. Now, we joke about gout all the time. It's got a reputation as a sort of humorous disease, but it's really no laughing matter is it?

WAREING: Not at all. It can be extremely painful.

WHITE: Indeed, you yourself . . .

WAREING: And potentially debilitating, if left untreated.

WHITE: Yes. You described it as like having a boulder dropped on your toe over and over again.

WAREING: Yeah. Or a heavy log. Pretty excruciating.

WHITE: It always seems to start in the toe, doesn't it? Why is that?

WAREING: Well, it's mainly to do with gravity. Gout is caused by excess uric acid in the blood, which will eventually settle in lower extremities as . . .

WHITE: Hold that thought Giles. We're going to take a quick break here. If you have any questions for Giles Wareing, or any personal experiences of gout you'd like to relate, the number to call is 0207 222 3131, or of course you can email us at d.white@alltalk.co.uk

-transcript break-
[THEME MUSIC]

WHITE: We're back, I'm Duncan White and I'll be with you right up to two o'clock. We've got traffic and travel at twenty past the hour, and right now I'm here with Giles Wareing, journalist and gout sufferer, and we are talking, appropriately enough, about gout. What d'you take for it, Giles? Are there such things as gout tablets?

WAREING: The standard treatment for symptoms is with NSAIDs, but there are also . . .

WHITE: NSAIDs – what are they when they're at home?

WAREING: Sorry, it stands for, uh, let me get it right . . . non-steroidal anti-inflammatory drugs. That's anything from ibuprofen to aspirin, and a variety of prescription medications, although it . . .

WHITE: And, as we said at the top, more and more young people are being affected by gout – although I gather it's still people like yourself, more in the forty to fifty age range, who are most at risk. Is that right?

WAREING: I'm just forty.

WHITE: Well, you don't look a day over it, mate.

WAREING: I'm not. Today's my birthday.

WHITE: [laughs] Great stuff. So, if you have any questions for Giles about his gout, or you just want to wish him a happy birthday, the number to call is 0207 222 3131. That's 0207 222 3131. Just had a thought. Interesting question for you Giles. Do you think all this low-carb business, Atkins et cetera, could be responsible for the huge rise in gout in the younger generation?

WAREING: I'm not sure about Atkins specifically, but

certainly there's an idea that rapid weight loss can lead to a gout attack. If the kidneys are put under strain then obviously that interferes with their normal function, and . . .

WHITE: And before you know it a nation of low-carb dieters becomes a nation of gout sufferers.

WAREING: Well, sort of.

WHITE: Sobering thought. Don't deny yourself those spuds, friends, or you could end up like Giles here. What foods shouldn't we be eating then, if we want to avoid the dreaded gout?

WAREING: Obviously alcohol is a factor, red meat, shellfish, certain vegetables, such as asparagus. Dairy products, interestingly, can be of some benefit. They, uh . . .

WHITE: Well, you can take my asparagus away any time. Absolutely hate the stuff. And not just because it makes your . . . well, we won't got into that. We've got David from Loughton on the line. Hello David!

CALLER: Yes, hello, Duncan. I'm a gout sufferer, on and off for nine years or more, and I cannot believe that someone who purports to be a so-called gout expert would recommend aspirin as a remedy.

Because any doctor will tell you that gout can actually be exacerbated by aspirin. I'm really shocked that such dangerous advice is being put out on the airwaves.

WAREING: I don't think I did recommend it.

WHITE: I think you might have, mate. It sounded like it to me.

WAREING: Well, I'm sorry if I was misunderstood. I did say that aspirin was an NSAID, which it is, but I didn't mean to suggest . . .

WHITE: So you shouldn't take aspirin for gout, then.

WAREING: Yeah. No. I mean, I think he's right, you shouldn't.

CALLER: Absolutely not, it's . . .

WHITE: As always, consult your doctor before taking any medication. Thanks for the warning there, David from Loughton.

WAREING: It raises uric acid levels in the blood for some reason.

WHITE: OK, today's subject is gout, the number to call as usual is 0207 222 3131. We've got traffic at

twenty past, news at the top of the hour, I'm
Duncan White, and here's Carole to tell you a bit
about tonight's special edition of sports chat live . . .

-transcript break-
[THEME MUSIC]

WHITE: Good afternoon, you're listening to the
Duncan White Show, here with you until 2 PM,
traffic coming up. With me today is Giles Wareing,
a freelance journalist and self-appointed gout
expert. And today also happens to be his birthday,
so it's jolly nice of him to come down. Many happy
returns, Giles.

WAREING: Thank you.

WHITE: We've got an email from Dennis in Ruislip
who says, 'How do I know if I've got gout?' I
gather, Giles, that the symptoms are pretty
unmistakeable.

WAREING: You could say that.

WHITE: Now talk us through your own gout, Giles,
because you've written about this. It all begins with
this terrific pain in your big toe . . .

WAREING: That's right.

WHITE: The pain is absolutely searing, isn't it? You described it at one point as being like hot butter through a knife. I have absolutely no idea what that means [laughs], but I'm happy to take your word for it.

WAREING: Well, it's difficult to describe.

WHITE: Worst pain you've ever felt?

WAREING: [pause] That's hard to say. Pain is relative. And you don't really remember pain. But bad. Even the weight of the bed sheet is unbearable.

WHITE: Right. Ouch. So you hobble off to the surgery, in terrible agony, and they, how do they know it's gout?

WAREING: Unfortunately a solid diagnosis takes a bit of time. They need to do a blood test, an X-ray, possibly draw off a bit of fluid from the joint.

WHITE: So how long is it before you get the results of all that?

WAREING: Well, if they misplace the samples, like they did with mine, it could be several weeks.

WHITE: Typical! [laughs] Typical NHS. So when did you finally get them?

WAREING: Actually the final results just came in this morning.

WHITE: [laughs] Unbelievable!

WAREING: Well . . .

WHITE: And what are they looking for, exactly?

WAREING: Uh, you'd basically be looking for raised levels of uric acid in the blood, but this isn't conclusive on its own, which is why they often take a bit of . . .

WHITE: So your problem is, you've got too much of this stuff in your blood. What can they do about that?

WAREING: Yes, so they . . .

WHITE: What's high, then? How high was yours?

WAREING: Actually my levels appeared to be relatively normal.

WHITE: That's a bit of a mystery, isn't it?

WAREING: As I say, it's not a conclusive measure. So they check the joint fluid under a microscope,

because it could also be something called
pseudogout.

WHITE: Pseudogout! [laughs] What's that, when you
pretend you've got gout so you can get a disabled
parking badge [background laughter]?

WAREING: Not exactly, no. Pseudogout is caused by
a different sort of crystal build-up, but in many
cases it's . . . it's worse than gout. It can be worse
than gout. It's basically a form of arthritis, with
gout-like symptoms.

WHITE: Pseudogout! You could not make it up
[background laughter]. Debbie is now hysterical.
She's come in to do the traffic and now she's crying
with . . . Debbie, you're supposed to stay quiet!
Calm down, dear!

DEBBIE: [unintelligible]

WHITE: I know. Debbie will be giving us the traffic at
twenty past, if she can pull herself together by then.
In the meantime we're here with journalist Giles
Wareing, who is suffering from something called
[laughs] pseudogout. Debbie's setting me off now.
Do you often get this sort of reaction, Giles, when
you tell people you've got pseudogout?

WAREING: I don't have pseudogout.

WHITE: Sorry, I got a bit confused there when Debbie started [laughs], when she started her rather indecent sniggering. What have you got, Giles? What is wrong with you, exactly?

WAREING: I don't know.

WHITE: You don't know?

WAREING: No.

WHITE: Let's take another call. We've got Corinne, I believe, on the line. Are you there, Corinne?

CALLER#2: Hi there.

WHITE: How you keeping this gloomy November lunchtime?

CALLER#2: Fine, thank you

WHITE: Good stuff. And what was your question?

CALLER#2: I just wanted to ask – my husband has had gout for some time – I wondered if your expert, in his own experience, had experienced side effects from any prescription NSAIDs, as our GP is reluctant to prescribe them for that reason.

WHITE: Interesting question. Giles? Any side effects?

WAREING: I don't know.

CALLER#2: Sorry, what was that?

WHITE: He said he didn't know. The problem is that we've just discovered that Giles doesn't actually have gout at all. At least I think that's what we've discovered. Do you really not have gout, Giles?

WAREING: No.

CALLER#2: So what is he, an impostor?

WHITE: [laughs] Good question. Giles, are you an impostor? [pause] Giles, are you . . . Giles?

CALLER#2: Does he get some sort of kick out of wasting people's time?

WHITE: We'll have to leave it there I'm afraid, Corinne, thanks. My thanks also to journalist Giles Wareing. I'm Duncan White, and you're listening to 98.6 London AllTalk. Traffic and travel after this.

-transcript ends-

I don't know why I started crying then and there. It normally only ever happened in the car. The inward drift to which I am prone at times of stress came upon me after I made the aspirin mistake. Going in knowing I hadn't got gout, I'd opted to play the dispassionate disseminator of useful information, but my confidence was shattered by the error. I began to tune out. I suddenly realized that I had not walked the dog that morning. I thought of my children, my small boys, at school, in the world, vulnerable. I considered the possibility that my wife didn't love me anymore. I thought of the bubble of air working its way through the heating system, ever upwards. I wondered who the first-worst journalist in Britain was. I wondered why no 1804 dollars were minted in 1804. I thought of Stick lying stiff and flat in next door's garden, the wind lifting his fur. I began, at that moment, to feel truly middle-aged, to pour my shapeless fear into the mould of it. In this new context the fear made sense: to be old, to be afraid, to think of death every day, that seemed neither morbid nor cowardly, just appropriate in the circumstances. It occurred to me that age and fear were part of the same thing, indivisible, an age-fear continuum. Also, I hadn't eaten anything. The first tears landed on the foam windguard of the microphone. I could just hear them in my headphones.

Amanda was very nice about it.

'Don't worry,' she said. 'We all have our moments. I fainted and fell off the back of a bus once.'

'Did you?'

'Yeah. It was really embarrassing.'

'I melted down on live radio. Thousands of people will have heard it.'

'Not likely. Duncan's numbers are shit. And they turned off your mike straight away, after that first heaving sob. Anyway who cares, right? Just a stupid programme at

Friday lunchtime. No big deal.' She smiled brightly, in a way that so perfectly concealed her pity that I felt tears rounding the sides of my eyeballs again. I blinked, coughed hoarsely and smiled back.

'Do I get paid for this?'

When I got home Caroline was in the process of distributing four large piles of flowers among every vase we owned. Or she owned. I couldn't really claim any share in the vases. I watched her for a while. She worked with an unhurried, assembly-line efficiency, but also with a clear eye for balance, tilting her head as she decided if one more or one less bloom should finish off an arrangement. Discernment without frustration. What must that be like?

'Where have you been?'

'On the radio.'

'Oh. How did it go?'

'As well as can be expected.'

'So will you be helping me at all today?'

'I have a bit of work to do yet.'

'Do the dog first, will you?'

'Yeah.' I started for the door, then turned around and went back into the kitchen. Opening the drawer where all the plastic bags were, I selected a sturdy white one from a computer outlet, and quickly examined it for tears or holes.

'What's that for?' asked Caroline.

'The greater good.'

*

A black slash of cloud was moving over Roundworm Park, its eastern edge sharply delineated against the flat cashmere sky beyond. The park itself was empty except for one of the regular professional dog-walkers, who was being tugged slowly round the path on his bicycle by a mixed-breed team of eight, while he chatted into a wire hanging from his ear. Philippa fell behind, sniffing at stinking puddles. On the far leg of the loop the rain spat into my face and wetted the knees of my trousers. A blue plastic bag snagged in the bare branches of a tree waved limply in the breeze, as it had for the last five years. I wheeled around in time to see the dog coming out of her posture, about a hundred yards away.

I strode over purposefully, drawing the bag from my pocket as I went, but the dog was now trotting in small circles, moving away from the spot. By the time I arrived I didn't know where to look.

How is a person supposed to find a dog turd in the middle of a field? How long is a good citizen required to search? I looked around the park. The dog-walker was at the opposite end. A few schoolboys were hanging about the entrance. No one to see that I was even showing willing. I was about to give it up when a particularly large turd presented itself. Odds were it didn't belong to Philippa, but ownership didn't seem important. Put one down, pick one up: that is how we save the park. I put the bag over my hand inside out, and gingerly gathered it in.

Only one of the schoolboys remained at the entrance when I approached. He was staring at me from under his grey hood. He was absurdly tall.

'Yo, I need to borrow your mobile phone.'

'I don't have one.'

'You don't have a phone?'

'Well, actually, I do have one, but I haven't got it with me.' He shifted from foot to foot impatiently, still staring. It occurred to me that I was being mugged, albeit in an entirely desultory fashion. I looked around for the dog.

'What about money? You got money?' His sneer kept sliding off his face, leaving a mildly panicked expression behind. He was also drenched, and the wrong side of sixteen for this sort of thing, but his height remained intimidating. His two companions, both much smaller, stood under the bus shelter down the road, smoking and monitoring his progress.

'No. No money either. Trust me, I haven't got anything you want.' He took a cautious step toward me, eyes down.

'What's that, then?' He pointed at my plastic bag with one pocketed fist. I'd meant to put it in the bin, but I'd been too busy reviewing my disastrous radio performance in my head.

'This? It's a . . .' I was, to be honest, embarrassed by the truth, and tried to remember what the computer bag had originally held. 'A four-port USB hub.'

He snatched it with alarming speed, thumping my palm hard with his finger tips, and ran diagonally over the road in the direction of the bus shelter. At his approach his two mates caught sight of him and sprinted off ahead, the three of them shouting at each other as they went. A fourth boy on a too-small bicycle watched them go by and then sped after them. I looked down and saw the dog standing next to me.

'Where were you?' The thumping of my heart filled my ears, but as we crossed the road I smiled for the first time in perhaps four days. I could feel the skin stretching to accommodate the grin.

10

TWAT MEETS TWAT

Started by moretoastplease at 10.12 AM on 29.10.04
Today our favourite very bad writer Giles Wareing interviews the celebrated very bad writer "Chair" Fitzpaine. Can anyone think of a more profligate way to waste newsprint?

Grotius – 10.37 AM on 12.11.04 (92 of 109)
Sorry for the delay. Been very busy. Here's a bit:

There is nothing like a drop of Irish whiskey taken in the warmth of an Irish pub, spare in its décor but filled with laughter and song. For centuries this ancient drink has inspired the musicians and storytellers of the Emerald Isle; though the Scots would doubtless dispute it, the Irish have a solid claim to being the inventors of this golden spirit, which they called uisce beatha, *or the water of life.*

I find it difficult even to type it out. Can I stop now?

---

moretoastplease – 11.02 AM on 12.11.04 (93 of 109)
It makes me hurt. More please!

Salome66 – 11.11 AM on 12.11.04 (94 of 109)
It's like something off a website listing B&Bs in
Kerry

Grotius – 11.23 AM on 12.11.04 (95 of 109)
. . . legend has it that St Patrick first brought the
secret of distillation to Ireland. Certainly there
is evidence to suggest that the alembic – a
primitive pot still used in the Middle East to distil
perfume – was prevalent in Ireland from the sixth
century . . .
I think we know Mr Wareing too well to put
much faith in this particular historical timeline . . .

Lordhawhaw – 11.28 AM on 12.11.04 (96 of 109)
Get to the part where the leprechauns come in

Salome66 – 11.41 AM on 12.11.04 (97 of 109)
How many pages before the first mention of the
craic?

---

recidivist – 11.50 AM on 12.11.04 (98 of 109)
This is my new favourite thread!

Grotius – 11.55 AM on 12.11.04 (99 of 109)
I've got a meeting in a minute. You'll all have to
wait . . .

Except for Salome: *"good whiskey, good friends, good craic . . ."* page 7. Not bad.

---

moretoastplease – 11.58 AM on 12.11.04 (100 of 109)
100! I thank you . .

---

recidivist – 12.04 PM on 12.11.04 (101 of 109)
How do you do italics?

PavlovsKitty – 12.15 PM on 12.11.04 (102 of 109)
Oh my God! He's on the radio!!!! Giles is on the radio!!!

Salome66 – 12.17 PM on 12.11.04 (103 of 109)
What? Where? Why?

PavlovsKitty – 12.22 PM on 12.11.04 (104 of 109)
It's over now. I didn't know it was him until the end. Some stupid health thing on AllTalk, but GW seemed well out of his depth.

---

moretoastplease – 12.29 PM on 12.11.04 (105 of 109)
He'd be out of his depth standing on a damp tea towel. What's AllTalk, pray tell?

Salome66 – 12.40 PM on 12.11.04 (106 of 109)
local London talk radio. Lowest common

denominator broadcasting *par excellence.* You're missing nothing.

What did he sound like, Kitty?

---

moretoastplease – 12.52 PM on 12.11.04 (107 of 109)
We have LCD radio up north as well, my love. And electricity.

PavlovsKitty – 12.58 PM on 12.11.04 (108 of 109)
like you'd expect – middle class, arrogant, up himself, full of shite. Perhaps a bit older than I'd imagined, or maybe ill.

Gotta go. Lunch beckons. What's with this weather?

---

recidivist – 1.01 PM on 12.11.04 (109 of 109)
more italics! Teach me!

Back / Top / Add a comment

There was another present lying on the bed when I went downstairs: a stiff, understated white shopping bag graced with a small, indecipherable logo. Inside was a shirt, flower-patterned with red stitching along the collar and cuffs, unashamedly ornate, a party shirt. As I unfolded it I was not surprised to see that it was much too big. Caroline never let size get in the way of her notions about what

I should wear; if she thought the style suited me, she would not have been dissuaded by the fact that they didn't have it in medium. There was no card, but it was a gift which came with an implicit instruction: put this on.

I thought again about the guitar, which fell into a different category of giving. Caroline would have looked on it as a pathetic male indulgence, an aid to self-absorption, an embarrassing, undignified hobby. The guitar was therefore a tangible demonstration of her capacity for self-sacrifice, a token of her unconditional love. That I had never expressed the slightest interest in owning a guitar was beside the point; she had given me something she didn't want me to have. At least, I thought, it meant something. My presents to her never managed to embody any complex emotional transaction. I bought them, and she took them back.

I cut my neck in two places shaving, and had to wait for the blood to stop running before I could put on the shirt. In the meantime I examined my face for the casual damage of age. There were a series of tiny folds in front of each ear, where the tug of gravity had pulled the skin downward, past the boundaries of elasticity. It had also brought the brows down onto the lids, and opened the eye sockets along the bottom edge. The skin no longer clung to the jawline; everything was slowly coming away, buckling and pouching like poorly hung wallpaper. Don't think about it, I thought. This is just what happens. This is how people come to look like their dogs.

*

'So glad you could make it,' said Caroline. She paused to switch gears. Sarcasm was so entrenched in her that she had to make a deliberate effort to sound sincere. 'That looks nice on you.'

'The collar looks a bit big,' I said.

'Only if you do it up, you prat.' She undid my top button and tugged at the wings of the collar. 'That's better. I'm going up to have a bath and get dressed. Why don't you go and spend some time with your children for a change?'

The sitting room was uncommonly tidy. There were flowers and clean ashtrays on every surface. An antique blanket from some chest or other had been hung across the back of the couch to hide its stains and rips. A scented candle sat lit on the piano, to mask the mysterious smell that lingered in that corner of the room. The boys were in their pyjamas, curled up one behind the other on the couch, staring intently as several forms of poorly animated Japanese merchandizing – replicas of robot toys I'd often stepped on – did battle on the telly. It occurred to me that of late I had only ever seen my children in their pyjamas, and that this was not because I was too busy, but because they were.

'Is this a video, or real telly?' I asked.

'It's a DVD,' said the older one.

'A pirates one,' said Freddy.

'They don't look like pirates.'

'He means it's a pirate DVD.'

'Where did it come from?'

'Colin brought it.'

'Oh. It's my party tonight, you know.'

'I know, Dad,' said the younger one.

'Of course we know.'

'How was violin?'

'Fine.'

'How was tae kwon do?'

'Fine.'

'Did you go to Billy's after?'

'Sssh, Dad.'

'Sorry.' I sat down between them, and watched.

Insofar as I could follow the cartoon, I was annoyed with it. Even taken as one long battle scene, it lacked any sort of contiguous narrative. When outmanoeuvred, the robot combatants simply transformed themselves into something else entirely – a dinosaur, a bulldozer – in order to gain the upper hand. In their new guises enemies sometimes became allies in order to defeat a creature which threatened them both. All this required detailed explanation, which duly arrived in the form of a breathless running commentary from a clutch of stiff, big-eyed cartoon children who sat on the sidelines. It wasn't clear whose side they were on.

'Now Mobatak is winning again,' said the older one.

My eye was caught by a picture on the side table, a framed, scarred snapshot of Caroline and me lying together, seemingly asleep, on a patch of scrubby grass somewhere in Devon. It had been taken fifteen years before and captured a rare moment of tranquillity from a weekend during which we had actually argued almost non-stop. We had been seeing each other for less than a year, and I had just begun to fear that our relationship would always be difficult, shot through with streaks of unhappiness and punctuated by periods of emotional estrangement. Several months later, after yet another big argument, we had sat up late to discuss the possibility of a permanent parting of the ways. In a desperate bid to prevent a split I'd told her that I didn't care that we fought, that the stress and the unhappiness were endurable because I'd long since realized she was the one for me. The memory gave me a shiver of horror. I remember her looking down at the table, and in a voice as resigned and defeated as any I'd heard her use, admitting she felt the same: there was no one else. This was the true extent of our compact, a pledge more binding than our subsequent marriage vows. We had, over time, developed new and ingenious methods of defeating each other's will, new ways to hurt, but our base alliance was renewed whenever the world seemed sufficiently ranged against us. We had become different people in the intervening years, but our agreement that night, of which we never spoke again, still bound us together like, like . . .

'What are those two things called?'

'Jeddera and Mobatak.'

'Which is which?'

'That's Jeddera. Do you know what his power is?'

'No.'

'Super strength.'

'Ah.'

Caroline called from the top of the stairs. She was standing on the landing in a towel, flushed and damp.

'I completely forgot about the meeting,' she said. 'You've got to go.'

'What meeting?'

'The Forp meeting. The park thing. I promised one of us would turn up, and I forgot all about it.'

'Now?'

'Just run over for twenty minutes and say you can't stay. I promised her, what's her name. The woman with the lame Alsatian.'

'Won't people be here in twenty minutes?'

'I looked her in the eye and promised her. Yesterday.'

The play hut on the western corner of the park had been closed to children for two years, although local delinquents frequently found their way past its padlocked steel doors. A single security light, bent skyward on its bracket, illuminated nothing but the precise angle of the rain. The interior shone with the cold blaze of fluorescence. I thought about not going in, but someone came up behind me.

'What a night, eh?' said a woman I recognized as the woman Caroline spoke of, the woman with the lame Alsatian.

Inside the meeting was already underway. 'This is Caroline's partner,' said the Alsatian woman. The various murmured greetings were tinged with disappointment, as if everyone had turned out especially to see Caroline. 'I'm sorry, I've forgotten your name!'

'Giles,' I said, in the vaguely apologetic way one learns to say a name like Giles. I pulled up a child's chair and sat down near a glowing space heater. Someone handed me a photocopy of the minutes of the last meeting. The room smelled of mildew and scorched dust.

'It's totally ridiculous, innit,' said a man with diagonally parked teeth.

'They've already spent half the grant money on consultation,' said an elderly woman, with a tremulous, rather grand voice.

'Well, I mean they got to justify their existence somehow, don't they?' said a pale young man with orange dreadlocks.

'And they're still talking about football pitches and basketball courts. There are already eight basketball courts just the other side of Cows Lane,' said a voice behind me. 'I never seen anyone on 'em.'

'It don't need much. All it really wants is somebody to cut the bloody grass once a fortnight,' said someone else.

'And collect the burnt scooters in the morning.' I hadn't quite meant to say it aloud.

'Amen,' said somebody, to general laughter and several nods of approval. I was immediately suffused with a sense of fellow feeling. I felt proud of all of us for turning up on this forbidding November night. There was no reason this small group of concerned and determined citizens couldn't turn the park, our park, around. Our strength lay in our basic common sense. Not for us the overblown schemes of some useless quango with time on its hands and a budget to dispense with. All that was required was a bit of regular maintenance, some judicious landscaping, new benches and bins, enough funds to reinstate the mother and baby club, perhaps even a little cafe with some tables near the front gate.

'What about this quad-biking thing? You know what that'll do,' said the man with the diagonal teeth.

'There are currently no plans to introduce quad-biking at Roundworm. That's what the lady on the parks committee told me last week.'

'You'll have all them fucking gypsies up here, pardon my French, stealing everything that ain't nailed down.'

'I have to go,' I said. As I tried to get off the tiny chair the door opened, spattering a noticeboard with stray rain. In stepped a beautiful woman with long red hair and translucent, arresting grey-green eyes. Everyone stopped talking.

In stepped Darby's mum.

Only one person had arrived by the time I got back: Patrick Gallet, an old and unattractively punctual friend of Caroline's. I could hear him bellowing in the kitchen before I opened the door.

'Here he is,' said Caroline. 'Where the hell have you been?'

'Ah! The gout sufferer returns!' shouted Patrick.

'Where you sent me. Hello, Patrick.'

'Been getting involved in the local community, I hear. Very appropriate for someone of your age.' His voice was loud and preposterously deep. I could feel it in the bones of my fingers as we shook hands.

'I said twenty minutes,' said Caroline. Her eyelashes were thickened with mascara, her lips a glossy bruise.

'I know, but they took one look at me and made me their leader. I couldn't just run off.' I took a glass of red wine from a previously poured row.

'So what is it, trying to improve that horrible park?' asked Patrick.

'No, we're trying to halt all improvement. We're afraid better facilities will attract gypsies.'

'Oh no. Was he there?'

'He was.'

'What's this?'

'It's very boring,' said Caroline.

'I'm just going to run up and shut everything off in my office,' I said, taking my glass with me. 'Shan't be a moment.'

TWAT MEETS TWAT
Started by moretoastplease at 10.12 AM on 29.10.04
Today our favourite very bad writer Giles Wareing interviews the celebrated very bad writer "Chair" Fitzpaine. Can anyone think of a more profligate way to waste newsprint?

---

moretoastplease – 2.25 PM on 12.11.04 (110 of 126)
every inch a twat then?

Lordhawhaw – 2.33 PM on 12.11.04 (111 of 126)
Ay, evr'y inch a twat

---

moretoastplease – 2.46 PM on 12.11.04 (112 of 126)
Wish I'd heard it.

LOLOLO – 3.01 PM on 12.11.04 (113 of 126)
It would have brought a whole new element to our collective loathing

---

Salome66 – 3.18 PM on 12.11.04 (114 of 126)
Your wish is my command. Here's a link:
www.all-talk-radio.co.uk/prog/duncanwhite/
12.11.04/ . . .

---

moretoastplease – 3.46 PM on 12.11.04 (115 of 126)
OMG it's TOO HORRIBLE for WORDS!

FritsZernike – 3.55 PM on 12.11.04 (116 of 126)
Car crash radio at its finest!

Grotius – 4.02 PM on 12.11.04 (117 of 126)
Can you have car crash radio? I somehow feel a visual element is necessary. You need to see the slow motion twisting of metal, the flying pebbles of glass. Car crash television, yes. But radio? Or am I being pedantic?

Salome66 – 4.09 PM on 12.11.04 (118 of 126)
No more than usual. You'd have to agree it has all the aural elements of a car crash . . .

---

recidivist – 4.16 PM on 12.11.04 (119 of 126)
Hi everyone.

FritsZernike – 4.20 PM on 12.11.04 (120 of 126)
Why would anyone agree to go on the radio to talk about something they know nothing about?

---

moretoastplease – 4.23 PM on 12.11.04 (121 of 126)
That's our Giles! Forty years old and still stupid!

Salome66 – 4.24 PM on 12.11.04 (122 of 126)
Hello, recidivist. Figured out the italics, I see.

---

recidivist – 4.27 PM on 12.11.04 (123 of 126)
Yes thanks.

Salome66 – 4.33 PM on 12.11.04 (124 of 126)
I love the idea of pseudogout. Was there ever a better fit between man and complaint?

FritsZernike – 4.41 PM on 12.11.04 (125 of 126)
Too bad he doesn't actually have it.

---

moretoastplease – 4.56 PM on 12.11.04 (126 of 126)
What's that weird shuddering noise right near the end? I've listened to it 4 times.

Back / Top / Add a comment

I bled the radiator in my office, the highest in the house, while the doorbell rang once, twice, three times. The black water jetted out of the valve onto my shoes. There was no more air in the system.

The party gathered pace rapidly, enabling me to move through it in a trance, nodding, smiling, shaking hands and kissing cheeks, assuring people I would return momentarily, avoiding anyone who could detect my unease. I tried to imagine the party as someone else's, to look at it through the eyes of a guest. I tried to imagine it as my party, and that didn't work either. I'd seen two or three of the younger girls from the paper walk in, assess the situation, and then slip into a corner to discuss an immediate exit strategy, but almost everyone else was there for the long haul, exhibiting the sort of forced abandon people reserve for someone else's fortieth. People will have fought over late-night babysitters. They will have rung up drug dealers on mobile numbers so old they will have had to add an extra 7. There would be cocaine here, somewhere, but I, as the official honouree, felt destined to be overlooked when it came to dishing it out. I wasn't sure how I felt about this. I had intended to stay relatively sober, but the glass in my hand was already my fourth, and I could feel myself switching to autopilot. Caroline passed me in the hall and hissed, 'I don't believe it. The Skeldings brought their fucking baby!' before slipping upstairs. I went into the back garden and cadged a cigarette from Patrick Gallet.

'You don't look happy.'

'I'm not. Why should I be?'

'Exactly. You're fucking forty.'

'I feel like crying.'

'It's your party. You can cry if you want to.'

'It's like celebrating a kidney infection.'

'Exactly.' Patrick was beginning to slur a bit. 'Let's go and do a line. That'll cheer you up.' I loved Patrick. He knew how to take a hint.

'I'm not sure I ... let's just casually ...' Someone touched my shoulder. It was Ken from the paper.

'Great party,' he said. 'So how does it feel to be officially middle-aged?'

'Really marvellous,' I said. 'And I can't wait to die.' Ken told me a story about work which made no sense as I watched Patrick's back disappear inside. When I went in later I couldn't find him. I joined a small group where Caroline was firmly in command.

'How are you, Giles?' asked a woman who I'd never seen before. I glanced at Caroline, who rolled her eyes in an abbreviated fashion, without stopping her story.

'Fine. How are you?'

'Really good. A bit weak. The recovery's been very slow.'

'I'll bet,' I said. I had no idea what she was talking about.

'Oh my God,' said Caroline suddenly. 'What the fuck is she doing here?' I looked over. Darby's mum was standing on the other side of the room with her coat on.

'Oh. I invited her,' I said.

'You invited her,' said Caroline.

'Sorry, I forgot. She was at the park thing. She only lives round the corner.'

'Well, you deal with her.'

Darby's mum had already reached us by then.

'Hello, Caroline. Hope you don't mind me barging in like this.'

'Hi, Sarah. Of course not. I gather you saw Giles at the meeting.' Sarah. It was the first time I'd heard her name.

'Yes. We're leafleting together next week.'

'Really.'

'We got bullied into it,' I said.

'It's my fault,' said Sarah. 'I got a little overenthusiastic, trying to do my bit.'

'I see,' said Caroline.

'Hello,' said Patrick Gallet, sticking his head into the circle.

'Sarah, this is Patrick,' said Caroline.

'Hi,' said Sarah.

'Giles!' said Patrick. 'You're looking great! Well done, mate!' He was patting me insistently on the chest and stroking my right arm. Then he winked at me.

'Thanks,' I said. The doorbell went.

'That'll be the Skeldings' taxi,' said Caroline. 'Go and tell him they'll be right out before he fucks off.'

Someone had already opened the front door. The cab driver stood in a bewildered pose on the threshold, smiling awkwardly.

'It'll be just a few minutes,' I said. 'They've got a baby.' I held my hands apart one over the other, as if to estimate the height of a newborn. The driver looked at me uncomprehendingly. I might have been telling him that his passenger was an owl. I walked back into the sitting room.

Caroline, Sarah and Patrick had disappeared. I stood near the fire, listening to snatches from three or four conversations, trying to look caught up in private thoughts. My eye was caught by a small grey square card on the mantelpiece: the invitation to Chair Fitzpaine's book launch. I picked it up and stared at it for a moment. Then I put it in my pocket and went back to the front door. The driver was still standing there, hands clasped tightly before him.

'OK,' I said. 'I'm ready. Let's go.'

11

The Surgery was somewhere in Vauxhall, and I was obliged to stop the taxi not once but twice in order to get more cash. It was after 11.00 when I finally got there, but people were still making their way gingerly past the bouncer who guarded the entrance and up the narrow red-painted stair-well. Another bouncer opened the heavy door at the top, into a long, low-ceilinged room lined with upholstered banquettes. Most of the crowd was congregated at the opposite end of the room, against a glowing orange bar. I'd only begun to realize how much I'd already had to drink. The room had a persistent tendency to pitch for-ward, as if on a following sea, unless I kept one eye shut.

'Giles! You made it! Fantastic shirt.' It was Fitzpaine, looking extremely animated. The tops of his glasses were misted over with steam.

'Hi. Thanks. Sorry I'm so late.'

'Don't worry. What you need is one of those.' He grabbed a tall green drink from a passing tray. 'Here.'

'What is it?'

'Mostly rum.'

'Cheers.' Lime juice stung the corners of my mouth. The room began to come about. 'Very nice.'

'The party or the drink?'

'Both.'

'There are a lot of people here you should meet.'

'Are there?' I doubted there were many people there who thought they should meet me. He spoke again, but I couldn't make out the words against the music. I laughed and nodded, as if he'd said something funny which was also very true. An elegant elderly woman swam up alongside us.

'Mark, I really think it's time I went home now.' She spoken in crisp English consonants padded with laconic American vowels.

'Are you sure? Mum, this is Giles Wareing. The guy who did the interview for the newspaper.'

'Nice to meet you,' I said.

'I thought that was a very nice interview,' she said. 'Very well balanced.'

'Thank you.'

'Mum, stay here and I'll go and sort you out a taxi. Giles, look after my mum for a minute.'

'Of course.' I smiled at her and looked out into the crowd, letting an awkward gap in the conversation blossom and ripen. The whole room now seemed to be on the back of someone who was climbing a flight of stairs. 'You called him Mark.'

'What?'

'Didn't I just hear you call your son Mark?'

'Oh! Yes. Well, that's his real name. I guess I'm the only one who still calls him Mark.'

'So Cheriton is what, his middle name?'

'Yes, his second middle name. He took it as a sort of, as a nom de plume, I suppose. I think he started doing it at Cambridge, to be different. Did you know him then?'

'No. We've only just met recently.'

'I see. Can I ask you, do you think he's on something tonight?'

'I wouldn't know, I'm afraid. I just got here.'

'Oh, right.' She dragged her tongue across her teeth slowly. Mark Something Cheriton Fitzpaine came up between us, from behind.

'Taxi's on its way. I'll come with you to get your coat. Giles, grab another drink, mate. I'll be right back.'

'It was nice to meet you,' she said, looking at me as if we had shared a sad secret, the death of a long-lost mutual friend.

'And you.'

The man with the tray was nowhere in sight, so I approached the bar and stood at the back of the three-deep crowd, waiting to be absorbed by it. I let my thoughts drift back to my own party. My birthday party. My fortieth birthday party.

Standing in front of the gas fire, listening to the conversations of others and staring at Cheriton Fitzpaine's invitation, I had toyed briefly with the idea of leaving before my brain began automatically to enumerate the reasons I had to stay. The last of these was that I needed to wait for my mother's annual call from Florida, which because of the time difference, a concept she had never fully grasped, usually came some time after eleven PM. Then I realized that she would not be ringing me this year, because she was dead. That tipped the balance. I left.

She had been ill for about six months when she and Bruce came over to see a doctor in Oxford who was meant to offer some glimmer of hope, but who instead delivered a prognosis more final than her American oncologist was prepared to disclose. She stayed with us for four days, looking and acting impossibly well while Bruce sat silent and rheumy-eyed in a chair, looking far older than his near eighty years. We tried to get her to stay for Christmas, but she was determined to fulfil her final wish, which was to die in Florida, far away from family and old friends, in a clean white hospital. The end was not long in coming. I arrived in time to speak to her, but I didn't say any of the things you're supposed to say. I just stood there, useless and frozen, like Bruce.

The smell of the hospital room stayed with me for months. Some day my sons would have to sit by my death bed and listen to my own morphine-tinged reminiscences, but when? Next year? In ten years? Twenty? Forty? It seemed mad not to be armed with such vital information at this stage of the game. How far through my life was I?

'Hey. This is Sunita. Sunita, this is Giles.' Cher Fitzpaine had come up behind me again, drilling a knuckle into my shoulder. He had with him a tiny, beautiful woman.

'Hello.'

'Sunita is one of the best literary agents in London. Giles is a fantastic writer. He wrote that thing for the paper, the interview.'

'Oh, yes?' said Sunita. I nodded. I suddenly wanted Sunita to be my agent very badly.

'Have you got a drink, Giles?'

'Not yet, no.'

'I'll see if I can find a waitress.'

'Are you the one that has the gout?' asked Sunita.

'No,' I said. 'That wasn't me.'

'Let's go over there,' said Cher.

I sat down at a banquette in a group which contained people I dimly recognized as famous writers. The novelist Becket Hitch and the drug poet Perry Freak were deep into some sort of argument about Iraq. I helped myself to cigarettes from a packet on the table. I remember some woman laughing loudly at something I said, but I don't remember what it was. I remember the room inflating and deflating like a huge lung. I remember knocking over a drink, but no one really minding, except the person whose drink it was. I remember getting the hiccups, and trying to concentrate on making them go away. Then I remember looking up and the place being nearly empty. And Cher Fitzpaine standing over me with his coat on.

'Come on,' he said. 'We're going on.'

Scene missing.

12

I've had to skip a day in this diary already, which doesn't say much for my dedication. My absence was due to an altogether forseeable illness, of which more never. Caroline is still not speaking to me, but I sense a slight thawing. When one turns 40, one is entitled to some behavioural leeway. Or so I will maintain.

My investigations continue apace. Searching on usernames shows what other sorts of thread people frequent – often giving clues about interests/background/locale/job, if any – but it's very time-consuming, & means wading through page after page of dross. Some of these losers post 50 times a day. Nevertheless profiles are slowly beginning to emerge. For example:

FritsZernike – Male. Lives Manchester. Student or recent graduate, UMIST. Chose as his username the name of the 1953 Nobel Prize winner for physics. There seems to be no significant reason for this. My guess is he found a list of winners on the net somewhere, in alphabetical order, and chose the last one. There is a person called Frits Zernike who manufactures ice cream shaped like fruit in Connecticut, but this appears to be a coincidence.

Likes – particle physics, the Cure, real ale, cycling.
Dislikes – London, organised religion, Giles Wareing
Email address suggests real first name is David. Second name may begin with K.
I don't know what I'll do with it, but I find just compiling this information rather soothing.
The Chord of the Day is Cdim.

*

A Tale of the Tape

Giles Wareing Laments the Demise of VHS

So this is it, then. A major electronics retailer has announced that it will no longer stock VHS video recorders. In the States several video rental chains have already stopped carrying VHS tapes. These are but the most obvious signs of a format on its way out. Mark my words: we will miss it when its gone.

The VHS tape will fade gently into obscurity, outflanked by the DVD format, with its superior quality and ridiculously cheap machines, much as the humble cas-sette tape was erased by the CD. VHS was never the format of choice for videophiles, but then it was never aimed at them. It was aimed at the rest of us. By way of saying goodbye, let's take a final look back at the format that won a war, and conquered the world.

Magnetic audio recording has its roots in the 19th century, the first working devices employing spools of steel wire instead of tape to store sound. With the advent of tele-vision came the demand for a cheap and reliable method of storing video images for later broadcast, but the technology didn't exist. In its early days all television was broadcast live. In America, a country which sprawls across four time zones, televised dramas were routinely performed twice – once for each coast.

Initial attempts to adapt the principle of audio tape recording to video faced a seemingly insurmountable problem: the higher frequencies needed to produce images meant that the tape needed to whiz across the recording head at high speed – up to 90 miles per hour – which was not just impractical but vaguely dangerous. You don't want to be in the room when a machine like that goes wrong.

The solution to the problem was a tidy innovation: the magnetic head was mounted on a spinning drum so it could record in a series of high frequency vertical stripes as the tape wound gently past. Even then it took four heads to lay down and play back sufficient information to produce picture and sound, until some bright spark got the idea to mount the drum at an angle to the oncoming tape so that a longer diagonal band could be recorded with each sweep of the head. Practical video recording was born.

But this new technology was far beyond the reach of the ordinary consumer. Commercial video machines were prohibitively expensive and required a degree of expertise to operate. Early efforts to produce home systems, such as the demonstrated-but-never-launched Telcan reel-to-reel machine (1962), or the pioneering-but-doomed Cartrivision system (1972) convinced many that the idea was too far ahead of its time. The future appeared to belong to non-recordable video discs.

Sony, however, stuck with tape, introducing the Betamax system in 1975. VHS, a rival system developed by JVC, was launched less than a year later. Today we tend to think of the "format wars" of the late 1970s as the triumph of marketing over quality, but early consumer tests showed that the public couldn't distinguish between VHS and the allegedly superior Betamax. Indeed, the differences were all but imperceptible on the televisions of the day. VHS, like the audio cassette before it, was a perfect example of what is known as sufficient technology – if you're only recording last night's Nationwide, how good does the picture have to be?

VHS recorders were by and large cheaper than their rivals (though not by any stretch cheap – the first machine offered in the UK cost approximately £2,200 in today's coin). The format offered longer-playing cassettes – up to 3 hours – and, crucially, the machines were quick to appear in hire shops. Consumers weren't stupid; they saw that only one format would survive, and many chose to lease machines rather than end up owning an expensive loser. With more VHS machines in homes, the growing – and largely unanticipated – market for renting films saw VHS become the dominant format.

A third rival format, V2000, also appeared, but it never really entered the race. By 1980 VHS had 70 per cent of the market. Betamax had its best year in 1984, selling 2.4 million units and actually clawing back a bit of market share, but a few years later it was all over. In 1988 Sony gave in and started making VHS format video recorders.

Beta limped on, improbably, into the 1990s. In fact, the machines were manufactured in Japan until 2002. It was the VHS cassette, however, that became the clunky, chunky, not-very-funky standard. The machines were reliable, the tapes surprisingly robust. While many adults never quite mastered the VHS player, for a whole generation their operation was second nature. Children learned to work the video before they could talk.

The technological advances which have put paid to VHS come at a price. Tape recordings tend to deteriorate over time, but they do so gradually, unlike the all-or-nothing DVD, which can be rendered unplayable by a single scratch. Video boxes line up nicely on bookshelves, while DVDs are stored in those God-awful CD racks that designers never stop inventing. The VHS recorder is also, in an age of no-moving-parts microchip technology, reassuringly mechanical, and perhaps one of the last devices in the home that you can bang with your fist to any advantage. Try smacking your new DVD player next time it acts up, and see how far it gets you.

The sun hung low and bright. A sharp wind got up under the cover of next door's motorcycle, inflating it into the shape of a giant squatting cat. A freshly dumped mattress was impaled on the railings to the left of the park gates, a stack of unmatched drawers on the pavement beside it. It was not yet eight thirty, and the SUVs of smart Kensington ladies were still lined up along Roundworm Road. They came early, before the traffic wardens, to let their lurchers befoul the unpoliced scrubland. They wore knee-high wellies and waxed coats, and called their dogs Odin and Daisy. Caroline referred to them as the Ladies Who Lurch. With the start of parking-enforcement hours fast approaching, most were already back at their vehicles, going through the elaborate routines they maintained to keep mud off their car interiors: changing shoes, banging boots, wiping down dogs, spreading blankets. It was rare for me to be up and out this early. I usually waited for the park to retreat into its familiar seediness.

Caroline and I had not spoken since Saturday lunchtime, when she'd told me to get up and take the children to the fucking swimming pool. Consequently she had no idea where I'd disappeared to on Friday night, nor was I privy to her suspicions. Not knowing how my own birthday party finished up, I wasn't even sure that she'd noticed I was gone. I was confident we would begin speaking today. She would almost certainly have information to impart.

Back at home I put on coffee and stalked the ground floor while reading the paper. The animals followed me from room to room with their usual impudent expectancy. A subeditor had added a preposterously clichéd last line – 'Farewell then, VHS . . . ' – either to fill space or because they thought my ending noncommittal, but the piece was otherwise untouched. Someone in Birmingham had found a decomposed body in an upstairs room of a house they'd just bought. Unfortunately the skeletal remains had not been picked up by a survey. In retrospect the first sentence of the third paragraph, a stray bit of information left over from a chunk of text I'd excised myself, should have been cut as well. It was unnecessary and confusing. The subs should have spotted it. Coffee spat into the upper chamber of the pot.

TWAT MEETS TWAT
Started by moretoastplease at 10.12 AM on 29.10.04
Today our favourite very bad writer Giles Wareing interviews the celebrated very bad writer "Chair" Fitzpaine. Can anyone think of a more profligate way to waste newsprint?'

LOLOLO – 11.12 PM on 12.11.04 (127 of 148)

The sound of a barrel being scraped, perhaps?

StGurnard – 2.43 AM on 13.11.04 (128 of 148)

This thread is fucking hillarious

---

moretoastplease – 8.51 AM on 15.11.04 (129 of 148)

Morning all. Just enjoying a light rye toast with honey. Nice weekend?

Grotius – 9.28 AM on 15.11.04 (130 of 148)

Morning, toastie. Very nice, thank you. I trust we've all had a chance to digest GW's latest verbal turd.

---

recidivist – 9.36 AM on 15.11.04 (131 of 148)

The VHS thing? What a load of *bollocks.*

Salome66 – 9.55 AM on 15.11.04 (132 of 148)

Confused, pointless, factually suspect – it certainly bears all the usual hallmarks.

Grotius – 10.09 AM on 15.11.04 (133 of 148)

Suspect? More like just plain wrong. Beta machines were far cheaper in the 80s, especially after VHS established dominance, and the technological superiority of the former was unquestionable – that's why it was still in use until a few years ago.

PavlovsKitty – 10.16 AM on 15.11.04 (134 of 148)
"much as the humble cassette tape was erased by the CD . . ."
Did you see what he did there? Cassette tape? Erased?

Grotius – 10.24 AM on 15.11.04 (135 of 148)
And he completely overlooks the lawsuit brought against Sony by Universal and Disney over the legality of home taping, which gave VHS manufacturers an unfair advantage from the outset.

PavlovsKitty – 10.27 AM on 15.11.04 (136 of 148)
That ending is truly pathetic: "Farewell then, VHS . . ." Yuck.

Salome66 – 10.29 AM on 15.11.04 (137 of 148)
Er, we'll take your word for it, Grotius.

Grotius – 10.41 AM on 15.11.04 (138 of 148)
Sorry. Bit of a specialist subject of mine.

FritsZernike – 10.45 AM on 15.11.04 (139 of 148)
". . . no-moving-parts microchip technology . . ."
What? Has he never seen the little DVDs going round and round?

---

moretoastplease – 10.57 AM on 15.11.04 (140 of 148)

As Sal said, it's par for the course: a few random "facts" culled from the internet, slapped down in no particular order and mortared together with the charmless, leaden prose for which our man is so justly famous. And now I've wasted 5 minutes of my life reading it.

Salome66 – 11.07 AM on 15.11.04 (141 of 148)
And yet you must admit, toastie, it does conjure up a rather powerful image: that of a hapless, talentless, balding middle-aged man sat alone in a darkened attic, staring at a screen and clacking his way toward death one lazy cliché at a time.

---

recidivist – 11.12 AM on 15.11.04 (142 of 148)
Farewell then, Giles Wareing. We won't miss you when you're gone . . .

---

easyGeoff – 11.19 AM on 15.11.04 (143 of 148)
Spot on with 139, Salome. And I ought to know: I've met him.

Back / Top / More / Add a comment

'Are you prepared to talk about where you were till eight o'clock in the morning?' Caroline had come noiselessly up the stairs. I quickly closed the Internet window and turned around. She was staring at me intently. I turned back to face the screen and counted to six.

151

'I just couldn't handle it here,' I said, trying to sound troubled. 'I'm sorry.'

'Where were you?'

'At a book launch.'

'You were at a book launch until eight a.m.?'

'I don't know where I ended up. I don't remember much of the evening, to be honest.'

'That is unacceptable. There were forty people here. I had to tell them you'd gone to bed.'

'I'm sorry.'

'Who was the girl who answered your phone?'

'When?'

'When I rang you at two a.m. in a complete panic.'

'I don't know. I don't remember that.'

'You ran off with Patrick's cocaine.'

'What cocaine?'

'He said you disappeared with it.'

'That simply isn't true.' EasyGeoff said he had met me. Where had he met me?

'All right. I am willing to dismiss Friday as some kind of one-off, turning-forty, my-mother-died-eight-months-ago, nervous-breakdown stupidity. But if you ever do anything like that again I will leave you. You have had your last warning. Do you understand that?'

'Yes.'

'If you need help you should get help. You can't carry on as you are.'

'I'm fine.'

'You don't act fine.'

'But I will be fine.'

'Right. That's all I have to say. I'll let you get back to your porn site. You're picking up today, by the way.'

'It's not a, it's just this . . .' She was already gone. I cupped my hands over my nose and mouth, pressing the tips of my index fingers into the corners of my eye sockets. EasyGeoff said he'd met me. Where?

I tried to return to the thread, but I'd been disconnected. The small broadband icon at the bottom of the screen, a simple rendering of two computer screens connected by a jagged bolt of lightning, was covered with a big X. I wiggled the wire coming out of the modem, which sometimes did the trick, but nothing happened. I scrabbled through the papers on my desk, looking for the pad with the helpline number on it.

Where had easyGeoff met me? Did I know easyGeoff? I had a sudden memory of being in a minicab next to Cher Fitzpaine, post-book launch, with Perry Freak in the front seat.

Cher asks me for a light and I obligingly dip my fingers into my jacket pocket, pulling out not matches but a small rectangle of wrapped-up magazine. It is, of course, Patrick Gallet's cocaine, which he had clearly slipped into my pocket, deeming a sly wink sufficient explanation of his actions. By the time I find it, however, I am incapable of putting two and two together, and far too drunk to experience genuine surprise. I hold the wrap in front of Cher Fitzpaine's nose. He takes it and opens it out, then deftly folds it up again.

'Well, you're a fucking dark horse, aren't you, Giles?' he says. 'Perry, we can cancel our first stop. Tell him to go directly to your place.'

I went downstairs and found the jacket I wore that night hanging in the closet. There was a rolled-up tenner in the pocket, which probably also belonged to Patrick, but nothing else. In the other pocket was a blister pack of small white pills. Where did I get them? Who was easy-Geoff? What did he look like? Where had he met me?

There are other people at Perry Freak's flat. I don't know whether they've been invited or if they are always there. Cher and I snort lines off the back of one of his books. He's got a whole box of them with him. As I lean forward I see that the white trail is partially underlining the words ' "... Destined to be one of those rare books which comes to represent a whole generation." – Giles Wareing'. We are drinking neat room-temperature vodka. Perry Freak is playing a penny whistle with his nose. At some point Fitzpaine grabs me and starts shouting, 'Stopping calling me that! Stop fucking calling me that!' But I keep saying it. I keep calling him Mark.

At some point I volunteer to go out and get more fags but when I see it's already nearly dawn I just keep walking. I see three large and distinctive tower blocks in the distance which I know to be near my house and I head in that direction. They are not the right tower blocks. Eventually I happen across a road I know, making it possible to piece together a route home, but it is farther away than I think. I have to walk with my head tilted to one side.

The helpline number was nowhere to be found. I turned off the computer and turned it on again – the solution for everything. The screen came to life. The icons began lining themselves up along the bottom: the clock, the plug, the little speaker, the tiny medical-bag logo of my anti-viral software. The modem's icon appeared, and the computer went ping. Problem solved. I fingered the blister pack of pills. Who is easyGeoff and where did he meet me?

I am more or less sober when I get home, but I do not have any keys. It is Saturday morning, 7.20 a.m. according to my phone. I do not wish to ring the bell. The dog is whimpering on the other side of the front door. I urinate into the gravel by the bins, and walk to the park.

I can see the black-haired woman dragging her trolley down the path toward me. I want to turn around immediately and leave the park, but my legs will not carry me any farther. I am not as sober as I thought. I sit down on the bench, feeling suddenly faint. She approaches with painful slowness. I stare straight ahead, trying to focus on the blue plastic bag in the tree. She sits down next to me. We sit in silence for a long moment. The sun has yet to rise over the houses across the road, but it's unusually warm and still, the air almost stuffy. I feel the pleasant coolness of sweat drying on the back of my neck.

'Where's your dog?' They are the first words I have ever heard the woman speak. She has a strange, guttural accent, the vowels tightly knotted, something Slavic, primitive and mysterious, rooted in a murky past of dead religions and inhuman cruelty. I am almost too afraid to answer her.

'She's at home,' I say finally.

'Still asleep, eh? That won't do, will it?' Actually, she's Scottish.

'No'.

'Did you want half, then?' I look over, expecting her to
be holding a limp sandwich or a doughnut, or maybe an
orange, but her hands are empty.

'Half of what?'

'Half a gram.'

'Of what?'

'Whichever.' I look up and down the park. We are the
only people in it.

'No thanks.' My head is beginning to throb. My toe
hurts. My nostrils feel like they are packed with sand. And
I am thirsty, so very thirsty. 'What else have you got?'

'Not much. I don't tend to keep a big variety in the
trolley. Just pills, mostly. Bit of E, a few Viagra. Some new
ones from America.'

'New ones?'

'These.' She pulls them out for me, a blister pack of
seven. 'Penny-glows, they're called.'

'What do they do?'

'I've no idea. I've got loads of them. Someone told me
they were goin' to be big, but no one bloody wants 'em.
Here.' I turn them over; the foil backing is stamped
'Panaglos'.

'Panaglos?'

'I dunno how you're meant to pronounce it, to be
honest.'

'Are they painkillers?'

'No, it's some kinda anti-depressant. Brand new.
They're meant to have a sort of, what do you call it, a cult
following. Take 'em. Free sample.' She cackles indulgently,
like a witch among friends.

'Thanks,' I say. She fishes through her trolley, finger-nails scraping at the fabric from the inside. Finally she pulls out a tightly accordioned leaflet.

'You'd better have this,' she says. 'In case there might be what do you call it. Contraindications.' The sun finds a gap in the terraced houses across the road, a scaffolding yard, and casts a pale stripe across the grass. There is one more thing I want to ask her. I am not sure if I dare. The encounter has the fragility of a dream.

'Why are you speaking to me? You've never spoken to me before.' She smiles a mirthless, reflexive smile, a facial tic.

'Thought you might be a copper. But Colin says you're all right.'

I double-clicked the Internet icon and the talkboard came up instantly. It had been my homepage for the last fort-night. Where had easyGeoff met me? Who was he?

Grotius – 11.32 AM on 15.11.04 (144 of 158)
I once wrote a study of the format wars for a marketing quarterly, so I find the factual inaccuracies especially irritating. Perhaps I should just let it go.

Salome66 – 11.36 AM on 15.11.04 (145 of 158)
Sorry geoff – did you say you'd MET Giles Wareing? How can you have kept this from us? When? Where?

---

moretoastplease – 11.44 AM on 15.11.04 (146 of 158)
Tell us! We have a right to know!

Grotius – 11.51 AM on 15.11.04 AM (147 of 158)
Yes, I think we'll need all the gorey details straight away.

StGurnard – 11.52 AM on 15.11.04 (148 of 158)
Still at it? all this bile directed at one pathetic hack

Salome66 – 11.57 AM on 15.11.04 (149 of 158)
Did you speak to him? Did you let on you knew who he was? What does he look like?

Grotius – 12.12 PM on 15.11.04 (150 of 158)
That's 'straight away' as in 'right now'.

---

moretoastplease – 12.23 PM on 15.11.04 (151 of 158)
easyGeoff, where are you?!!!

StGurnard – 12.34 PM on 15.11.04 (152 of 158)
Christ, don't you people have anyhting better to do with your time? Doesn't anyone have a job to go to?

PavlovsKitty – 12.42 PM on 15.11.04 (153 of 158)
Of course we do. I'm at work right now!

Salome66 – 12.46 PM on 15.11.04 (154 of 158)
Me too!

Grotius – 12.55 PM on 15.11.04 (155 of 158)
I can't help noticing, StGurnard, that you seem to
find yourself at a loose end this Monday lunchtime.
Could it be that you have you no job to go to?

---

moretoastplease – 12.57 PM on 15.11.04 (156 of
158)
Could it be that you are, in fact, Giles Wareing?

PavlovsKitty – 12.57 PM on 15.11.04 (157 of 158)
Is it lunch already? I'm off!

Salome66 – 1.09 PM on 15.11.04 (158 of 158)
easyGeoff . . . calling easyGeoff . . .

Back / Top / Add a comment

I had been absentmindedly fiddling with the blister pack
in frustration, running my thumb along its regular bumps.
Suddenly a bump gave way, and a single white pill burst
through the protective foil, through the O in Panaglos, and
skidded across the desk. I snatched it up and swallowed it.

13

The older one emerged from the gates wearing his usual aspect of pained resignation, the Wareing default countenance – my mother's face, although her expression also carried a trace element of disgust, just as mine was tinged with mild alarm. Age sharpened and set the features, so that one's face came to look profoundly disappointed, even in repose. One day the wind changes, and it sticks that way. Freddy came bounding out behind him wearing a bright yellow sticker, and overtook him.

'Hello, Dad.'

'Hello. What's your badge for? Good work?' He puffed out his chest and leaned to one side, the better to display it. I bent over. The badge said, 'I Have Bumped My Head'.

'Again?'

'Darby pushed me, that's why.'

'Perhaps I'd better have a chat with Darby's mum.'

'Or maybe her dad.'

'Yes.' I had never even considered the possibility of Darby's dad. The older one sidled up.

'Mrs Benny wants to see you.'

'And who is Mrs Benny?'

'My teacher.'

'Oh, right.' A man in a suit, somebody's father, walked by and waved.

'Hey, great party. Did you have a good time?'

'I can't remember.'

'That's how all the best parties end. See ya!' Someone who could only be Mrs Benny approached, her face a picture of false apology.

'Hi, Mr Wareing,' she said, looking down at the top of the older one's head. 'We've had to have a bit of a chat about the games console, I'm afraid.'

'Ah. Which games console?'

'This one.' She produced the boy's block of wood from behind her back and handed it to him. 'We don't allow them on school grounds. It's policy.'

'It's a bridge support. From a train set.'

'We thought it violated the spirit of the law, if not the letter.'

'It's a piece of wood.'

'I'm aware of that, but he was playing with it during literacy hour, and getting distracted.' I watched him switch it on by pressing firmly on a black square drawn on one side, and then wait while it warmed up. 'If he could just leave it behind when he comes to school, that would be really really great.'

'You'll never see it again,' I said. 'I promise.'

I rang Caroline at the bookshop to break the news.

'You haven't.'

'He's been told off for bringing a block of wood to school.'

'We decided we wouldn't.'

'Well, we changed our mind. It can be for his birthday.'

'Which is four months away.'

'I know that.'

'They'll fight over it.'

'No they won't. I bought them each one.'

'Oh my God. How much did that cost?'

'If you add in all the games we got, a lot.'

'Giles, what is wrong with you? Are you going through some kind of actual thing?'

'Dunno.'

'Because that really is all we need.'

I looked at the boys, one on each sofa, furiously pushing buttons which caused little squelching explosions to punctuate the chirpy electronic music emanating from their consoles. Their eyes were intent, but glazed, alight with an eerie concentration one does not associate with children.

'Who loves Daddy best of all?' I shouted. Neither of them looked up.

'Me.'

'Me, Dad.'

TWAT MEETS TWAT

Started by moretoastplease at 10.12 AM on 29.10.04

Today our favourite very bad writer Giles Wareing interviews the celebrated very bad writer "Chair"

Fitzpaine. Can anyone think of a more profligate way to waste newsprint?

Lordhawhaw – 2.11 PM on 15.11.04 (159 of 170)
If you don't like the thread, StGurnard, you can always leave.

PavlovsKitty – 3.24 PM on 15.11.04 (160 of 170)
I think he has

---

moretoastplease – 4.44 PM on 15.11.04 (161 of 170)
easyGeoff not been in yet?

Grotius – 5.01 PM on 15.11 04 (162 of 170)
He seems to be toying with us.

---

moretoastplease – 5.12 PM on 15.11.04 (163 of 170)
dum dee dum

---

easyGeoff – 5.23 PM on 15.11.04 (164 of 170)
Sorry about that! Things just went haywire at work. Always like this in the run up to Christmas. Yes, I did meet GW – at a party, at the weekend. I'll tell you about it later, when I've gone home. It's too good a story to dash off between urgent emails!

Salome66 – 6.10 PM on 15.11.04 (165 of 170)
I'll have to wait til tomorrow, as I'm going out tonight, but I look forward to it.

---

moretoastplease – 7.17 PM on 15.11.04 (166 of 170)

It had better be good

---

easyGeoff – 8.35 PM on 15.11.04 (167 of 170)

Right –

I have a mate who lives with a literary agent and I got him to take me along to the Cher Fitzpaine book launch. Not that I like Fitzpaine, but I heard Perry Freak was going to be there, and I've always fancied him (so I have a thing for skinny, pale, drug-addled men. What can I say?). It was at a nightclub in Vauxhall, the Surgery, and it wasn't til very late that some drunken idiot came & sat down at our table, spilling drinks, stealing fags, making unfunny, rude remarks and generaly looking like he was about to vomit all over everyone. Only later, when some of us went on to Perry's flat (score!), did I realise that the sweaty, balding drunk who took my last Marlboro Light was in fact our Giles. He and Fitzpaine just sat in a corner argueing (didn't get close enough to hear what it was about, & frankly didn't want to – something about a guy named Mark) and at one point nearly got into a fistfight, I think. In the end Perry sent GW out for some fags & when he left shouted "Right – nobody answers the door!" He never did come back anyway.

Sadly, Perry is not even a little bit gay. You'd think he'd at least be bi!

StGurnard – 1.09 AM on 16.11.04 (168 of 170)

ffuck off u tawts

StGurnard – 1.11 AM on 16.11.04 (169 of 170)

twats

Salome66 – 9.58 AM on 16.11.04 (170 of 170)

Brilliant story, brilliantly told, geoffrey. Always immensely satisfying when real life lives up to your dearly held prejudices. GW just had to be a pathetic, boorish drunk, didn't he? Why so angry, StGurnard? Bit close to the bone?

Back / Top / Add a comment

16.11.04

I took another one of the pills today. The pack was sitting there on the desk, one blister already exploded. Later it struck me as a slightly stupid thing to have done, but no ill effects, or indeed any effects thus far.

The online vilification continues apace; with no dissenters apart from StGurnard, who is of course me. I thought I had created a complex character – embittered, brutish, misanthropic, but with a fierce sense of natural justice – whose frank views might flush out a few sympathizers, but I was rumbled almost immediately. Any outright attempt to defend GW seems destined to be met with derision; only blanket disdain is tolerated. I thought about complaining to the website directly, but I don't want to draw any extra attention to the existence of the thread. My only hope at this stage is that no one but the most dedicated participants is reading it. It seems I will need yet another alter ego (& with it another webmail account), and a new strategy.

Today's profile:

easyGeoff. 27 or 28, gay, lives 'Stoke Newington-slash-Dalston'. Works for unnamed PR agency, email address given indicates real first name is Geoff, surname or middle name begins with C. Twice mentions he contributes occasional film and DVD reviews to a popular movie website. A search of the archives of Hairinthegate.com turns up a Geoff Church (3 reviews in all), who is described as 'a writer who lives in North London.' Directory enquiries lists one G Church residing at 49 Grayton Road, N6.

Likes: le theatre du grand guignol, Simone Signoret, Perry Freak, Eurostar, mushy peas, gin

Dislikes: pseudointellectuals (oh, please), GW, beer, Leicester, all televised sport barring snooker.

The chord of the day is Db7#9, which sounds vaguely wrong even after you've checked to make sure your fingers are in the right place.

14

Like the gout, the phantom smell first visited in the night. It was partly animal, with a hint of burnt toast and a faintly toxic edge. The characteristics of the odour shifted as if to evade identification; a smell that didn't want you to know what it was, or where it was coming from. It generated a series of random memories, of feeding a goat in a zoo, a saucepan left to boil dry, of a certain brand of defunct felt tip. It was all of these things and none of them. Whatever it was, it had been strong enough to wake me up. It seemed to be coming from the window, or perhaps my fingertips.

'Do you smell that?'

'Hmmmph,' said Caroline, rolling over.

'That. It smells like someone is burning a pumpkin. But not quite.'

'I don't smell anything,' said Caroline. 'Shut up.'

I was alarmed at first, but I knew better than to trust my symptoms. I would not be seeing the doctor about this. There would be no more doctors.

The wind was northerly and bitterly cold. The leaflets whipped like loose sails as I held them out, and this made people reluctant to take them. Darby's mum was stationed at the park's other entrance. Occasionally we caught each other's attention and she smiled and shrugged as if it was all great fun. My fingers were turning white. Even in the cold clear wind the shifting smell clung to me: an old apple in a car ashtray, the air from inside a bicycle tyre, with a whisper of childhood medicine.

'Join the Friends of Roundworm Park,' I said mechanically to a woman who I knew full well spoke no English, thrusting a leaflet in her hand.

I looked over and saw that Maria had appeared on her bench. The dog was already standing in front of her. I walked over and sat down.

'All right,' she said, looking at the dog. It was still strange to hear her speak.

'Yeah, you?' The smell became sharper, more synthetic: the sticky side of packing tape, held directly under the nose.

'Fine. Cold today.'

'I know. I'm absolutely freezing. Listen, I wondered: have you – have you got any more of those pills, the ones from America?' She glanced past me toward the gates, and stuck a fag in her mouth.

'They doing the trick, are they?'

'I don't know, really. Have you got any more?'

'Plenty. I can't fuckin' give the things away.'

'How much would you want for, say . . .'

'Quid each.'

'Right. Well, I've only got ten on me, so let's . . .'

'Not just now.' I looked up. Darby's mum was approaching us.

'I'm all out!' she said, smiling and flashing empty, lavender-gloved hands. Her cheeks were stained pink with the cold. 'Shall I take half of what you've got left?'

'Oh. OK,' I said, handing her a stack of more than forty leaflets. 'Some of mine blew away.'

'Would you like to join the Friends of Roundworm Park?' asked Darby's mum, craning her neck theatrically to indicate that she meant Maria. 'Help to make it a nicer place for everyone who uses it? Sorry, I don't know your name.'

'I like it the way it is,' said Maria, staring straight ahead, her voice reduced to an ominous rasp. The smell took on a sudden, terrible weight: chestnuts roasting on an open sewer.

The phone rang.

'Wareing. What are you doing?' Brian, the features editor.

'About what?'

'About the fucking Burberry War.'

'Barbary.'

'Is it done?'

'No.'

'When can I have it?'

'I don't know. When do you want it?'

'Tomorrow?'

'I didn't think you liked the idea.'

'I said yes, didn't I?'

'You said it sounded boring.'

'So what you're saying is you've had a whole week and you've done fuck all on it.'

'No, I . . .'

'Look, I want to run this thing next week. When can I have it?'

'Tuesday?'

'Urgghh. OK, but early Tuesday. How are you, by the way?'

'Fine.'

'How did your party end up? I had to go on to another thing.'

'I don't know.'

'Sounds like it was fun.'

Over the course of an afternoon's Internet research into the Barbary War I learned that Panaglos was one of a 'new wave' of anti-depressants which were chemically unrelated to the myriad SSRIs and SNRIs on the market. The neurochemical mechanism of its anti-depressant effect was not known. It had become a cult drug in the US, thanks largely to unfounded claims that it produced 'giant erections', possibly based on some clinical evidence of priapism in a small percentage of males. It remained unlicensed in Europe and unpopular with doctors in America, although it had a small but utterly devoted following among US depressives. The leaflet boasted the usual clutch of contradictory side effects – drowsiness and insomnia, excess salivary flow and dry mouth, increased and decreased libido – but on various

Panaglos forums users talked of stranger, more subtle symptoms: 'involuntary surliness'; 'revelatory dreams'; 'palpably improved phrase-turning ability' (Christ, what must he have been like before?), 'diminished consequence awareness' and 'olefactory hallucinations'.

It was the last one I had been searching for. Phantom odours were mentioned by several Panaglos users; in most cases they seemed to fade after a few weeks. I had not experienced any of the other side effects. In fact the only thing the pills seemed to do was to remind me to keep taking them. Perhaps that's all a pill really needs to do.

A quick British Library catalogue search turned up five books on the subject of the Barbary Wars, so I made a vague plan to go there early in the morning, though I had not crossed its threshold since a wasted week I'd spent researching nineteenth-century Irish whiskey taxation three years before. This time, however, I felt oddly empowered by the challenge: five days to produce a coherent essay on a war I'd only just heard of.

SUPER BEST DRY CLEANERS (or, THE SECRET GW NON-APPRECIATION SAFE HOUSE)
Started by Salome66 at 12.31 PM on 18.11.04
Quick! In here!

Salome66 – 12.34 PM on 18.11.04 (1 of 20)
Criticise everybody's least favourite journalist in the company of like-minded detractors. Don't show anyone else the secret handshake.

---

moretoastplease – 12.46 PM on 18.11.04 (2 of 20)
Ooh, it's lovely and warm here!

Lordhawhaw – 1.06 PM on 18.11.04 (3 of 20)
Is this what I think it is?

---

moretoastplease – 1.08 PM on 18.11.04 (4 of 20)
It's so big inside!

Salome66 – 1.11 PM on 18.11.04 (5 of 20)
Welcome, GW haters! Biscuit, anyone?

---

moretoastplease – 1.23 PM on 18.11.04 (6 of 20)
And yet from the outside it looks like an ordinary
disused dry cleaning establishment!

---

recidivist – 1.27 PM on 18.11.04 (7 of 20)
clever that

Grotius – 1.47 PM on 18.11.04 (8 of 20)
I was just thinking about starting up a hideout like
this myself. Well done, Sal

Lordhawhaw – 2.33 PM on 18.11.04 (9 of 20)
What happened to the old thread? It was heading
for 200 posts, last I looked.

Grotius – 2.51 PM on 18.11.04 (10 of 20)
It was pulled. Someone (I won't say who, lest he
search on his name and find us here) went on a bit

of a rant, at one point actually inciting people to hunt down and kill GW. People objected and it all got very messy.

---

recidivist – 3.12 PM on 18.11.04 (11 of 20)
StG*rnard, I'll wager

---

moretoastplease – 3.20 PM on 18.11.04 (12 of 20)
Precisely, although I think he's banned anyway. It's odd because he began by playing devil's advocate, actually defending GW.

Salome66 – 4.15 PM on 18.11.04 (13 of 20)
To the extent that most of us thought he *was* GW

---

sammy'sdot – 5.02 PM on 18.11.04 (14 of 20)
Who is GW and why don't we appreciate him?

---

recidivist – 5.15 PM on 18.11.04 (15 of 20)
If you have to ask, you'll never know

Salome66 – 6.23 PM on 18.11.04 (16 of 20)
He's just an exceedingly bad writer working for a certain newspaper who, while actually rather unremarkable, has become for some of us a potent symbol of everything that's wrong with everything. We're avoiding using his name only because we wish to protect the discussion from saboteurs, but you ought to be able to figure it out.

PavlovsKitty – 6.31 PM on 18.11.04 (17 of 20)
first name rhymes with piles

---

sammy'sdot – 6:44 PM on 18.11.04 (18 of 20)
what's this thread doing in the fashion folder?

---

moretoastplease – 8.21 AM on 19.11.04 (19 of 20)
shhhhhh!!

Grotius – 8.19 AM on 19.11.04 (20 of 20)
Haven't heard from GW in a while, have we? Could
he be on holiday?

Back / **Top** / **Add a comment**

15

In its new context everything about Maria's behaviour made sense. She normally settled on her bench sometime before nine and received visitors until about midday. People of varying class and age – stone-faced men, truant teens, mums with prams, etiolated junkies – took turns to sit down and chat, until the subtle exchange took place under the guise of passing a lighter or a packet of fags. Instead of queuing, customers hovered in a complex holding pattern, strolling and back and forth, sometimes chatting amongst themselves. I sat down on a bench on the other side of the park to watch the stately parade of transactions, waiting for a comfortable opening to present itself. I wanted more pills, pills in bulk, pills in reserve. The dog lay under the bench, gnawing a piece of timber into fragments.

'Hello, mate.'

I looked up and saw Tony, a man whom Colin had once drafted in to repair two of our sash windows. He had his dog on a lead – an ancient collie that walked with a pained, stiff-legged gait – and an extra-tall can of cider in his free hand. Tony was generally silent and sullen in the mornings, charming and voluble by lunchtime and incoherent by sunset. Judging by his bright smile, I guessed that he was already on his second can.

'Hi, Tony.'

'How you keeping, then, all right? How's the family?'

'Yeah, they're fine.'

'How's them windows holdin' up?' He let go of the lead and sat down. The dog didn't move.

'Still working.' It had taken him eight weeks, but he had done a beautiful job on them in the end.

'Terrible innit.' With his can hand he made a generous sweeping gesture as if to indicate everything in his field of vision.

'Yeah.'

'This used to be a nice park when I was a kid. There was a pond over there, and a bandstand. And they had a park keeper. He had his little hut just by the gate there.' A lean, fidgety black man got up from Maria's bench and walked off toward the road. He was wearing bedroom slippers.

'It's a shame.'

'Fucking tell me it's a shame. It's cause we're on the border between the two boroughs. No one gives a shit.' He pushed his heavy glasses up on his nose, revealing a small pink plaster at the bridge. Then he offered me the can.

'No, I won't. Actually I will.' The cider was warm and smelled of pine disinfectant mixed with stale tobacco, but then so did everything else. With notes of burnt ginger and compost. The boy with the hood entered the park riding a four-wheeled mobility scooter, going faster than I would have thought possible on such a machine. His two mates chased after him, but fell behind as he took the corner and sped up the path toward us. Then he stopped abruptly and glared at me.

'You gave me a fucking turd.' The scooter's flank was emblazoned with the words Ventura Shopsprinter II.

'Well, strictly speaking, you stole my turd.' There was an edge in my voice I didn't recognize.

'Stole your what?' said Tony.

'How you like me to give it back you, motherfucker?'

'Did you bring it with you?'

'You dissing me now?' He leaned forward in the scooter's chair, as if he might stand up.

'Of course not,' I said. 'How could I have anything but the utmost respect for you? You're clearly a genius.'

'We don't want no trouble,' said Tony.

'No, that's right. We don't want any trouble. Keep the turd. It's yours.'

The boy climbed off the scooter and took a step toward us. From under the bench the dog emitted a low growl, as she did whenever she suspected someone might try to take her stick. I felt unable to move, or unwilling. I couldn't quite tell which. The boy took another step and the growling grew louder. He took a step back and it stopped altogether. A fat girl wheeled up on a pink bicycle.

'The cops is outside the chemists,' she said.

'So?' The boy tugged his hood forward, remounted the scooter and headed overland toward the far corner of the park, where there was a gap in the chain-link fencing.

'Fucking kids,' said Tony, tossing his empty cider can

over his shoulder. A police car poked its nose gently through the front gates. Maria waved at them as they passed her, tyres straddling the path and leaving a curly wake of mud and chewed turf. Only then did my heart begin to pound so hard that it made my head move slightly. The smell snuck up and pounced: old mackerel in new bin liner. I closed my eyes and leaned forward, resting my elbows on my knees, breathing slowly.

'Hi.'

I looked up and saw Darby's mum standing in front of me with a puppy on a string.

20.11.04

Today's profile: Salome66.

Real first name unknown. Surname unknown. Significance of username unknown. '66' may indicate birth year (making her 38) or it may not. Web-based email address only. Frequently posts on poetry threads. Claims to write poetry but posts no examples and provides no links. Lives South London. Posts of hers on some of the longer threads go back to 2002. Describes self as 'mature student' but also seems to have a job. Appears to be well-travelled, well-read, politically engaged, intelligent, articulate, sophisticated and possessed of a romantic soul.

Likes: blank verse, Wallace Stevens, Mexican cuisine, dogs, peonies, Cornwall.

Dislikes: 'all forms of coffee apart from the blackest espresso', Prince Charles, GW

Interesting Fact: in a thread entitled 'Where Do You Sit in the British Library?', Salome66 claimed, on March 2004 at 4.17 PM, that she always sat in the low 4000s of Humanities 1.
   The Chord of the day is B.

16

SUPER BEST DRY CLEANERS (or, THE SECRET GW NON-APPRECIATION SAFE HOUSE)
Started by Salome66 at 12.31 PM on 18.11.04
Quick! In here!

PavlovsKitty – 11.53 AM on 19.11.04 (21 of 28)
Or perhaps they've sacked him at last.

FritsZernike – 2.22 PM on 19.11.04 (22 of 28)
Or maybe he's ill, God forbid

ThisDistractedGlobe – 1.06 AM on 20.11.04 (23 of 28)
No, I feel certain that he's taken some time off to work on a serious, nay groundbreaking bit of journalism which will rescue his reputation from the clutches of mediocrity.

Salome66 – 10.21 AM on 20.11.04 (24 of 28)
Spot on, ThisDistractedGlobe! He means to win us over! The pathetic workings of his tiny mind are all too transparent! I can hardly wait for his 3000-word

life-changing effort to hit the stands. What will it be about, I wonder?

Grotius – 10.39 AM on 20.11.04 (25 of 28)
The perfect martini?

---

moretoastplease – 10.55 AM on 20.11.04 (26 of 28)
How pears are always either too ripe or not ripe enough?

Salome66 – 11.02 AM on 20.11.04 (27 of 28)
Nice username, btw, TDG. Hamlet, isn't it?

ThisDistractedGlobe – 12.24 PM on 21.11.04 (28 of 28)
It is, lady.

Back / Top / Add a comment

Colin was painting the insides of the kitchen cupboards with an off-white undercoat. They were all open at ninety degrees; their handles lay in a pile on the table.

'Hello, Guy. All right, mate?'

'Can't complain. Tea?'

'If you're havin' one, mate, please.' The smell of paint was strong and strangely appetizing. I had ceased to trust my nose's assessment of anything. The kettle started its throaty exhale.

'Do you know anything about tracking people down, Colin?'

'How d'you mean?'

'Like if someone you needed to find had changed their name, and all you had was an email address or, I don't know, some sort of Internet username.'

'Don't talk to me about the Internet, mate. Me son-in-law's give me his old computer, and he's hooked me up wireless like, so I don't even pay for it. Just comes out the air. But I can't make fucking heads or tails of the thing. I daren't even turn it on, you know what I mean?' The kettle burbled urgently and then flicked off.

'Yeah. I mean I guess there are ways to get a name and address from an email – you usually have to give them your details when you sign up, your post code. But I don't know how to do it. And I'm not sure it's strictly legal.'

'Well, I can ask Gary, me son-in-law, cos he knows about computers and that. And he ain't strictly legal his self, if you know what I mean. But you'll have to write it down for me. Like I said, I know fuck all about it.'

'It's not important. I just can't find this person.'

'What d'you want 'em for?' It was a good question.

'It's someone I used to know, and I might want to get in touch again, but then I might not. I don't want them to find out I'm trying, you know what I mean?'

'A lady, is it?'

'Well, it is a lady, but it's not that sort of situation.' Colin put down his brush and produced a roll-up from behind his ear. He guarded the lighter with a cupped hand as if he were outside.

'Tell you what. Give me what you got and I'll see what Gary can do.'

'Thanks.' I set his tea down on the counter next to him. 'There you go. Three sugars.'

'Ta, mate. That's handsome.'

24.11.04

Last night I dreamt I was dead. When we were children we used to assure each other that you could not be dead in a dream, that you would always wake up first, but as I lay there and felt the life ebbing out of me, felt my vision dissolve and my breathing become a pointless exercise, it seemed as if I had passed the point of a return to consciousness. There was a sense of my brain flickering out, not at all unpleasant, but definitely irreversible. Then came one final, shuddering exhalation, and that was that; I was forever freed from the need to breathe. I became a single point of consciousness, infinitely small, floating in a straight line. After a while even this sense of motion evaporated; I was moving at the speed that everything was moving. I slipped the bonds of meaning, a last shard of energy resolved into the background hum. And then I woke up.

Several hours later the idea that I am dead has not quite left me. I can feel my heart beating, see my hands moving, but there has been a definite dissolution of consequence, a sense that I am no longer really here. Or that I am utterly here, stripped of any illusions about past or future, existing only in the present. I have a strong urge to refer to myself in the third person. He thinks it seems more appropriate somehow. Don't get him wrong: he knows he hasn't disappeared, or become other. It's just that there is a new sense of distance that needs to be acknowledged, the first person once removed. He keeps telling himself that it's the drug. This must be how it's supposed to make you feel (he thinks): unconquerable, immortal, shielded from death by death's own embrace, a zombie, a vampire. He no longer sees himself in mirrors. He sees someone else. When he was a child they used to say: when you die in your dreams, it means you're dead.

Today's profile: Grotius – Prolific poster on a range of topics, with an opinion on everything. Definitely over 30. Computer games designer, or reviewer, or both. Lives outside of London somewhere, but within easy reach. Appears to have once had something wrong with one of his testicles, which he refers to on several health threads without going into specifics. Hugo Grotius, it transpires, was a 17thC Dutch theologian, jurist and all-round Enlightenment figure – possible clue to first name, or perhaps he wishes to demonstrate that he shares similar ideals, or simply that he knows who Hugo Grotius is. Has a cat named Megan. Left-handed and rather idiotically proud of it. Voted Lib Dem in last election for 'strictly local reasons'.

It's possible that he may have known Salome66 prior to their internet acquaintance. Though they never say so outright, there is an assumption of ease between them. He is pompous and pedantic, but he invariably defers to her.

Likes: gaming, cats, ping pong, chess, Japanese food, Klee, Star Wars.

Dislikes: dogs, GW, SUVs, ITV, unnecessary capitalisation. The chord of the day is B again.

THE LAST POEM YOU READ
Started by RhymeMaiden at 10.39 PM on 09.05.03
What was the last bit of verse you digested?
Did it make you feel sad, happy, comforted, tested?
Discuss it here.

Salome66 – 11.22 PM on 24.11.04 (1361 of 1373)
That's weird. Stevens is probably my favourite poet

ThisDistractedGlobe– 11.25 PM on 24.11.04 (1362 of 1373)
He was always a favourite of mine, but I hadn't read any of his poems for years. I can't think what made me pull the book down off the shelf tonight, after all that time. But I'm glad I did.

Salome66 – 11.28 PM on 24.11.04 (1363 of 1373)
Where else do you post, TDG? I haven't seen you around much.

ThisDistractedGlobe – 11.31 PM on 24.11.04 (1364 of 1373)
I've been lurking for months, but was too shy to post until v recently, as you'll see if you do a search.

Salome66 – 11.35 PM on 24.11.04 (1365 of 1373)
As if I would! Why so shy?

---

dubstar24 – 11.36 PM on 24.11.04 (1366 of 1373)
'Mystery Bruise' by Perry Freak. Absolutely fucking fantastic.

ThisDistractedGlobe – 11.39 PM on 24.11.04 (1367 of 1373)
Dunno. Everyone on here seems so self-assured, and I'm not

Salome66 – 11.40 PM on 24.11.04 (1368 of 1373)
A studied pose in every case, take my word for it.

---

dubstar24 – 11.41 PM on 24.11.04 (1369 of 1373)
any other Freak freaks out there tonight?

Salome66 – 11.45 PM on 24.11.04 (1370 of 1373)
Perry Freak isn't a poet. He's useless, fatuous, self-regarding, post-literate druggie who thinks that putting random line breaks into an adolescent diary rant constitutes verse.

ThisDistractedGlobe – 11.48 PM on 24.11.04 (1371 of 1373)
Amen. I should go to bed. I've got to be at the British Library bright and early.

Salome66 – 11.51 PM on 24.11.04 (1372 of 1373)

God, I haven't been there in months! I feel so lazy.

---

dubstar24 – 11.53 PM on 24.11.04 (1373 of 1373)

fuck all of you ignorent monkeys

Back / Top / Add a comment

17

The phone rang.

'How's the history lesson coming?' It was Brian the features editor.

'It's taking a bit longer than I thought it would. There's a lot to digest.'

'We did say this week.'

'You want it to be good, don't you?'

'This week would be better.'

'I'll, I'm.'

'I've got something else for you in the meantime.'

'What?'

'Would you describe yourself as an Alpha male?'

'I don't know.'

'You know what I'm talking about though, right?'

'I know what an Alpha male is. I just don't know if I am one.'

'It wasn't a trick question.'

'I'm just not in a position to answer it.'

'Well, you'd probably know if you were one. So let me tell you what we want. Some professor of something up north somewhere has said that, something like, that Alpha males are now at a profound disadvantage in our feminized society. Their aggression is evolutionarily counterproductive in the modern world. For which reason they're not being selected.'

'I still don't know what I am.'

'Forget about your midlife thing for a second and listen. Everyone in the office this morning was talking about how you only ever hear about the Alpha males, but no one ever talks about the Beta males, or the Delta males or whatever.'

'Uh-huh.'

'So what we want from you,' he said, leaving a pause which probably signalled that something else was already claiming his attention, 'is the whole Greek alphabet, all the males from Alpha to Omega, but funny. Get it? A funny male Greek alphabet. All the male types in fifteen hundred words.'

I inserted a thoughtful silence. 'It won't work.'

'I love your enthusiasm. It's fucking infectious.'

'You can't do anything with Greek letters. You can't even make puns with them.'

'Twelve hundred words.'

'Can't do it.'

'You're definitely not an Alpha male, by the way. I'd put you somewhere around Tau.'

'I don't even know where that comes.'

'So I'll leave this in your hands. Be funny. Gotta go.'

Darby's mum had appeared in the park with her puppy three mornings running, and insisted on walking all the way round the path with me, slowing me down, compromising my sullen privacy and asking a lot of questions about pet care for which I had no answers. Her dog was short-legged and long-necked, a lurcher–cairn cross, she said, with scrubby brown fur like a dry-clean-only jumper that had been through the wash a few times. She called it Jackie, a name which it did not appear to recognize, and coaxed it forward with a succession of organic dog treats. We proceeded by inches.

'What sort of food do you give her? Wet? Dry?'

'I don't know. Whatever there is.' It was surprisingly cold and I had underdressed. The edges of the puddles were rimed with muddy ice.

'Don't you worry about her diet? Come on, Jackie. Come on, boy.'

'She's a dog. She eats curry takeaways off the road.'

'How do you stop her doing that?' She lurched backward as the puppy stopped to sniff a tree stump. As I stopped and turned the wind found its way between the buttons of my shirt. I reached for the top button of my jacket, knowing it wasn't there.

'I don't. I consider it a public service.' She smiled at the ground and I looked everywhere but at her. We walked on in a silence which felt entirely open to interpretation; companionable, or awkward, or some combination of the two. I had never been quite able to decide whether I found Darby's mum enchanting or irritating. We reached the secluded back turn, where the ground was still crunchy with frost underfoot.

'So, have you got a lot on this morning?' she asked.

'I never have a lot on.'

'Do you want to come by for a cup of tea?'

I let the dog back into the house on the way, which felt like a conscious decision to prepare for the possibility of betrayal, but half an hour later, sitting in Darby's mum's half-ripped-out kitchen with my fingers laced round a cup of tea, things had taken on an innocent, neighbourly tone. The situation seemed insufficiently wrong for me to have bothered, and I felt like going home. I leaned against her new fridge while she sat at the table and peppered me with questions about work and family.

'And whose idea was Philippa?'

'The older one. We had a nanny called Philippa. We'd only just sacked her a month before.'

'Aww. And he loved her.'

'That's what you get when you let a three-year-old name a pet: a dog called after a fat South African girl with a drink problem.'

'She's lovely, though. I could walk her for you sometimes when you're busy, seeing as I've now got to be out there anyway.'

'Yeah maybe. And I can easily take, um, Jackie if you need.' She came and stood just too close to me, face to face. I felt the skin on the back of my neck tingling, heating up.

'I could give you a key,' she said. 'In case no one's here.' I looked into her eyes and felt them pulling me forward. My heart leapt in my chest, and then seemed to stop altogether.

'OK.' She touched my arm. She held my arm. She was holding my arm. Time froze for a second, poised on a knife-edge of transgression. I knew I would agree to anything she wanted. I felt myself about to switch electricity suppliers.

'Could you come by and get him tomorrow at about ten?'

'Yes.' Anything.

'And if anyone asks, could you please say that I was with you?'

18

Beta, Gamma and Beyond

The Alpha Male is passing into history, says a new report, a victim of his own aggression in our increasingly feminised society. So who will take his place? Giles Wareing looks at the complete list of contenders, from Beta Boy to Omega Man . . .

Alpha Males, as any media scientist will tell you, are yesterday's news. According to Professor Rick Ferris at the University of Leicester, the qualities normally associated with Alpha Maledom – aggression, competitiveness, obsession with status – put him at a distinct disadvantage in our feminised society. When selecting mates, today's women are looking further afield, and well down the Greek alphabet. But what are these other males actually like? Here, for the uninitiated, is a rough guide.

Beta Male – expensive, better quality alternative to the Alpha Male, all but wiped out in the so-called format war of the early 1980s, when women decided that the rougher, readier version was perfectly acceptable for day to day home use. Now perversely fashionable in a retro sort of way.

Gamma Male – radiates a strong electromagnetism which is in fact incredibly toxic. Good first boyfriend material, especially if you're trying to upset your parents, but not much use for anything else.

Delta Male – Soulful, brooding sort sometimes known as Mississippi Delta Male. On the plus side: good sense of rhythm, often possessed of an earthy authenticity. On the minus: perpetually depressed, may own a guitar.

Epsilon Male – genetically predisposed to throw like a girl, but otherwise normal. One to watch.

Zeta Male – made up largely of men who dress as superheroes to get their point across.

Eta Male – like the Alpha Male, Eta Male is hungry, driven and single-minded, but only when it comes to food. Their 'Survival of the Fattest' strategy has long been regarded as tactically flawed, but some scientists are predicting that they will one day rule the Earth.

Theta Male – a grouping which includes all actors and directors, working and resting. Best avoided.

Iota Male – Iota Male is, generally speaking, a little bit better than most of the men you meet. Or perhaps a little bit worse, but not enough to make much difference one way or the other. Seventy-five per cent of the male population fall into this group.

Kappa Male – all you need to know about them is they wear baseball hats, indoors and out, and are therefore either twats, or bald, or both.

Lambda Male – describes himself as a 'house husband' because it sounds better than 'agoraphobic'.

Mu Male – outwardly normal, but cat-loving to the point of suspiciousness.

Nu Male – he has taste, he keeps himself clean and well-groomed, he likes children, appreciates Abba, is attentive, sensitive, funny, charming and clever, and he unloads the dishwasher without being asked. No living examples known.

Xi Male – virtually indistinguishable from Nu Male, but sadly gay.

Omikron Male – He reads whole articles about watches in men's magazines, and is therefore of no consequence in the wider scheme of things. Ignore at your leisure.

Pi Male – Possessed of an awkward, complex and ultimately unknowable personality best expressed in terms of the relationship between the circumference of a circle and its radius. Precisely how one expresses this is unclear; perhaps by wearing a T-shirt that says Pi Males Go On and On Forever Without Repeating.

Rho Male – Includes all hypochondriacs, fainters and men who never learned to swim.

Sigma Male – Encompasses most men now working in the growing scapegoat sector.

Tau Male – Comprises men still looking for work in the scapegoat sector.

Upsilon Male – It's all vegans from here on down, by the way.

Phi Male – All men who are evolutionarily hampered by unat-tractive phobias: mice, spiders, birds, specific foodstuffs.

Chi Male – Can't drive and therefore unsuitable for mating, but Chi males do make lovely pets.

Omega Male – the one you wouldn't go out with if he was the absolute last man on earth, although given the options, perhaps you ought to cross that bridge when you come to it.

I rang Ken from the paper.

'Hello?'

'You left out Psi.'

'Hello, Giles. Say that again?'

'In the "Alpha Male" piece. You left out one of the letters.'

'Which one?'

'Psi.'

'Ah. Well, it was a wee bit long, so we just took out the least funny gag. Personally I think it's stronger for it. The drawings are great, don't you think?'

'You can't cut a whole letter out of an alphabet piece. It's unethical.'

'It's the Greek alphabet. No one'll notice.'

'You think people don't know the Greek alphabet?'

'Did you?'

'Do you know how much shit I'm going to get for this?'

'How much? From who?'

2.12.04

He is getting low on Panaglos. The inadequacy of his supply provides a potent distraction. He can't think. He can't work. The woman who supplies him with it has not appeared on her bench for two days. People with more pressing addictions are sitting there with desperate faces, drinking from tall tins and getting into arguments. He tries to listen to snatches of their conversation, but they fall silent when he passes. He still has almost a week's worth of pills left, but he can't concentrate on anything but getting more. He's not himself, and he wants to stay that way.

Today's profile:

PavlovsKitty. 26, female, in the process of moving from London to Edinburgh. Single, owns a snake, real name Hannah Mytton. Has a weblog in which she publicises her opinions on certain celebrities, the details of an on-off relationship she's having with a medical student called C, and her belief that most of her interpersonal difficulties are digestive in origin. There is a regular section written from the point of view of the snake.

Likes: snakes, mangoes, country music, Keanu Reeves, in spite of herself.

Dislikes: yellow, GW, simple carbohydrates.

The chord of the day is still B.

The puppy barked continually while I fiddled with the two locks, and by the time I'd opened the door he'd peed on the mat. A tiny bit of me hoped I might find Darby's mum there waiting for me, poised to act out some sexual fantasy that first required me to let myself in. Instead I found a small turd in the kitchen. I cleaned up thoroughly, letting the chore fuel my resentment. I then dragged Jackie down to the front gate where I'd tied up my own dog, and the three of us set off. Philippa, unused to her lead, spent the entire journey trying to pull it from my grasp with her teeth, while Jackie refused to make any forward progress at all. Eventually I had to pick him up and carry him.

Maria was not on her bench. I let Philippa off the lead but she took this to be another stage of the game: she jumped for it and tried to take it off me, and when I finally got it coiled up she began to growl and bite at my shoes. I heard a strange chirping sound, like muffled crickets. My chest began to pulsate, and I felt a sense of rising panic before I realized it was my mobile going off. The children changed the ringtone regularly to ensure maximum alarm on my part. I hadn't answered it in nearly a week. It must have been in my coat the whole time. It was Caroline.

'Hello?'

'Where are you?'

'In the park. Get off!'

'Hello?'

'Sorry. The dog is biting my shoe.'

'Is Sarah there with you?'

'Who?'

'Sarah-Darby's-mum. She told me only this morning that she walked her dog with you most days.' I hadn't realized the lie would be tested so soon. Did it even apply to Caroline?

'Oh. Yes. She is.'

'Ask her if she still wants me to pick up Darby this afternoon. Tae kwon do's cancelled so I can if she wants.'

'Tae kwon do is cancelled? Why?'

'Like you care.'

'Actually she's just run off across the field after Jackie.' Jackie was, in fact, eating a discarded chicken wing at my feet.

'I don't have her mobile. Just ask her and then text me.'

'Text? I don't even . . .'

'Menu, select, select, select.'

'OK.'

'Oh and also. We've been asked to dinner by the . . .' Something hit me hard in the shoulder, from the rear. The mobile floated free from my hand. The dog yelped. A bicycle appeared on the path in front of me moving away at speed. I recognized the tall hooded boy immediately, even from behind. I watched as he tucked my phone into the pocket of his coat and then stood up to apply pressure to the pedals, weaving from side to side as he accelerated.

Jackie made a hideous choking sound. My right shoulder blade felt hot. Philippa was limping in small circles while attempting to inspect her left rear leg. The bike passed behind a stand of trees at the rear of the park and never emerged. Jackie produced a small heap of sick. My heart began to thud melodramatically, unaware that it had missed the moment. Then I felt a shudder go right through my frame, twisting my shoulders and unlocking both knees. I resisted the urge to sit down on the ground.

SUPER BEST DRY CLEANERS (or, THE SECRET GW NON-APPRECIATION SAFE HOUSE)
Started by Salome66 at 12.31 PM on 18.11.04
Quick! In here!

PavlovsKitty – 10.56 AM on 2.12.04 (38 of 52)
unbelievably weak

---

recidivist – 11.09 AM on 2.12.04 (39 of 52)
What must it be like to the purveyor of such shite?

Grotius – 11.24 AM on 2.12.04 (40 of 52)
Not just pointless and unfunny, but snide and downright offensive. It retreads lazy, idiotic stereotypes about bald men and cat lovers (I happen to be both) and its whole tone is crypto-homophobic.

ThisDistractedGlobe – 11.49 AM on 2.12.04 (41 of 52)
And he left out Psi

Grotius – 12.04 PM on 2.12.04 (42 of 52)
Well, spotted TDG! I hadn't even noticed that. How predictably stupid.

---

easyGeoff – 12.08 PM on 2.12.04 (43 of 52)
I agree. Nasty, homophobic, unfunny, lame.

Salome66 – 12.21 PM on 2.12.04 (44 of 52)
Hi all! I noticed the missing psi as well, TDG. One
less terrible joke to wade through, at any rate.

ThisDistractedGlobe – 12.25 PM on 2.12.04 (45 of 52)
Shouldn't someone complain about the mysterious
missing Greek letter? Make our Giles own up to his
stupidity? Isn't a letter to the editor in order?

Salome66 – 12.31 PM on 2.12.04 (46 of 52)
Good idea. Let the paper know they have a fool in
their midst. Although I can't believe they don't
know it already.

---

easyGeoff – 12.45 PM on 2.12.04 (47 of 52)
I've half a mind to start a 'Sack GW' petition

---

recidivist – 12.52 PM on 2.12.04 (48 of 52)
I'll sign it.

Grotius – 1.11 PM on 2.12.04 (49 of 52)
How's this:
      'To the editor: Surely even a journalist as
slapdash as Giles Wareing must be able to procure
a complete Greek alphabet from somewhere (Beta,

Gamma and Beyond, Dec 2)? What excuse could he possibly give for leaving out the letter Psi? I'm not complaining, mind: one less vile stereotype or hackneyed joke can only be considered an improvement. Would that he had left out a few more.'

Salome66 – 1.14 PM on 2.12.04 (50 of 52)
Brilliant.

ThisDistractedGlobe – 1.19 PM on 2.12.04 (51 of 52)
You must send it, Grotius.

Grotius – 1.23 PM on 2.12.04 (52 of 52)
I already have.

Back / Top / Add a comment

I lay on my side on the sofa with both boys draped over me like snakes, finger pinched in my book, watching a polar bear eat a seal. The dog was curled up on top of my feet, and though I could not reach it without upsetting the pile, there was a glass of wine on the floor in front of me. It struck me that this was as close to perfect happiness as I was likely to get, that this quiet half-hour before bedtime might end up being a high point in my brief existence, perhaps the high point.

Caroline was on the phone in the kitchen speaking in a theatrical voice. Someone's husband had walked out, sending shock waves through Caroline's group of friends. Normally they would take vindictive pleasure in enumerating the peculiarities which doomed a particular union to fail – his dullness, her unbridled stupidity – but this example seemed closer to home: a marriage run aground while on a similar course to their own. Everyone was picking over the wreckage, looking for clues. For the last five minutes Caroline had been saying the same thing over and over, stressing different words: 'I mean, *what* did she fucking think?'

'Mum sweared,' said Freddy.

'I heard her,' I said. He plugged his thumb back in.

'Dad, is that real?' said the older one, looking up from his games console and pointing at the television. A lifeless, deflated seal. Blood staining snow.

'Yes it is.'

'What did she fucking *think*?'

'Mum sweared again.'

'I know.' I shifted and felt Darby's mum's house key stab me in the thigh.

'I thought polar bears were nice.'

'Well, they need to eat,' I said.

'They should just eat fruit,' said the little one.

'There isn't any fruit where they live,' said the older one.

'Well, they should move where there is.'

'You're so stupid, Freddy.'

'I'm not stupid, you're stupid!' shouted Freddy. He began to stand up suddenly, one foot on my ear.

'Ow! Don't fight on me,' I said. Freddy sat back down, stuck his thumb in his mouth and put his head on my shoulder. The older one turned his attention back to his game. The baby polar bears gambolled in a blizzard. Caroline strode into the room, phone in hand, looking pensive.

'Helen thought your thing was funny today,' she said, picking up my wine glass and draining it.

'What thing?'

'I don't know. Something about Greek men. She said it made her laugh.'

'They left out Psi.'

'Who is Sy?'

'Who's Helen?'

'Christ. Never mind.' She put the glass down. 'What're you reading?'

I stood the book up on my chest to show the cover.

'Wallace Stevens.'

'Since when do you read poetry?'

'I read poetry. I do.'

'Where did it come from?' She smiled indulgently, as if I were a child doing something cute.

'I ordered it.'

'Huh.'

She clapped her hands four times and scooped Freddy up. He gave a grunt of irritation, but then settled limply into the contours of her shoulder like a sack of rice.

'It's bedtime. Come on, you.'

'Mum, I haven't even died yet!' said the older one, still working the buttons furiously with both thumbs.

'OK,' said Caroline. 'You come up when you die.'

When she'd gone I opened the book at my finger, which had gone white. My lips moved slightly as I read.

19

The paper printed Grotius's letter, it seemed to me, with a sort of barely suppressed delight. It was signed K Mabey, Bedford. I stared at it for a while, pronouncing the words under my breath. It could have been a pseudonym, of course, but it had the dull ring of the actual, especially Bedford.

It took less than a minute to come up with an address: directory enquiries' online service listed only one K Mabey in Bedford, at 45a Penshurst Road. Penshurst. There was a line from a poem – 'Thou art not, Penshurst, built to envious show' – but I couldn't remember the rest, or who wrote it. This was Grotius. He was found. I scribbled the name and address down in my journal, under his profile. It was like having a hank of his hair.

I decided it would be easier to leave Philippa behind when I went to collect Jackie, and then pick her up on the way to the park. The less time I spent in charge of the both of them the better. Once off the lead Jackie followed me so closely that I was in constant danger of stepping on him. Philippa trotted off in a lazy S, nose brushing the ground. Maria was sitting on her bench for the first time in four days. Next to her was a dishevelled young man who appeared to be asleep in his own lap.

'Got your fancy woman's dog I see,' she said, lighting a long brown fag.

'She's not my fancy woman.' I tried not to sound annoyed, but I didn't quite pull it off. 'Where have you been?'

'I had a few things to take care of here and there. Admin, do they call it these days.' She let out a jolt of a cackle that dissolved into a cough, reverberating with a distant interior thunder.

'Oh. Did you . . .' The man next to her shuddered, then spat on the ground between his knees.

'Don't mind him. All right, John?' John let out a broken, ratchety groan. I sat down gingerly on the far edge of the bench and looked straight ahead as Maria rummaged in her trolley. The day was bright and cold. Fresh dog turds gave off plumes of steam. I thought about Maria sitting out here all winter at her age, whatever it was. Sixty? Seventy? I couldn't have guessed.

'There you go,' she said, handing me a small white box which rattled as if less than full. Inside were three foil-backed blister packs with seven chambers apiece: twenty-one small pills, three weeks' worth of Panaglos.

'Is that it?'

'Got a problem with my supplier,' she said, lighting a fag. 'They've banned it now in America, you know. Too many suicides.'

'Oh.'

'Don't worry. I'll sort it. You've got yourself enough there to get you through the holidays.'

John let out another groan. A puddle of drool was collecting between his boots.

'Isn't there something you could give him?'

'I'm not givin' him anything when he's in that state. Fuck knows what he's taken already.' There was a loud crack. Across the park four small boys in rucksacks had managed to pull down a small tree, snapping it at its base. 'Totally out of control,' said Maria. 'Little cunts. I blame the parents.'

'I had my phone stolen in here by some kid just yesterday.'

'What sort?'

'It was an old one. Pay-as-you-go. Not worth much.'

'No, I mean the one who took it. Was he a black feller?'

'He's just a kid. Mixed race, or Asian, I don't know. Tall kid who's always in the park. I think he has it in for me.'

'I know the one you mean. Leave it with me. That's sixty you owe me, by the way.'

I handed over three twenties. John muttered something unintelligible. I got up to leave and stepped on Jackie.

The following week passed in a gentle blur of mornings in the park, afternoons at my desk and nights of wine and television. The phantom smell had settled down, or rather mutated into a manageable, occasional whiff of something acrid and soapy. Outdoors it came and went on the breeze as if from a great distance, hardly something I could call my own anymore.

The days had obligingly shortened, becoming easier to fill. Without a mobile I was serenely out of touch. I checked my office line once a day, but vowed only to return messages of the utmost importance, and to my mind none qualified. With no fresh material to criticize, the talkboards had gone quiet on the subject of Giles Wareing. Another five days without comment and the thread itself would be deleted, I gathered, in an automated house-keeping exercise. On Friday I finished the Barbary War piece in the early afternoon and emailed it through. I checked the talkboards, strummed a few chords, checked the talkboards again: nothing. Then I decided to call it a week. I went downstairs to consult the fridge and the TV listings.

The older one was scratching at his violin in the kitchen while Caroline looked on. The refrigerator was suspiciously empty.

'There's nothing for supper,' I said.

'And why do you think that might be?' asked Caroline.

'I can't do this,' said the boy.

'You're doing really well,' said Caroline. 'Try using a bit more bow.'

'I don't know,' I said.

'Because we're going out.'

'My neck hurts.'

'Out where?'

'To Helen and thing's,' said Caroline, rolling her eyes elaborately. 'I've told you.'

'No you haven't.'

'Well, we are.'

'Mum, my neck hurts.'

'Perhaps your father could monitor your practice for once in his life. I'm going to have a bath. The taxi is bringing the babysitter at eight.'

I adjusted the neck of the boy's pyjamas so that it protected his collarbone from the metal clamp of the violin's chin rest and sat down in Caroline's vacated chair. A yellow exercise book filled with a dense and looping script lay open in front of me.

'It says you need to pay particular attention to your tone on the A string. Which one is the A string?'

'*That* one,' he said, his rolling eyes a perfect imitation of Caroline's.

Helen lived somewhere to the north and east of us, in a street nearly identical to ours but subtly grander, with mature trees and a better class of parked car.

'Nice,' I said thickly as the taxi crept along looking for the house number. I already felt sleepy and detached, the sharp tang of toothpaste catching at the back of my throat.

'You couldn't pay me to live up here,' said Caroline, who considered whole swathes of London to be blighted by a certain not-quite-rightness: too posh, too shaggy, too suburban, too Edwardian, too central, too south. By her standards our own neighbourhood was indefensible. The taxi stopped. Caroline passed the driver some coins rolled up in a tenner.

'What's Mr Helen called?' I asked, pushing the doorbell.

'Can't remember,' said Caroline. 'Shit.'

'Hello!' said Helen, whipping open the door. I recognized her as the woman who brought the boys home on Wednesdays. 'Come in!'

We followed Helen along the hall to the kitchen. The table was set for eight. I didn't know whether to be relieved or not. The room was empty, but there were voices and cigarette smoke wafting in from the open garden door. One of them was oddly familiar: clipped and robotically jovial, like something off the radio. A tall, stooped, bottle-shaped man stepped in gingerly, as if entering a china shop. He was the one who had asked me if I'd had a good time at my party at the school gates. I'd told him I didn't remember, and he'd laughed. I glanced at Caroline, who mouthed the word 'Martin'. It was all coming together,

'Hello, Giles,' he said, walking towards me. 'Good to see you again.' His voice was high and gentle; not the one I'd recognized.

'Hi, Martin.'

Another figure entered from the garden as I smiled and shook Martin's hand. I made an effort not to look over his shoulder.

'There you are,' said Helen. 'Caroline, do you know Cher Fitzpaine?'

Martin gave me a glass of wine. Other people arrived almost immediately: a pregnant woman in a shawl and her wary-looking partner, both of whom claimed to have seen me somewhere before.

'You're the one with the white dog,' said the wife. 'I've seen you in that park – what's it called?'

'Roundworm.' I felt instantly uncomfortable. What had she seen me do? Had she seen me drinking cider on a bench with Tony? Lying in the tall grass and crying? Buying drugs from the local dealer?

'Ah yes,' said the husband-or-partner. 'North-west London's premier dog toilet.'

'That's the one.'

I pretended to give the subsequent discussion about dogs and dog people my full attention, stringing some of my hoariest anecdotes into a monologue which I injected into gaps in the conversation like joint compound. When I wasn't speaking I nodded appreciatively while stealing glances of the room beyond. It wasn't until fifteen minutes later, having freed my captives, that I finally came face to face with Fitzpaine.

'Hi.'

'Giles. We're speaking, are we?'

'Yes,' I said. 'I am speaking now, I think.'

'It's just that I called you last week, but you . . .'

'Did you? I didn't . . . that's really . . . well, my mobile was stolen. That'll be it.'

'So that wasn't you who told me to fuck off.'

'No.'

'It didn't sound like you. He also called me something which I had to look up on the Internet.'

'What was it about?'

'I'm not telling you. It's disgusting.'

'No, I mean why did you ring me?'

'I wanted to invite you to my stag night. I'm getting married next month.'

'Oh. Wow. Nice.' I looked around the room for something like a fiancée, desperate to know what sort of woman would agree to marry Cher Fitzpaine. There was only one possibility: a small girl in a heavy green velvet dress with her back to us.

'I got a little paranoid after the phone call,' he said. 'Especially because I wasn't really sure how we'd left it the last time we saw each other.'

'I don't remember either.'

'Good. So I really hope you can come. Just a small thing, you and me and Perry and whoever.'

I didn't understand why he was inviting me to his stag night. Did he have so few friends? I didn't know him well enough to ask him, let alone to say no. I hoped it was on a day when I had plans, even though I had no plans.

'I'm flattered. When is it?'

'I'll let you know.'

'You can't sit me next to my husband,' said Caroline loudly. 'We're barely speaking.' Martin came over with a bottle of white wine and I held out my glass.

'Oh. You were on red,' he said.

'It doesn't matter.'

'So are people still slagging you off on that chat-room thing?' asked Fitzpaine. I concentrated on my glass as Martin filled it, wondering if I could get away with not responding.

'Did I tell you about that?'

'In some detail.'

'Did I. Well, yes, I guess they still are.' He began to walk toward the garden door. I followed helplessly.

'So what are you going to do about it?' he said, once we were outside. He offered a cigarette, and I took it.

'I think it's dying down, actually.'

'I wouldn't count on it. There's one guy on there who really seems to hate you.'

'You've seen it?'

'Yeah, well you said it had something to do with the interview, so I tracked it down.'

'They don't like you much either.'

He smiled. 'No, but the last time I looked it was really all about you, and all rather malicious and personal. I suspect some of them might be people you know.'

'Nah, I think it's just a group of freelance malcontents. The Internet has a way of bringing them together.'

'Don't just let it go. Pursue it. Find out who they are. I would.'

'I suppose.' I had an awful premonition: I suddenly knew exactly what he was going to say next. I willed him not to say it, clenching and unclenching my jaw. He examined the ash of his cigarette from all sides and then looked up at me.

'We're kindred spirits, you and I.'

No we aren't, I thought. We really aren't. I tried to drain my wine glass, but it was already empty.

A wave of laughter reached us from inside, Caroline's voice riding on top of it.

'And he didn't even have gout in the fucking first place!' she said.

I woke up the next morning to find a tiny little figure looking at me.

'Dad, I want Shreddies,' it said.

'Um, OK, good.' My throat felt as if I'd swallowed a length of rope.

'Dad, get up.' He tugged on the duvet.

'I am. I am.' I sat up on the edge of the bed. My head began to whirl.

'Dad, you're naked.'

'So I am.' So I was.

'I can see your willy.'

'Yes.' I looked over my shoulder at Caroline, who lay motionless, a strand of her hair glued to her lower lip. Perhaps we'd had sex. My mood instantly lightened, even as my temples throbbed.

'What was it you wanted? Porridge?'

'No Dad. Shreddies.'

'How about a nice thin gruel? Great way to start the day.'

'Shreddies I said!'

'Ah. You don't fancy gruel. What about Clams Casino, then? A lot of people say it's not a breakfast thing, but I . . .'

'No!'

'Suit yourself. Me, I don't like anything too heavy in

the morning. Just a handful of hemp seeds and a glass of my own pee.'

'Get him his fucking Shreddies,' said Caroline.

I poured the cereal, made the coffee, fed the animals and brought in the newspapers. The boys ate their breakfast in silence in front of the kitchen telly, then moved to the bigger telly. Caroline appeared at about nine.

'Christ, my head,' she said.

'Hmm.'

'What is it you do in your office by yourself all night?'

'When?'

'When we got home you went straight up to your office and stayed there for ages.'

'Just checking my email.' I didn't remember coming home, or paying the babysitter, or going up to my office, or anything.

'Uh-huh. And what were you shouting about last night?'

'When?'

'You were shouting at that woman. The pregnant woman married to the guy with the terrible jumper.'

'Oh.'

'Yes.'

'She, uh, she accused me of being a glass-half-empty person.'

'Right.'

'Whereas she was, she maintained, a glass-half-full person.'

'So you shouted at her.'

'No, I just said that glass-half-full people are missing the point.'

'Which is what?'

'Which is that the glass is half empty.'

'I see.'

'And getting emptier all the time.'

'Yours certainly always is.'

'What use is boneheaded optimism in the face of bleak inevitability?'

'Hmm. Did you tell her you just turned forty by any chance?'

'I don't remember.'

Caroline pulled a mug out of the cupboard, during which time I had another premonition. I felt like I knew what was she about to say. I became more and more certain of it as she poured her coffee, sat down and started to thumb through the papers. Was she so predictable, or was this another side effect of the Panaglos? I stared at the top of her head as she read.

'Well,' she said finally, pushing aside one newspaper section and retrieving another from the pile. 'Your little friend Cher Fitzpaine is a bit of a twat, isn't he?'

Word for word.

I found my clothes from the previous night in my office, along with a bottle of wine on its side. An empty glass, fogged with fingerprints, stood next to the computer. A veritable crime scene. There was also an illegible note lying on the keyboard, scrawled on the back of a printout of the Greek alphabet. The first line was just decipherable: 'don't forget'. It was already too late for that. This was followed by a bunch of capital letters and a row of exclamation marks. Initially I thought the letters might be chords. Perhaps I'd been struck by inspiration in the night. Naked inspiration. I picked up the guitar and worked through them: C, F, A . . . It didn't sound good, but I was prepared to give it a chance. The next one looked like Db, but that seemed unlikely: I didn't know Db. Then D, then G. I played it through twice, taking an educated guess at Db, before realizing that the Ds were Ps and the small b was an L: CFAPLPG. What could it mean?

With what had now become a rather familiar feeling of achey foreboding, I turned on the computer.

SUPER BEST DRY CLEANERS (or, THE SECRET GW NON-APPRECIATION SAFE HOUSE)
Started by Salome66 at 12.31 PM on 18.11.04
Quick! In here!

ThisDistractedGlobe – 1.42 AM on 11.12.04 (62 of 72)
where is everybody?

ThisDistractedGlobe – 2.01 AM on 11.12.04 (63 of 72)
???

ThisDistractedGlobe – 2.09 AM on 11.12.04 (64 of 72)
all alone

---

easyGeoff – 2.13 AM on 11.12.04 (65 of 72)
Hi TDG. Big night?

ThisDistractedGlobe – 2.15 AM on 11.12.04 (66 of 72)

yyes a bit

---

easyGeoff – 2.19 AM on 11.12.04 (67 of 72)

Just got in meself

ThisDistractedGlobe – 2.21 AM on 11.12.04 (68 of 72)

ditto

---

easyGeoff – 2.24 AM on 11.12.04 (69 of 72)

that time of year innit. you going to the CFAPLPG?

ThisDistractedGlobe – 2.31 AM on 11.12.04 (70 of 72)

the what

---

easyGeoff – 2.37 AM on 11.12.04 (71 of 72)

The Combined Film And Poetry London Pre-
Christmas Get-together. Just an excuse for local
posters to meet up and get pissed. Second annual.
There's a thread about it in the Books folder. You're
one of the poetry lot, aren't you?

ThisDistractedGlobe – 2.57 AM on 11.12.04 (72 of 72)

I geuss so.

Back / Top / Add a comment

20

On Monday morning a small white envelope appeared on the mat, postmarked locally and addressed to 'the occupier' in a small, shaky, old-fashioned cursive. The letter inside was written in the same crabbed script at a jaunty angle to the edge of the notepaper. There was no salutation, signature or punctuation:

I am writing you this letter to let you know that the chap that has been seen entering your house recently looking as a decorator has a police record he is a well known figure in the area and has a reputation for violance theft intimidation and many other vices a friend of his was found murdered some weeks back he has served time in prison his kind do not believe in working for a living they steal and corrupt and intimidate to live their lives I hope you dont let him work his way into your home lying is an art to his kind and his is as good as it gets dont be fooled by this person remember his kind dont do anything for nothing and dont be Fooled by the London accent he is irish

I do hope this letter has been some help to you

I didn't know what to make of it. It was impossible to guess at the accuracy of the claims, or the motives of the author. It certainly seemed a suspect piece of neighbourly advice. I quickly decided that I wouldn't mention the letter to Colin right away. Perhaps less wisely, I decided not to tell Caroline about it either.

The phone rang while I was getting dressed.

'Wareing.' It was Brian, the features editor.

'Hi, Brian.'

'What the fuck am I supposed to do with this thing you sent me?'

'Um. I don't know.'

'It's three thousand fucking words long.'

'Well, it's about two-eight, actually.'

'And hardly your usual thing.'

'No. I guess that was partly the point.'

'It's all serious and weighty.'

'Sorry.'

'We like serious and weighty, but we have people for that. More than we need, in fact.'

'But.'

'What we have a shortage of is people who can do sixteen hundred words about going to a naked dinner party.'

'That was three years ago.'

'Still your finest hour, I think.'

'Maybe.'

'Listen,' he said, suddenly sounding weary, 'I think I might be about to do you a huge fucking favour, but I still have to work out why I should bother.'

'OK. Do I say thank you now?'

'Not yet. I'll call you back in an hour.'

I had to get to Jackie before nine thirty or he shat on the floor, and in my haste to leave I forgot my own house keys. Passing the house again on my way to the park, with Jackie under my arm, I glanced up and saw Philippa staring forlornly from the boys' bedroom window. I mouthed the word 'sorry' and carried on.

Maria was on her bench with a client, so I started off in the opposite direction, pausing only to wave. She gave a discreet nod, or perhaps not even that; it was hard to judge from such a distance. Jackie sniffed at the base of an overflowing bin for a good ten minutes, but without my keys I was in no hurry. The air was cold but the sun was out, the sky a hard eggshell blue. I paused every ten paces or so and eventually he came along behind. It took us half an hour to walk our way round to Maria's bench, by which time she was alone. I sat down.

'I've got something for you,' she said, fishing deep in her bag. I hoped it was more Panaglos – my future at that point only seemed to extend as far as my supply might last – but the thing she pulled from her bag was the wrong shape. 'This yours, then?'

I looked at the object, which for a moment seemed unnameable, though plainly familiar, as if there were a fogged spot on my brain.

'Oh my God,' I said. 'My phone.' I took it from her and examined it, still not sure it could really be mine.

'You're very welcome.'

'How did you get it back?'

'That's not your problem.' She said this with a cold finality that both irritated and frightened me. I thought of the letter on the mat. I was too old to fall in with a bad crowd.

'I need more pills,' I said, trying to iron the desperation out of my voice as the words emerged.

'Next week,' she said. A noise emerged from deep in her chest like an old deck of cards being shuffled.

I rang Caroline as I left the park.

'I'm driving.'

'I've locked myself out, that's all.'

'I'm about twenty minutes away. How are you talking on your stolen phone?'

'Oh. I found it.'

'So it wasn't stolen.'

'No it was, but I got it back.'

'What do you mean you got it back?'

'It was returned to me.'

'By who?'

'Someone in the park.'

'I don't understand. How the ... shit, there's a cop behind me. I have to go.'

'OK. See you in twenty minutes.' She was already gone.

Philippa was still in the window, shifting her weight anxiously on her front paws and yawning with overexcitement. As I walked past the stupidity of the situation struck me like something cold, a snowball in the back of the head.

Guilt coursed down my spine but the Panaglos neatly erased its track as it went. Emotions still came, but they no longer left a mark, which was something.

I undid the lower lock first, because I could never remember whether the upper one was clockwise or anti-clockwise. Today the door simply opened. Perhaps I'd left the upper lock undone. That would have been the smart thing to do. Jackie nosed between my legs and scuttled off toward the kitchen. I took two steps into the hall to hang the lead over the banister and as I turned to go it occurred to me that I was locked out of home. Caroline would be at least twenty minutes, probably more like forty. I thought about sitting on the cold steps with the dog yelping on the other side of the door. I decided a quick cup of tea at Darby's mum's house would use up the right amount of time. I followed Jackie in and filled up the kettle.

The window behind the sink was spattered with plaster, and there was a thick layer of wood dust on the sill. In the tiny garden scraps of cabinetry were leaned up against the wall. The new refrigerator was in its slot, but otherwise the room looked much as it had on my last visit except, I suddenly noticed, that there was a man sitting at the kitchen table staring at me.

'Hello!' I said, too brightly, attempting to force an air of normality on the encounter. A jolt of surprise had gone through me which I feared may have had involuntary physical manifestations. My feet may have briefly left the floor.

'Who are you?' he said. His voice was deep and smoky.

223

He was dressed in a white shirt, arms folded, black hair combed straight back. A suit jacket hung on the chair behind him. The sharp sideways light from the window created a lattice of illuminated dust which hung in the air between us like a gate.

'I'm Giles,' I said, taking a step backwards. 'Freddy's dad.'

'Ah. Sarah walks the dog with you every day.' He smiled a smile of recognition which was in no way reassuring.

'Yes. Well, most days.'

'Not today, though.'

'No, she had a, she was busy I guess.'

'Doing what?'

'I'm not sure, actually. She just called. Texted.'

'Funny. I keep ringing her but her phone's off. Darby got hurt at school. I had to go and get her.' I wondered briefly if Freddy might have been implicated.

'Is she all right?'

'Nothing serious. A greenstick fracture. She's asleep.'

'That's good.' Glancing across the room and down the hall, I saw that the front door was still wide open. In the whiteness beyond the threshold the blurred shape of a pedestrian crossed from right to left, and I heard the sandy scratch of shoes on the pavement, like two quick punches.

'You have a key.'

'Sorry? Yes, you know, in case . . .' The name stuck in my throat. '. . . Sarah, can't, walk Jackie for some reason.'

'Like today.'

'Like today, exactly.'

'Very kind of you.'

'Oh, not really. I have to be out there anyway,' I said, forcing a smile. 'Rain or shine, unfortunately.'

'Because you have a dog too.'

'Yeah.'

'Where is it?'

'Where's what?'

'Your dog.'

'Oh! Right. She's uh, she didn't, I usually drop her off first on the way back. I live just ... it makes the whole thing less of an ordeal.'

'I see.'

'Actually today I managed to lock myself out before I'd, so she didn't even ... I guess I'll have to go out again later.'

'You seem quite at home here.' He was very big through the shoulders, I noticed.

'Not really. No, as I said I'd locked myself out, and it uh ...' I stopped. Neither of us said anything for while. The sun faded abruptly, and the gate of dust disappeared. I noticed the square of red, worried skin on his forehead.

'I don't know where my wife is,' he said, fixing me with a stare. 'Does your wife know where you are?'

I took a few slow breaths while looking down at my shoe, trying to work out what should come next. Jackie stuck his nose into a gap between the dishwasher and an adjacent, unfinished cupboard and exhaled sharply. I became aware of the clock ticking and looked up. He was staring at me, Darby's dad, as if he would never blink again.

I fished around in my pocket, drew out the fat key tied on its loop of purple ribbon, placed it on the worktop and walked out: the most immediate solution to the most pressing problem. That was what I liked about Panaglos. Whenever circumstances became too awkward to handle, it sent a message along your skin, a reminder that the emotional consequences of your actions had become negligible. Don't undo the knot, it said. Just cut the rope.

I sat on our front step nursing a cup of coffee from the corner cafe and trying to ignore the dog whimpering on the other side of the door. The house across the road was having a basement dug on the cheap, basements being the latest innovation in space optimization in this neck of the woods. I watched the foreman berate his two labourers in an Eastern European language, telling them off for not bringing up enough earth in the night. My phone played a snatch of an unfamiliar pop song.

'Hello?'

'Got your phone back.'

'Yeah, just got it back. Amazing.'

'I only gave it up cos it was clappin'.'

'Yes.' I paused. 'Who is this?'

'Why don't you get a better one, then I can take that off you next time, you fuckin' . . .'

I turned the phone off. Colin pulled up in his white mini–van, striped along its flank with the blue paint of another vehicle. I watched as he patted himself, produced a disabled badge from his breast pocket and slid it onto the dashboard. I thought about his reputation for violence, theft, intimidation and many other vices. I hoped he had a key to the front door. And I also sort of hoped he didn't have one.

IT'S TIME TO SET A DATE FOR THE CFAPLPG*
Started by Psalmanazar at 10.09 AM on 7.12.04
* that's the Combined Film And Poetry London Pre-Christmas Get-together! Come one come all!

PavlovsKitty – 9.31 PM on 11.12.04 (87 of 96)
It's a shame cos I'm coming to London anyway but my Eurostar ticket is for that evening. If only it was the day before!

Psalmanazar – 8.48 AM on 13.12.04 (88 of 96)
The 21st was the date most people seemed to agree upon. The proximity to Xmas is problematic, I know, but we're aiming to accommodate as many non-Londoners as possible, since the rest of us are here anyway. If it helps we plan to start early – about 3 or so.

ThisDistractedGlobe – 11.45 AM on 13.12.04 (89 of 96)
Where is it? Who's going? Can anyone come?

---

easyGeoff – 12.02 PM on 13.12.04 (90 of 96)
You've got to come TDG!

Psalmanazar – 12.10 PM on 13.12.04 (91 of 96)
It's at the Badger in King's Cross, TDG. Details
upthread.
The guest list is by no means final, but so far it
looks like this:
easyGeoff
RhymeMaiden
agitprop
LadyMintCake
Hellomynameisjanice
ChildeHarold
marco9xe
Grotius
sammysdot, a 'definite maybe'
me . . .
. . . and hopefully you, TDG

ThisDistractedGlobe – 12.24 PM on 13.12.04 (92 of 96)
I'll have to see

---

sammy'sdot – 12.27 PM on 13.12.04 (93 of 96)
Is Salome66 coming? I've always wanted to meet
her.

ThisDistractedGlobe – 12.26 PM on 13.12.04 (94 of 96)
I don't know. She's local, isn't she?

Psalmanazar – 12.31 PM on 13.12.04 (95 of 96)
Haven't heard from her, but you're right – she's integral to the proceedings. Salome66, come out, come out and RSVP!

PavlovsKitty – 12.48 PM on 13.12.04 (96 of 96)
I suppose I could see if there's a later train, maybe swing by on my way . . .

Back / Top / Add a comment

The phone rang.

'OK, you can thank me now.' It was Brian.

'Thank you. For what?'

'Your piece. I got someone to take it.'

'Who?'

'Claire Pleasance, who does the *Sunday Review*. Do you know Claire?'

'No.'

'Don't you? Anyway, I saw her at the weekend and she said she was having a real problem finding stuff to fill the section over Christmas, you know, ahead of time. They always do, apparently.'

'Uh-huh.'

'So I called her just now and convinced her to put your gigantic Barbary War thing on the front for the 26th. How great am I?'

'Boxing Day.'

'The front. I told her it was really good.'

'No one reads the papers on Boxing Day.'

'You really are a model of fucking gratitude.'

'Sorry. Thank you.'

'You get paid. That's the main thing, isn't it?'

'Yes.'

'I told her eight hundred, so don't take less.'

'OK.'

'Now, I need you to do something for me.'

'Uh-oh.'

'You're gonna love this. This is gonna be great.'

'Can I say no now?'

'No. Listen: Giles Wareing is going to infiltrate the BDAC.'

'The what?'

'The British Drivers' Action Council, the extremist motorist organization.'

'Never heard of it.'

'You must have. They're brilliant. Some junior transport minister called them terrorists last month. You've got to check out their website.'

'OK, I will.'

'I think this story requires the Wareing magic.'

'Who said no?'

'No one.'

'Why isn't Phil doing it?'

'He's, he didn't want to. But it's because of his column. He's got too high a profile for undercover.'

'You need a nobody.'

'Not just any nobody. Look at the website.'

'I will.'

'Then you have to call Wayne, who is – get this – a disgruntled former member of the High Wycombe chapter. I'll just warn you now that he's extremely weird, and possibly dangerous. But he says he can get you into the Milton Keynes group. Margot will email you a bunch of stuff in the next hour.'

'OK.'

'It won't go in until after Christmas, but you need to get going on it.'

'I will.'

'Happy motoring, and don't take less than eight hundred from Claire.'

'I won't.'

After I hung up I became aware of Colin scraping at a wall somewhere below, his tuneless whistling at once breezy and menacing. He was doing the stairs, working his way up toward me.

Claire Pleasance offered me five hundred, and I took it.

I walked the dog in the dark. An end to the mystery of Salome66, it seemed, was at hand. I'd been wasting my time sifting the Internet for clues; all I had to do was pitch up at a particular pub on a particular evening and there she would be. Provided, of course, she turned up. But why would I go? What would be the point? What would

I be seeking? Chasing people down on the Internet was one thing. The energy required to do it was almost nil, and the personalities one encountered were mere shades. I wasn't sure I was ready to accept the fact that these people actually existed, that Salome66 could be a human being rather than a personal demon sprung from my own forehead. I couldn't even remember the last time I'd set foot in a pub.

I decided I wouldn't go, and made a promise to myself to obey my own proscription. Normally cowardice would have been more than sufficient to keep me away from the Badger on the night in question, but the Panaglos made my behaviour difficult to predict in advance, just as alcohol made my behaviour difficult to remember in hindsight. I could not, for the moment, be sure what I would do, or even what I had done. I was travelling through life in the frosted, rolling bubble of the present which, for the moment, was how I liked it.

A cyclist shot past in a kaleidoscope of strobing red and reflective yellow, his tyres juddering along the ragged stony edge of the path as he skirted round me. As soon as the darkness up ahead reclaimed him I went down on one knee and waited for the panic to subside. Blood climbed into my head, making it pound. Eventually I felt the dog snuffling through my pockets.

After I put the children to bed I looked at the BDAC website. Only one of its pages was updated regularly, with a weekly message from the founder, Robin Royce, most recently predicting that road-user charging would cause widespread rioting. A separate page for the Milton Keynes chapter contained nothing of interest apart from a months-old local newspaper story about a speed camera that had been set alight. Salome66 had yet to make an appearance on the Christmas Drinks Thread.

21

I was making the children's tea when Caroline came home from the bookshop on Tuesday, dragging shopping bags and cold air into the kitchen. I was concentrating on trying to chop a soft onion with a dull knife.

'I hope our dinner is this elaborate,' she said.

'It depends on what you decide to make.'

Caroline reached into her bag and handed me the magazine from a Sunday paper we didn't normally read, folded open to a picture of a bereft-looking middle-aged woman in a pashmina standing alone in a country lane.

'Did you see this?' she asked. I scanned the enlarged opening paragraph: the woman in the picture had discovered that her husband of ten years, a stockbroker, had been downloading child pornography.

'No, I missed it.' I could tell she wanted me to read further. The police had arrested the stockbroker as part of an international sting operation, tracing him through his credit-card details.

'It's interesting, isn't it?'

'I guess.' The wife stood by him at first, but the irrefutable evidence was there on his hard drive: thousands upon thousands of images. I switched to slicing garlic, lightly pounding the cloves with the flat of the knife, as I had once seen on television, to free them from their skins.

'Around the time of his fortieth birthday,' said Caroline in her archest singsong, 'he became distant and uncommunicative, and began drinking heavily. He stayed up late using the computer, sometimes all night. Phone bills showed that he was on the Internet for hours at a time.'

'I use it for work.'

'That's exactly what he said.'

'We pay a flat monthly rate anyway. And I'm not a paedophile, by the way.'

'I'm not saying you're a paedophile, I'm saying that something is clearly going on that you're not telling me. You're behaving oddly, even for you. You spend hours alone up there, at night. You're distracted, silent and curiously uninterested in sex.'

'Is that a complaint?'

'Not necessarily.'

'Because I dare you to complain about my lack of interest in sex.' In truth the accusation gave me pause: so complete had been the erasure of my libido that I had barely noticed it.

'You say your phone's been stolen, then suddenly you have it again. Something is going on. If you're depressed . . .'

'I'm not depressed. I'm overjoyed.' I did not see how I could not begin to explain things to her – the Giles Wareing haters, the Panaglos, the phantom odours, the enveloping sense of dislocation, the Combined Film And

Poetry London Pre-Christmas Get-together. Suddenly it all seemed too, I don't know, technical. Caroline was wearing a mask of detached, almost professional concern, but I could see I was beginning to scare her. I realized that an immediate, confident denial of some sort was called for. Something eminently deniable.

'I am not having an affair with Darby's mum, if that's what you think.'

Caroline looked taken aback, but not in quite the right way.

'I'm sure you aren't,' she said. 'She's far too busy knocking off Jake and Justin's daddy.' I paused to absorb this information.

'The guy with the pirate beard?'

'No.'

'Who's the guy with the pirate beard?'

'He's the new boyfriend of Melanie's mum.'

'What does Jake and Justin's father look like?'

'What do you care?'

'Does Mr Darby's mum know?'

'I don't know. You're changing the subject.'

'What subject? You accused me of being a paedophile, and I've denied it. What else is there to discuss?' The mis-direction had been transparent, but effective enough. I could tell by her expression – though she was trying to hide it – that she was too weary to pursue it further.

'We need to talk about Christmas,' she said finally.

'What about it?'

'You know that we're going to my sister's.'

'Yes,' I lied.

'Well, the children break up on Friday, and she's happy to have us from Saturday teatime. I don't see any reason to hang around London, do you?'

'I have to work.'

'You can work from there.'

'I have something important on the twenty-first,' I said, staring intently at the chopped garlic. 'It just came up.'

'You really are beginning to test my fucking patience, Giles.'

'The extremist car people. I have a meeting with one of them. It's work.'

I watched Caroline fiddle with her keys. She stopped suddenly and looked up at me, searching my eyes for something I hoped the Panaglos would conceal. I found I could stare back for as long as she could, as if watching her through some remote apparatus, feeling a tug of emotion that would not register on my face. I wanted to say something, if only to acknowledge a bond that was still strong, but she spoke first, three words, three simple syllables, delivered flatly.

'The shed leaks.'

IT'S TIME TO SET A DATE FOR THE CFAPLPG*

Started by Psalmanazar at 10.09 AM on 7.12.04

* that's the Combined Film And Poetry London Pre-Christmas Get-together! Come one come all!

Salome66 – 2.42 PM on 14.12.04 (131 of 143)

my ears are burning

Psalmanazar – 3.01 PM on 14.12.04 (132 of 143)
Sal at last! Say you're coming!

Salome66 – 3.11 PM on 14.12.04 (133 of 143)
Dunno. Things are a bit hectic at work right now,
and the Badger's off my manor.

Grotius – 3.14 PM on 14.12.04 (134 of 143)
That's hardly an excuse. Some of us are travelling in
from the burbs.

---

easyGeoff – 3.50 PM on 14.12.04 (135 of 143)
Go on Salome. You know you want to. Film, poetry
and the bulk of the GW-hater's collective.

---

hellomynameisjanice – 6.03 PM on 14.12.04 (136 of
143)
You know what? I'm really excited about this!

ThisDistractedGlobe – 11.23 PM on 14.12.04 (137 of
143)
I may boycott the event if Salome66 doesn't
promise to turn up.

Psalmanazar – 8.45 AM on 15.12.04 (138 of 143)
Fantastic idea! The F&P get-together is hereby
suspended until we receive Salome's RSVP in the
affirmative.

RhymeMaiden – 9.30 AM on 15.12.04 (139 of 143)

Salome, Salome please say yes!

I've already gone and bought a dress!

---

easyGeoff – 10.10 AM on 15.12.04 (140 of 143)

GW-haters walk out in sympathy!

---

hellomynameisjanice – 10.24 AM on 15.12.04 (141 of 143)

please don't cancel it . . . please . . .

Salome66 – 10.45 AM on 15.12.04 (142 of 143)

Oh go on then

ThisDistractedGlobe – 10.49 AM on 15.12.04 (143 of 143)

Hooray!

Back / Top / Add a comment

In fact Wayne from the British Drivers' Action Council wanted to meet me straight after I rang him, in a supermarket coffee shop off a roundabout just shy of the M25, to which I was obliged to take a very expensive minicab.

'If you're gonna join the BDAC, you're gonna need a car,' were his first words. I found him sitting at a small round table, his shoulder pressed against the large window through which he must have witnessed my arrival. He was imposingly built, wearing a tie and a checked shirt under a plum-coloured fleece and, rather incongruously, glasses with delicate rectangular frames. The shadow of a sharp widow's peak was indelibly etched on his shaven head.

'My wife has it,' I said, hanging my coat on the chair opposite. 'Coffee?'

'Latte.'

When I rejoined him I put my notebook on the table, but there was something about the way he stared at it that made me decide not to write in it.

'So,' I said. 'How did you get involved with the BDAC?'

Wayne swallowed a few times and looked out the window. Mist and rain blurred the view of the supermarket car park. Tiny trees bobbed in the wind, pulling against their wooden stakes. An empty trolley drifted past.

'When my divorce came through I was very depressed,' said Wayne. 'I'd just turned thirty and it seemed like my life was over.'

'Uh-huh.'

'I just felt like I wanted to do something about something, you know?' He had a habit of pursing his lips when he'd finished speaking that made him look almost girlish.

'So you joined a motorists' rights group.'

'I joined lots of things, all sorts – pro-hunt, anti-wind. I fancied all that Fathers of Justice business, dressin' up and makin' a bit of mischief, but I ain't got no kids. Then I met Rob at a rally to stop that asylum detention centre gettin' built, you know, the one up there.' He pointed behind him, at the wall.

'This is Robin Royce, the head of the BDAC?'

'Yeah, but he weren't then. He'd only just started kapok.'

'Kapok?'

'KPOC. Keep PowerPoint Out of Church. He was about to convert to Catholicism over it.' Wayne gave a mirthless chuckle here, and shook his head from side to side slightly. 'So he got me doin' photographs for his website – I had all the gear, it's a hobby of mine – and we became friends from that, I guess.'

Links to and from other websites, according to Wayne, connected them to an expanding network of wide-ranging, essentially male disaffection. Royce sought to capitalize on this tide of unfocused anger.

'We set up about six different websites – it don't cost much – one was an anti-EU thing, one was smoker's rights, fuck the metric system et cetera. But it was the BDAC site that got all the page impressions, hundreds a day sometimes. This was just after them petrol protests. There was fifty-three guys turned up to our first meeting. When we issued a press release last March, four national newspapers reported it.'

'This is claiming responsibility for the five torched speed cameras.'

'Yeah, that's right. To be honest we only done two of 'em. The others was what do you call it, copy cat.'

'Good publicity, though.'

'Yeah, well, if you want people to listen, you got to get their attention first.' Wayne took off his glasses, rubbed one eye furiously, and put them back on.

'So why did you leave?'

'Well, officially I ain't left. But I had a disagreement with Rob, cos I thought we was gettin' too much into the violent side of things. We had lads comin' to meetings lookin' to bust up traffic wardens and that. Just hooligans, you know, blokes who get a kick out of hurtin' people, who bounce from thing to thing, wherever they can find trouble.'

'They don't care about the issues at stake.'

'Exactly. I tried to discourage all that, but Robin, the power went to his head. He likes havin' his own little army of nutters.'

'Sounds dangerous.'

'Well, this is the thing. My girlfriend Karen, she wanted me to quit. We'd moved anyway, so I told Robin it was too difficult, and he went and made me like a liaison, I'd guess you'd call it, to the Milton Keynes chapter, cos I'm in Luton now, not too far.' His rubbed eye, the left, had begun to redden and swell. 'I've been to two – no three – meetings up there, and they're exactly the fuckin' same, if not worse.'

'So you thought it was time to blow the whistle,' I said, my mind beginning to wander slightly.

'Well, this is it, you see. Whup. Hang on.' Wayne produced a mobile phone from somewhere inside his fleece and put it to his ear. 'Yeah,' he said, refusing to meet my gaze throughout the protracted silence which followed. 'So when is this?' he said finally. 'No, it sounds good. What time? Yeah. Cheers, Graham.'

'What was that?' I asked.

'Meeting tomorrow. You should come. Sounds like they're plotting something.'

'Right. OK.' I was about to say I couldn't make it, but the possibility that I might be finished with Wayne and the BDAC by tomorrow night seemed preferable to stringing this piece out over the holidays. 'Where is it?'

'Give me your mobile number and I'll text you the details,' he said. 'And for Christ sake come in a fucking car.'

A Christmas tree had been delivered in my absence, left lying on its side on the gravel near the bins in a girdle of green netting. The children arrived home at four and demanded that it be put up.

'The dog needs to go out,' I said.

'We'll take her,' said Caroline.

'Yeah, Dad,' said Freddy. The older one, locked into the right-to-left-scrolling world of his games console, had to be turned around and led out by the hood of his coat.

In the far corner of the garden a runaway tangle of clematis, honeysuckle and Virginia creeper had for ten years deposited its leaves onto the lower end of the gently sloped shed roof. This became, in turn, a pile of sodden compost which grew heavier every year. The wet finally found its way through the roofing felt, rotting the plywood and the slender struts beneath, creating a structural weakness akin to a mushy spot on an apple. At some point in the autumn after a heavy rain, the mushy spot had given way, and the huge pile of detritus fell through. After fifteen minutes of clawing through the wet mess in the dark, with rain pouring through the hole onto my back, I located the Christmas-tree holder. A dozen dead snails were floating in its brimming base. Underneath the floorboards were the consistency of poached fish, flaking away from the nails at a touch. Once granted a foothold, decay proceeded with unseemly haste. The shed had the sweet smell of a mausoleum, of flesh returned to benign clay. Carrot slithered between my ankles. I shouted, 'Fuck!' and fell backwards into the lawn mower.

22

The extraordinary meeting of the Milton Keynes chapter of the British Drivers' Action Council was held in a dusty function room above a chain pub. There were no more than a dozen people present, including myself and a blonde woman in a tiny white leather jacket who appeared to be someone's date. I found Wayne sitting at the back behind a steam tray, looking sweaty and fretful.

'Robin's here,' he said, indicating with a barely perceptible nod the leftmost of two men who sat at a folding table facing the sparse assembly. The BDAC founder was waxily bald, with a close-cropped white beard and thick hexagonal glasses which accentuated the profound misalignment of his eyeballs. He was wearing what appeared to be a padded fisherman's vest with several pens and pencils stuck into the breast pocket. As he finished reading from a piece of paper in front of him, he hugged himself and looked about the room with his chin stuck out imperiously, as if he could only see through the bottom half of his glasses. I settled my neck into the collar of the ugly dark green fleece I'd donned for the occasion. It bore the logo of an obscure Irish whiskey on its breast.

'Welcome, everybody,' said Robin explosively, as if to

quiet an unruly crowd, though in truth he had only broken an uncomfortable silence. 'I know you usually meet on the first Wednesday of the month here, and I'm sure there were quite a few people who couldn't make it on such short notice.' Without pad or tape recorder, I could only try to memorize a few key phrases. He described the Labour government as the 'enemy of the British motorist', intent on trampling the rights of drivers in a bid to 'secure the blessings of environmentalists, Europe and the PC lobby'. He painted cities in general, and London in particular, as places where honest citizens suffered under 'the tyranny of the pedestrian', spitting out the last word as if it denoted an illegal and disgusting predilection. He talked of green protesters using lottery money to block traffic and turf over high streets. He talked of direct action, of months of planning on the part of the flagship High Wycombe chapter, and finally, of something called Project Roadworks.

'I will now hand the floor over to Graham,' he said, 'who's been coordinating the project from the beginning.' The man next to Royce stood up.

'Basically, and I think everybody here understands this, we want to take our message to London,' said Graham, to a small, lopsided burst of applause, 'to show this government that we will not put up with higher petrol prices, lower speed limits, speed cameras as a form of taxation, or any other attempts to undermine drivers. This protest, however, has a specific message, which is: we need more roads and we need them now.'

This was met with a series of loud claps from two

younger blokes at the front who clearly imagined a protest that would, with any luck, turn nasty.

'We are going,' said Graham, 'to engage in a little road-building ourselves.'

'Where?' asked someone.

'In an as-yet-unnamed London park. And we would like this to be the first joint direct action between the two chapters.'

'Exactly how much road are we talkin' about building?' asked the man with the blonde date.

'We reckon we can get enough tarmac for roughly thirty yards of single-lane roadway, depending on how much time we get on the night.'

'So this is a stealth operation.'

'Very much so. Very much so.'

I knew I would have to ask a question for the sake of the piece and I wanted to get it out of the way. I raised my hand slightly before speaking.

'Hi. I'm just wondering if this sort of gesture might backfire with the public?' All eyes turned toward me. 'Paving over parkland. Will that get Londoners onside?' I glanced over at Wayne, who looked horrified. The two guys in the front exchanged faint smiles.

'You're from London are you, erm?'

'Giles,' I said. 'Yes.' I looked down for a moment. Wayne appeared to be attempting to rub a hole into the back of his hand with his thumb. 'I run a multimedia equipment-hire firm, and these petrol increases are destroying my business.'

'Well, Giles,' said Graham, 'first of all, the support of Londoners is not our primary aim. We're trying to open everyone's eyes to the need for a major road-building scheme in this country.'

'OK.'

'Secondly, we're talking about fairly minor damage here – just a thirty-millimetre wearing course laid right on the ground. We want it to look the part, that's all.'

'I see. When does all this happen?' One of the two guys in the front row whispered something into the ear of the other.

'Soon,' he said, lifting his eyebrows to indicate he was addressing the whole group. 'Anyone who is interested in Project Roadworks can come downstairs for a drink afterwards. We're going to need all the help we can get.'

I stayed for an hour, just long enough to register my interest in the direct action, to hear Robin Royce tell an appalling anti-Semitic joke and to decide that I wanted nothing more to do with the story. No one had even seen the big black SUV I'd hired.

I woke up to find a packed bag next to me on the bed. Caroline was sitting at the kitchen table drinking coffee and flipping through some kind of brochure.

'Tired, are we?'

'I've been on assignment,' I said, the last word scraping a sore patch at the back of my throat.

'How did it go?'

'We're planning a big direct action. The less you know

the better.' Freddy appeared at my elbow, twisting a banana out of the fruit bowl.

'Dad.'

'Yes, Freddy.'

'What is direct action?'

'Should we get a basement, do you think?' asked Caroline.

'It's just something desperate people do when they can't think of any other option,' I said. 'They aren't happy with something in their lives and they don't know what else to do, so they do this drastic thing.'

'I know, but it can increase the value of your property by twenty per cent.'

'I was talking to Freddy.'

'Is it like shooting, though, Dad? Do you shoot people?'

The dog nosed open the door and let out a pleading yawn.

'She needs to go out,' I said.

'Yes. And after that perhaps you could do something with the boys while I do absolutely everything else. You're not going to see them until ... when are you coming, exactly? Any idea?'

'Wednesday.'

'Wednesday.'

The cup holder sprang out for the twelfth time. The tinted passenger window went down, and then up again. The door locked and unlocked in quick machine-gun bursts.

'This is a cool car,' said the older one.

'It's not ours, though,' I said. 'It's just hired.' I looked over the expanse of black bonnet, through the heavily tinted windscreen, down onto the road from what seemed a great height. This was not a car for crying in. It was a tool of aggression, offering the indiscriminate mowing down of pedestrians as an alternative method of working through any issues a man might have with the world.

'I wish I was in the front,' said Freddy.

'On the way back you can be,' I said. The older one turned his attention to the radio.

'Where are we going, Dad?' asked Freddy.

'To get some roofing felt.'

'What is roofing felt?'

'It's . . . I don't know what it is, exactly. It's weird. It feels weird.'

'Is that why it's called roofing felt,' said the older one. 'Because it's for roofs and it sort of, felt, a bit weird when they invented it?'

'Maybe.'

'Yeah, I think that's why,' said Freddy. 'That is definitely why.' The window went up and down again. And again.

I stupidly had not reckoned on the DIY superstore being a popular Christmas destination, forgetting that they sold decorations, lights, fake trees, wrapping paper and a large range of depressing gift items. It was a difficult landscape to negotiate at the best of times, made worse by the drifting, dozy crowds clotting the aisles and the boys' insistence that I invest my pound deposit on a huge flatbed trolley they could both ride on. The Christmas aisle was the widest but also the most clogged. As I made my slow progress toward the back of the store, the boys stood up, grabbed at things and took them on board for examination: an electronic dancing Christmas tree, a musical snow dome, strands of tinsel, a faux Victorian angel, extra-long matches, two boxes of crackers. I asked an elderly male employee, whose ponderous, avuncular temperament was unsuited to the chaos of both the aisle and the season, where the roofing felt was. He stood frozen in thought for some time while a queue of bad-tempered shoppers built up behind him. I couldn't hear his answer.

'Freddy!'

Darby was sailing towards us on a similar flatbed trolley, wearing a dirty cast on her right wrist and a large Santa hat that flopped from side to side by means of a concealed motor. Her mother was almost unrecognizable in a black woollen hat with long ear flaps ending in tassels. With her mane of hair concealed she looked small and ghostly pale.

'Dad, look, it's Darby!'

'Yes, I can . . .'

'Hi-YA!' Having extracted a tube of wrapping paper from a passing display, Freddy struck Darby on the shoulder as she drew up on the port side.

'Hi,' said Darby's mum wanly. 'Just doing a little last-minute . . .'

'DIE!' shrieked Darby, grabbing the tube from Freddy and bringing it over her head dramatically. Freddy snatched two more tubes and held them out in an X, blocking the blow.

'It's a nightmare, isn't it? I hate Christmas,' I said, for something to say. Freddy's next swipe missed Darby, but the follow-through cleared the shelf behind him of its clear plastic reindeer ornaments. Other shoppers made disapproving faces.

'I gather you met Nick the other day,' said Darby's mum, biting her lower lip uncertainly. I noticed for the first time that her teeth were slightly grey. 'At the house.'

'Yes. We didn't really . . .'

'Take THAT!' shouted Freddy, knocking off Darby's Santa hat. Another trolley prodded me in the back of the calves. The aisle had come to a standstill around us. Darby boarded our trolley and pushed Freddy into the shelves, which rocked backwards alarmingly. As they righted themselves several dozen discounted red baubles rained down on Freddy. He began to cry.

'Oh, Darby,' said Darby's mum.

'I think we should probably . . .' I scooped up Freddy in one arm and began to push the trolley forward. As I moved away Darby's mum smiled weakly at me over her shoulder, mouthing the words Happy Christmas.

Only when I cleared the aisle did I realize I'd lost the older one. I resisted the urge to scream out his name above the oppressive yuletide music. 'Where's your brother gone?' I asked Freddy.

'He probably went to the wood,' said Freddy. 'He really loves wood.'

I piloted the trolley to the far corner of the store, where I found him helping himself to bits of scrap timber from a large bin.

'What are you doing?'

'I need these,' he said, holding out a square of MDF and a rectangular slab of pine.

'What for?'

'I'm making a computer.'

I was used to being at home without Caroline or the children, but the absence of the dog made the house seem disturbingly empty, as if it was between owners. The windows dulled as the last of the powdery daylight dissipated outside, casting a smeary gloom over the kitchen. In the oppressive silence I felt dangerously inconsequential, as if the cells in my body might any minute start drifting apart from one another. The mundane rhythms of family life gave my sense of self its contours; in their absence it held no defining shape. Already I regretted staying behind. I looked up at the remains of the kitchen clock, its black and white face smudged with darkness. They'd been gone an hour and a half.

SUPER BEST DRY CLEANERS (or, THE SECRET GW NON-APPRECIATION SAFE HOUSE)
Started by Salome66 at 12.31 PM on 18.11.04
Quick! In here!

Salome66 – 12.02 AM on 19.12.04 (79 of 87)
I don't know. I guess the trick is to confront your own mortality without being, I don't know, consumed by it.

ThisDistractedGlobe – 12.08 AM on 19.12.04 (80 of 87)
I knew there must be a trick to it

Salome66 – 12.14 AM on 19.12.04 (81 of 87)
Well, it will sound stupid but I find that poetry helps.

ThisDistractedGlobe – 12.15AM on 19.12.04 (82 of 87)
It doesn't sound in the least stupid. Any recommendations?

Salome66 – 12.23 AM on 19.12.04 (83 of 87)
I'm not sure what to suggest. Emily Dickinson is good on mortality. Works for me, but I realise it's a personal thing. The wrong poem can sometimes make you feel worse.

ThisDistractedGlobe – 12.26 AM on 19.12.04 (84 of 87)
I doubt there exists a poem capable of making me feel worse, but thanks.

---

easyGeoff – 12.44 AM on 19.12.04 (85 of 87)
Lighten up, you two! It's almost Christmas!

ThisDistractedGlobe – 12.48 AM on 19.12.04 (86 of 87)

Merry Christmas everyone. Fuck Giles Wareing.

Salome66 – 12.53 AM on 19.12.04 (87 of 87)

Amen. And good night.

Back / Top / Add a comment

Going to the park without the dog on a crisp, clear sunny morning seemed an almost perverse luxury. When I looked over from halfway round I saw Maria sitting on her bench. Had she been there all along? I squelched my way across the grass and sat down beside her.

'Where's your doggy?' she asked. The sun was low and warm and in our faces. Small puddles in the dimpled mud at our feet evaporated with an audible crackle.

'She's gone to the country,' I said. 'I don't suppose you've got my . . .'

'Not yet. Fucking Christmas post. Next few days, I expect.' The hooded boy who stole my phone shuffled through the park gate and along the path away from us. Occasionally he dipped his head down and to the right, as if were trying to peer at us from under his arm.

'So what brings you here on a Sunday morning?' I asked Maria.

'Sundays is smackheads, mostly.'

'Ah.'

'Poor fuckers.'

'Yes. Nice day, though, isn't it?'

'Something in the air.' The boy stopped in front of a bench directly across the park. A slight rise in the middle of the muddy expanse between us cut him off at the knees. He appeared to be staring into his upturned palm.

'Well, they keep saying it's going to snow, but it doesn't look like it to me.'

'Somethin' sinister. Trouble brewin'.'

'Yeah. I usually feel that right before Christmas. Like everything is about to go very, very wrong.' My phone gave off a single reverberating chime, heralding the arrival of a text message. I fished it out of my pocket and pressed SHOW. A single word appeared on the screen; the word that Cher Fitzpaine had had to look up on the Internet. I'd tried to look it up myself a few days later, without success. At least I knew how it was spelled now.

On Monday I stayed in bed until it got dark again, dreaming of snow filling up the shed, and consequently Tuesday seemed to arrive ahead of schedule. I sat in my office all morning, trying to will some kind of reprieve. The phone rang. It was Brian.

'How are the moto-terrorists?'

'They've accepted me as one of their own.'

'Well done. Got anything good?'

'Not yet. There's some kind of direct action happening after Christmas, but they're being very need-to-know about it. They want to build a road in some park.'

'Fantastic. We'll need to get some pictures of you.'

'I don't see how that's going to . . . well, maybe I can work out something with Wayne.'

'I'd rather use someone from the picture desk, but I guess we don't want to blow your cover.'

'Too fucking right. These guys exude menace.'

'Good. Keep me posted.'

The light in the house was sepulchral, even at midday. Purplish clouds pressed against the windows. I heated up some soup and read the previous day's paper. All the stories seemed improbable and alien, as if the world had been propelled into the future, or the past. Scientists were searching the Antarctic for antimatter. A Mexican football club had been prevented from signing a woman. The police had plans to moor a prison hulk on the Thames. Sikhs were rioting outside a theatre in Birmingham. My mobile rang. I answered it with extreme hesitation these days.

'Hello?'

'It's chair.'

'Sorry?'

'It's . . .'

'Oh, hi, Cher. What's up?'

'It's tonight.'

'What is?'

'My stag do. You, me, Perry, drink, drugs.' I couldn't think quickly enough.

'I have a thing.'

'What thing?'

'A work thing. A Christmas thing.'

'Miss it.'

'I can't.'

'Of course you can.'

'You haven't given me much notice, have you?'

'Sorry, but you've got to come.'

'I can't.'

'You can't skip some lame Christmas party to come and get wasted with me and Perry? On my stag night?' I hated my new friend Cher Fitzpaine.

'It's . . . it's not a work thing. It's to do with, um, the, with the Internet thing. The talkboard thing.'

'The people who hate you?'

'Yeah, some of them.'

'What is it?'

'I don't know, they're meeting up and I was going along to, sort of, go along. Or. I don't know.'

'Brilliant! Go and tell them what a bunch of fucking cunts they all are.'

'Well, I don't know about that. It's not like they're even all the same . . .'

'What time does it end?'

'I don't know. Closing time, I suppose.'

'No problem. Perry never surfaces till about then anyway. See you at the Tyburn at eleven thirty. I want to hear how it went.'

'I don't know.' He was gone. That's when I first realized I was actually going to the Combined Film And Poetry London Pre-Christmas Get-together.

23

At three thirty it was already dark, and from the outside the brightly lit pub appeared to be extremely quiet. Inside, however, the noise level was reassuringly constant, and though the central bar wasn't busy, several large gatherings were underway at pushed-together tables, most of them clearly work-related. I didn't spot the Combined Film And Poetry London Pre-Christmas Get-together at first, because what seemed the safest vantage point from the bar offered an impeded view of the pub's deepest recesses. I spotted them on my first trip to the loo. Several copies of that day's paper, which people had clearly brought along as identification, were piled haphazardly on the three tables. There was a large, loud woman wearing a bit of tinsel in her burgundy-dyed hair and a large white T-shirt with RHYMEMAIDEN printed across the front. The rest of them – about six in all – were anonymous-looking, spanning an age range from late twenties to early fifties.

I returned to the bar, ordered another half and pretended to be engrossed in a damp tabloid. A man with wild black hair, little round glasses, a four-day growth of beard crawling down into his collar walked in and strode eagerly toward the back, removing his coat as he went. A round of muted cheers greeted his arrival. A middle-aged woman left. Twenty minutes later a slight girl in a neat pink coat came in rolling a small suitcase behind her. I took her to be Hannah Mytton, aka PavlovsKitty, twenty-six, the person who called me 'middle class, arrogant, up himself, full of shite', en route from Edinburgh to Paris. In the pocket of my coat was a list of likely attendees, copy-and-pasted directly from the talkboard. Mentally I crossed her off it.

But who, apart from RhymeMaiden, were the others? Was Salome66 among them? Would she turn up at all? Another trip to the loo barely gave me a chance to take in the scene: they looked ensconced but awkward, a stiff, posed tableau of revelry.

At five o'clock, according to my tally of their comings and goings, they were down to four people, none of whom were likely to be Salome66. At 5.20 PavlovsKitty made her excuses and tottered off with her suitcase. I accidentally caught her eye as she walked past, and my skin began to hum with fear. I was too close to all of this, to all of them. I was risking recognition, confrontation, embarrassment, all for reasons I had barely taken the time to contemplate. What was I doing? My face heated up like a radiator; my bowels suddenly felt dangerously loose. I drained my fourth half-pint. Or fifth; I'd lost count. I had to go. I put my coat on outside and headed off in the direction of least resistance.

My phone rang. It was Caroline.

'We're roasting chestnuts,' she said. 'Where are you?'

'Sitting in a grubby cafe in King's Cross, drinking the worst cup of coffee I've had in a long time,' I said, accidentally locking eyes in the mirrored wall with the man who made it for me.

'Are you with your car terrorists?'

'My who? Oh. No. I'm waiting for them. They're late.'

'Typical. Do you want to talk to your children at all?'

'Yes. Of course.' After what sounded like a scuffle, the older one came on the line.

'Hello,' he said, his small voice bearing a large, dead weight of indifference.

'Hello,' I said, appropriating a bit of his flatness. 'How are you.'

'Fine.'

'Having a nice time.'

'Hmmm.'

'How are the chestnuts?'

'Disgusting.'

'What did you do today? Have you been out to see the . . .'

'Freddy wants to talk to you.'

'Oh. OK, well, be good, and I'll see you tomorrow, probably later on in the . . .'

'Dad.' It was Freddy.

'Hello.'

'Hello, Dad.'

'How are you?'

'Fine.'

'So what's been going on there? Anything I . . .'

'What?' he shouted, but not at me.

'Hello?'

'Dad, Mum says can you bring my do-wave.'

'Your what?'

'My do-wave. From off my bed.'

'Your, sorry? I don't think I know what you . . .'

'What?' he shouted, again not at me. 'Oh yeah. Dad I mean my duvet. Please can you bring it.'

'Yes, I'll bring it. Can you just put Mum back on the . . .'

'Bye.' The line went dead.

When I returned, armed with a cheap paperback from a remaindered bookshop up the road, the pub was heaving, its windows steamed and running with drips. The three tables at the rear were crowded with bottles and pint glasses and torn wrapping paper: some of these people – strangers outside the Internet – had actually brought each other presents. Why would people who hid behind pseudonyms and deliberately smudged their personal histories so readily submit to face-to-face encounters? Why, after taking full advantage of the remove offered by the talkboards, risk intimacy?

I found standing room at the bar from where I could see a slice of the action. They were now at least a dozen strong. RhymeMaiden was still there, as were several young men any one of whom could have been easyGeoff, who would almost certainly recognize me from Chair Fitzpaine's book launch if I got too close. I strained to hear voices I might attribute to Psalmanazar, agitprop, hellomynameisjanice, but the clamour was too general. I pretended to stretch my neck in order to study a disembodied hand or half a face, searching for a clue that might allow me to rule someone out. Across the bar an overweight, older man who was clearly alone was beginning to take an interest in my interest in the crowd at the back. I hid my face behind a pint glass, muttering, 'Get a life,' softly into the beer as I sipped. When I looked again he had returned to the magazine he was reading. I took my turn to stare: he was at least ten years older than me and wearing a dress shirt with a graph-paper pattern which accentuated the swell of his mass. He had cut himself shaving just below his ear. His grey-brown hair was parted in the same manner as mine, revealing a tapering strip of scalp which reached almost to his crown. It was the kind of baldness, incomplete and off-centre, that made you look unwell. Was I as bald as that? I would be, one day, but how soon? I was looking so hard at his head that I didn't notice at first that he was now staring back. I pulled out my paperback, a flimsy edition of *Barchester Towers*, opened it to the middle and read the same two lines over and over:

Mr Quiverful. She wished to see Mrs Proudie. It was indeed quite indispensable that she should see Mrs Proudie. James Fitzplush

It was RhymeMaiden's squeal that alerted me. I looked up and saw her enfolding a woman in her arms, with elaborate and exaggerated affection. I looked away and heard her say something. I heard the group introduce themselves in near-unison. I could almost feel the expansive spread of smiles all round. I began to suspect that Salome66 had arrived. The clock above the bar made it ten past nine.

'Same again?' The barman was pointing a discreet finger at my empty glass. My stomach was taut with liquid.

'Why not?'

From my vantage point the putative Salome66 was now reduced to two black-clad calves ending in a pair of chunky suede boots. The rest of her was hidden behind a pillar. A small table with one stool opened up, and I took it. I could feel the eyes of the fat man at the bar on me as I made the switch. The view of Salome66 was no better, but I could see more of the party: there were three easyGeoff candidates, RhymeMaiden, a likely sammy'sdot, an obvious LadyMintCake, a potential Grotius, and a grey-haired woman in a poncho who could have been anyone. I consulted the list in my pocket. With PavlovsKitty come and gone, the woman with the suede boots was, by elimination if nothing else, almost certainly Salome66. My heart began to thud wildly. I was incredibly close. I took out my book and tried to calm myself down with controlled breathing, repeating the words in my head like a chant:

Mr Quiverful. She wished to see Mrs Proudie. It was indeed quite indispensable that she should see Mrs Proudie. James Fitzplush

At nine thirty one of the possible easyGeoffs left. At quarter to ten I went to the bar for another drink and noticed that the fat man was gone. By the time I'd finished that drink two other easyGeoff candidates were winding stripey scarves around themselves, preparing to leave. This, I realized, was my chance. I grabbed my coat and ducked out the side door. I made a wide, anti-clockwise circuit in the streets behind the pub, trying to get authentically cold. The pavement in front of me kept leaning one way and another, making it difficult to navigate. After ten minutes I re-entered the pub through the main door and, feeling very off-balance, walked directly to the back, toward RhymeMaiden, who was easing herself out of her seat and between two tables, toward the black-clad calves and the suede boots sticking out from behind the pillar, toward a fast approaching point of no return. I suddenly thought: what if they had seen me standing at the bar? Or sitting at the table pretending to read a book? But it was too late. I was upon them.

'I'm so late!' I said, a little too loudly, to no one. 'I got stuck at a work thing. I've basically missed it, haven't I? I can't believe it.' I held my breath. Time seemed to suffer a sudden loss of traction.

RhymeMaiden slowly turned and looked at me, her eyes wide with alarm. The gray-haired woman in the poncho, who was now also wearing a purple woolly hat, drew her bag to her chest defensively. I decided to address RhymeMaiden directly.

'I'm. Sorry, I'm, uh . . . I'm ThisDistractedGlobe. And

I'm late. I'm sorry. Is this not the thing? Am I making a fool of myself?' A look of recognition began to break across her round, friendly face. Then a smile.

'Oh my God!' she said. 'TDG! It's TDG! You made it!' And then she hugged me. I was taken aback, but there was something oddly genuine in this over-the-top greeting. 'It's so great you came. Let me get you a drink.'

'No, I'll get the drinks. Does anybody . . . ?' I looked at the grey-haired woman, who was now pulling on a coat.

'That's Janice,' said RhymeMaiden, 'aka hellomynameisjanice, who is sadly just on her way back to Wimbledon.'

'Goodbye, mynameisjanice,' I said, reaching out to shake her hand. RhymeMaiden laughed. Janice gave me a hollow smile. I looked at the floor and caught a glimpse of one suede boot.

'And I'm RhymeMaiden, as you can tell by the shirt, real name Anne – don't worry, I don't actually speak in verse, not usually anyway – and I don't know if you know . . .' She pointed into the corner at a man I hadn't noticed. It was one of the potential easyGeoffs, young and chiselled and, in this case, sporting modishly long sideboards and a light spray of spots. I must have miscounted them on their way out. Was it him? Did he recognize me? I smiled as he fixed me with a look of pure, clinical hate, a stare so piercing it seemed to create an exit wound at the back of my head. Then his eyes rolled up toward the ceiling and his eyelids dropped like wonky blinds, one slightly further than the other.

'Psal-man-a-zar,' said RhymeMaiden carefully. 'Or just

Tom, if you like. He organized the whole event, as you know, but then he took the festivities at too fast a pace, poor lamb. We were just debating what we should do with him, actually.'

I turned around the other way, back toward the suede boots, and there she was: younger than I'd expected, but then I'd assumed that the 66 referred to the year she was born, which would have made her thirty-eight. Her hair was brown and straight and shoulder length, her skin pale and flawless. Her eyes shone black in the dim light, pupil indistinguishable from retina, with a strange mocking intensity and a slight myopic cast. Was this her?

'So you,' I said, extending my hand toward her, 'must be the one and only Salome66.' She slid her fingers into mine and opened her mouth to speak. I saw that her two front teeth crossed slightly, in a manner which struck me as impossibly elegant, even rather artful. She seemed to be toying with some teasing response.

'That's me,' she said finally, holding her lips slightly apart.

'But I'm guessing your real name isn't Salome.'

'No. It's Kate.'

'Hello, Kate.' It was her. It was her!

'And I'm guessing that your parents didn't christen you ThisDistractedGlobe,' said RhymeMaiden.

'No,' I said, thinking slowly. 'My name is Robert.'

'Pleased to meet you, Robert,' said RhymeMaiden. 'Mine's a V&T, when you're ready.'

*

I ordered a glass of red wine because I couldn't hold any more beer. I could see the two women whispering to one another while I was at the bar. Psalmanazar-Tom had fallen asleep, leaving RhymeMaiden-Anne to take charge, a job she clearly relished. She offered me a seat next to her.

'Grotius, agitprop and easyGeoff were, I guess, the big no-shows,' she said, 'especially considering how they all made a point of saying they'd definitely be here. No other real surprises apart from the discovery that marco9xe is an absolute twat in real life, but I'd had my suspicions about that. Anyway it's been great, really great.'

Every time I looked over at her she was looking at me with that strange, open-mouthed half-smile, her arms folded in front of her grey V-neck jumper. She seemed to be logging my reaction to everything. Perhaps she knew who I was. That makes one of us, I thought.

'What are you reading?' she asked, pointing at my coat pocket with an elbow.

'Oh, it's, uh, Trollope. *Barchester Towers*.' I felt pinned down by the admission: middle class, unadventurous, smug, constantly seeking refuge in the familiar. I couldn't even defend the choice, because I'd never read any Trollope in my life. I tried to wriggle out from under it. 'The character names are really stupid.'

She smiled her half-smile again, and I felt something tidal pulling at my insides.

'Have you come far?' she asked.

I was slow to answer, my stare having become snagged on the slight cast in her eye. I imagined that at work she wore unflattering wire-rimmed glasses, and I was charmed by my own supposition. 'Not too far,' I said. 'From the west. Way out west.'

'Time, please!' said the barman.

'We should really do this again,' said RhymeMaiden, noticeably drunk now. 'A post-Christmas, post-family debrief. But with only the good people from tonight. No Marco, none of those dimwits from earlier. Us four, and maybe a few others. No mentioning it on the boards.' Psalmanazar lifted his head and said something utterly unintelligible.

'When?' asked Salome/Kate.

'Can we squeeze it in before New Year?' asked RhymeMaiden. 'Are we all back for New Year?'

'I'm not sure where I am,' I said, not intending it to seem quite so general a statement. Salome/Kate laughed a light obliging laugh.

'Time, please!' shouted the barman, with some aggression. I noticed how bright the place had become.

I gave them both a concocted email address, but one I was confident I could establish by morning – Robert-tesq1965@bubblenet.co.uk – making myself a year younger while I was at it. Between us RhymeMaiden and I got Psalmanazar/Tom outside. Salome66 – it really was her! – followed us out with her hands in the pockets of her coat, her face an inverted, inward-looking mask of amusement.

'Kate, you'll need to come with me to get Tom home,' said RhymeMaiden. 'Here, hold him up.' She hugged me, suddenly and with some force. What had I done to earn this affection? 'Nice to meet you at last,' she said. 'See you next week, I hope.'

'I'll be there,' I said, not sure if I was lying or not.

I turned to look at her. Standing up she was quite small and rather more buxom than she had initially seemed, and a little unsteady on her feet, but the same, quiet self-possession remained. This was definitely her.

'It was a pleasure to meet the legendary Salome66,' I said, shaking her hand with awkward intensity.

'Call me Kate, please,' she said, tilting her face up toward mine, making her reply seem both a sharp rebuke and an invitation to kiss her. I didn't, though.

I stood on the pavement smiling and blushing with success, my arm tentatively raised to hail a taxi. I had found Salome66. I had met Salome66. I had spoken to Salome66. What's more, she seemed to like me. I felt as if I had slain a ghost. A lone taxi light curved into view and brightened as it approached. I stuck my hand higher. I wanted nothing more than to go home and smile to myself in bed. The taxi pulled up and the window slipped down. Then I remembered I wasn't going home.

'The Tyburn Club, please,' I said, the smile decaying on my lips.

'It's probably very local,' said Perry Freak, lighting a cigar with a cigarette. 'Exclusive to West London, I should think, perhaps even peculiar to a single estate.' He looked down at my phone again. 'But I think it would be safe to say that he's calling you a faggot.'

'Single estate,' I said. 'Like olive oil.'

'Perry considers himself the country's leading authority on street slang,' said Cher Fitzpaine, returning from the bar with three more tequilas. 'When in reality he only knows enough to buy drugs.'

'Fuck off,' said Perry. He blew smoke onto my phone, while fingering its keys. Despite Fitzpaine's assertion that Perry did not venture out before eleven, it was clear that they'd both been at the Tyburn most of the afternoon, drinking and alienating the staff.

'Some words actually derive from the choices made by the phone's predictive text facility. The lazy twats go with whatever option the phone gives them, rather than type out what they mean; book instead of cool, for example. Or aunt instead of cunt.'

'Interesting,' I said, testing my voice. I'd had one tequila and Cher had already passed me his small wrapped-up rectangle of magazine paper. I'd been too paranoid to take any; I'd just gone into the loo and washed my hands elaborately before returning the packet unopened. I felt sloppy, slightly ill, on the verge of tuning out.

'But because none of the little fuckers can read, they mispronounce the new word, and then someone else misspells the mispronunciation, and so on. A dialect of Chinese whispers.'

'You're making it up,' said Fitzpaine.

'I tried to write a predictive poem once, but it was bollocks.'

'I don't want to talk about poetry. I want to hear about Giles's big showdown.'

'It wasn't a showdown,' I said. 'Showdown' felt thick in my mouth, a pre-slurred word.

'Were they there? The Giles Wareing haters?'

'Some of them.'

'So what did they say when you walked in?'

'They didn't know it was me.'

'Incognito. I like it.'

'I never intended to reveal myself. I just wanted to see who they were.'

'And?'

'And I saw.'

'You're being difficult now. Here's your tequila.'

'I couldn't. I can't, really.'

'Yes you can. It's my stag night. So who were they?'

'They were . . . they were people. Ordinary, nice, intelligent people.'

'So where does that leave you?'

'I don't know.' I downed the tequila and, with some effort, held it down.

'It's not important who they are,' said Perry. 'Who are you?'

'Yes,' said Cher. 'Who the fuck is Giles Wareing?'

'What is Giles Wareing,' said Perry. 'What does he stand for?'

'Where does he come from?'

'Where is he coming from?'

'What does he mean?'

'What do you mean, what do I mean?' The room began to undulate unpleasantly.

'What does he do? What does he think?' asked Perry.

'It's no use trying to fuck with my head,' I said. 'I won't remember any of it tomorrow.'

At 10 a.m. the need to pee finally drove me from bed. There was no going back to sleep. My skull felt as if it was tightly packed with coins. My throat had rusted shut. Opening the curtains did little to dispel the grainy penumbra which hung round the bedclothes. Outside the world was drowsing in senescent half-light, like a terminal patient whose day has dwindled to a few hazy hours of painful recollection. The Victorian gas-effect street lamp in front of the house blinked on and off, unsure which direction time would take when it finished standing still. I went up to my office and took a Panaglos. There were four left.

I saw the scribbled email address on the back of my hand: roberttesq1965@bubblenet.co.uk. As I'd presumed I had no trouble registering it, along with the password salome66. I made coffee, got dressed and set off to the park in hopes of obtaining a fresh supply of pills.

Long before I reached the park I could see the police tape threaded through the rusted iron fence, its loose end flapping listlessly from the left gatepost. Beyond the entrance I could see the yellow-and-white forensic tent squatting directly over Maria's bench. A policeman, his high-visibility coat luminous in the matt midwinter gloom, stopped me going any further.

'Sorry, sir. Park's closed.'

'What's happened?'

'Homicide. Last night.'

'Who was it?'

'I'm not able to answer that, sir.'

'Someone local? I live just up there.'

'A woman, sir. Elderly. I can't tell you any more than that.' I watched as a man in white-paper overalls emerged from the tent and bent his head while addressing a colleague. I could see high-visibility coats dotted round the whole park, the acid, depth-defying yellow of policemen, but also of traffic wardens, of cyclists, of street-sweepers, of all who do not wish to be run over. 'I'm afraid I'm going to have to ask you to remove yourself to the opposite side of the street, sir.'

'How was she killed?'

'We're trying to establish that at the moment.'

'Christ. I live just up there.'

'Then perhaps I might suggest that you go back up there.' But I couldn't go home. I had to go Christmas shopping.

24

Caroline's sister's farmhouse rambled erratically along the slope of a hill. I had never quite got its measure, knowing only the route from the kitchen out past the pantry and up the back stair two flights to the attic bedroom where we were always berthed. Her husband did something financial and European, and he spent part of every week, probably most of every week, in Brussels. The whole holiday spun on the axis of his heroic and still uncertain return. He would arrive, with any luck, immaculately dressed and laden with shopping bags, sometime after dark on Christmas Eve. My arrival on the evening of the 22nd barely caused a ripple. Caroline and her sister were more interested in my copy of the evening paper. They pored over it at the kitchen table while I lay on the sofa in the corner watching regional news: portents of drought, teens being hit by trains, a brave dog's birthday party.

'It's unbelievable,' said Caroline. 'In our grungy little park!'

'I never liked that area,' said her sister.

'What was she doing sitting there in the first place, at seven a.m., in the dark?'

'That's just when they found her, though. She might have been there all night.'

'I wonder who she is. Who do you think she is?'

I realized, from a slightly annoyed stress on the 'you', that Caroline was addressing me. 'I don't know,' I said. 'Could be anyone.'

'He's in that park every day with the dog,' said Caroline.

'The cops wouldn't tell me who it was,' I said.

'Well, you're useless at that sort of thing.'

'I have no talent for disrupting murder enquiries in order to obtain gossip.'

'Oh, it's awful. I'm glad we're here.'

'I'm glad you're here,' said Caroline's sister.

I waited until they went back to parsing the picture captions before I helped myself to another whisky. My toe started to ache again.

The older one woke up the next day with a temperature. I volunteered to stay behind with him, to miss the visit to Father Christmas, the trip to the golf range and the tree nursery, the last minute sweep of the nearby retail village. I wrapped him up in a blanket and brought him down to the armchair in the kitchen. I made him hot drinks and cold drinks and toast, searching for plates and cups in the unfamiliar cupboards. I sat with him and watched cartoons and giddy holiday versions of dull daytime programmes. I stared out of the window into the distance where the pale pink sunlight clipped the tops of faraway hills, and thought about the tent squatting over Maria's bench. I had three Panaglos left.

Caroline's mother arrived in the afternoon, trailing scent and glitter, and largely taking over care of the boy. My brother-in-law burst through the door at seven fifteen on Christmas Eve, to be greeted with cheers from his children and mine. I drank a bottle and a half of the fine wine he brought with him while wrapping seventy-five small stocking trinkets in green tissue paper and saying almost nothing. I walked the dog around the edges of his property in the dark, falling over twice. I went to bed early, alone.

On Christmas morning my eyes itched with tiredness. I observed proceedings through the dirty windscreen of my own self-obsession, thinking about Salome66, Maria, my dwindling supply of pills. Caroline loved the scarf I had bought her, which came as a terrible surprise; I'd rushed into a shop I knew she liked and grabbed the first thing I saw. The shop assistant had already wrapped it by the time she told me it cost £450. I bought it anyway, assuming that Caroline would hate it. If I could deliver it safely and keep hold of the receipt, I could return it before the credit-card bill arrived, and disaster would be averted.

'I love it.'

'You do?'

'It's beautiful. What's it made from?'

'I don't know. Something rare. I wouldn't wear it outside.'

'Don't be ridiculous. It's a scarf.' She wrapped it round her neck and smiled to herself.

Caroline and the boys gave me a phone, a fancy one with a built-in camera and a smooth sliding action.

'I bought it after yours got stolen,' she said. 'How was I to know you'd get it back?'

'It's very nice,' I said, although it actually struck me as too nice; extremely desirable, eminently thieveable. 'Thank you.'

'Well, you needed to upgrade anyway. You should see his old phone. Show them your old phone.'

My mother-in-law left before lunch, in order to be at Caroline's half-brother's house for supper. My brother-in-law was gone by the time I got up on Boxing Day morning, off to Japan by way of London and Prague. I took up my station on the sofa by the telly in the kitchen, armed with a Bloody Mary. After breakfast everyone else went off to a freezing little playground, Caroline resplendent in over-sized wellies, stained, borrowed puffa jacket and £450 scarf. When the house had been silent for a few minutes I took my last Panaglos and waited with mounting dread for the next thing to happen.

I awoke to the slamming of the front door. It was pitch black and for a moment I thought I was at home in bed, facing the window which faced the street which led to the park where Maria had been killed as she sat on the second bench along as you head anticlockwise round the crumbling path. There were voices and footsteps heading in my direction, muffled but getting louder and more distinct.

The light snapped on. The room instantly whirled through a hundred and eighty degrees and stretched and became Caroline's sister's kitchen.

'There he is, all alone in the dark,' said Caroline.

'All alone,' said Caroline's sister.

'Dad, why are you in the dark,' said Freddy.

'Here,' said the older one, approaching sullenly and depositing something on my chest. The newspaper.

'This one's not very well again,' said Caroline, ushering him from the room. Freddy turned on the television and sat on my shins. Caroline's sister's kids raced past in a blur, arguing.

'They're always fighting,' said Freddy.

'He hasn't even done the logs,' said Caroline from the other room.

'News, all news, so so boring,' sang Freddy, turning up the volume.

'That's all right,' said Caroline's sister, from somewhere. One of her children was hitting the other one, upstairs. Caroline appeared at the door.

'You haven't even done the logs,' she said.

'I forgot.'

'Cup of tea,' said Caroline's sister, striding back on, stage right.

'Cup of tea,' said Caroline.

'Cup of tea.'

'Cup of tea.'

The newspaper felt flimsy and insubstantial, just two lean sections and a magazine. At the top of the front page, after Your Complete Guide To The Sales and Our Bumper

Boxing Day Quiz and In The Magazine: The Year That Was 2004, were the words Giles Wareing On America's Forgotten Pirate War. I got up and held the Review section under the bright light above the kitchen table. Most of the page was taken up with a reproduction of a painting of the USS *Philadelphia* in flames.

> Just after nightfall on February 16, 1804, the US warship *Intrepid*, commanded by Lieutenant Stephen Decatur, sailed into Tripoli harbour virtually unnoticed; the vessel was in fact a Tripolitan ketch, recently captured, renamed, refitted and, to add to the grand deception, presently sailing under British colours. The few members of the crew who were allowed on deck were disguised as Maltese sailors. Beneath the elaborate ruse Decatur's mission was simple: to enter the harbour, board the captured USS *Philadelphia* and burn it. This daring, if somewhat inglorious, assignment was to be a turning point in America's first war as a nation . . .

It occurred to me that I might have written a new introduction for the Boxing Day paper, perhaps recounting an incident from exactly two hundred years previous, 26 December, 1804, when William Eaton, along with his detachment of US Marines and a hastily raised army of local mercenaries, would have been heading overland with the slightly crazy intention of capturing the Tripolitan city of Derna. This was the expedition supposedly funded by the US Mint's entire output of 1804 silver dollars. But of course there were no 1804 silver dollars minted in 1804. Why not?

Well, it was too late now. My eyes flitted across the words I knew almost by heart, alighting here and there on fragments, on minor changes.

The Mediterranean ran like a fault line between Christendom and Islam, the semi-autonomous city-states of the North African coast serving as the westernmost reaches of Ottoman influence. A tangle of treaties between the European powers and the various regents, pashas, deys and beys who ruled Morocco, Tunis, Algiers and Tripoli had more or less enshrined piracy as a tool of Barbary diplomacy; Britain regularly stumped up handsome tributes to secure the safe passage of its merchant ships. Part of the price America paid for its independence was the loss of that protection . . .

There was a sentence missing in there somewhere, although I couldn't remember what it was, so I could hardly claim the paragraph was poorer for its absence.

. . . Adams and Jefferson, who would become the second and third Presidents of the United States respectively, continued to disagree over the most expedient (and least expensive) solution to the ongoing Barbary problem – an imitation of European pragmatism or a demonstration of force? In those early days, however, the debate was largely moot: the fledgling American government was unable to authorise funds to satisfy the Barbary states' lavish demands for tribute, much less to raise a navy capable of taking them on . . .

I missed my original mention of the Articles of Confederation, the pre-constitutional document which gave the government its minimal authority, but I supposed brevity and narrative continuity were the main priorities. This was a Boxing Day slice of history, not an exam paper. I skipped to the last paragraph:

> . . . Jefferson's preference for an honourable outcome, even at considerable cost – perfectly captured in his phrase 'Millions for defence, not one cent for tribute' – coupled with his insistence on regarding the wider world through the prism of American idealism, would be the starting point for every subsequent foreign conflict. The Barbary conflict, for better or worse, defined the American nation's reasons for going to war, reasons which have today proved just as contentious, and just as blinkered, as they were two hundred years ago.

I'd added the 'and just as blinkered' at the last minute, fearing that the piece had a slight pro-American bias. But in the cosy pages of the Review section – on a cold and politically neutral winter's eve – the conclusion seemed a model of balance and authorial detachment, sufficiently weighty without being too pretentious, almost as if it had been written by someone else. I couldn't ask for more than that.

I wondered what Salome66 would make of it, wherever she was. I wondered how it would be received generally. I allowed myself to believe that in the sleepy, newsless week between Christmas and New Year, the article would get rather more attention that one might normally expect. I imagined being invited on the radio to set America's current foreign policy in the context of its historical adventures. I would have to do it over the phone; I was with my family in the country. A television news programme, perhaps reeling from a last-minute cancellation by a minor government minister who'd decided to extend his skiing holiday, might even ring to see if I was available to give them five minutes on US relations with Tripoli then and now. I would have to check the trains. I thought about what I would say. '*Of course one must be careful in comparing Qadafi with the likes of the Tripolitan Pasha Yusuf Qaramanli, but I suppose both rulers did manage to cling on, even to maintain diplomatic ties with America, despite direct military efforts to remove them from power* . . .' I thought about what I would wear. I imagined subsequent overtures from a publisher who would probably be surprised to find I was not at work on a book already. A television series on the subject might follow. I imagined the Giles Wareing Haters' Club seeing it and simply melting away, collectively dumbstruck, individually embarrassed to have got me so incredibly wrong. Freddy tapped me on the neck and said something about a giant salami on the television.

'A giant salami,' I said. 'How funny. Does it have a face?'

'Not a salami, Dad. A tsunami.'

The death toll rose with every news update. In contrast the first shaky images, recorded on tourist video cameras and uplinked around the world, were strangely benign: disarranged beach furniture; water-logged streets; a wave breaking on a terrace filmed from the safety of a balcony.

I stared at the screen and tried to stop myself wondering how many people in Britain had for some reason yet to hear of this terrible tragedy, and what percentage of those people might be discussing something interesting one of them had just read about the Barbary War, and what proportion of that percentage might be in some way connected to the publishing industry. I pinched my leg to make myself stop. I wondered again why there were no 1804 silver dollars coined in 1804. I thought about Maria sitting dead on her bench under a yellow and white tent. I felt a shudder of horror and wondered if the Panaglos had already begun to leave my system. I found myself searching for something appropriate to say, but common sense prevailed, and I kept silent. I had no gift for the appropriate. I found myself wondering what Salome66 was thinking at this precise moment. I found myself saying, 'I have to go back to London tomorrow.' Caroline looked up at me with a kind of blank contempt.

25

From: anne.jarett@gyre&gimble.com
Date: 27 December 2004 15.38
To: roberttesq1965@bubblenet.co.uk
Subject: <no subject>

Hi. It's me Anne (aka RhymeMaiden) from the other night. Kate and I are trying to drum up support for another pub meet. Can you do 29th or 30th? Same place, 8 oclock. No pressure. Hope your Christmas went well. xAnne

29.12.04

Evidently he picked a bad time in his treatment to come off Panaglos; he had hoped that having reached the other side of the myriad and widely publicised withdrawal symptoms, he might be able to reclaim first person status. But three days in he has experienced no dizziness, no headaches, no suicidal ideation, no auditory hallucinations telling him to harm himself or others, while the bifurcation of Giles Wareing has become, if anything, more pronounced. Simply to continue to be Giles Wareing requires an increasingly indulgent suspension of disbelief.

And there is the night fear, a dramatic version of the foreboding he has experienced all his life. His head plays host to terrible scenarios, almost abstract constructs of fear: a stranger's baby leaning dangerously off an imaginary bridge; a sudden realisation that he has inadvertently committed a jail-worthy offence; a visit from the police of a foreign nation where torture is routine; fire consuming a family through his negligence – anything to engender terror, to send the heart racing, to drench the twisted bed sheets in sweat. These are not dreams. They come, unbidden, while he lies awake in the dark, alone, as if they were meant for someone else.

Then he sits in the bath all morning, until the water goes cold, while the cat paws at the drips from the tap. In their brief time alone together he and the cat have reached an uneasy détente, like the one between the British navy and the Barbary potentates, a pragmatic truce based on mutual mistrust. It is the day of the second pub meet, and he must find some way of using up the daylight which still stretches before him. He cannot contemplate visiting the park without the dog – he has only got close enough to see that the tent is gone – so he must find a chore to drive time forward, to get to the next thing.

The contents of the shed were spread all over the back garden's muddy strip of grass: the two watering cans, the lawnmower, the broken hedge trimmer, the wet sack of compost, a deck chair with a rotted seat, the half-handled rake, a box of tiles, the folding wallpaper table that I put my foot through three summers ago, the old kettle, a wicker basket containing seven different brands of slug poison. I stood on the ladder, which stood on the hard standing beneath the hole in the shed floor, my head poking out through the hole in the roof.

The two cheesy joists came away at a pull. Two new ones, sawn off a length of treated pine, slotted neatly into the empty metal brackets at the top of either wall. I also fixed some shorter lengths along the top of the walls between the brackets and wedged three little cross beams between the new joists at intervals, to give me something to nail into.

The section of thin plywood was imperfectly measured and did not quite fit into the trapezoidal slot where I had cut back the damaged roof: two long shards of wood jigsawed out of the top of the wallpaper table were needed to fill in the gaps. From underneath there was something strangely satisfying about the resulting messy patchwork, stone-washed daylight leaking through the cracks. It was only meant to be a temporary stay against decay, because a shed is not forever. A middle-aged man may plausibly hope to outlive his shed.

Everything I knew about the correct application of roofing felt came from the label on the roll which was sitting in the kitchen because I had read that roofing felt became difficult to manipulate in cold conditions. I dragged it outside, cut off a generous length and laid it the long way across the lower half of the gently pitched roof, allowing it to drape luxuriously down either side. The recommended glue was black and thick and all but impossible to apply with the plastic mini-trowel provided, but the short, big-headed galvanized roofing nails were a pleasure to drive. A second section, overlapping the first by six inches as per the diagram on the label, was sufficient to cover the roof. After that it was a matter of slicing off the excess, nailing round the edges on all four sides and tacking the flimsy pine flashing back in place. A light rain began to fall as I worked, gathering into drops which rolled off the felt obligingly.

Colin was standing in the open garden doorway when I turned around, holding one of his three phones. Colin had a system with his phones: one in either breast pocket, a third on his belt at his hip, which was his business phone, his decorator's phone. I didn't know what his other phones were for, but one had a furtive ring, a suppressed chortle which hinted at an array of non-legitimate interests. The other made no noise at all. It just skittered about on the kitchen table when he left it there in the mornings, dancing perilously toward the edge.

'Colin.'

'All right, Guy?'

I had tried to disguise the start he gave me as a sudden realization that I had forgotten something, after which I turned back toward the shed, leaned in and retrieved the hammer. This now struck me as a mistake. Had I unconsciously selected a weapon? Would he consider it provocation? I held the tool as unaggressively as possible, with the claw hooked over two fingers.

'Fine, yeah, fine. Good Christmas?'

'Yes, thanks, mate. Handsome. Didn't expect to find anyone here, over the holidays.' He brandished his phone, the large one, encased in a vinyl pouch dotted with undercoat.

'No. I had to come back. For work. What can I do for you?'

'I thought I might borrow your steps, the small ones, if you don't mind, mate.'

'It's, yeah, of course. They're just there by the shed. I was fixing the roof.'

Colin strolled over and appraised the roof on tiptoe. 'Nice job you done there,' he said. 'Handsome.'

'Thanks.'

'You've heard about all that business in the park, have you?'

'Yeah, I did hear, yeah.'

'Fucking horrible,' he said, folding the aluminium ladder with a snap. 'That's brilliant, cheers.'

'It was Maria, wasn't it?'

'Yeah, that's right. Bad business all round.'

'She had enemies, I suppose.'

'Well, we all do, Guy. We all do.'

'Is there a funeral or something? Because I would like to, um, pay my respects.'

'Don't go nowhere near that, mate,' said Colin, fixing me for perhaps the first time in our acquaintance with a long, level gaze, his eyes still blue reservoirs of untapped malice. 'The cops'll be all over it.'

*

There was a picture of Maria on the front of the local weekly paper, under the headline 'HORROR OF MURDER IN THE PARK'. It was a blurry, over-enlarged snap of a slightly younger, smiling Maria, cropped tightly in an attempt to disguise its festive origins, although the lower edge of a paper hat and a slice of tinsel-draped pub-bar background were still discernible.

> Residents in the Roundworm and St Jerome wards suffered an apprehensive Christmas weekend after a local woman, Maria Gagliardi, was found murdered in Roundworm Park early on the morning of the 22nd. Police are appealing for witnesses in the incident, which follows a recent sharp rise in violent crime in the borough. A police spokesman said people should take sensible precautions when using the park after dark.
>
> Mrs Gagliardi, 52, was originally from Glasgow and had been a longtime resident of Melplash House on the nearby Hardy Estate. She is survived by her daughter Irene.
>
> If you have any information about this or any other incident please contact Trainee Det Con Tamatra Price on 020 8674 8998.

Someone was reading the story over my shoulder, which I found unnerving enough to leave the Tube a stop early and walk, past the British Library and into the unfamiliar tangle of streets south of Euston Road, a page torn from my mental map of London. In this way I happened across the pub by accident, rather earlier than

I had expected, the momentum of the surprise carrying me through the doors before I had given myself a chance to reconsider. I had seen Salome66. I had spoken with her. I had touched her hand. What else was I intending to do? What was the point? But it was too late now. I was already inside and she had spotted me.

For a moment I saw her, at the back of the room, as she was, unadorned by the mystique I had built around her: small and mousy, almost plain, encased in a shapeless, high-necked jumper of indeterminate brown, her static-charged hair riding up on itself at the back. But then she stood up as I approached and she smiled her half-smile and I saw her crossed front teeth and I felt my insides slip again. I noticed that her black eyes were not black at all but a deep, glossy grey shot through with dark green, like some rare, gaudy marble, or moss on wet slate. We stood facing each other, too close for people who shake hands when they meet, and just too far apart for people who kiss, doing neither.

'You're here,' she said. 'We didn't know if you got the email.'

'Just got back from . . . Christmas. A couple of hours ago.' I felt a sudden shiver of embarrassment at our being strangers, at our acquaintance not having automatically deepened since our last meeting. This chore lay ahead.

'Robert!' shouted RhymeMaiden. 'You made it! Come here and give me a kiss at once.' I obliged and then turned to the young man next to her, who was not, I realized, the drunken Psalmanazar of the previous meeting. He was blond and balding, his spots concentrated along the jawline. 'This is Andrew. Andrew of the North. Known online as moretoastplease. He's come all the way from Manchester!'

'Hello,' said Andrew. His accent had a built-in sneer.

'Hi.'

'Robert is TDG, you know,' said RhymeMaiden.

'Oh. Hello.'

'Hi.'

So we sat down, four members in good standing of the Giles Wareing Haters' Club, and we discussed the tsunami, the still mounting death toll, whole islands that had been submerged, the friends of relatives and relatives of friends who had been on holiday in Thailand and Malaysia, how they had all escaped narrowly, been somewhere inland when it hit, how extraordinary it was that so many people went all that way just for Christmas, what kind of impact this huge increase in long-distance air travel has on the environment, and how it was all part of the same thing, the planet heating up, but actually probably not, because earthquakes don't have anything to do with global warming, do they? No, this was different. An act of God. No place to lay blame. A brief, sober silence. Another round of drinks.

We went on to talk of other things, of Christmas sales, the horror of being back at work, this thing about naked people we were all missing on television. We talked about everything and anything, except the obvious single thing we all had in common: our deep, abiding hatred of Giles Wareing. I tried to think of a way to raise the subject of him.

'Where's the loo?' asked Andrew.

'It's just round there. Turn right by the guy who's sitting next to the menu. The one who looks like some sort of Barbary pirate.'

'Thanks.'

As the evening wore on it became clear that Rhyme-Maiden and Andrew had had a previous encounter at a get-together in the spring, and that she had more or less summoned him to London for this one, and that while he was officially staying with a friend from university, RhymeMaiden intended to see to it that he didn't make it back tonight. By the third round she was devoting herself full time to the task of chipping away at the remains of his reluctance, though the beer was doing most of the work. Salome66 and I were left to make conspiratorial eyebrows at each other.

'So,' I said. 'What's the 66?'

'What?'

'Why the 66 in Salome66? You're clearly too young to have been born in 66.'

'I was born in 1972. If you're trying to flatter me, you're fucking up.'

'So then what is the 66 for?' She gave me a withering look.

'It doesn't mean anything,' she said. 'I actually wanted three sixes, but I hit the wrong key.'

'Oh, right.' I thought about changing the subject to poetry. Then I remembered I didn't know anything about poetry.

Instead I persisted with more general questions, and slowly the life of Salome66, or rather Kate Horan from

Midhurst in West Sussex, began to spool out of her. She had a brother named Adam. She was half Jewish and half Scottish, she said, making the two sound mutually exclusive. But really she was just English, she said. There was no use denying it. She worked for the Charity Commission. The pay was terrible. She wanted to quit and travel. She spoke Spanish, not very well. I couldn't extract what I wanted from this information. I couldn't find a reason to discount her estimation of Giles Wareing as equal to shit. Or a reason to respect it. I thought about unmasking myself right then, just to see what would happen.

'Another round?' asked RhymeMaiden rhetorically. 'I'll get them.'

'I'll give you a hand,' said Andrew.

'What about you? Where are you from?' asked Salome66. It was time to tell the story of Robert. It seemed advisable to get it out in one go.

'Well,' I began. 'I was born in East Sussex, as it happens. But we left when I was five months old. I was mostly raised in the States. My dad's American.'

'You don't sound American.'

'No, I know, but I used to. My parents got divorced when I was twelve, and I ended up coming back here with my mother. Then she got remarried and I went back to New Jersey for a year, but then I came back here to go to University. Cheaper. My mum had married this other American guy, and so she eventually ended up back in the States with him. But I stayed here.'

'You sound totally English to me.'

'I know. I'm sort of ashamed of it, to be honest.' There

was something strange in her eyes, a mixture of disbelief and admiration, as if being from New Jersey were an exotic and desirable condition, too wonderful to be true. The story of Robert was having an unintentional effect.

'So do you visit your parents a lot?' She was smiling her half smile, teeth crossed.

'My mother's dead,' I said, 'but my dad is . . . my dad's still in New Jersey. Still in the same house. I haven't been over there to see him in a while.' Here I left a dramatic but ultimately inconclusive pause. 'We don't really, I don't know. It's weird.'

I told her I worked in advertising, but that I was writing a novel, or trying to write one. As she began to talk animatedly about an ex-boyfriend who had been a some-time actor, some-time writer and, she hinted, a full-time bastard, and who now made furniture and had his own shop in Exmouth Market, I began to feel my presence in the room diminishing, absence stealing over me in the old familiar way. I started to think about the callousness of my deception, and my lack of an exit strategy. I thought that, on balance, I could probably forgive Salome66 her hatred of the journalist Giles Wareing, given that I agreed with much of her criticism and that I had successfully tricked her into liking the real Giles Wareing, at least in the guise of Robert of East Sussex and New Jersey. I could now go for the Reveal, as they called it on TV makeover pro-grammes, or I could disappear. Or I could let myself be drawn in deeper, though from my point of view this presented only danger. Her eyes had reverted to their former blackness, shining as if freshly polished.

'Were you Stella?' asked RhymeMaiden, setting a full pint in front of me.

When the lights came up there was talk of going on somewhere, but I claimed an early breakfast meeting, a type of appointment I had only read about. RhymeMaiden and moretoastplease seemed impatient to tend to their own rendezvous. I stood up and Salome66 stood up, and because I have no gift for the appropriate, I said, 'You really are short,' and she said, 'Shut up,' and elbowed me playfully. Then I saw that a strand of her hair was stuck to her face near her chin. I really wasn't thinking clearly when I reached out and moved it out of the way.

26

The alchemic conversion of all emotions into pure, distilled anger. This is the first major side effect of withdrawal. Fear turns to anger. Guilt is anger. All is anger. Anger pounds at his temples as he stalks around the park. Injustice, frustration, sleeplessness, impotence, boredom and the current international situation are all met with anger. Even hunger induces anger. In his anger this process seems to him a step in the right direction, although it also makes him even more angry.

The Chord of the Day is Fmaj7.

Not only was the tent gone, but also the bench, bolts sheared off flush with the base of the concrete slab on which it once rested. A yellow MURDER placard stood nearby, chained to one of the iron stanchions of the dog-run fence. The park was blanketed in a still, cold mist, the dog invisible just ahead of me. Two women who had been jogging but were now walking approached from the opposite direction, one of them talking ceaselessly: 'You know, as long as you lay it all out for her, she has what I call good organizational skills. Put her in a different situation and she's fucked. And that is exactly what I . . .' The fog swallowed up the words.

I had been for the previous two days the subject of many telephone calls between friends, chiefly because I'd called Nick Skelding a fat cunt at Patrick Gallet's New Year's Eve party. I didn't really feel a part of the drama because I didn't remember much of it, only the anger welling up as he spewed forth one of his received opinions on something. Apparently I'd taken issue with it, and in turn he'd called me a Zionist, which proves just how little he understood my position, in that I regarded the whole of the Middle East and its long history of troubles with a cold and unyielding indifference. But I didn't say that, apparently. Apparently I'd said, 'I'd rather be a Zionist than a fat cunt.'

The notion that there was something deeply wrong with me was, I understood, gaining wider currency, but I didn't care and I was enjoying not caring, although it also made me angry. Of course there was something wrong with me. I needed some Panaglos and I didn't know how to get any.

On my second circuit of the park I was telling myself that it was OK that I had said it because Nick Skelding was, and always had been, a fat cunt. I became so distracted that I began an almost unprecedented third circuit of the park, whereupon I again came across the spot where the bench had been removed, the crime scene, to find the tall boy with the hood crouching down in the protective fog and spray-painting his tag onto the bare concrete slab: TNT, with the N leaning over like a lightning bolt. Was it tribute or desecration? I didn't care. Anger, never far away, welled up again.

'TNT?' I asked. He stood up.

'What the fuck.'

'Does it refer to the explosive?'

'What the fuck you on about?'

'Trinitrotoluene, I think it stands for. Or maybe it's just your initials.'

'Fuck off.' Fear rose in me and became anger, which made me even more afraid. What was I doing?

'Right. Oh, hey. I got a new phone. Check it out.' I took it out of my coat pocket and demonstrated the sliding action. A sequence of rich polyphonic tones brought tidings of operational status. 'Nice, huh?'

'You think I won't take it off you?'

'It was incredibly expensive, I think.' I held the phone up between us, as if to appraise it. My heart was flying along now, and I was getting a little dizzy. I started to hear chanting in my head: *in the middle, in the middle, in the middle* – in a distant voice I didn't recognize, and the voice started to rise and fall in pitch; it was singing, *in the middle in the middle in the middle*, some odd, looping, half-familiar tune. Was this a fresh withdrawal symptom? Had I read about auditory hallucinations?

'Man what the fuck is wrong with you?'

'I have to go, actually.'

'Gimme the phone.'

It was getting louder: *In the middle in the middle in the middle . . .*

'I got a knife.' Then and there came my first brush with suicidal ideation.

'I don't believe you. Show me.' Actually I don't think I did say it, but I think that I was about to say it. Or did I say it?

In the middle in the middle in the middle of . . . Of what?

A foot slapped into a nearby puddle and Colin's lime-green windcheater emerged from the fog, heading in the direction of the gate. His head appeared a moment later.

'Hey, all right, Guy?' he said cheerily as he passed. 'Keepin' outta trouble?' The boy's face turned suddenly wary, and I accidentally took his picture.

THE EVER-TERRIBLE MR GILES WAREING . . .
Started by easyGeoff at 10.56 AM on 04.01.05
. . . has made his bid for immortality with a lengthy piece for the Sunday paper over Christmas. Is this as bad as it gets, or can he write worse than this? http://doturl.com/a4jts

---

recidivist – 11.28 AM on 04.01.05 (1 of 12)
Oh he can write much worse than that. Not sure anyone else could, though.

PavlovsKitty – 12.02 PM on 04.01.05 (2 of 12)
Happy New Year, all. Been looking for you all morning. Our old clubhouse has been pulled down!

FritsZernike – 12.10 PM on 04.01.05 (3 of 12)
Yes, there's been a massive thread cull over the holidays. Must be trying to clear space on the server.

PavlovsKitty – 12.13 PM on 04.01.05 (4 of 12)
It's like a chat desert on here

Grotius – 12.24 PM on 04.01.05 (5 of 12)
I read that piece of shit on Boxing Day. A complex period in history reduced to a tired 'West v Islam' struggle in an attempt to cobble toget5ther some lame (and biased) analogy about the present situation in Iraq.

FritsZernike – 12.30 PM on 04.01.05 (6 of 12)
I clicked on the link but I didn't get very far. Life is too short to waste it wading through prose like that.

---

easyGeoff – 12.41 PM on 04.01.05 (7 of 12)
It's essentially a long-winded recounting of the Barbary Wars (US v various N African potentates) twisted into an absurd defence of current US foreign policy.

Salome66 – 1.04 PM on 04.01.05 (8 of 12)
I stopped reading the Sunday papers about a year ago, and if that link is anything to go by I made the

right decision. Giles Wareing has, as we predicted, tried to raise his game and in the process has made an utter fool of himself. I can't tell whether the pro-US bias is blatant propaganda or the accidental result of GW's sheer inability to make himself understood, but it's dreadful either way.

Grotius – 1.55 PM on 04.01.05 (9 of 12)
My greatest fear is that, far from recognising GW's awfulness, the editors have decided to turn him into some kind of serious commentator in 2005.

Salome66 – 2.23 PM on 04.01.05 (10 of 12)
Or perhaps the Barbary article was the last straw, and they finally intend to get rid of him. To my knowledge his byline hasn't appeared yet this year. Early days, I know, but we can hope.

Grotius – 2.39 PM on 04.01.05 (11 of 12)
Right. WareingWatch is on. First to spot a GW piece wins.

---

easyGeoff – 2.58 PM on 04.01.05 (12 of 12)
where's TDG today? You'd expect him to have something to say about this.

Back / Top / Add a comment

11.01.05

---

*The nature of the withdrawal is to freeze time at a point of
maximum hopelessness. He wakes up and every day is
Wednesday. The sun does not bleach the gap in the curtains
a little earlier each day. The house is quiet and empty for
infinite periods. The darkness which finally descends belongs
to the day before, it is recognisable as yesterday's evening. The
same programmes appear on television each night. A woman
who dresses badly is taught to dress well. A crazed toddler is
brought to heel by a stern nanny, her good work all but
undone by backsliding parents just after the second break.
The wine erases the rest. When he wakes up he is in bed and
it is Wednesday again.*

The phone rang. It was Brian.

'Happy New Year. How's the car thing going?'

'Fine. Nothing much happening.'

'Now listen. You know we're doing this big arts thing.'

'No.'

'Well, we just heard about this sculpture in Switzerland.
A giant toilet. Thirty feet high. '

'Wow.'

'And the idea is that it's moving to a park in Glasgow
this summer. Or Edinburgh. I can't remember.'

'So you want me to write an amusing essay about the
state of modern public art.'

'No. We want you to go to Switzerland to sit on the
giant toilet.'

'It doesn't sound . . . it doesn't.'

'It'll be a great picture.'

'I'm a forty-year-old man.'

'I know. It's inherently comic.'

'No.'

'Don't say no. You'll only need to do five hundred words. Less.'

'No.'

'We'll pay you a lot.'

'No.'

'Come on. It'll be fantastic.'

'Absolutely no way.'

'Please say yes.'

'No.'

'Do you want to think about it?'

'No.'

'I'll call you back in half an hour.'

The line went dead. I sat with the dial tone humming in my ear. *In the middle in the middle in the middle in the middle in the middle . . .*

I was sitting in the kitchen staring at my hands when the front door opened. Caroline's keys landed on the hall table with a metallic splash.

'To what do we owe this depressing little scene?' asked Caroline. The older one scuttled under her arm and disappeared behind a cupboard door. Freddy leaned his face into my shoulder.

'I have to go to Switzerland to sit on a giant toilet.'

'When?'

'Wednesday. Tomorrow. Back Thursday.'

'That's funny, Dad,' said Freddy. 'A giant toilet!'

'Don't say toilet,' said Caroline. 'What about picking up? I'm at the bookshop tomorrow.'

'I don't know, I'll . . .' I trailed off. Caroline wore her special tolerant expression, a practised look of exasperation held in abeyance.

'I hate these biscuits,' said the older one from somewhere inside the cupboard.

'Just one,' said Caroline, putting on her thinking frown. 'It's fine. I'll sort something out with Marcy. It's fine. A little notice would have been nice. Has this dog been out?'

In the park the TNTs had begun to proliferate. One now obliterated the yellow police sign. TNT was scrawled along the backs of benches in black marker, and sprayed at intervals along the pavement in bruisy automotive primer.

At the far end of the park, behind a rise where spindly birches emerge from a tangle of brambles, there was something else new: a small Christmas tree, no more than two feet high, freshly transplanted into the cold mud beside the path. It was listing slightly, with a few strands of tinsel still hanging from its branches. It looked unbelievably forlorn in the premature, gathering twilight. I stared at it for a bit, wondering if it would survive the winter, while the dog faced east and opened her nostrils to the oncoming breeze.

A laminated sign at the gate announced a meeting of

the Friends of Roundworm Park, to discuss 'proposed improvements, security issues, and vandalism'. It flapped about on its string like a bird trying to escape from a snare. I saw a hooded figure approaching from the direction of the shops. I turned and sprinted for home.

27

Basel airport was a model of clinical efficiency, a glittering agglomeration of clean surfaces. It seemed an ideal habitat for people temporarily shorn of identity, a place where I thought I might live quite happily, drinking coffee and chatting to strangers whose grasp of English was purely functional. Cold steel sunlight streamed horizontally through the windows as I sat hunched over my laptop, trimming the toilet piece to its barest essence. I left myself no room to describe the background of the young German artist, Karl Knabe, our dawn meeting in the square, the fruitless search for a longer ladder, the protracted argument with the security guard, or the intense flirtation conducted between Karl and Sophia the raven-haired Italian photographer while I sat perched above them on the rim of the outsize bowl. As I excised each line the whole humiliating episode seemed to withdraw into unreality. All that remained were the exact dimensions of the giant convenience, some idle speculation as to its larger meaning and a couple of mentions of how cold it was. I emailed it across at a lean four hundred and fifty words.

*

My return flight was delayed, delayed again and then finally cancelled. I called Caroline.

'The plane is stuck at Heathrow, apparently. Mechanical issues.'

'Christ,' she said. 'So what are you going to do?'

'They've already put me on the first flight tomorrow. Back to the hotel, I guess.'

'Oh well. I suppose we'll just have to struggle along without you somehow.'

I went to the airport bar, bought a beer and sat down to check the talkboards. There were two new posts in the latest Giles Wareing thread:

THE EVER-TERRIBLE MR GILES WAREING . . .
Started by easyGeoff at 10.56 AM on 04.01.05
. . . has made his bid for immortality with a lengthy
piece for the Sunday paper over the holidays. Is this
as bad as it gets, or can he write worse than this?
http://doturl.com/a4jts

PavlovsKitty – 8.22 PM on 12.01.05 (16 of 17)
Still nothing from GW. Maybe he's in rehab with his
friend Chair Fitzpaine

Salome66 – 10.05 AM on 13.01.05 (17 of 17)
If it keeps the talentless twat out of the papers, I'm
glad he's seeking help.

Back / Top / Add a comment

A new email pinged into my inbox:

From: kate.horan@charitycommission.gov.uk
Date: 13 January 2005 10.09
To: roberttesq1965@bubblenet.co.uk
Subject: pub again

Hi. I know it's ridiculously short notice but if you're not
doing anything tonight I thought you might want to meet us
at the Badger. Say 8? xKate

I compared the times of the last post and the email.
Salome66 had in the space of a few hours called me a twat
and then invited me to the pub. I wrote a post of my own
and pressed the Refresh button repeatedly until I saw it
appear:

ThisDistractedGlobe – 10.44 AM on 13.01.05 (18 of
18)
Talentless twats like GW don't seek help; they just
self-medicate themselves against the realisation of
their own mediocrity so they can continue to turn
out drivel at the prevailing word rate in order to
fund their pointless existences. Mark my words –
he'll be back, and soon.

Back / Top / Add a comment

And then I wrote an email:

From: roberttesq1965@bubblenet.co.uk
To: kate.horan@charitycommission.gov.uk
Subject: Re: pub again

I'll be there. Robert

And then I went and paid over the odds for a flight on another airline scheduled to land at London City airport at 19.05 GMT.

I was at the bar when she walked in, alone.

'Hi.'

'Hi.' Our eyes met briefly before we both looked away; an embarrassed acknowledgement that in the time between our last meeting we had become strangers again.

'Anne got stuck at work. She decided to go straight home.'

'That's too bad.'

'Do you want a drink?'

'God yes. A pint of whatever. Are you going some-where?' She was looking at my suitcase. I had intended to stow it at King's Cross left luggage, a plan which I only then realized I'd completely forgotten about.

'Uh, no. Just been somewhere. New York, for an ad

shoot.' I had said I was in advertising, hadn't I? How specific had I been about my job description?

'You came here from the airport?'

'Yes. No, actually. I got back yesterday, and went straight in to work, but then I forgot to take my case home.'

'Ah. So did you see your dad while you were there?'

'Not this time. Things were just too hectic. Maybe next time.'

We sat down at the table right at the back, the same table, even though the pub was virtually empty. She drank quickly, talking about a problem she was having at work. I nodded until she fell silent.

'You don't talk about yourself much,' she said. 'Not like most men.'

'I haven't got much to say for myself, I suppose. You're nowhere near as opinionated as you are online.'

'No one is, are they?'

'I don't know.' She leaned close to me.

'Let's forget about our online selves,' she said. 'We don't really need them now, do we?'

'No. But we did have this whole other, this other avenue before we . . .'

'I'm beginning to think it's a complete waste of time anyway.'

'Well, I'm inclined to agree. I've always thought people online, they have this tendency to say they hate things, they hate certain specific . . . when really they don't even care, they just want to join in. You know what I mean?'

'I may even give up.'

'Me too.'

'Good. Now tell me about growing up in America.'

And so I told her. I told her of the ping and pock of tennis balls through the open window and the great piles of leaves burning on flat square lawns and of snow which lasted for weeks and the smell of fish which always clung to the docks and the smell of skunk which sometimes drifted through the woods. And I kept going until a soft grey mist descended reliably over my brain.

28

I woke up in a white bed which took up most of a white room, in my pants. The walls were bare. A naked bulb hung from the ceiling. The sky behind the net-curtained window was the colour of wet plaster. A door at the foot of the bed was slightly ajar. Where was I? Was I in hospital?

Another door somewhere opened and closed. There was the sound of keys jangling, followed by footsteps and a soft knock at the door opposite.

'Hello?'

'Hello?' It was Salome66, carrying two tall cardboard cups, a blue plastic bag hanging from one wrist. 'I thought you might want coffee.'

'Oh. Thank you.'

'Or rather I thought you might need coffee.'

'Yes.' Only then did I realize how much my head hurt. 'Hmmm.'

'Quite a night.'

'Yes it, yes. Quite a night.'

'Do you cry like that a lot? After you . . . ?'

Two questions presented themselves, though I suspected I should not ask either: Cry like what? After I what?

'No, I . . . I don't know what was going on.'

'I get sick sometimes, but I usually pass out long before that.'

'I don't know where it came from.'

'You know, I think it might have been to do with your dad. Because you were talking about your dad a lot right before that, and all your regrets and stuff, but you seemed fine, just a bit drunk, and then when I came back from the loo, you were just, I don't know, weeping.'

'Sorry.'

'It's OK.'

'Where am I, by the way?'

'Darkest North London. Stokest Newington.'

'Really? I thought you lived south of the river.'

Her features set in a manner designed to cloak irritation. I supposed that repeating information gleaned from a public Internet forum, no matter how innocuous or freely offered, somehow demeaned her idea of our friendship. Or whatever it was we had now.

'I used to,' she said. 'I moved last year.' She tipped a newspaper out of the plastic bag and gazed at the front page. 'This is a much nicer flat.' I noticed she was still wearing her pyjamas under her coat.

'Yeah, I love what you've done in here.' She smiled without looking up.

'I haven't really had time to decorate.'

'It's fine. I thought I was on a locked ward.'

She laughed and slipped the front section of the newspaper free from the others, then lay across the bed, propped on one elbow to read it, flipping the pages slowly.

Her pyjama top rode up, revealing an inch of belly. My libido chose this moment to return, after an absence of over two months.

'Cher Fitzpaine in rehab again,' she said. 'Why is that news? Who cares about that fucking waste of space?' I smiled broadly. I was lying in bed with Salome66 while she called Cher Fitzpaine a waste of space. I felt like I was in love.

'Not your favourite author, then?' I said, with a knowing drawl that I hoped might encourage her to take off her coat.

'Of course not. Does anyone like him?' She casually flipped over another page and took a sip from her coffee.

'No, I don't think anyone does. I was just remembering that thing you said on the talkboard about him and his equally talentless friend.'

'I thought we'd given up the talkboards.'

'It was just a funny thing about him and . . .'

'Look. I'll make you a deal. You quit posting for, I don't know, Lent. And I will too.'

'I guess.'

'Promise?'

'Why not? I can quit any time I want.'

I grabbed the second section and pretended to read the computer ad on the back while stealing glances at her, at the inch of exposed skin, imagining the moment a minute or two hence when she would finally take off her coat. I flipped the section over. Its front page bore a large photograph of a middle-aged man sitting on a giant toilet holding a flapping copy of Wednesday's *Basler Zeitung* and staring directly into the lens while wearing an expression of pained resignation. The words '2005: The Year In Art' were picked out in yellow against the azure sky. Below, in slightly smaller letters, it said, 'Giles Wareing Contemplates die Supertoilette.'

I turned the paper back over and perused the computer advert intently for some minutes, blood coursing audibly past my ears.

'Sorry, what time is it?' I said finally. 'I've really got to get to work.'

No one was home but the dog. I felt as if I hadn't slept in a week, but I parked my suitcase in the hall, turned around and went straight back out to the park, treading the morning post into the mat. The air was bitterly cold and intermittently held tiny snowflakes which darted about like insects. The number of TNTs on the pavement had nearly doubled since I'd last been round. The anger rose up in me again; anger like envy, anger like shame. As I reached the back bend I saw that a broad puddle of water had gathered at the base of the little Christmas tree, which was leaning badly, tinsel shivering in the wind.

Caroline was sitting at the kitchen table when I got back, looking at the front of the second section of the newspaper.

'It's absolutely freezing out there,' I said. 'I think it was warmer in Switzerland.'

'Well, I hope you're pleased with yourself.' She began to open the post.

'I don't know how I feel. It was so humiliating it was almost liberating.'

'I think it proves you deserve a pay rise.'

'I think it proves I'll do almost anything for the money they pay me now.'

'Speaking of money,' said Caroline, slitting open another envelope. 'I can only guess what we owe . . .' She stopped and stared at the piece of paper in front of her. 'Oh my God.'

'What is it?' But I could see what it was well enough from where I was standing. It was a credit-card statement. My credit-card statement.

'Oh no,' she said, her voice cracking a little. 'What have you done?' What damning evidence did she hold in her hands? The flight into London City? That was only yesterday! How could it appear on the statement so quickly? Was it something older? Had I used the card for something illicit before? I knew I should say something.

'What is it?'

Caroline continued to stare at the statement, as if checking the figures, but I could see tears gathering in her eyes. Eventually one of them fell onto the paper. She hardly ever cried. Perhaps once a year, always because of me.

'Giles, what were you fucking thinking?' she screamed. 'That I wouldn't see this?' I was still in my coat and my bag was packed and standing in the hall. The moment was all set up for my ejection from the house. I opened my mouth, but that was all.

'Are you deliberately trying to destroy us?' She was beside herself now, crying and sniffing and trying to catch her breath. 'How could you do it!' she shrieked. I rubbed my face and prepared to confess all: Salome66, the lies, the meetings, the unmissed flight, the blanked-out night in another woman's bed, everything, starting, if necessary, with the pain in the toe.

She was angry now, fuming. She stood up, crumpled up the statement and threw it at me.

'How could you pay £450 for a fucking scarf!'

THE EVER-TERRIBLE MR GILES WAREING . . .
Started by easyGeoff at 10.56 AM on 04.01.05
. . . has made his bid for immortality with a lengthy piece for the Sunday paper over Christmas. Is this as bad as it gets, or can he write worse than this? http://doturl.com/a4jts

---

Salome66 – 3.22 PM on 13.01.05 (19 of 35)
Talentless twats like GW don't seek help; they just self-medicate themselves against the realisation of their own mediocrity so they can continue to turn out drivel at the prevailing word rate in order to fund their pointless existences.

A fairly harsh assessment, TDG. Not saying I disagree with a word of it, just that you seem even more bilious than usual. Feeling OK today?

Grotius – 3.41 PM on 13.01.05 (20 of 35)
I think he's hit the nail on the head, myself

Lordhawhaw – 3.46 PM on 13.01.05 (21 of 35)
Seconded.

FritsZernike – 5.10 PM 13.01.05 (22 of 35)
Hear hear

Salome66 – 1.07 AM on 14.01.05 (23 of 35)
GW strikes me as a tragic figure in many ways. I can
just imagine him crying himself to sleep every night,
railing against the cosmic injustice that rendered
him so unable to string a few sentences together,
and the cruel twist of fate that resulted in his being
employed at the very thing he is worst at.

Lordhawhaw – 9.13 AM on 14.01.05 (24 of 35)
And yet it's we who suffer most.

RhymeMaiden – 10.02 AM on 14.01.05 (25 of 35)
Hi TDG! Sorry I couldn't make it last night! Hope all
went well (nudge nudge)

---

recidivist – 10.24 AM on 14.01.05 (26 of 35)
that doesn't rhyme

PavlovsKitty – 10.32 AM on 14.01.05 (27 of 35)
Oh my sweet companion in Christ!!!!!!! Whos seen
this mornings paper!!!!

Lordhawhaw – 11.10 AM on 14.01.05 (28 of 35)
Haven't opened it yet. Why?

RhymeMaiden – 11.26 AM on 14.01.05 (29 of 35)
Not I, not I, I'm sad to say
I didn't pick one up today
(the newsstand had none left to proffer
Thanks to special CD offer).

---

recidivist – 11.27 AM on 14.01.05 (30 of 35)
thats better

PavlovsKitty – 11.36 AM on 14.01.05 (31 of 35)
Second section, front page: GW sitting on a giant
loo!

FritsZernike – 12.21 AM on 14.01.05 (32 of 35)
Oh my God! It's true! And not looking too good on
it, I might add.

Grotius – 12.54 AM on 14.01.05 (33 of 35)
What's this?

FritsZernike – 1.20 PM on 14.01.05 (34 of 35)
A typically worthless GW effort about some
sculpture in Switzerland. Facetious, simplistic and
sneering. I've always liked Knabe's work myself.

RhymeMaiden – 3.14 PM on 14.01.05 (35 of 35)
Arse. The article's online but not the pic.

Back / Top / Add a comment

I went to the extraordinary meeting of the Friends of Roundworm Park because Caroline thought one of us should, meaning me, and I was in no position to argue. Due to recent events it was very well attended. A community liaison officer was there to answer questions about the murder.

'We haven't made any arrests as of this point in time,' he said. 'Our investigation is continuing, but I'm afraid I can't comment on that any further. At the same time I would urge anyone who thinks they have any information about the incident to come forward.'

'Are we going to get any kind of protection for the park?' asked someone. Others made guttural noises of assent.

'While we urge people to exercise extra care and attention when using the park, especially after daylight hours, we have no reason to suspect that ordinary park users are in danger.'

'How can you say that?' shouted a woman. 'Someone was murdered! A woman, sitting on a bench!'

'At present we believe the incident was the culmination of a long-running dispute, rather than a random attack.'

'What the hell does that mean?'

'I can't say any more about it, I'm afraid.'

'We've got all sorts in that park out there,' said the man with diagonally parked teeth. 'Vandals, muggers, drug addicts, villains. We got gang graffiti going up now, and you know as well as I do what that means. They're claiming this park as their territory.'

'It used to be safe to walk round here.'

'We're very aware of the ongoing vandalism issues with respect to the park, and we are working with the local community to find ways of addressing it.'

'Once a day the police drive round, if that. I ain't never seen any of 'em so much as get out the car.'

'We're reviewing our patrol policy at the moment, in light of community concerns about low-level antisocial behaviour in the area of the park, especially just after school hours. In addition to that we've . . .'

'Is that what you call it now, someone being murdered? Low-level antisocial behaviour?' There were embittered, triumphant guffaws.

'Something needs to be done!'

'As I said previously . . .' He pressed on, letting the waves of anger break over him until the crowd exhausted themselves, in line with his job description. I sat at the back and absorbed their useless anger, silently soaking it up and making it mine.

THE EVER-TERRIBLE MR GILES WAREING . . .
Started by easyGeoff at 10.56 AM on 04.01.05
. . . has made his bid for immortality with a lengthy
piece for the Sunday paper over the holidays. Is
this as bad as it gets, or can he write worse than
this?
http://doturl.com/a4jts

ThisDistractedGlobe – 11.49 PM on 15.01.05 (36 of 38)
You can see it, my friends, in the sallow skin, the
thinning hair: this is a man in an advanced state of

decay. And in the eyes, behind those dull, puffy eyes, is the fear of Death. Giles Wareing, this ageing mediocrity, simply isn't up to the task of confronting his own pointlessness. But even he must know that his life means nothing, and that he will die a coward.

---

recidivist – 12.02 AM on 16.01.05 (37 of 38)
and he can't write

ThisDistractedGlobe – 12.22 AM on 16.01.05 (38 of 38)
and he can't write

Back / Top / Add a comment

The phone rang. It was Ken from the paper.

'Hi, Ken.'

'Great pic last week. Way to cling to your dignity.'

'Thanks.'

'Listen, I'm just ringing round to keep people abreast of what's going on since Brian's departure.'

'Brian's what?'

'You must have heard.'

'Brian left?'

'Last Friday. Where have you been?'

'I don't know.'

'Well, anyway. He was eased out last Friday.'

'Eased out.'

'By a security guard. A mere formality these days.'

'Right.'

'Don't worry, though. For the moment Margot is acting features editor and everything is running smoothly, more or less. We're not sure who will come in to replace Brian, but all freelance contracts will be honoured. When does yours run out, by the way?'

'The end of February.'

'Oh. Well anyway, I am as of today officially acting deputy features editor, in which capacity I am calling to ask about your auto-terrorists piece.'

'Brian said I didn't have to do it,' I lied.

'Brian isn't here anymore.'

'He said if I did the toilet thing he'd let me off it.'

'The thing is we're extremely short of copy at the moment.'

'In any case I was waiting for their next direct action. Haven't heard anything for about a fortnight.'

'Can you push them along a bit?'

'That would be unethical, wouldn't it?'

'End of February, did you say?'

I took the dog to the park. The day was clear and windy. Freshly replaced green council bin liners inflated and stood like bell jars above the rims of the barrel-slatted bins. A piece of junk mail flitted past like a crippled butterfly. The dog whirled in and out of the tall grass in search of quarry. The change was immediately noticeable: along the pavement every example of TNT had been altered to read

TWAT, crudely but legibly, using a near-matching shade of automotive primer. Not only did this counter each discreet act of vandalism with a direct insult, it created a reasonable expectation that any new tags would be similarly adjusted. I'd missed a few, however. I would need more paint. Overnight the puddle around the Christmas tree had frozen solid. Its surface was dusted with little brown needles.

29

Over the next fortnight I slipped into what could be called Withdrawal Proper; the sense of dislocation I had been experiencing proved to be a mere preamble to an all-consuming despair punctuated by profound memory gaps. The snatch of song running through my head – *in the middle in the middle in the middle ...* – became more persistent; occasionally it seemed to emanate from else-where, from other rooms, from passing cars, from inside cupboards. It kept me awake at night as I tried to remember, or imagine, what came next.

It was not an entirely unproductive period, however. I walked the dog as normal. I wrote a six-hundred-word piece about the decline of the moustache. At some point I made a start on the shed floor, although I abandoned the project as soon as I calculated the amount of work involved. As ThisDistractedGlobe I posted such vitriol about Giles Wareing's moustache piece that I received a formal email warning from the talkboard moderator.

During this period I also convinced myself that only the consummation of my relationship with Salome66 could heal my riven self. At night my libido raged as it had not done for months, making intemperate demands. I often dreamt of this consummation and several times I woke up believing the dream was real, and that I was cured. I also realized, even in my dislocated state, what a mad idea it was. Her subsequent postings seemed to indicate that she either hadn't seen the toilet picture or hadn't recognized me in it, but there was no way to be certain. I sent her an email apologizing for my weeping and my abrupt departure, included my mobile number and spent an hour debating whether or not to press Send.

Then the phone rang.

'Hello, is that Giles Wareing?' At that point it sounded like a trick question. 'Hello?'

'Yes. It is.'

'Giles. This is Victoria Monahan, from Collop & Sprague.' Publishers.

'Oh. Hello.' Cher Fitzpaine's publishers.

'Giles. I've been meaning to ring you for some time, having long been a big fan of your work. In fact I meant to ring you several weeks ago, but we've just moved offices and things are rather hectic.'

'Oh, right.'

'Giles. Let me tell you what I'm proposing, and then you can tell me what you think. I had an idea for a book that we'd really like you to do, based on that brilliant piece you wrote last month.'

'Really.' I couldn't believe it. This was the phone call I'd dared to imagine that Boxing Day. This was even how I'd imagined it, more or less. The broad blanket of despair began to lift at the corners, letting in light and air.

'I just enjoyed it so much, and on the day I was ringing

up everyone I knew and telling them to read it. I just thought it was, you know, really so in tune with the times.'

I wondered what the Giles Wareing haters would make of my six-figure book deal.

'Well, that was the point I guess. Not just to entertain, but to make it relevant to the current situation.'

'Which is why we thought it would make a great book.'

'It's funny, actually I had the same thought at the time.'

'Well, there we are. Great minds think alike. You know, I should have rung you straight away, but it's all so crazy round the holidays.'

'That's OK.'

'The only problem, Giles, is that I fear we could have used the extra time. I mean, if we're going to get the book out for next Christmas.'

'Next Christmas? How long a book are you thinking of?'

'Well, that depends on you, really. As long as it's done by the end of March.'

'The end of this March?'

'I mean the basic structure is there. You've got all the Greek men there, Alpha to Omega. Except, what is it? Except Psi, someone pointed out.' There was a long pause during which I re-examined the conversation in full.

'Yes,' I said finally. 'A subbing error.'

'Well, now you can remedy it. Just needs fleshing out a bit, really.'

'Yes.'

When I hung up I realized I'd pushed Send by accident. Salome66 had my number.

A Sunday morning at the end of January: a sudden coming-to, head throbbing. The kitchen table was covered in a drift of breakfast cereal. In the sitting room the television was blaring. I was holding a newspaper. Two more speed cameras had been torched, one on the A303 in Wiltshire and one near Maidstone. The head of the British Drivers' Action Council, Robin Royce, denied any responsibility for the damage, but claimed such actions were an example of 'the chickens coming home to roost'. He said the A303 camera had long been a target of motorist anger because of its placement at a point where the dual carriageway ended, the site of a proposed road-expansion scheme which had been abandoned by the government. The Maidstone camera, he said, had been deliberately hidden behind a stand of trees. I wondered why Salome66 had not called or returned my email. Perhaps it was for the best.

Caroline appeared in the doorway in her pyjamas, scratching her ribs in a strangely alluring manner. She read for a moment over my shoulder.

'Stupid old cunt,' she said. I presumed, for the moment, that she was referring to Robin Royce. She walked over and peered into the coffeepot. 'Did you enjoy the party last night?' I had no memory of any party.

'I suppose.'

'The food was good, wasn't it?' I had the feeling she was trying to trip me up.

'Hmmmm.'

'I don't remember coming home. Do you?'

'No.'

'The babysitter must think we're a terrible pair of old alcoholics.'

'Well, she would have a point.'

'And then you, you took the dog out, didn't you? At what time was it? I don't even like going into that park in the day after what happened. You were there for, it seemed like hours, and I couldn't sleep.'

'I have the dog with me. It's fine.'

'That dog, are you mad? That dog would happily go home with your murderer.'

'Well, the murderers don't know that.' Caroline poured herself a cup of cold coffee and stuck the mug in the microwave. While she waited she stared out of the window at the frosty back garden.

'And where the fuck is Colin?' she said finally. 'He hasn't been around for weeks.'

The older one walked in carrying the two bits of wood he'd bought from the DIY store before Christmas. On one he had carefully drawn a computer keyboard in pencil.

'Dad, will you help me?' he said.

'Erm.'

'Go on,' whispered Caroline as she passed by with her coffee. 'Help him make his computer.'

'All right,' I said. 'Let's have a look.'

I retrieved a few scraps of wood left over from the

shed-floor project, which I screwed to the back of his wooden monitor so it would stand up by itself. I found an old phone and cut off the curly wire, using it to connect his keyboard to his monitor by means of two roofing nails. I produced a broken mouse from an ancient computer and drilled a hole into the back of his monitor where he could plug it in.

'Looks good,' I said. He nodded. 'What else?'

'Screen.'

'What should be on it? What do you want to do with your computer? Play games?'

'I want to write articles on it.'

I went upstairs and printed out the moustache piece, cut out a section from the middle of the page and glued it onto his monitor. I peeled a sticker off my computer which advertised the brand of microchip within and stuck it on his.

'There. What do you think?'

'Good.' He stared at his screen, suppressed a funny little smile, and clicked the mouse.

The park was full of posters. They were stuck to trees, poles, gates and bins. They blew about on the grass and flapped in the mud. They were pasted at intervals along the wall that ran up the boundary of the adjoining estate. This was not unusual. Homemade posters featuring a missing cat or dog with glowing eyes often sprang up overnight, bleaching out or blowing away over the weeks as hope died. These posters featured a person. I crouched down to look at one which had stuck to the wet pavement. It was a photograph of the boy in the hood, staring straight ahead, looking bemused. All the posters were the same, the same photo and the same writing, which said 'Have you seen this TWAT?' in a plain bold font. I didn't remember putting them up. I barely remembered making them. The wind blew an ominous chord through the chain-link fence.

My phone rang in my pocket. It was Wayne from the BDAC.

'Hi, Wayne.'

'Did you see the thing in the paper this morning?'

'I did. Nice work.'

'Nothing to do with me, but in any case, Robin's decided to strike while the iron is hot.'

'To capitalize on the publicity.'

'Exactly. And also a truckload of tarmac has become available.'

'When?'

'Tonight.'

'That's not much notice, Wayne.'

'Yeah, my fault there. I was ringing your old number all last week. Forgot you had a new phone.'

Then I realized: I had given Salome66 my old number.

The rest of the day was one of frenzied preparation: looking for dark clothes, gloves, a blank pad, my tape recorder and most importantly, my old phone. Caroline looked on disapprovingly as I ran up and down the stairs.

'It's Sunday. You should be spending time with your children.'

'I'm always here.'

'You're never *here*, Giles. You're never anywhere.'

'This is the last thing. Tonight is the last thing. Then it's done. Have we got anything like a balaclava?'

I finally found my old phone under Freddy's bed, the battery dead. I plugged it in up in my office and waited a minute before turning it on. There were six new messages.

The first was from Brian, inviting me to his leaving party on Saturday, which was evidently where I'd been the night before.

The second was from Wayne, asking me to call him.

The third was from the boy in the hood, calling me that word again.

The fourth was from Cher Fitzpaine, announcing that he was allowed visitors from the first of February and asking me to come.

The fifth was from Salome66: 'Hi, Robert, this is Kate, sorry I didn't call before, I was away for the weekend, call me on this number when you get a chance, bye.'

The sixth was from Wayne again, asking me where the fuck I was.

I met Wayne in a hotel bar just off the North Circular. He was visibly nervous, and drinking a large whisky.

'Everyone's meetin' in an hour in the parking lot,' he said. 'I got you here a bit early cos I wanted to tell you something.'

'What?'

'I ain't comin' tonight. You're on your own.'

'What do you mean?'

'I told you I was gettin' out. I'm going to Cornwall with my girlfriend for three weeks, and then I ain't tellin' you where I'm going after that.'

'I said I'd keep your name out of it.'

'They'll soon realize it was me that helped you. I don't care if they do, cos I'm gone.'

'What about pictures? You were going to take pictures.'

'I'll give you my camera. It's pretty straightforward to operate. Anyway, it's officially BDAC property.' He laughed, drained his whisky, ordered another. I told the barman to make it two.

'Kate, this is Robert. I'm so sorry I never rang you back. I didn't get your message until today, my fault, but anyway, sorry again. It's Sunday, call me on this number when you get a chance, bye.'

I stood out in the nearly empty lot alone, back to the cold wind, watching the traffic crawl over a roundabout, the mournful blare of bus horns ringing against the grimy underside of the A406 overpass, and wondering who would choose to stay in a hotel sited here. Perhaps it was full of people who had travelled this far and simply given up. People who had run out of will. Or petrol.

A huge red SUV pulled up and the window came down, revealing Graham's head. Up close his skin was rough and pockmarked, hair and face all one colour, as if he were sculpted from sand.

'Where's Wayne?'

'He's not coming,' I said, 'he's done his back or something.'

'He fucking never,' said Graham. 'I had a feeling he'd bottle. Get in.'

I could see Robin Royce in the passenger seat, his preposterous pipe stuck into his white beard, glasses glinting in the dark. I got in behind Graham and found myself sitting next to one of the big lads from the Milton Keynes meeting.

'I've got the camera anyway,' I said. 'For the website.'

'Right,' said Graham. 'But you don't take any pictures of me, or of Robin. This is not an official BDAC action. Got it?'

'Yup. No problem.' Someone tapped me on the shoulder. I turned around and saw the other big lad from the meeting. A bolt of paranoia shot through me. Could they know I was a traitor? What if they were taking me somewhere to take care of me?

'You got a vest?' he asked.

'No.'

'Here you go, then,' he said, reaching into a box and pulling out a reflective yellow vest and handing it to me. 'Large. They're all fucking large, innit.'

'Job lot,' said the big lad next to me, grinning.

'But won't we be a bit, um, conspicuous?'

'That's the idea,' said Graham. 'You walk into a park wearing all black, some member of the public reports you for a pervert. With the vest on you're so obvious that you must have a good reason to be there. You look like a cop, or a security guard, or a maintenance guy. Or even a bin man. It gives you a purpose, so people ignore you. They think someone who's up to something, he'd never wear high-visibility clothing like that.'

'Reverse psychology, innit,' said the big lad in the back.

'The Israelites of Hampstead won't know what hit them,' said Robin. I saw Graham wince as he looked right before entering the roundabout.

'So the park is Hampstead Heath?'

'An out-of-the-way corner of it,' said Graham.

'I hope it's not one of those gay-sex spots,' said Robin.

'I don't think it is, no,' said Graham, wincing again reflexively.

'We wouldn't want to be paving over any queers,' said the big lad next to me.

'No,' I said. 'That would send the wrong message.'

We came off the North Circular just after the M1. My phone rang as we were going through Golders Green.

'Hello?'

'Robert?'

'Who?'

'Robert? It's Kate.'

'Sorry, couldn't hear very well. Hi.'

'You have a new phone number.'

'Yeah.'

'How are you?'

'Fine. You?'

'Fine. I was hoping I might get to see you.'

'Oh, OK, yeah, absolutely. When?'

'Well. What are you doing tonight?'

'I'm a, I'm just on my way to a thing. In Hampstead somewhere.'

'What time does it finish?'

'I don't know, to be honest.' Graham looked at me out of the corner of his eye.

'Why don't you come here after?'

'It might be quite late.'

'It doesn't matter. Just come when you're done. Do you need the address?'

'Yes.'

Perhaps I'd been right about tonight, I thought. Tonight would be the last thing. The last thing and then it's done. All the last things.

I didn't really know where we were: parked along an anonymous brick wall, with the expanse of the heath looming invisibly behind it. Graham had got out of the car to confer with someone in an idling lorry.

'And now we've reached the point where we're all meant to believe that every other person is homosexual,' said Robin, 'when in fact the opposite is true.'

'What do you mean,' I asked, 'by the opposite?'

'Exactly what I said.'

'That every *other* person is a homosexual?'

'What?'

'Surely the opposite of every other person is every *other* person.'

'I mean that every other person isn't gay.'

'That's saying the same thing, isn't it?'

'Of course it isn't.' Graham knocked on my window and motioned that we should all get out.

There were nine of us in all grouped at the back of the lorry, staring at a large black mass covered by a tarpaulin. The air smelt strongly of oil and smoke and coal fires, overpowering but somehow strangely tempting. After a moment it struck me: this was the phantom smell come to life, no longer evasive and disturbing, more like a bracing whiff of hellfire.

'What we have here,' said Graham, in a pleasant professorial voice, 'is five and a half tonnes of bituminous macadam, or bitmac for short, liberated yesterday from a council works depot by Raymond, thank you, Raymond.' Raymond, who stood holding a rake, beamed and dipped his head. 'Normally, as you know, roads are machine-laid hot, but this was an unsuitable method for our particular requirements. So what we've got tonight is a workable, wearing course type of aggregate which can be laid by hand using shovels. Any questions so far?'

'Why hasn't it gone hard?' I couldn't help myself. I was curious.

'Good question. This is what we call slow-cure, or deferred-set bitmac. It's what councils use to patch up potholes and footpaths and the like. Which is good for us, cos we're laying this right on the grass, gypsy-fashion. Lucky it's been quite dry of late, is all I can say.' He paused to light a cigarette. Two beeps emanated from his vest pocket.

'So Team B,' he continued, 'if all's gone according to plan, is in the park now laying out some kerbing. When they text me they're done, and I think that was probably them just now, we will go in just up here, drive slowly up to the site, position the wagon between the two kerbs and slowly dump the bitmac as we roll along. Then the rest of you will distribute it about evenly with shovels. Raymond and I will come in behind with the rakes, and when we're satisfied it's all proper, we'll call in the roller. Everybody mind yourselves in the dark down there. We don't want any accidents.'

Team B had earlier cut the padlock off the barrier and replaced it with one of their own. Graham opened it with a key and the lorry moved through, followed by a small pickup, with the rest of us walking behind. The lorry crept along the edge of a ridge, headlights out, before turning and heading steeply downhill toward a lower path, violently tearing the branch of a tree as it passed. I felt the camera in the pocket of my coat and grabbed it, turning it on as I pulled it out. Wayne had set it on night vision for me, and as I looked down at the screen I saw my own feet walking along, glowing white. I tipped it up in the direction of the ghostly parade ahead of me, the towers of the City fiery in the lower distance, and pressed the button. The camera produced an old-fashioned, pre-recorded clicking sound, but no one turned around. I pressed it again, and then returned it to my pocket.

After ten minutes we reached the site: two lines of concrete kerbing laid out like a runway, north to south. The lorry stalled as the back went up, dumping the whole load of bitmac in a pile in the centre. Graham ordered me and one of the big lads to fill wheelbarrows for the others. I kept up a steady rhythm, humming along under my breath to the little looping song in my head: *in the middle in the middle in the middle in the middle* ... Shovels chopped and scraped in the darkness. As the pile receded my legs and back began to burn with tiredness. Even so, I was enjoying myself. The bitmac was still warm at its centre; the smell was intoxicating. I began to imagine an alternate existence, where I worked on the black stuff all day and came home to Salome66 at night, muscle-bound and stinking of tar. We would have no Internet access. We would drink cheap wine and watch terrestrial television. Life would be happy and uncomplicated, and the spectre of death would recede.

'What is that shit you're humming?' The big lad had stopped shovelling and was staring at me.

'I don't know.'

'Well, it's fucking annoying.'

I was switched to wheelbarrow duty after about half an hour, with the mission of filling in any holes or shallow spots, but in the dark it was almost impossible to see what I was doing. I stuck to the edges, topping up along the kerbing and taking more pictures when I could; pictures of Graham and Raymond raking at the far end of the little roadway, pictures of Robin Royce smoking his pipe, pictures of myself wearing a disapproving expression, with my back to the action.

When we'd finished the lorry and the wheelbarrows were driven away to be dumped somewhere. Raymond continued to rake while the rest of us were taken down a narrow path to where the pickup had been concealed against the thick undergrowth.

'Everybody take a sign and drag it back up there,' said Robin. 'And then we'll figure out exactly where they should go.'

The one I took was a passable facsimile of a motorway sign which read 'Exit Labour'. The others said 'Speed Limits Kill', 'Cameras Criminalise Car Owners' and 'DfT's Road to Nowhere: Expect Delays'. We laid them out on the ground while Graham and Robin deliberated over the exact positioning.

'It will have considerably more impact if you place it here,' said Robin, shining his torch on a patch of ground at his feet.

'But a real exit would be on the left,' said Graham.

'Well, it's hardly a motorway, is it? I suppose we can switch these two round, but I still think Expect Delays has got to come last.'

The wooden stakes on which the signs were mounted could not be driven into the cold, hard ground. In the end we had to dig holes for them. As I crouched down to scoop dirt back into the hole around one stake, I felt something touch my elbow. I turned around and came face to face with a Labrador with a tennis ball in its mouth.

'Jesus fucking Christ!'

'What is it?'

'What's happened?'

There was a faint whistle in the distance and the dog

turned and trotted off, disappearing into the blackness after just a few feet. 'It was nothing,' I said. 'Sorry.'

The final rolling phase proceeded with excruciating slowness. The hand roller was petrol-driven and noisy. Some of the kerbing shifted and had to be knocked back into place. Even in the dark I could see that Graham was getting twitchy, that he longed to hurry the driver as he went about methodically re-securing the roller to the truck bed with chains and belts. Instead he took out his phone and made a call.

Robin Royce produced a rectangular stencil and a can of white paint and proceeded to lay a broken white line up the centre of the road. I took a few pictures of him at work, and a few of the finished product, which did indeed look like a slice of B-road transported to the middle of a field, steaming lightly after its fantastic journey.

'Looks good,' I said to Graham as we stood back a few paces to take it all in. 'So is that it now? Are we done?'

'Not quite,' said Graham, looking up toward the ridge where a bouncing light was growing more intense by the second. Then a whining engine could be heard, growing louder and throatier. All at once the light became two sharp beams as the car turned right and began racing down the hill toward us. I looked at Graham, who was smiling. 'Team C,' he said.

The car was a clapped out-looking Volvo with the words 'Pro Road Agenda' picked out in white on the bonnet. As it came to a halt halfway down the new road surface I thought I could see its tyres sinking slightly into the still-soft bitmac. The interior light snapped on as the doors cracked open. The two men in the front seats were wearing balaclavas. They jumped out, leaving behind a passenger in the back seat: a small, balding man wearing what looked like a pyjama top under a black coat. He was staring straight ahead, blankly, as if terrified. He seemed to be looking directly at me.

'Who's that?' I asked, hearing an unexpected vibrato in my voice.

'Jonathan Abel MP,' said Graham. 'Junior Transport something or other.'

'I didn't know we had an MP on board.'

'We don't. He's the worst of the anti-roadies.'

'What, you mean they've . . . ?'

'Well, he didn't know he was coming out tonight, put it that way.'

'Ah.'

'He's our front-page guarantee.' The two men in balaclavas jumped into the pickup, which then drove off.

'Fucking fantastic,' I said. 'I'm just going for a slash.' I took six calm, deliberate steps in the direction of some bushes just below us. And then I ran. I ran right through the bushes. I ran as fast as I could for as long as I could into the bituminous black night.

30

I ran without purpose, changing direction with each fresh wave of panic, running away from light, away from sound. What did they mean to do with him? Sirens blared in the distance, and I ran from them.

Eventually I began to tack north and east. I saw a church steeple silhouetted against the sky, and then the outlines of houses. I came to the edge of the Heath, to a long narrow path which communicated with the street. I walked for an hour without consulting a single sign, heading vaguely east until my sense of direction evaporated entirely. I tried to stick to small, residential streets but I ran up against railway lines and had to retreat to main roads in order to cross them. I walked across other parks. I climbed a few fences. I walked through car parks. I crossed Holloway Road and Hornsey Road, deep into uncharted territory. I became convinced that I was going too far north, then too far south. At one point I was certain I was heading back toward the heath, and I nearly turned around.

Then all at once I was somewhere I'd actually been before: Stoke Newington Church Street. I headed in what I supposed was the direction of the station. I found the street, then the number. There were four bells. I pressed the two middle ones long and hard. Then again.

'Hello?' It was her.

'It's me, Robert.'

'What are you doing? It's three in the morning.'

'Sorry. You said it didn't matter how late.'

'I know, but I didn't mean ... I've got ...' The buzzer drowned her out. I pushed the door open and pawed my way up the stairs in the dark, prepared for transgression. She was standing silhouetted in the doorway, wearing a bathrobe and looking smaller than ever.

'I've got to be up in less than four hours, you know.'

'Let me in.'

'What are you wearing? What have you been doing?'

'Please just let me in.'

The sheets are crisp and clean, freshly changed. It is gentle, an act of completion rather than of passion, a little sombre, a little tentative. It has been a very long time for both of us, and we are being careful not to freight the act with too much significance. But how can it not be significant? If nothing else it brings us to a point where what happens next is far from obvious.

Sunlight filled the room, penetrating the duvet and filling the space under it with pale green light. I rolled over and took hold of her from behind, skin against skin, and pulled a bit of her hair aside to kiss her neck.

'Christ,' she said. 'It's quarter to eight. Why didn't the fucking alarm go off?' I sat bolt upright and pulled her hair further aside. It was Caroline all right. 'Why are you looking at me?'

'Because you're beautiful.'

'Fuck off.' She slid over and grabbed the clock. 'The battery's fallen out the back again. You need to wake them up and get them dressed. I have to do two packed lunches and a camel costume.' She got up and stomped into the bathroom. For a moment I thought I might have dreamed the previous twenty-four hours, but there were my jeans on the floor, black with tar up to the knees, lying on top of a reflective vest.

The park was bright and cold. Most of the TWAT leaflets featuring the boy in the hood were now skidding along the ground in the breeze, but a few were still in place on tree trunks and fences. The dog chased a flock of pigeons up into the air and then ate the bread that had been left for them. My mobile rang in the pocket of my jeans. It was Ken from the paper.

'I don't suppose you've seen the news this morning?'

'No, I haven't even looked at the papers yet.'

'So you won't know that a group calling itself Pro-Road Agenda has built a stretch of road on Hampstead Heath overnight.'

'Really.'

'And they've kidnapped some MP and handcuffed him into a Volvo parked on the bit of road, in order to protest Labour's anti-car bias.'

'Wow.'

'They claim to be a radical offshoot of the British Drivers' Action Council. Isn't that your lot?'

'Yeah, that's them.'

'So my question is, Giles, how come you didn't know about this?'

'I did.'

'Then why weren't you there?'

'I was.'

'And why didn't you arrange for a photographer to go with you?'

'There wasn't time. But I did take quite a few pictures myself.'

'I see.'

'Good work, did you mean?'

'We need eighteen hundred words by four.'

'OK.'

'Email me the pics as soon as.'

I saw the boy ahead of me on the path, wearing a school uniform in place of his usual hooded top, scooping up leaflets and stuffing them into a rucksack. I stopped walking. He stood up and stared at me, looking deflated. I stared back. Then I turned and walked in the direction I had come. Along the way I noticed that the little Christmas tree was dead.

THE EVER-TERRIBLE MR GILES WAREING . . .
Started by easyGeoff at 10.56 AM on 04.01.05
. . . has made his bid for immortality with a lengthy
piece for the Sunday paper over the holidays. Is this
as bad as it gets, or can he write worse than this?
http://doturl.com/a4jts

Lordhawhaw – 1.26 PM on 30.01.05 (44 of 49)
Well, I'll say this: it wasn't actually that bad. I just think he missed a trick. That BDAC lot are worthy of crucifixion, and Wareing let them off the hook.

---

easyGeoff – 1.55 PM on 30.01.05 (45 of 49)
Are you joking? It was TERRIBLE. As a writer GW is hopelessly under-equipped for serious journalism. I'm surprised they printed it.

PavlovsKitty – 2.13 PM on 30.01.05 (46 of 49)
Agree with his Lordship. A competently written article – FOR ONCE – and a worthy target.

Grotius – 3.09 PM on 30.01.05 (47 of 49)
I thought it was shit. GW trots out the usual cliches about the road-building lobby, and his insinuation that the BDAC is full of disgruntled racists is ridiculous and counterproductive. You may not agree with them, but why should their protests be any less legitimate than the anti-road lot?

Salome66 – 5.32 PM on 30.01.05 (48 of 49)
That picture gave me the creeps. The night vision makes GW look like some ageing ghost, something that visits you in nightmares. Is it the spectre of spent prose, the evanescent shade of a washed up, middle aged hack, the troubled soul of a non-entity searching vainly for meaning? I mean it – I stared

at it for hours, and I saw something there that really frightened me. It was like meeting GW in real life.

---

easyGeoff – 7.15 PM on 30.01.05 (49 of 49)
He's an ugly fucker all right.

Back / Top / Add a comment

Over the course of the next week I received two texts from Salome66 on my old phone, one apologizing for not letting me in, and the other trying to arrange another date. I ignored them both. Cher Fitzpaine rang on the morning of the 7th of February.

'Hi, Cher.'

'Did you not get my message about visitors?'

'I got it.'

'On the whole when you get a message from someone who is in a vulnerable state, don't you think you should reply?'

'I'm sorry.'

'So when were you thinking of coming?'

'Well. I hadn't made any plans to come, actually.'

'I'm all alone here. Are you trying to jeopardize my recovery?'

'I don't think you're supposed to say things like that.'

'Come tomorrow.'

'I can't.'

'Come Wednesday.'

'I don't even know where you are.'

'Garston House, just outside Exeter. It takes no time on the train.'

'I don't . . .'

'I'm reaching out,' he said. 'It's very important to me that you come.' There was a raw, pleading edge to his voice that made me loathe him. Nevertheless I felt constrained by the shackles of normal human conduct.

'All right. Wednesday afternoon. Anything I should bring?'

'Two hundred Silk Cut.'

'All right.'

'Don't say you're coming and then not come.'

'I'll be there.'

'And don't forget the fags.'

The midday train was empty but for a few students wearing headphones. The weather had turned in the night; the sky was clotted with heavy cloud. Railway-blighted back gardens quickly gave way to industrial estates, their long corrugated roofs crusted with yellow-white lichens. The countryside came and went in flashes, broken up by timber yards, hulking retail sheds and high walls of stacked, parti-coloured cubes of compressed rubbish. The sun occasionally broke through to illuminate specific features of the landscape: a row of rusted cattle troughs, a tree in the middle of a field, a cluster of cars in an otherwise empty car park. I watched some forlorn corner of a golf course flee past and thought about replying to the latest text from Salome66, the one that said, simply 'were r u?'. But I didn't. I thought about the boy in the park, in his school uniform, and the look on his face as he stuffed the leaflets into his rucksack. I thought about my boys in their school uniforms, sitting in their respective classrooms, learning about the Victorians, or verbs, or why things freeze. I wondered why there were no 1804 silver dollars coined in 1804. I listened to the song in my head, which had appropriated the rhythm of the speeding train: *in the middle in the middle in the middle in the middle in the middle . . .*

The taxi from the station left Exeter and plunged almost instantly into disquieting rusticity, along wet, narrow lanes with grass growing up through the tarmac in the middle, through villages with short, made-up-sounding names. A large manor appeared briefly on a hill before we headed deep into the cleft of a valley, over a bridge and up again, proceeding through a tunnel of trees, until a discreet sign pointed us up the long drive leading to Garston House.

Cher Fitzpaine was alone in the dining room, enjoying the end of a late lunch. He wore a black cardigan over a crisp, pale grey shirt. His hair was combed wet and he looked suspiciously tanned.

'Hello, Giles. Good to see you. I liked your piece about the moto-terrorists the other day. Very amusing. Have something if you want. The food isn't bad.'

'Is this really rehab?'

'Rehab, detox, whatever. I'm trying to finish a book, and this is a good place to write. It's deeply unfashionable. No one comes here.'

'I'd imagined more of a twelve-step type regime.'

'It's what people expect to happen to me. If the press want to call this rehab, I can't stop them.'

'Actually I think you can.'

'Did you bring the fags?'

'Yes. So you're free to come and go from here, is that right?'

'Well, theoretically, but I don't have a car. What's been the reaction to the road-building piece? I like your jacket.'

'I don't know. I presume the BDAC aren't too happy, but I haven't heard from them. They liked it at the paper, I guess. Which is good, because my contract is up at the end of the month.'

'I meant, you know, on the Internet. The Wareing Hate Club.'

'Oh. I haven't really looked,' I lied.

'How is all that going? What happened with the girl, Salome? You saw her again?'

'Yes. Twice.'

'Where?'

'At her flat.'

'Oh my God. You got into her flat. Christ! You had sex with her!'

'No, I didn't. I nearly did. I mean, I'd resolved to, I went there intending to, but it was late and she had work the next day and, well, now I'm glad I didn't. I consider it a narrow escape.'

'Wait. You didn't have sex either time?'

'No. The first time, I was ... the thing is, I was fully prepared to commit adultery. I'd made the mental leap in my head, and it gave me a scare.'

'I didn't realize you were so conventional, Giles. That's very interesting. So what happens next?'

'What do you mean?'

'When do you go for the whole "I am Giles Wareing" scenario? Do you do it in person, or on the Internet, where the others can read it? Or both. Both might work.'

'I'm not telling her. That's it. I'm done. It's over.'

'That's a terrible ending. Where's the closure?'

'The point is, I don't care what they say anymore, now I've seen who they are, who she is. She's just a normal, lonely woman. All that vitriol is just an exercise. She didn't care about the talkboard, really. In fact she decided to give it up.'

'But she kept on posting.'

'Well, yes.'

'And so did you.'

'A bit. But I'm done with it now. Finished.'

'That's what you say. I think there's more to come here.'

'The talkboard thing was a pointless obsession. I just needed to work through it.'

'This won't do at all,' he said, sounding almost professorial. 'It needs a final resolution.'

'What do you mean? Why do you care?'

'You need to see her again, I think. One more time.'

'What is this new book about?'

'It's a modern tale of middle-aged disaffection, with a technological twist. I'm moving onto a new level.'

'Me. You're writing about me.'

'I'm writing about a man. A man in a similar situation.'

'You've been following the talkboard thing all along?'

'Avidly. You're ThisDistractedGlobe, of course. I'm safe in assuming that, aren't I?' A horrible realization began to creep over me, spreading from the pit of my stomach.

'Which one are you?'

'I need to keep tabs on what happens in real life, though. Frankly, I was hoping you'd be a bit more forthcoming.'

'You're one of them. Which one?'

'Perhaps I'll have to track down Salome66 myself in the end. You did it. How hard can it be?'

'You must be easyGeoff. He only cropped up after I told you about the talkboards. He said he'd met me at your book launch.'

'It's a good name, isn't it? Perry gets the credit for that. I've copyrighted it, just in case.'

'You've been manipulating the whole thing from the beginning.'

'Not at all. I've just given things a kick from time to time, whenever it went a bit quiet, or I thought you were in danger of not following through.'

'You pretended to be one of them just to perpetuate all that . . .' I stopped and took a cautious breath. I did not want to be sick in front of Cher Fitzpaine. 'I can't believe you did this to me.'

'What are you talking about? You did the same thing. You criticized yourself to fuel their hatred. How fucked up is that? It's a brilliant detail.'

'You can't turn my life into fiction.'

'Why not? It's a great story. Up to a point, anyway.'

'Because, apart from anything else, you're a terrible writer.'

'A lot of people feel that way about you, I've heard.'

'I meant to tell you that your novel was a piece of shit, by the way.'

'Number nine on Amazon this morning.'

'I'm going to talk to a lawyer about this.'

'Yeah, you probably should. I have.'

Raindrops shivered sideways along the train window, blurring the scenery outside. My revulsion at the prospect of being a character in a Cher Fitzpaine novel had turned to anger, and then to something even more disturbing: curiosity. Why hadn't Salome66 stopped posting as promised? Why did she hate Giles Wareing so much? How would she react to the news that I was Giles Wareing? Did she already know who I was? Was she playing some kind of game with me? Was she, perhaps, a confederate of Fitzpaine's? Could it be that I had spent the last few months being insufficiently paranoid?

It was just after six when the train pulled into Paddington. I took the Tube to Liverpool Street, got onto another train bound for Stoke Newington, and picked my way to her flat in the rain. If nothing else, I thought, I have got to know the area quite well. There was no answer when I pushed the bell, or when I rang her mobile. I didn't leave a message.

She appeared just after eight o'clock, weighed down by a rucksack and two bags of shopping. I stood up slowly, stiff with cold.

'Robert.'

'Sorry. I tried to ring.'

'I forgot my phone this morning. Here, take these.' She handed me the shopping bags and pulled out her keys. We walked up to the flat in silence. I had neglected to think about what I was going to say. She started to put her shopping away, unfamiliar packages from a health-food chain. I looked around the flat, noticing things I hadn't seen before: a picture of her parents standing next to a hot-air balloon; a framed drawing of a cat; an old Hoover held together with packing tape; a pile of newspapers in a green recycling box by the door. Something was missing.

'Where's your computer?'

'I don't have one. I just use the one at work.' All that invective, I thought, dished out on company time.

'There's something we need to talk about,' I said, not quite knowing what it might be. She came and stood in front of me, arms folded, and fixed her dark marble eyes on mine. I thought about pressing ahead with the sex idea, but then I thought of Fitzpaine's book. He would not have the satisfaction.

'I know what it's about, Robert. I know you've got a wife, or a girlfriend, or something.'

'Oh.'

'You show up here at weird hours, unannounced. You don't answer your phone for days. You don't call, and then you do call. I know you're hiding me from somebody.'

'Yes.'

'I thought I didn't mind, as long as I didn't know the details. I was sick of being alone. But I guess it's not an ideal starting point for a relationship.'

'No. It isn't.' I unfolded her arms and held her close to me. I decided not to rule sex out for the time being.

'So I assume you're here to end it before things go too far.'

'Not necessarily.' We kissed. I closed my eyes and felt the cross of her front teeth against my lips. Here I am, I thought, embarking on an affair after all, beginning a double life. The life of Robert. The affair of Robert and Salome66.

'Wait,' I said. 'How can you not have a computer?' She looked at me.

'It's not compulsory, is it?'

'A lot of the time you post in the middle of the night. You can't be at work then.'

'Oh God. I thought we'd agreed to forget about all that.'

'We did, but that didn't stop you carrying on, did it?' My anger flickered to life, a low, steady flame.

'What?'

'Salome66 hasn't exactly been slacking off, I've noticed.'

'Robert.'

'You couldn't quite kick the Giles Wareing Hating habit.'

'Christ. It's really important to you all this, isn't it?'

'And it isn't to you?' I was speaking quickly, trying not to lose my grip on the words. 'Why do you hate Giles Wareing so much? What is it about him? Where the fuck is your computer?'

'Robert, I'm not Salome66.'

'Oh yes you are. You can't hide behind some alter ego. It's not fair. You wrote all that stuff, so don't make out it's some kind of exercise, some kind of pose. If you can't confront your own opinions, don't express them. Even the dreadful Giles Wareing deserves better than that.'

'No, I mean I'm not Salome66. I don't post on that website. I never have.'

'What?'

'I'm just a friend of Anne's. She wanted me to come to her talkboard meet, to rescue her in case it was full of weirdos. But she was having a good time, so I stayed.'

'But you said you were Salome66.'

'I know. I felt like I shouldn't be there, like I didn't belong. You were actually the first person to talk to me the whole night. I thought it would make it easier if I pretended to be one of the people who was supposed to be there.'

'So who is Salome66?'

'I don't know. It was just a name you said. And I said yes. I'm sorry. At that point I didn't think I was ever going to see you again.'

'Why didn't you tell me before?'

'Because I didn't think it fucking mattered! I didn't realize you were obsessed with her!'

'Hang on. Was she there that night, do you think?'

'I don't care! I don't care who Salome66 is, and I don't care who Giles Manning is!'

'Giles Wareing.'

'Christ. Who the fuck is Giles Wareing?'

I walked over to the recycling box. I found what I was looking for about a third of the way down. Giles Wareing Joins the Moto-Terrorists of Hampstead Heath. There I was, staring into the lens with white eyes, shovel in hand. I held it up.

'This is Giles Wareing.'

'He looks like a ghost.'

'Giles Wareing is a forty-year-old freelance journalist.'

'And why should I care about Giles Wareing?'

'You shouldn't, I suppose. No one should.' She looked at me, and then at the picture.

'Oh Christ. Because you're Giles Wareing. That's you.' She took the paper from my hand and looked at it closely. 'I actually read this.'

'Really? What did you think?'

'So what were you doing? Stalking someone who slagged you off on the Internet?' This struck me as a fairly concise summation of what I had been doing. It was odd that I had never thought of it that way before.

'No, not stalking. I just wanted to . . .'

'What were you going to do to her? To me? Oh my God.'

'Nothing, I didn't have any kind of . . . none of this was planned.'

'You should leave.'

'Then I found myself attracted to you, which was extremely confusing. I'm sorry. This is as weird for me as it is for you.'

Do you know what? You have no idea how fucking weird this is for me. Get out.'

When I was halfway through the door I turned to look at her once more. Her eyes had gone black and shiny, and wet. She looked back down at the paper.

I walked along in the dark for while, head down in the vague direction of the Tube station, thinking about what I had done, trying to gauge its effect, wallowing in the full flush of an emotion I had not experienced for several months: guilt. After five weeks the Panaglos seemed to be in its final half-life throes. I was my old, depressed self.

This was not, on the face of it, a particularly good time to come back into possession of one's capacity for guilt. I had coldly misled a woman on the flimsiest pretext of revenge, who then turned out to be someone else entirely. I had been distant and self-indulgent and dishonest. I had neglected my family and my work while I pursued a pointless obsession. I knew I had done other things which I couldn't even remember.

My phone rang. I thought it must be Caroline, wondering where I was, but the number was withheld.

'Hello?'

'You slimy little cunt.'

'Yes?'

'You'd better be watching your back, Wareing.'

'Who's this?'

'We're not through with you.'

'Is that Graham?'

'I don't take kindly to being made a fool of.'

'I didn't make you a fool, Graham. If that is Graham.'

'We know where you live.'

'Do you?' I had reached the entrance to the station.

'When we come for you there won't be no warning.'

'Sorry, but isn't this a warning?'

'You're nothing, Wareing. Nothing but a grubby, shitty, cowardly, washed-up, useless hack.'

'I know. It's been a real journey.'

'Don't you fucking . . .'

'Can you hang on just a second, Graham?' I stepped back, lifted my right knee and hurled the phone high into the air, watching it spin end over end, up and out of the cone of misty drizzle under the street light, into the roiling, sulphur-tinged darkness. I felt a lot of things go with it. Graham, for a start. Kate. An indifferent freelance writing career. My brief love affair with Panaglos. My first forty years. The possibility of redemption, with its attendant yoke of fear. Perhaps now I could start again, afresh, anew.

The was a loud report, and a sharp screech of tyres. My phone had come down onto the windscreen of a passing car, bouncing into the road and shattering into a dozen pieces. The driver, a large, bald, red-faced man, jumped out of the car and looked around for someone to hit. To hell with starting anew. I decided it was time to go home.

The house was dark. The only light came from the kitchen, from the shaded bulb which hung just above the table.

I found Caroline sitting under it with a glass of red wine in front of her. The bottle on the worktop was somewhere between half and three-quarters empty, the exact level obscured by the label.

'What time d'you call this?' she said. The readout of the microwave clock was hovering in the darkness behind her.

'Eleven twenty-seven.'

'That's slow,' she said, unintentionally elongating the vowel. Then she gave me a lie-detector stare. 'Where have you been, Giles?'

'I went to visit Cher Fitzpaine. I told you.'

'Till now?'

'I got hungry, so I had a curry in Exeter. And then the train was late.' It sounded terrible even as I said it, but I was stuck with it now. I hoped it would be the last lie I had to tell. In any case, she decided to accept the premise for the moment.

'I don't understand how you have time to nurture some celebrity twat writer when you don't seem to have time for your family.' I took a glass from the cupboard and emptied the rest of the bottle into it. A little bolt of panic shot through me.

'If you're worried about the shed floor . . .'

'I'm not talking about the sodding shed floor. I'm talking about your children.'

'What do you mean? I sat with Freddy last night and helped him with his homework.' The song started up in my head again. *In the middle in the middle in the middle.* I looked around for another bottle.

'You sat opposite him and read the paper. And anyway

I'm talking about the older one. You never engage with him.' I wasn't entirely sure what she meant by engage. It didn't sound like something I'd be good at.

'Yes I do.'

'No, you don't. He sits there in his room, typing on his wooden computer, pretending to be you. You don't even call him by his name.' The song got louder, making the argument difficult to follow. What should I say next?

'I don't call anyone by their name. I don't call you by your name.'

'You don't call him by his name, and I know why. We both know why.'

'Do we.' I suddenly felt exhausted. I had to stifle a yawn.

'It's because of your dad. I didn't choose the name; you did. You demanded it.' *In the middle in the middle in the middle . . .*

'We agreed.'

'You wanted to name him after your father, like you were. That's fine.' An emotional rasp entered her voice. 'Stupid American tradition, but that's fine.'

'Yes.' My gut was urging me to leave the room, but I was frozen to the spot.

'Robert Giles Wareing.'

'I know his name.'

'Robert Giles Wareing the fucking *third*.'

'I apologize for that.'

'Anyway. I don't know what your fucking crisis is about because you never say anything. Whether it's about being American or not being American or your mother dying, or

your poor father – ' at first she seemed to pause dramatically, but it became clear that she had the hiccups – 'sitting
there, in that tiny house in New Jersey, by himself.'

'He not alone. He's got what's-she-called. Angela.'

'How do you know? You haven't spoken to him in
over a year.'

'I don't want to talk about this.'

'It's not like he walked out on you. Your mother is the
one who ran off.'

'I'm too tired to do this now.' In truth, I felt a little
faint. The song was now loud enough to blot out everything; everything but Caroline's wobbling, saw-toothed
voice.

'Maybe you can't deal with him because it makes you
angry with your mother and you can't handle that. And I
don't know why I'm crying when you aren't.'

'I can't handle this.' *In the middle in the middle in the
middle in the middle . . .*

'But it's not his fault. You shouldn't take it out on *him*.'

'I'm going upstairs.'

'Or on your son.'

As I made my way unsteadily up to my office the song
seemed to expand in either direction, but I couldn't quite
get hold of the tune, or any other words. I began to realize
that it existed outside my head, that somewhere there
was such a song. I sat down in the chair and turned the
computer on. I took a few minutes to get control of my
breathing, which had become rapid and shallow. Then I
typed it into the search box: 'in the middle in the middle
in the middle'. Then I hit enter.

And because the Internet was what it was, and is what it is, a messy electronic mock-up of the collective unconscious, a huge, humming exo-consciousness, a disorganized jumble of every stray thought and memory that has ever been tapped into a keyboard, the void answered back, responding to nothing more than three common words typed three times in succession, to the simple, desperate plea: what is this?

They were song lyrics. They were, in fact, the title of a song: In the Middle, In the Middle, In the Middle, written for the New York State Department of Safety. Because it was the Internet, I easily found the rest of the lyrics, even the chords. I found people expressing a nostalgic fondness for this 1960s public-safety advertisement on talkboards and in chat rooms. I learned of every instance where it had been sampled by an obscure rap group. Thanks to the Internet, I was even able to listen to it through wasp-fuzzy speakers built into the edges of the laptop's keyboard:

Don't cross the street in the middle in the middle in the middle in the middle in the middle of the block . . .

I had a strange memory of watching it on television with one of the boys – the older one, but when he was much smaller – on my knee, both of us singing along, but it was from a strange perspective, the TV nothing more than a squarish blur, and the voice that was mine was not mine. When the song was finished I clicked again.

Don't cross the street in the middle in the middle in the middle in the middle in the middle of the block . . .

And then I realized that the voice that was not mine was my dad's, and that I was the boy on his knee, and we were singing our favourite song together, or at least the bit of it that I knew: *in the middle in the middle in the middle in the middle.* We were in the house in New Jersey, the same house, with the fish-shaped coffee table on iron legs, and the butterfly chair, and the big black dog that was also just a blur. There was an orange winter light seeping in under the shade, and me and my dad were singing.

I put my head down on the keyboard and cried. I don't know for how long. This time I didn't really want to stop.

31

I woke up some time after nine, feeling exhausted but strangely unencumbered, without the usual filmy haze between me and the world. I lay back and listened to the silence wafting through the house. I would call my dad within the next few weeks, make tentative plans to visit. I would spend more time with Bobby, perhaps take him somewhere at Easter, just the two of us. I would be a good father. A good son. A good man.

A familiar sense of defeat quickly swamped this bout of optimism. I would almost certainly not call my dad this week. I could spend more time with Bobby, but the idea of engaging with him filled me with dread at the possibility of failure. No matter what resolutions I made, I knew I would continue to drift away from my children, from Caroline, from my life, and then I would die. As I smiled grimly at the idea of an ending so deeply unsatisfying to Cher Fitzpaine, I became aware of a persistent scratching sound invading the silence of the house, like something trapped in one of the walls. It stopped. I held my breath and listened. After a minute it started again. I slid out of bed and opened the curtains, and found myself face to face with Colin, who was on a ladder scraping down the window frame.

'All right, Guy? Didn't wake you up, did I?'

By the time I had showered and dressed, Colin was making himself a cup of tea in the kitchen, his white hair full of off-white paint chips.

'Colin. How's it going.'

'Not bad, mate, not bad. Might have to put a blowtorch on that ledge out there. The paint don't want to shift, know what I mean?'

'You haven't been around for a while.'

'No, I took a bit of time off. It seemed like a good time to lower my profile locally, as they say.'

'Shall I not ask?'

'I'd appreciate that, ta. So how you been keeping, mate?'

'Fine.'

I took the dog to the park. There was a new bench where Maria's once stood, a sturdy, straightforward assemblage of chunky hardwood planks and black steel. When had this happened? I'd been going to the park several times a day for years, logging the smallest changes, and yet something as profound as a new bench could appear without my prior knowledge. From a distance I could see that three or four cheap petrol-station bouquets had been laid on it. As I approached I noticed the small brass plaque screwed to the back. I bent over to read it. It said, 'Made by Offenders Subject to Unpaid Work in the Community'.

'Hi.' I turned around. It was Darby's mum.

'Hello.'

'It's awful, isn't it? Really awful.'

'Yeah.'

'You knew her, didn't you? I remember you sitting here with her.'

'I knew her a bit. Not very well.'

'She seemed quite popular.'

'Well, she was an important part of the community.'

'You could tell. There she is! Hello, Philippa!' The dog wandered up, her tail oscillating at high speed. 'What a good girl!'

'Where is, um, Jackie?'

'He's with Nick. Gone up to his parents in Northumberland for a few days. His dad's in a bad way.' I thought about my dad and wondered what kind of way he was in.

'Oh. Oh dear.' Darby's mum looked up at me with her pale, lightly freckled face, and her steady electricity-provider-swapping stare.

'Are you very busy?' she said. 'Do you want to come round for a coffee?' My toes curled up in my shoes.

'I can't today,' I said, after a long, wavering pause. 'Maybe next time.'

Colin was just coming down from the ladder when I got back.

'Hold up, Guy,' he said. 'I forgot to give you this.' He had a piece of paper in his hand.

'What is it?'

'It's that address you wanted. That email you give me, remember? Before Crimbo, weren't it. My son-in-law tracked it down straight away. I ain't had a chance to give it to you.'

I took the paper and unfolded it. It was the same piece of paper I'd given Colin. Next to Salome66's Internet email address was scrawled 'Mabey – 45a Penshurst Rd Bedford MK417ZU'. The name was vaguely familiar. And Penshurst. Thou art not, Penshurst, built to envious show.

'Oh shit.'

I ran upstairs to my office and found my journal under a pile of old bills and unread newspapers. I turned it over and flipped backward, past the third-person ramblings, the suicidal ideation, the mid-life whittering, until I found it scrawled at the bottom of the profile of Grotius: K Mabey, 45a Penshurst Road Bedford. He and Salome66 shared an address. Salome66 lived in Bedford.

I ran downstairs again, panting and wild-eyed, patting myself for keys as I pulled open the door.

'Damn!'

Colin looked down from ladder.

'Something wrong?'

'Yeah. I need to go to Bedford, right now, but Caroline's got the car. Shit, and I don't have my phone. I need to, I don't know, I need to . . .' I looked around me stupidly, making fists and then wringing them out.

'I can take you if you want,' said Colin matter-of-factly.

'Really?'

'You're paying a hundred for the day whatever. Painting or driving, it's up to you, mate.'

It was midday by the time we hit the M1. Colin's minivan rattled alarmingly at speeds over fifty miles per hour, and his habit of driving while talking on one of his three phones and simultaneously consulting a clipboard jammed with wrinkled scraps of paper was far from reassuring. Loose change skittered about in the well between the seats. A St Christopher medal swung from the rear-view mirror. Everything in the car was in motion except the speedometer needle, which lay dead against the peg below the zero.

'So, where're we going exactly,' said Colin, hanging up his phone after a protracted argument with someone over the precise definition of eggshell.

'Penshurst Road, but I don't know where it is.'

'And who're we goin' to see?'

'I'm not sure.'

'Well, I'm glad you've thought this through. What the fuck . . .' The traffic up ahead was at a standstill. Colin slammed on the brakes, causing the van to change lanes spontaneously. After a final skid we drew slowly up to the back of the queue. I was terrified and hungry, powerless to resist saying the words that swam around my head.

'Colin, I don't know if I should tell you this.'

'I don't know if you should either, mate.' He put the wheel between his knees and rolled a cigarette.

'But a couple of months ago I got a note.'

'A note.'

'A note about you.' He let the car slip forward a few feet while lighting his fag.

'Come through your letter box, did it?'

'Yeah.'

'Tiny little writing?'

'Yes.'

'Did it say I was a murderer?'

'Not in so many words.'

'Did it say I was Irish?'

'Yeah. It did.'

He leaned over and yanked open his glove box. He rummaged through it even as he tried to get into a lane that was moving slightly faster.

'There,' he said. 'Like that?' He flipped an envelope onto my lap which appeared to be an exact copy of the one I'd found on the mat.

'Just like that. Who sent them?' He frowned solemnly. Traffic was beginning to move again, albeit slowly.

'Me downstairs neighbour. She's not right in the head, if you know what I mean. Depressed or something. We had a dispute about noise after I put me new floors down, blonde wood. And then one day she come up and tells me her old man had moved out cos o' me. Cos I wouldn't put carpets down! Screaming and shrieking something awful. I know why her old man left. He was a cunt and all, but never mind.'

'Has she sent a lot of them?'

'About a dozen, I s'pose, over the last few months, wherever she sees I'm workin'. It ain't very good for business, I can tell you.'

'Must be difficult.'

'It's not very nice, no. A person who don't even know you writing horrible things about you.'

'I can imagine.'

'And you've got no idea how many fuckin' people have read it.'

'Exactly.'

'After a while you go a bit mental with it, you know?'

'You lose your point of reference.'

'Yeah. If you like.'

'Until you start to believe it yourself.'

'Well.' He frowned, flicked ash through the top of the window. 'I didn't start thinkin' I'd murdered someone if that's what you mean.'

'No, of course not. Neither did I. But are you Irish?'

'Ha! Pure pikey, mate. Right. Here we go: Bedford, twelve miles.'

Penshurst Road was part of a development to the north-west of the town centre, a maze of squat terraces faced with brick the colour of bled flesh, with an eccentric numbering system all its own. Artfully curved streets snaked off a central artery. The buildings were featureless but for bolted-on steel balconies attached to the second-storey windows, and little porches over the doors. Everything else was parking.

'Thou art not, Penshurst Road, built to envious show.'

'Come again?'

'Nothing.'

45a was a ground-floor flat with its own front door. Colin pulled up outside, blocking in two cars, and instinctively patted himself for his disabled badge.

'What's next?' he asked.

'I don't really know.'

'Well, who have we come to see?'

'I don't know that either.'

'Well, how do we find out?'

'We need to get them to come to the door, I guess.'

'And then what?'

'It depends.'

'Christ, I'm glad you're in charge. Come on, then.' Colin grabbed his clipboard and got out. He opened the van's back door and indicated a large cardboard box. 'Grab that.'

'What is it?'

'It's a lavatory pan. Cracked. Useless.'

'It's heavy.'

'Lift with your legs.'

The clear plastic door buzzer, lit from behind, held a small strip of paper onto which the word MABEY was hand-lettered. This was it, I thought. Maybe. The box was going soft where my damp hands held it. Colin snapped the letter box three times, which caught me by surprise. I froze, the box slipping from my grasp by millimetres. After a moment the speaker above the button crackled. Then it said 'Hello.' The voice buzzed as if bounced off a sheet of foil, genderless, disembodied, robbed of inflection. A ghostly electronic whisper answering from the void.

'Got a package here for next door, mate,' said Colin. 'All right if I leave it with you?'

'What?' The word was formless, an interrogative parp from a toy trumpet.

'A package. For next door. They ain't in.'

'Oh. Yeah, hang on.'

My heart thudded off the ensuing seconds. I was losing

the box. Finally the door clicked and then opened inward
with a little suctiony squeak. There was a waft of cologne
and cats.

'Whoa,' said a man's voice. I couldn't see anything over
the far edge of the box.

'It's heavy and all,' said Colin. 'All right if he pops it
inside?' I felt a cat winding itself around my ankles, and
suppressed a shudder.

'Yeah, yeah, fine. Just bring it ... let me just ... hang
on, I'll ... this way. Come back in, Pepper.'

I stepped into the dark hall, which was so narrow that
my elbows brushed both walls. I kept going, forcing the
man backwards and through a lighted doorway to the left.
I followed.

'Anywhere is fine,' said the man.

The room was lit mainly by screens. Two computer
monitors, one twice the size of the other, stood side by
side on a huge table covered with papers, bits of electronic
gadgetry and plastic soft-drink bottles. At one end of the
room a giant wide-screen television stood in front of
the front window, teeming silently with up-to-the-minute
financial information. Another television stood on a stand
in the corner, glowing blue. The carpet was covered with
boxes and stacks of magazines. The high-tech office chair
appeared to be the only seating.

'Anywhere you can find. Sorry it's so ... I work from
home.' I put the box down against the wall, and stayed
crouched there for a moment

'Computers, is it,' said Colin from somewhere behind
me.

'Computer games,' said the man. 'I test and review them.' I stood up and turned around. 'Is there something I need to sign?' he asked.

We both froze, our embarrassment temporarily suspended by the raw dawning horror of recognition. It crept over me from the edges in, like a chill.

'You.' It was him who spoke first, but it was what I would have said if I had regained the power of speech: you. It was, for the moment, all there was to say.

He was wearing the same grid-patterned shirt, or one very like it. He looked, if anything, even fatter standing up. And there was that unmistakable parting in his lank hair, the broad delta of skin that made him look ill. It was the guy from the pub that first night; the one who'd sat opposite me at the bar and stared.

'You're . . .' I'd never said Grotius out loud before. I wasn't sure how it was pronounced. 'You went all that way down to the pub that night, but you never joined the group.'

'Yes. I'm not the most prepossessing fellow in the flesh, so I thought I'd watch for a bit first, see how things stood. They all seemed so young to me. You were doing the same thing, I take it.'

'Sort of. How old are you, fifty? Fifty-five?'

'Thereabouts.'

'And you write about computer games?'

'It's a huge industry, expanding exponentially. And who the fuck are you, exactly?'

'I'm ThisDistractedGlobe.'

'Uh-huh. And why are you here?'

'I'm looking for Salome66.'

'Ah. You're an Internet stalker.'

'I suppose I am.'

'Well, you found her.'

'You.'

'I am Salome66, among others.'

'How many others?'

'Sometimes it's useful to have more than one username. I expect you know that.'

'Uh-huh. But Salome?'

'I picked it after I got kicked off a new media website for bullying – just giving some wanker a hard time. I wanted to see if I could get away with more with a girl's name.'

'And could you?'

'Oh, Christ yes. I sketched out a sort of personality, gave her a few likes and dislikes, and she could do no wrong. She started as a sort of parody – liberal, single, bookish – but after a while she became like a person. She got email. Her inbox was always full. People wanted to be friends with her. So I made her a friend of mine. If I say something in a forum as Grotius, and she agrees with me, then everybody takes me seriously. She's an invaluable tool.' He pronounced Grotius with a hard T: groaty-us.

'You don't think it's deceitful?'

'On an Internet forum? It's all deceit. Everybody lies. Everybody is more strident than they are in real life. People make up opinions just to get attention, just to belong. All anybody wants is for the Internet to answer back, so they don't feel alone. Now they're all blogging, putting their fucking diaries online, blah blah blah, today I shat my pants. In the old days it was a conversation at least.'

'So you don't really like Wallace Stevens.'

'My ex-wife did. I've only read a bit online, enough to maintain the charade, but you've got to admit he's a brilliantly pretentious choice.'

'Yes.'

'So look, I'm sorry your Internet girlfriend isn't real. I apologize for being a man, but I don't swing that way, and I'm not...'

'But you do hate Giles Wareing.'

'Well, I don't know about hate, but he's a pretty...' He stopped and stared, in the same sullen, intrusive way he had stared across the bar.

'Oh my God,' he said 'You're him. Are you? You are! I knew I fucking recognized you that night. Giles Wareing. So what is this, some undercover piece about your Internet enemies?'

'This is not a piece. This is real.'

'Real. I don't like the sound of that.' He frowned at the floor deliberately, as if suppressing a smile. Colin cleared his throat in the doorway.

'He's a pretty what? I'm a pretty what?'

'Lousy writer? Will that do?'

'In what way?'

'Is it normal for journalists to do this? Does this happen a lot?'

'What's wrong with my writing?'

'I don't know, let me see – it's clichéd, uninspired drivel, like most of the rest of the newspaper.'

'Why single me out?'

'Why not? You're an averagely bad writer. You're emblematic of the problem. You have a silly name.' Surprisingly there was no sting in this. Averagely bad I could live with.

'OK.'

'That's it. If I knew you were coming to confront your demons, I would have prepared a more cogent assessment.'

'I didn't come to confront my demons. I just wanted to see what they looked like.'

'Well, this is what they look like. They're a lonely, divorced, middle-aged guy with grown kids who don't speak to him, who lives in Bedford. Now fuck off out of my house.'

I looked around for something to smash. I thought about spitting in his unshaven, jowly face. Neither of these things seemed appropriate. Simply walking out didn't seem quite right either, but that's what I did.

'Well, I didn't understand a single fucking word of that,' said Colin after about a mile of silence.

'It's complicated.'

'I could see.'

'How old are you, Colin?'

'Fifty-two next week, mate.'

'What's it like?'

'It's fuckin' awful.'

Darkness was gathering in the dips and crevices of the landscape. Rain began to hit the windshield. We lived, they said, in drought-stricken times, but the rain was always there, ever present, spattering away, taunting us. London would dry up, turn to desert, and still it would rain. The world sours deliberately, to make you mind leaving it less.

Colin let me off at the corner. I stopped to look at the clock in the off-licence, peering through the fogged-up window: five past six. The children would be having their supper, elbows on table, heads propped on open palms, forks held like spades. I would arrive home at supper time, like my dad always did, and touch the backs of my sons' necks with my ice-cold hands, making them squeal with delight. Except my hands were clammy from the car.

I rang the bell because I'd forgotten my keys. Caroline came to the door looking pale and serious.

'The police are here,' she said.

I wasn't at all surprised, although I had no idea why they'd come. It could have been any number of things.

32

It was a matter the police thought might be best dealt with at the station. They asked if I had a computer in the house, and asked if I would mind if they brought it along. They stressed that I was not under arrest, with added emphasis on the words 'at this time'. I looked at Caroline's ashen face. It seemed the wrong moment to utter the words 'I am not a paedophile'.

I sat in an interview room alone for over an hour, listening to footsteps come and go, listening to jocular exchanges between people who seemed to be on the verge of entering, but didn't. I watched the surface of a cold cup of tea vibrate in response to some commotion on another floor. I began to feel sleepy, though my heartbeat was skittish and shallow. Then all of a sudden the door flew open, creating pressure against my eardrums.

'Sorry to keep you waiting, Mr Wareing.'

There were two of them, a man and a woman. The man did all the talking. He was dressed in a suit and tie, and had a sheaf of paper in front of him. I felt like I was applying for a mortgage.

'You are aware, Mr Wareing, that you are here in

connection with a complaint of harassment made against you by a member of the public.'

'Yes.'

'That you on one or more occasions put up leaflets throughout Roundworm Park, with a picture of the gentleman in question on them.'

'Yes.'

'And the words . . .' He consulted the sheet of paper in front of him. 'The words have you seen this twat.'

'Yes.'

'Where did the picture come from?'

'I took it with my phone.'

'Without permission.'

'Well, it was an accident actually. The phone went off accidentally.'

He stared at me with a look of perfect blankness.

'And do you have this phone with you?'

'No. I don't have that phone anymore.' The woman looked at the ground, and then to the side, as if looking for places to look.

'Can I just ask you what was your motive behind this campaign of yours?'

'I don't know. He and I had had . . . sorry I don't know his name.'

'Mr Sayed.'

'We'd had a few run-ins. He'd threatened me on a couple of occasions. He stole my phone.'

'This is the phone that you took a picture of him with?'

'No, this was a different phone. A previous phone.'

'Is there a racial element to all this, Mr Wareing?'

'What? No.'

'Because we are very concerned that there may be a racial element to all this.'

'There is no racial element.'

'You are aware that Mr Sayed's grandmother was murdered in the park some months ago.'

'No. Yes, I mean, I didn't know they were related.'

'You are aware that Mr Sayed is a minor.'

'I don't know how old he is.'

'He's fourteen. You knew he was of mixed race?'

'I don't know. I guess so.'

'That his father was an immigrant?'

'No.'

'Who had been the subject of threats on the estate in the past?'

'No.'

'Do you have a problem with immigrants, Mr Wareing?'

'I am an immigrant.'

'We're very worried about the possible racial element to the situation.'

'There is no racial element.'

'OK,' he said. 'OK. OK.'

At some point the woman began to explain to me how things would proceed from here, but I had already begun to drift by then. I was thinking about Maria sitting dead on her bench, about Kate sitting up in her bed that touched three walls. I thought about Wayne sitting in Cornwall with his girlfriend, possibly in a trailer by the sea; about Cher Fitzpaine typing away on a tiny laptop next to an indoor pool, sunglasses in his hair. I thought about Amanda from AllTalk, and tried to imagine her falling off the back of a bus. I thought about my dad sitting in the house in New Jersey, watching the bird feeder through the window. I thought about the radiator key, and then I felt in my pocket, and it was there.

After some further hours alone I was brought something to sign, with the vague understanding that I had been cautioned in some official way, and that, although no one would quite say so, this was more or less the end of the matter as far as the police were concerned. They offered to let me ring someone, but I decided to walk home in the dark, a final act of atonement, a last chance for someone to do me harm, to challenge the stooped figure walking the mad streets in the middle of the night without a coat, and let him fight for his survival, win or lose. In the end I didn't see another person for the whole two-mile walk. I let the cold get into my bones and kill off the remnants of my anger. It felt strange, but not bad, to be sober.

I was surprised to see Caroline sitting in a pool of light at the kitchen table, drinking fizzy water from a tall glass. The fizzing was the only sound in the room. I got a glass from the cupboard and joined her. I looked at the clock. It was three in the morning.

'So,' she said.

'I have not been charged.'

'Not been charged with what?'

I found this impossible to answer. I didn't actually know the answer. So instead I sat down and told her the whole story, the entire story, beginning with the pain in

my big toe. I explained about the inward drift that makes
it hard for me to focus sometimes, as if she didn't know,
about the people who hated me on the Internet, the way
my sense of self had inadvertently become dependent on
outside forces, forces beyond my control. I told her why
I left the birthday party and a bit about Cher Fitzpaine's
book launch. She didn't flinch or interrupt. Occasionally
she looked away or refilled her glass from the large green
plastic bottle that stood between us, but mostly she looked
at me with intense concentration, a deliberate display of
listening.

Knowing I was being listened to, I made an effort to be
precise, to leave nothing out. I told her about Salome66.
I briefly explained the difference between a talkboard and
a chat room. I gave her a taste of what sorts of things were
said, a few salient quotes off the top of my head. I introduced the subject of my alter ego, ThisDistractedGlobe,
and gave some indication of the role he came to play. I told
her about the profiles of the usernames I kept in my journal.
I told her about the Combined Film And Poetry London
Pre-Christmas Get-together, described the scene in the pub
in some detail, paying particular attention to the appearance
of the fat man opposite who would figure in the story later.
I glossed over my description of Kate Horan slightly,
because it seemed prudent. I didn't, for example, mention
that her front teeth were slightly crossed.

I told her about Maria, who got shot, by no one knows
who, probably some rival drug dealer. I told her about
Panaglos, its side effects and contraindications. I admitted
that I had taken it without prescription for many weeks,

and tried to describe how it made me feel, cloistered within myself, permanently on standby. That wasn't quite right, but I only wanted to give her an idea. I told her about the phantom smells, the premonitions, the song that played in my head. She yawned a few times during this, but each time she returned her hand to her lap and resumed her attentive pose. So I carried on, grateful for the opportunity to come clean.

I told her about the boy in the park, about the day he stole my phone, about the deep feelings of fear and loathing which welled up in me whenever I saw him subsequently. I recounted the circumstances under which my phone came back into my possession. I mentioned the incident with Darby's dad, tried to make it seem funny in hindsight, although neither of us laughed, and confessed my shameful, selfish thoughts as the tragic events of Boxing Day were unfolding. I took a breath, paused and almost stopped there – thinking perhaps the rest could wait until morning – but Caroline was looking at me with a quizzical expression that made me keep going. I'd got this far now; more than halfway.

I tried to keep events in the proper order when I could, but sometimes they got tangled up, and I had to backtrack. For the purposes of concision I conflated the second and third pub meetings with Kate, and I skipped the bit where I spent the night at her flat altogether. I did not necessarily feel that it made the story less honest. I told her how I went out at night with a can of automotive primer bought from the petrol station next to the railway bridge, and amended the boy's graffiti. I told her about the final meeting with Kate, which I dressed up as an intentional confrontation and placed at a time slightly earlier in the day. The basic point was still there: that Kate was not, and never had been, Salome66. Nevertheless I got the sense that Caroline was beginning pick up on these minor lapses of candour. I pressed on, speaking more quickly now.

I told her about Cher Fitzpaine's book, and about him being easyGeoff, and this part I'm not entirely sure she understood; I hadn't really set it up properly. I told her about Colin giving me the address, courtesy of his son-in-law, Penshurst Road, which I remembered, I said, as the address of Grotius, hitting the hard T with confidence. I gave a rundown of my trip to Bedford with Colin – the note, I had to go back and explain the note from Colin's neighbour, and apologize for not showing it to her, which I would later – of Penshurst Road and meeting the fat man from the pub, who turned out to be the real Salome66, although real isn't quite the right word, I said, adding a sarcastic little laugh. And then I jumped to the poster campaign I had mounted some weeks earlier, how I had accidentally taken the boy's picture with my new phone, a picture which I chanced upon some time later, while trying to send a text. I told her how I had emailed the picture to myself and designed a crude leaflet on my computer, printing off several dozen full-colour copies and sticking them up all over the park. I described how perversely empowered it made me feel. I told her I barely remembered doing it the next morning, and partially blamed Panaglos-withdrawal for my memory gaps and my impaired decision-making. Though I take full responsibility, I said. I mentioned the police concern about the racial element, but only in passing. I told her how much better I'd been feeling since I'd left the station, and by way of conclusion I asserted my intention to be a fully engaged husband and father in future. I glanced quickly at the clock. I'd been talking for almost two hours.

'So you see,' I said finally. 'I'm not a paedophile after all.'

She stared for a moment, letting the seconds slip by, as if to make certain I was finished.

'That's interesting,' she said. 'Would you like to hear about my day?'

'Um. OK.'

She lifted her arm from her lap and slid something across the table, something oblong and plastic which spun on its central axis as it skidded toward me. When it stopped spinning I saw that it had a white circle in the centre, bisected by a light blue line.

'I'm pregnant.'

I stared at the blue line, clean and solid and straight, an emphatic denial of the possibility of error.

'Really?'

'Yes, really.'

I looked at her and felt a big grin well up in me, a grin which I thought wise not to display on my face for the moment. I opened my mouth, but nothing came out.

'If you say you don't remember having sex, I will fucking kill you.'

*

I should have slept, but I couldn't. I made some coffee and then took the dog down the road to the park. It was cold and the path was slippery with frost. There was, however, a faint sense of promise riding the still air, a sharp, metallic foretaste of spring. The sun had yet to rise above the railway line, but the heavy night sky was already washing out to the east, revealing a line of cloud retreating northward. The air was mildly intoxicating; it burned through despair, working on the animal parts of the brain to produce a sense, false or otherwise, of improving circumstances, an optimism utterly impervious to logic.

Caroline had been deliberately unenthusiastic.

'We have no au pair,' she said. 'And no money.'

'We can get one. We can get money. It'll be fine.'

'From where?'

'From my book deal. I have a book deal.'

'Since when?'

'Some publisher called me. They want me to do a book. I forgot to tell you.'

For the moment I was trying to keep a lid on my joy. I was suspicious of joy, and a little frightened of it. It was not part of my usual emotional repertoire, and I was only letting myself experience it in discrete chunks. There seemed to be some risk attached to it.

But I felt happy, there was no denying it, no repressing it. The dog dashed about crazily, paws smashing through the ice-glazed puddles, while I stood and finished the coffee in my mug. Dawn was imminent. Nothing, I thought, could better this moment, except perhaps if I'd thought to bring a hat.

Glancing across the park at the line of spindly, skeletal trees which stood either side of the path opposite, I saw something flash. The third tree along seemed to be sprouting leaves; a greenness crept outward along the branches, filling out the space from left to right, a bright, artificial, high-visibility green, incandescent, like a spot-lit blob of summer. I blinked a few times and looked around. A man in a heavy tartan jacket with a boxer on a lead was standing at the park's entrance, looking at the same thing. The horizon began to darken and dance in the spot where the sun was poised to rise. The green was now spreading to the trees on either side, shimmering in the half-light. The man let go of his dog and began to walk toward the trees. The sudden sprouting had a noise to it, like a distant train braking to a stop. I ran to catch up with him, so he wouldn't get there before I did. The dog saw me and came sprinting after.

We converged about fifty yards away from the trees, walking forward and looking straight ahead.

'What is it?' I asked.

'I don't know,' he said. 'I thought I was going mad for a minute.'

As we approached the whole middle tree seemed to be alive, quivering in a breeze that was not there. The trees either side remained incompletely green, twitching lightly at the edges. And then I saw. I don't why it took so long to figure it out.

'They're birds,' I said.

'Huh?'

'Look. They're parakeets. Hundreds of them.'

We slowed down about twenty feet from the tree, and then stopped. The noise, a magnified, pet-shop clamour, was suddenly overwhelming.

'I'll be damned,' he said. 'Look at 'em all. I never seen anything like it.'

'Me neither.'

'Where'd they come from?'

'I don't know. You hear about these giant colonies in London, but I've never . . .'

'Fuck me. It's like the jungle. How do they survive the winter?'

'I don't know,' I said. 'They just do.'

As we looked on the sun winked above the horizon, and without warning the whole flock disengaged itself and rolled off into the sky like a cloud of green ticker tape.

I took a feather home to show the boys.

Acknowledgements

'In The Middle, In the Middle, In The Middle' Words and Music by Vic Mizzy © 1998, Unison Music, USA

Reproduced by permission of EMI Music Publishing Ltd, London WC2H 0QY

I am indebted to Natasha Fairweather and Ursula Doyle, who saw something publishable in this book when it was still a deformed and unfinished thing, and to all the friends and family members who took the trouble to read it in various states of derangement. The manuscript, I mean, not the friends and family members. What they get up to in their own time is their business.